RAZON'S DAUGHTER

BY

LOWELL DUANE PABST

DEDICATION

This book is dedicated to Michael Anthony Scott: my best man. No other form of thanks will adequately express gratitude for undying faith. So much has been shared and now the culmination of putting this story to print.

I also wish to thank Nancy Ellis for her encouragement and instilling trust in the characters to lead me through the story to its conclusion, Susan Medina for believing in me, Lore Cossey for sharing the dream, and Nate Fletcher for endlessly asking, "Is the book published yet?"

PROLOGUE

Spent and resting in the warm glow of his first amorous union, the blade master remained enveloped within the comforting arms of the woman just made his own. In the ecstasy now his, he was drifting off into a deep sleep, content to have her gentle drifting fingers calmly caressing the creases of his brow. Those creases were embedded by the constant wariness of a warrior in an enemy land: tension, vigilance so opposite to the peace he was feeling now. He could feel her mind reaching deeply into his own, uttering the quiet thoughts, easing him back into the softness of the bed and washing his mind clear of fears, of concerns. How endearing were the images of life and joy within her encompassing charm.

Totally oblivious was he to the power of her spells as they robbed him of strength and life. His euphoric state left him unaware and defenseless, totally vulnerable to her guileful ways. She was sucking his life away amidst dreams of peace, home, and love.

Bound in lethargy, he felt the spasmodic jump of his lover at the sudden crash in the room. He failed to respond but with a groan, as she leapt to her feet instantly ready to meet this intrusion. Her screech of wrath only brought a muttered moan from his lips.

He sensed more than heard her deep-throated curses of infuriated anger at recognition of her assailant. A warrior of blue surcoat was charging her from the center of the room.

There was no warning, no footsteps nor opening of the door! How did he get into the room without my sensing it? The succuba questioned within. *There is barely time for me to act. My time....!* Rage prompted action.

Two towering reptilian creatures instantly materialized and were thrust between the woman and the warrior's attack—only a moment's step from wielding his sword upon her.

The warrior took the sudden arrivals in stride. With a full spin of body and a mighty upward swing, his bastard sword slashed full arc through the neck of the first creature. He continued his press.

Fear and hate brought burning bile to the pit of the woman's stomach. This warrior displayed none of the panic-driven fear; the mere appearance of these creatures was known to invoke in men. Comingled with the shriek of defeat and despair, she screamed, "I've not finished here!" Without alternative, she flashed her arms about her. "Another time and place," she hissed. "I will see my retribution!" and she vanished.

The warrior in blue noted the abrupt disappearance of the woman within a wavering chasm of deepest shadow. Having just dealt with the first of the creatures while it suffered from disorientation, he was confident in what was needed now.

He made a sudden sidestep to place himself between the second creature and the male form on the bed. This second creature no longer experienced any confusion; it stood potent and lethal.

The two combatants locked eyes.

Sensing a critical tension in the room, the bed-bound warrior struggled to rise. His weakened body could not generate even that much energy. He resigned to just watch, distant and unfocused. Through a visual haze, he had seen the first creature fall. Now the warrior in blue was moving towards the bed with sword poised to fight. Battle-hardened instincts and years of association with this swordsman made it obvious even in his stupor of thought that the warrior was protecting him from the second fiend. *I have to help*, he thought. Instead, the bed engulfed him as he lost consciousness.

The warrior faced the hulk from Hades, ready. He had fought these creatures once before. He was familiar with the raking claws and their intense desire to bite. He knew his fortune in having killed the first so quickly.

The swordsman in blue smiled. He was ready.

The creature lunged with an open palm. The claws of his immense hand extended like daggers from his scaled arm. The beast sought to drive the claws into the warrior's face.

The warrior parried the thrust, felt his muscles tense to swing. As he stepped into the motion, he noted the creature's other hand balled into a tight fist, ready for a sweeping hook to his body. Realizing the creature had anticipated his parry and was feigning a sacrificial strike for a sure kill, the warrior spared his strike. Instinctively, he ducked to the side with a deep swoop, bending at the knees.

The two giant arms swished dangerously just above the warrior's head.

Turning his shoulder slightly, the swordsman used the pent-up force from his bent legs to power his shoulder into the beast's midsection, driving with his legs.

The whumpf of breath from the creature's lungs was overpowering in acidic gases, blinding the warrior into a delay just enough for the creature to fall back a moment. It raked in a huge breath of air and bellowed in rage.

In a determined charge, the warrior sought to drive his bastard sword into its ribs and heart.

The creature's dodge-and-strike move allowed it to land a powerful blow to the back and shoulder of the warrior, throwing him soundly backwards on the floor; his sword glanced off the creature's side instead of rendering the heart blow intended.

"You are fast!" the warrior conceded, lying prone on the floor.

He pulled his knees into his chest planning a prone-forward jump to his feet. No time, he braced the bastard sword pommel to the floor as the beast lunged upon him to crush his head in its massive jaws.

The creature stared, open-mouthed, as it died upon the warrior's sword. The drool would permanently etch the warrior's chain mail with its acid.

The warrior used his pulled-up legs to help shove the weight of death off him in a push-and-roll, allowing him to stand and prepare for further battle.

Seeing all quiet, he turned his attention to the man on the bed. Noting the rhythmic breathing of sleep, the warrior wiped his blade off on the strewn bed covers and sheathed it in its place upon his back. After a brief time, the sleeping man began to stir. He was struggling to focus his eyes.

"Are you dead, dreaming, or just plain lazy?"

Recognizing the rebuff as a friendly jab, the sleeper struggled to come up with a retort. His usual quick response not coming to mind, he just looked at the warrior, smiled, and collapsed. *She was beautiful,* he mused as consciousness drifted away.

CHAPTER ONE

The gray of morning was overpowering the blackness of night. The half shadows would soon replace the period of all shadow. Coming to light were the murky tints of color. They were mostly shades of brown, dirty green, and charcoal of soil and buildings.

The young girl began to wake. Long, copper-colored hair fanned widely across her pillow. Her eyes opened and took in the spartan room. They focused on the window looking to the outside. The old, gnarled tree's branches blocked the dim sunlight from her;. She could hear the fluttering of birds outside. She listened intently to their hoarse squawks and chittering announcing the new day.

She arose from her bed, adjusting her night shift about her budding, youthful form. Today was the most important day of her life. She questioned her mixed feelings as she sought out the washbasin and towel to rinse the night's sleep away. She was excited about being initiated into an apprenticeship. It meant she would start her training to become as her mother. Looking at herself in the mirror, she forced a smile. *I should be happy today,* she scolded herself, *yet why is there this heaviness inside?*

She heard stirring outside her room. The girl felt her mother's presence just outside her room. She drew upon her will in preparation of her mother opening her door. I must be my best. *I must show Mother I can be as the others.* She dropped her head in remorse at the last thoughts she read when her mother decided against entering.

The youth's inner struggle returned as it had for the last several weeks. *My mother smolders inside with anger and fights to keep up a façade in hopes I will succeed.*

Bringing her trepidation to bear with sheer determination, she rehearsed aloud, "Mother will see. They will all see I can be as good as any of the others!" Once again, the girl drove away the hints of hesitation as she listened to the last fading steps of her mother walking away from her nest chamber.

The young girl could keenly sense the energy levels of living things. She could read thoughts; however, she could not fly. She had no wings. She could not change appearance from what she looked like now to the opposing smooth-skinned, rather bat-like features the women preferred here. She knew her mother could, at will, so could the other girls, even those younger than her. She knew that was partially why her mother was so bitter.

The girl finished her morning ablutions, took a deep breath, and opened the door of her room to face the day. She went downstairs to the gathering floor below. At the bottom, she greeted Reht, a massive scaled creature, cheerily. He uttered only an outward grunt from his rather enlarged jaws. However, his telepathic greeting was much more articulate and friendly. The girl accepted his peculiar behavior as one of his games. He was a Hert, a servant creature. He was also her friend. He was the only one who took an interest in or really tried to understand her, perhaps because he had been with her since birth. Children were rare and each one was assigned a Hert as a guardian and pseudo-nanny. The association was lifelong.

The girl responded to his greeting in kind, telepathically telling him about the birds she heard outside this morning. She liked the birds. Once she saw a bird of the deepest black, except for a bold splash of red on each shoulder. Its eyes were glistening black. It was a type of bird unknown to her and its rhythmic call was of finer tones than any she had heard. She was sure it was the same one when she found it beneath the old tree two days later lying lifeless.

The girl's mother called, "Cynderet, you have dallied the morning away in your laziness. You must hurry now if you want to make your first meeting with the Eldresses on time. They will not wait for you as I have had to these many years. You cannot fly. You will have to walk."

"Yes, Mother." Cynderet could tell Mother was still fighting for control of her anger. She sensed her mother's internal conflict between anger and apprehension; wanting to scream outright at Cynderet's racial divergence, and a determined effort to pretend a calm façade.

Cynderet was twelve years old. She grew up accustomed to reading her mother's feelings of conflict. She used them as a scale of equilibrium from which Cynderet judged all other feelings as highs of affection or lows of anger and danger. She could tell her mother was on the brink now. Generally, she could calm her mother telepathically by planting visions of her striving to be as her mother was. Today she knew better than to try; too much was at risk. Cynderet decided to be amiable and to do what she was told quickly.

Cynderet's mother knew the girl was different. The result was a continual surging of temper just below the surface of control. "I need to stay calm today," she said to herself. She was aware Cynderet was somehow keen to her feelings; if she were to give vent to her anger now it would put Cynderet at an even greater disadvantage in the testing for apprenticeship with the Eldresses.

"Hell's glory! If Cynderet were just normal!" she muttered to herself as she went up the stairs. "I should never have been burdened with this disgrace, this cripple. I am Luanta!"

Cynderet hurried with her morning meal and her daily duties. She rushed back upstairs to get dressed for the special occasion. Her mother waited at the top of the stairs and said, "Your clothes are set out for you on your nest. Reht will lead you to the Eldresses at Council Peak. Do not embarrass me or jeopardize your chances by being late!" She hissed. "I will leave now to join in the Preparatory Rituals. You will need to show all that you are as good as the others though you do not look as they do." Luanta held back the rest of her thought, nor look as capable.

Cynderet read it though. It heightened her inner conflict. Her mother was trying to protect her from something—what? After watching her mother fly away, she turned to Reht and asked, "Why would Mother think me incapable of apprenticeship?"

The question surprised him at first. He looked to her quizzically for a moment, noting the hurt there, and the fear. "Cynderet, your mother is concerned about much today. She is thinking of you. The Eldresses are the council leaders of your female society. They are the master teachers of the youth with sole power of law within the domain of the Shadow Plane.

"They control the Last Powers. Children, when of age, meet with the Eldresses to receive their blessings, to receive apprenticeship, and to be taught how to control the innate powers of the Society. Luanta is an Eldress, but only as a council can they declare law, approve the young for apprenticeship, or bestow the Last Powers. Luanta explained to you the Eldresses meet only one day a year to decide apprenticeships. Today is the Day of Least Shadow; the time the sun reaches its zenith. Today is the day."

Reht could see she was still confused but trying to understand her mother's apprehension. He continued, "Once a child is approved, she will be taken under the tutelage of one of the Eldresses for a period of six years. When the apprentice reaches eighteen, then she will once again face the council and prove she is ready to receive the Last Powers—the powers of Energy Feeding and Force Field Webbing. These two abilities remain latent in each individual until the council as a whole performs the ritual and makes a sacrifice. Your mother is anxious for you because the consequences of not being approved are severe." He sealed his mind to her, reading the rest of his thought.

"That is why Mother is being so careful about what she says or does," Cynderet mused. "I will have to be the best to be initiated into apprenticeship.

The Eldresses will be merciless if I show the least bit of weakness or hesitation." She recalled rumors from some of the other youth that she would not be accepted and would be considered an alien, not to be trusted.

"I want my mother to be pleased. She is so bitter inside. I do not know why I am so different, but I do know the only way I can get her to see past my differences is by becoming an apprentice. Mother once said something happened during my conception. Do you know what it was?"

"No, Little One. I was not there."

Cynderet stopped just before entering her nest chamber. Reht could read her question before she asked it and was prepared. He had been waiting for her to ask it a long time.

"Will I be an apprentice?"

"Little One, you are as prepared as any of the others. You must overcome your own fear and stand upon who you are."

Cynderet finished getting dressed and put on the heavy shawl she wore when outside to limit comments about her lack of wings. It was not uncommon to go around in human form on the Shadow Plane. It just was not the preferred appearance. Many felt uncomfortable in the feeding form here. They preferred to use it only when feeding.

Reht was there at the top of the stairs waiting for her. He sent her the thought that she looked acceptable to him. Her beauty in the human form, especially in the clothes her mother had provided, would impress the Eldresses. "They fit to show your female form the best. The physical charms of the human form are the principal assets used to charm the cowardly human male and draw him to nest."

Cynderet frowned at him, and sent back how silly she thought the whole "show" idea was. She felt rather uncomfortable in the strange clothing. They were not the usual bulky, full-covering types she normally wore. "The material is so thin I feel naked. It clings too close to my skin." She pulled the shawl closer about her neck and tied the ends together in a futile effort to cut out the draft she felt upon her exposed skin of chest and throat. "Why such a low neckline?" she asked.

Reht just shrugged.

He led her along the familiar aisles of the community. They passed between the stone structures the Energy Feeders called homes. She could see within each the wide open-air gathering areas, the stairs leading to the aboveground nesting chambers, each home guarded by the faithful Hert. The nesting similarities between the Society and birds had always intrigued her;.

The birds nested high in the trees and the Energy Feeders nested in chambers also aboveground.

They passed Harriant's home. She was finishing her last efforts to get ready for the council also. Her Hert was quietly waiting with head bowed in humility. Cynderet knew how Harriant treated her Hert. She felt a twinge of pity for him. The wounds of Harriant's last fit of angered lashings were still partially visible around the finer scales of his neck and face.

Cynderet set a faster pace to her steps. She sent to Reht her desire to arrive at the council site long before Harriant. Cynderet was sure this jealous vixen started most of the rumors about her. On several occasions, Cynderet had been able to confound Harriant with logic and reason when in discussion with the other girls. This shamed Harriant's insatiable ego and earned Cynderet her wrath and despising. So far, Harriant's only ability to retaliate had been in starting rumors of what would happen when the Eldresses found out Cynderet was less than normal. Well, today was the day. Cynderet wanted to be at the site long before Harriant in order to see how things were set up. She wanted to have time before the bantering started to see if she could come up with something to counter-balance her deformities.

Reht looked towards Council Peak in the center of the community. It was much higher than the homes. He knew each level of stairs was guarded by four of the Council Guard. They were the personal protectors of the Eldress Council and the military defense of the city. Council Guards were the only ones to actually bear arms, a short pole-arm blunt at the bottom end with foot-long cleaved, double-edged blades on the top.

Reht had been trained in the use of these weapons when he too had been a Council Guard under the command of Luanta. However, he had been released when given the guardianship of Cynderet. He could feel the training of weapon use even now in his arms. His mind quickly rehearsed precision maneuvers. He had been one of the best. Now, he was the guardian of the deformed child of the second highest member of the Eldress Council. He was glad.

She was smarter than the rest. She could also communicate without vocalizing words. He could talk to her and she could communicate back, no one ever hearing a sound. She respected him and valued his judgment. He felt the same about her. As she had grown older, he had watched her wisdom grow, so did his respect for her. There was more to this child than they knew. Yes, she was different, but the physical deformities were not the ones that held her apart. There was more to this child than even Luanta knew. He was pleased to be her protector. That meant his first responsibility was to her no matter whom or what came against her. He knew he would willingly give his life for her, die with her, if it ever came to that: but never after her!

They arrived at the massive portals of Council Peak ahead of the others. The portals were double doors twelve feet high and each five feet wide. Standing open, the massive doors were swung securely to either side, allowing passage through to the many flights of stairs leading to the top, the governmental center of the Eldresses where the initiation would take place. Although one could see the council area high above, this was the only entrance to the stairs. Four Council Guards stood within the foyer and before the stairs. One, obviously the captain, stood forward towering over Cynderet. He looked resplendent in his black-and-silver surcoat. His scaled skin shone iridescent in the late morning's light. The other three stood nearer the stairs with their weapons, the double-bladed pole arms of the Council Guard, at the ready. Only the captain was unarmed; his weapon was leaning against the far side of the portals. He recognized Reht and though Cynderet did not know him, he seemed to recognize her also. He welcomed them in and up with a polite bow and ushering movement of his huge, clawed hand indicating the stairs.

They proceeded up the first several flights of stairs. There were no enclosing walls to block their vision of the community below and around them, except for that portion hidden by the peak itself. The community was built in a type of bowl, a circular valley with Council Peak standing center most in the valley. The peak was a natural rise carved and built upon generations ago of finely crafted stone blocks. The stairs were the only passage up. Cynderet had been taught early on in life that there was a force field protecting the peak. Not even the Eldresses flew here. Everyone had to use the stairs.

They were little more than halfway up when Cynderet realized she was having difficulty breathing. She felt tired and her chest was heavy. She found herself taking quick shallow breaths. Fighting the intensity of her nerves, she forced herself to breathe more deeply in desperate effort to settle her nerves. It seemed to help at first, but the higher they climbed, the more difficult it was to take the next step.

It was with great relief the two reached the lower landing of the last flight of stairs. The Council Hert remained stoic in their duty stance, one standing straight in each corner. Here, Cynderet hesitated, studying them for a brief moment;. She turned and looked out to the city below. She wanted to bask in the last moments before reaching the top and the council area itself. Those last moments before her life would be changed forever by initiation into an apprenticeship. She enjoyed the feel of the coolness floating on the updraft of air as it dried the dampness of perspiration generated of exertion and anxiety. She took a few deep breaths, letting each out slowly in determined effort to relieve the last vestiges of exhaustion. She sensed the arrival of the other inductees at the foyer of the portals below. They soon would be starting up the stairs. She turned as if to see them. The flight of stairs she just finished blocked her view of the foyer below. Her mind told her they were coming up. She would have a little time if she hurried now.

She put action to thought—nothing happened—she could not move her feet; they seemed bound in place. She knew it was imperative to take the last flight up—to do it now. She could not. Her body felt as though it was against a wall. What was holding her in check? She looked around her more closely to see and feel.

She began to realize there were unseen, outside forces affecting her. They must have been growing stronger as she climbed. *It must have been my lack of concentration that prevented me from sensing them,* she thought. She opened her mind slowly to what was around her.

She felt the stone. It was ancient. She could feel its strength. The steps were worn from centuries of use. She opened her mind further, allowing it to feel of the wearing of the steps. The past began to open to her, revealing the padding of innumerable feet—feet similar to her own—trudging up, anxiety building in each shuffling step.

She permitted the visions to grow. She saw the feet and legs of generations before. Styles of clothing were just becoming clear when the voices hit her mind and simultaneously struck her heart. They were voices from the past, full of the emotions and apprehensions of those who had gone this way before. There was no happiness.

It made little sense to her. Struggling to sort through the morass of thoughts and feelings, she tried to read some of them to understand. As soon as she opened her mind for comprehension, they rushed in as strings of thoughts: a tangle of stress-mangled fears of the unknown. No single thoughts were clearly discernible above the din of time's keening collection.

The impact on her mind was powerful and fraught with feelings similar to her own enhanced by time and the repetition of succeeding generations. She had never experienced such intensity or numbers before. She did not know how to weed through it all. She could feel the physical effect impacting her control of her own body. Her determination so soon regained in her respite was dissipating fast to the onslaught of sensations causing her body's strength to waver. She realized the wall preventing her further passage was built from the misgivings experienced by these voices; these voices from the past—a living dismay, the resident remainder of the innocents enduring their own passage in exquisite foreboding of what lay ahead, all speaking of the same fear. Their building in strength over the last several flights of stairs now made it impossible for her to start climbing again. She shut her mind to the cacophony of emotions; she could still feel the constricting presence around her.

Cynderet could hear the excited chatter of the other inductees climbing behind. How was it they felt nothing? Could they not hear the voices, feel the keening? The others were coming quickly. She had to go on; it was imperative she reach the council site before the others. In desperation, she slammed her mind shut off those of the past and focused her energy on taking the first step up of this last flight.

She could not take the next step.

Reht sensed Cynderet's increasing difficulty in climbing each set of stairs. Several times he looked down into her face to see how she fared. He read the determination there: the tight lines about her mouth, the set of her eyes. She was putting all her concentration into ascending each step—one at a time. The higher they got, the more he could feel her inner will force her body to climb.

He could not feel the sensations she was, but he could feel their effect upon her. He could tell she was in the midst of a powerful struggle. She was fighting mind over body. He felt her impasse at the base of the last flight. He read her emotional battle with the feelings of those who had gone before. It was as if any who had passed had left a message for her to read.

Reht saw her pleading look to him. He read her send and took her hand to help her up. Strengthened in the union, they ascended together.

The feelings continued to grow. The emotional wall closed in upon her mind and crushed her chest, forcing her to take gasping breaths, ragged and irregular. She held tightly to Reht's hand, forcing her heart to continue beating. She felt herself losing consciousness as they reached the uppermost step. She had to do something. She remembered a game Reht taught her. She closed her eyes, created a void in her mind, and focused only on the void. Each time an emotion or thought entered, she pushed it out. She let nothing in until she was back in control of self. It seemed like a long time before she opened her eyes again. She did so thanking Reht for the different mind games he had taught her. She gave his hand a squeeze. She felt the dampness of her close-fitting clothing bathed in sweat. Her breathing was still labored, but the faintness was gone. She looked around.

They were standing just outside the entryway to the council area. Two pillars of stone rose before them with a vast courtyard beyond. It was completely open to the sky above. The sun shone almost directly overhead. The roof of a large building could be seen behind the courtyard. Its walls were hidden behind a black-and-silver drape. There were doors into the building on either side of the drape. There was a large open stairway leading down towards the building at Cynderet's left.

In the center of the courtyard was a large circular table that took up much of the space. The Eldresses were there, twelve of them. They were chanting with their arms extended, hands placed palm down upon the table. She could see her mother, second highest in rank, sitting just to the right of the Senior Eldress on the table's far side.

The entire courtyard was full of mental activity. She took another look at the drapery. Instinctively, she could feel the intense impressions of the past emanating from it.

Fascinated by a drapery acting as a resonator for those of the past, she timorously allowed herself to open up again just to understand. It was too tempting not to. However, this time, she felt prepared. She was very methodical in her process. She was not going to be overwhelmed a second time. Cynderet opened her mind by little bits.

The climb had been like a crescendo of perceptions, a heightening of intensity to this point. The drapery radiated a jumbled yet powerful force of feelings. Fear, pain, and loss were all there; none of joy or hope. "Why?" she breathed to herself. She opened a little more.

The emotions brought forward horrible images of suffering and loss. Her head began to hurt. All had something to say. "What?" she asked.

Her telepathic door opened just a bit more as she asked the question.

She hoped a voice or image would become clear. One did not. It was as if they had been waiting for her; they could wait no longer. She had asked her question and they answered—all at once. The impact was the careening screams of voices beyond number.

There were flashes of scenes and thoughts so fast she could not focus upon any specific one: heart-rending emotions were all she could perceive.

The messages all bespoke fear and pain. These two were universal culminating in a keening of loss. She felt she was beginning to understand.

Something awoke.

Something stirred that had not been noted before. A telepathic head reared. It roared in anger. Its repose had been disrupted. In rage, it crushed silence upon the voices of the past. It slammed an illusionary vault door shut. The voices within the drapery were sealed against further utterance. Tainted was the feel of the void.

Cynderet's head pounded; tears formed in the corners of her eyes. She squinted fiercely to hold the tears back and closed her mind to the impact of the keening and the subsequent void of silence. The whole experience was beyond any she had known before. She did not know what it meant or why. She thought it must be a test. She sought a diversion.

She resolved to focus upon the Eldresses and opened her eyes. They sat almost surrounding a dull, circular black table of stone. It was opened by a narrow passageway just in front of her with enough room to allow one person through into the inner circle of the table. None of the Eldresses sat on this side. It was full shadow around the table. The light of the sun seemed to be drawn into the table itself. The Eldresses sat on the far side chanting, heads lowered in deep concentration.

She began to feel something else, something new. It was different than the emotional bombardment. It was not the Eldresses. It was something she had not yet isolated—something was seeking her out.

A sleeping behemoth had opened its eyes and had found her before it. Cynderet could feel it watching her; a sense of curiosity backed by immense strength and power. It was making no effort to attack or even move;. Its purposeful intensity was felt as it made an almost playful attempt to penetrate her mind. The send was not vocal or in word images. It was of its own nature: intelligent, specific, not another emotional deluge. It felt coherent and articulate.

How could this be? she asked herself. Only Reht knew she was telepathic. He had taught her early on not to speak telepathically with the other Hert lest they learn of her ability and tell the Eldresses. He feared to endanger her further because she was already so different and deformed according to the standards of the Society. Cynderet realized this new entity was trying to get in to see, to explore her mind. It was not trying to communicate;. There was no effort to exchange thought or even note her ability to commune with it. In fact, its purpose was self-serving with its own intents. She held tight control upon herself, allowing its efforts to drift around the vestiges of her conscience as if smoke prodding for an opening. A tightening of pressure was felt against her mind's restraint. Malignant was the touch of it. Suddenly, Cynderet was afraid: these wiles served a purpose and that purpose was control! It was that same raging force that had silenced the voices of the past. Cynderet sought to drive it from her mind.

It was gone that fast. As soon as Cynderet recognized its efforts, it slipped away and was gone before her forceful drive was needed.

After a moment, in the emptiness of silence, it sent another probe—stronger this time, attempting to go deep into her being. She looked deep within her own mind and imagined a door shutting firmly about her thoughts. She felt the power of her vault door sealing and mentally saw the door firm against intrusion.

The sender changed its probe from force to a breath of cloud and tried to slip between the cracks of the door and frame.

She shut the door tightly seeing the door swell against its frame as if swollen with water. The hold was so tight that no light or air could get between. She saw the intruding tendrils back away from the door and depart to an area just beyond the limits of her thoughts.

She was glad she had practiced thought-sealing before with Reht when she did not want him to know what she was thinking. Sometimes it had been a game, other times to protect him from hurt at something her mother had said or done. He had teased her by trying to penetrate against her will. Through his coaching, she had developed mindlocks to seal him out and to do so at the least indication of attempted entrance.

He had been very pleased when she mastered her ability. Maybe this was why. Did he know more than he had let on? He had always been so purposeful in his training of her. Was this experience, this new probing, the reason why? She resolved to ask him later.

Cynderet could not feel any probes against her at the moment and sought to locate the source of the direct power. She opened the mental door and began to search within her mind, focusing on each person of the Eldress Council. Each was deep in concentration of the chant; however, she did sense that they were giving of themselves to something. In her mind, she saw an umbilical cord extending from each Eldress, reaching to some kind of dark shadow. It was huge, round. Its depth sank far into the mountain of Council Peak—into deepest darkness. It was all cloaked in total darkness.

Cynderet pierced the darkness. It was beginning to clear before her mind's eye. Yes, it was almost visible. It began to take shape: rounded, heavy, pulsing. It was alive. She saw it.

It saw her.

It attacked so quickly! Right at her mind!

She slammed the door.

She opened her natural eyes and saw the Table.

It was the Table. It echoed life; it was its own. It was alive! It had its own identity and echoed strong personal character and purpose. It radiated pain, death, screams of fear, and of loss, not of its own, but of others. It was pulsing deep within to the rhythm of the Eldresses' chant. It was feeding. It was feeding upon the energy of the Eldresses themselves.

The urge to turn and run was overwhelming. She looked behind her to the stairs downward. She must have started to move because Reht took her arm in his massive hand and held her. He rapidly sent the mental reminder that this had to be met. He was there with her; she had to see this through.

Cynderet looked up into his stern face and felt his pride in her. His thoughts of his faith in her were a calming balm. He reminded her of her mother; she too had trusted in her. Deformed or not, her mother had done all she could to prepare Cynderet for this moment. She had to stay.

The deciding factor came in the thought readings Cynderet had of Harriant and the other inductees who were beginning to arrive. She felt their aversion to this place. Their idle chatter had ceased at some time coming up the stairs.

Harriant voiced a tight grunt as she stopped at the top of the stair. However, Cynderet heard the actual scream of fright within her that emanated as the grunt. Harriant was fighting her own battle to stay.

They all stopped behind her. She turned to acknowledge their presence. Two nodded their greeting, but Harriant and her best friend just looked at her then away. The fifth was having great difficulty finding solace. She kept looking quickly in every direction with fear emanating in each rapid-eye movement. Her body jerked visibly. Cynderet could read their thoughts. None knew the secret of the Table. They only felt the power here and were frightened by it.

CHAPTER TWO

The sun was almost to its zenith. The community around the peak was clearly visible below. The shadows could be seen in their last moments of existence before vanishing beneath walls, trees, and terraces of structure. It was as if the shadows were slipping into the very walls.

Linnet, the nervous one, could not bring herself to stop looking around furtively. She was growing pale; waiting for the ceremony to begin. She locked her arm in that of her Hert to hold herself from collapsing. He was very careful to support her, but to make it look casual. The Hert appeared more aware of the proceedings than the inductees did. Each was doing what he could to make his ward look at ease and ready.

Without any prior warning or change of inflection, the chanting stopped. The Eldresses seemed to shake themselves in an effort to focus on what was going on beyond their deep trance. Cynderet sensed the Table going quiet and taking a listening attitude. It was pensive, waiting for things to proceed.

Ermentrude, the Senior Eldress, stood up and looked to the inductees and their Hert. She did not smile or acknowledge any, though she knew all. She just looked at them. She was taking stock of their appearances and possibly their outward demeanor. Cynderet wondered if she could see the inner thoughts of each as her sharp gaze rested long upon Linnet.

It took a moment for Linnet to realize she had been singled out. She felt the gaze first, then being caught up in the deep scrutiny, she was unable to move her eyes away, not daring to break the stare. Viewing from the side, Cynderet was keen to Linnet's battle between fear and reason; this struggle emanating in Linnet's uncontrollable quivering. Linnet was about to break as the intensity of the stare heightened. Panic was an instant from driving Linnet down the stairs when the stare broke and the Senior Eldress shifted her stare to Harriant. Cynderet noted Linnet's Hert tightening his grasp of Linnet as her knees suddenly began to buckle.

Again, the intense gaze took in all it could. This time, of Harriant, a long purposeful scrutiny attempting to go far beyond the physical. It seemed Ermentrude was trying to enter deep into Harriant herself.

The Senior Eldress went from one to the next, each the same. When she got to Cynderet, there was an immediate change. The intense scrutiny was there but something more. Cynderet felt the mental impulse of the Senior Eldress when Ermentrude recognized what was visually different about Cynderet.

"Why is this one in human form?" she asked of no one in particular.

Cynderet looked instantly to her mother. She read her thoughts of reluctance to speak because of her station as an Eldress. Cynderet realized that her mother would not be of any help here; she must answer this question and all others.

She looked to Reht. He sent, "Speak your mind."

Cynderet deliberately untied the scarf she wore and handed it to Reht. "I am dressed to demonstrate my persuasions for the hunt and felt that this display would be more important than the usual form. It reveals what I have to use in charming those who will succumb to feeding."

The response seemed to appease the Senior Eldress. She broke off the scrutiny. Without any other comment, she turned to the other Eldresses. "The zenith of our sun is upon us. Let us begin the ceremony."

All twelve stood up at their stations around the Table. Two of the Council Guard took position at the opening of the Table with weapons at the ready position. Two took position behind the Eldresses, their backs to the black-and-silver drapes.

"Call for the first of the inductees," the Senior Eldress ordered.

The Council Guard Captain who had been at the entrance portal came from behind the inductees where he had been standing unseen. He came to the center of the opening of the Table and called the first. It was Harriant's best friend, Shenet.

Shenet took a tentative step forward. She looked back to Harriant. Harriant gave a slight toss of her head, and Shenet took the several steps in the direction of the Hert. He stepped aside, allowing her clear passage to the center of the Table.

The Eldresses waited for her to take position and then sat down.

The Council Guard Captain recited Shenet's family lineage from memory to the council. Only the female progenitors were mentioned. The male, or human, factor was not.

When he finished, the Eldresses stared at her as the Senior Eldress had done earlier. However, this time, Cynderet felt the Table emit tendrils, probing inside Shenet's mind. Slowly, they worked, exploring what was there. After departing her mind and a slight pause, the probing returned, becoming more purposeful. Instantly, it plunged far inside and stopped to spread out like a fan, sending each frond to enter a different area; the penetration was aggressive and unmerciful. It started a purposeful search, for what Cynderet could not tell, but she felt Shenet's instant response: fear. Fear heightened as the probe unclothed each memory, each thought Shenet held in her deepest parts. The power of the probe forced a moan from her. Her eyes began to tear from pain as the probe sought even deeper.

She covered her ears in a futile attempt to stop the mind-search, thinking it was auditory instead of telepathic. She struggled to withstand the pain as long as she could. She began to shake convulsively. She lost control of her legs. Her knees shook as the intensity continued to increase. She crumpled to a kneeling posture, still pressing her hands tightly to her ears. She lost all control. She screamed in pain. The shaking of Shenet's body was obvious to all as she huddled there kneeling on the floor, weeping.

The Table revealed to the Eldresses' minds what it had learned in its probe. Cynderet was aware of a sense of fulfillment yet something more—a feeling foreign to Cynderet as the Table communicated with them. It was pleased with Shenet's strength and indicated it found her teachable. She would be accepted into apprenticeship.

Shenet ceased crying. The pain subsided almost immediately with the Table's release of her mind. She strove to quickly regain her composure. She looked to the Eldresses for some kind of sign of rejection, believing she had failed the test.

The Eldresses looked at her for a moment longer, then began to discuss amongst themselves who would be her mentor. It was decided that the most Junior Eldress would take her into her care and teaching.

Ermentrude informed Shenet she had passed the test and would begin training. She was introduced to the Eldress and was told she and her Hert would live with her mentor for the next six years. After which, she would once again come before the council to prove herself worthy to receive the Last Rites.

Shenet turned and left the Table's center. Her face was pale with deep red splotches on throat, cheeks, and around her swollen eyes. Her Hert came to her aid and helped her return to her station with the others. Harriant looked at her with a questioning, bewildered look. Cynderet read her thoughts of confusion as to what had happened and her personal resolve to be better and stronger. Shenet had fallen in Harriant's esteem.

The two who had greeted Cynderet were the next to be tested. In similar fashion as Shenet, they passed the test and were assigned to an Eldress for apprenticeship. Their Hert also went to aid them back to the group.

Harriant refused to even look at them. If it were possible, she lifted her chin even higher with each.

She was called next.

Cynderet watched Harriant pass through the entrance to the Table. While her family line was recited, Harriant boldly studied each face of the Eldresses seeking to impress them with her courage. Harriant believed the Eldresses brought about the ordeal; she had no idea of the living, mind-probing Table. Only Cynderet knew—and the Eldresses, she realized—the understanding bursting upon her thinking.

They did know. They had to! It was all a part of being an Eldress—to link with the Table. That was why the Eldresses could not make decisions, decree law, or stand in judgment without being in full council here at Council Peak. The Table was a part of the council; maybe it was the most important part. Cynderet realized then that she was going to try and find out. Her encounter with the Table was going to be different!

Harriant stood firmly before the council. She had observed the other three and was determined to be the strongest. Her personal resolve was her greatest strength. She saw the Eldresses look to her, into her, as if trying to see deep inside. She felt the beginnings of mental fingers probing into her mind. At first, it was not so bad, a slight tingle about the hairline and around the base of the ears. She allowed them to look all they wanted. She would be the best ever. There seemed to be a lessening to the probe's intensity.

She was beginning to think she had accomplished her goal; that the testing was over. A feeling of personal satisfaction was warming within when the sudden impact of the renewed probing pounded into her. It passed right through her resolve and penetrated deeply into her most hidden thoughts and buried weaknesses. It relished her instant fear.

The impact was so sudden it buckled her to her knees in the instant. Her head felt to be swelling beyond what her skull could endure. She felt the fingers of the probing grab unto her fear and pain. Their grip intensified, growing stronger and stronger. All turned black.

Harriant awoke to find herself sobbing, prostrate upon the stone floor. She realized she must have passed out;. The vestiges of blackness were still leaving the recesses of her mind as she became more aware of her surroundings once again. She was hearing sounds, but unable to discern what or from where. They came again. This time, some semblance of sense could be decoded. It was the Senior Eldress telling her to get up.

"You have passed and will be under my own personal tutelage. Arise and take your place with the other candidates."

The tone was straightforward with no emotion. Harriant tried to comply and found herself too unstable to rise beyond a knee.

Her Hert meekly tried to help her up. Harriant's usual attack at insinuating she was helpless was obvious for its absence. It was a weak and shattered Harriant who, holding to his offered arm, returned to her place with head down, unable to look except to her next shuffle of steps; her pride too shattered to dare look at another.

Linnet was next. Linnet did not pass. Cynderet recognized the initial exploratory probes. Linnet began sobbing almost immediately. She begged for someone to help her. Cynderet felt a desire to aid her, to cradle her through the ordeal. Reht must have picked up on it because he took her arm strongly in his massive hand and held her. When the second wave of probing lunged deeply within her mind, Linnet went into hysterics. In a spasmodic fit, she threw herself to the floor;. Her head careened off the edge of the Table. She fell to the floor in convulsions, arms and legs twisting and jumping of their own impulses. Blood soaked into her black hair and onto the floor of the Table's inner circle.

Cynderet blocked out the mental cries and visions of Linnet's mind as it gave up its last thoughts. Cynderet knew if she again opened her mind to the myriad of emotions in the council area, she would recognize Linnet's in the midst. Her thoughts of fear and pain would always be here, joined with those of before.

Cynderet was last. She had felt the probing of each of the others and felt sure of the sequence. She knew she was stronger than the others were. She witnessed each of their initiations in the Table's center: Harriant had tried to defy, Shenet had been submissive, Linnet—petrified. Cynderet resolved to be submissive to the first probe. She would allow her mind to be explored during the shallow perusal of the general areas. She would never willingly allow the Table to enter her innermost sanctuaries, those places she was only beginning to realize existed. This test would pass or fail on the superficial level only.

There was a warm burning within Cynderet's breast as a new firmness settled within: resolve—a sense of defined purpose and an exacting sense of agreement between what was to be done and her place within it. It was of a magnitude strange and alien to Cynderet. She liked the almost regal feeling of being united in mind and spirit. It was warm, almost hot within her bosom. A wall of sheer will grew, made of the strongest fibers. She saw them intertwine one with another, forming layer upon layer: flexible, but impenetrable. She was ready.

Cynderet heard her name called. She passed into the open area of the Table and heard the recitation of her lineage. She exchanged looks with Reht. His faith in her shown in his eyes; he was proud of her. A shared smile lingered as the recitation ended and Cynderet turned to face her mother. Noting Luanta's deliberate avoiding of eye contact, Cynderet decreed within her mind, "I will succeed, Mother. I will become an apprentice and make you proud. I realize now that there is much more that I must learn for some purpose neither of us really—" Cynderet closed her thoughts as she felt the Table's presence.

The Table caught the first bits of Cynderet's thoughts of her mother. It saw how Cynderet wanted to please Luanta and her need to be accepted. It also saw how Cynderet had carefully ended the thought and stole it away into the furthest recesses of her mind. The Table tried to follow only to have its efforts lost in a jumble of memorized squawking birdcalls Cynderet mentally recited to cover the trail.

The Table then sent its exploratory probing fingers into Cynderet.

She stood resolved, though she did not resist. She noted the Table's surprised impulse. After the earlier confrontation with her, it had expected her to fight all the way.

It hesitated just a bit at this variance of attitude. The Table looked around almost playfully just to see what thoughts and attitudes Cynderet had. It was not looking for anything specific, just looking to see what was there.

Cynderet followed the fingers searching within her mind. She kept a deliberate stoic sense about herself. She did not want to give the Table any idea of her plans before the second and more powerful penetration.

The initial probing ceased. The Table withdrew itself. Cynderet did not understand why this was necessary, yet the Table had done it with each candidate. Cynderet knew what would follow. She was aware the Table knew she understood what was happening. It also knew she had a power of her own. She had no idea what the Table would do about this knowledge, but she knew she had beat it once before. She waited.

The Table spoke to her. "It is you who denied me entrance earlier. You already know some of the secrets of the Society. Do you know what it all means?"

"No. I am new to the mysteries. I have come to be appointed an apprentice, to be granted the right to learn the powers of the Society. I seek to be as my mother."

"Your mother is one of the greatest. She is second only to Ermentrude the Ancient. She will become the Senior Eldress one day. She has gone through the testing, so have the others. If you would be as they, you too must be tested."

It attacked then, faster than Cynderet could imagine. It penetrated so deeply she could not slam the door upon it as she had done before. It was within, searching. Cynderet felt the imminent violation of her most private sanctums. She felt dirty and cringed inside. She tried to drive it out with a giant hand pushing against it. She felt she had it stopped when it became water and flowed through her fingers. She became a wind and blew at it, dry and arid. It became an ant and dug the spines of its legs into the floor of her mind, ducking its head down and proceeding against the wind.

Cynderet realized it was in, but she did not have to keep everything out in the open. She disguised her secrets as pleasant memories. She twisted their meanings so they would appear obfuscated and disjointed to the Table. She felt the Table laugh, not with mirth, but with scorn.

"You would block me with your puny thought-changes? I have entered the minds of even the greatest. Their thoughts became mine. Their fears, food for me to feed upon. You are the first to see me as I am. You are the Mind Child. Still, your mind shall open to me. Open or you will end up as Linnet. You are mine, Mind Child. Either way, I shall have you."

The Table opened to her mind the scenes of Linnet's dying again. It showed her quivering in panic and uncontrollable fear. The scene was clear when Linnet succumbed to hysterics and the Table's fury as it threw her to the floor, slamming her head against the Table's edge. Cynderet noted the distinct variant of the happening.

"Yes," the Table purred, "it was me. Her pathetic being, to think she would be even considered for apprenticeship. I drove her mad. She was worthy of only the vilest of loathing. Her spirit will dwell here, here with the others who will never become of the Society. Their place is of another, of another's needs and purposes. She is immured within these non-walled pinnacles until called to a new home." The vitriolic growl found its home, piercing Cynderet's heart.

The Table lambasted her with scenes of exquisite pain and suffering, the deaths of those before. Lives unable to endure the Table's probes. Minds that exploded behind terrified faces of youth so like her own. It drove her to the brink of insanity with a deluge of images, weakening her resistance with powers she had not witnessed before. Cynderet felt the pounding of her own panic building within.

The Table was winning. She was losing her will to resist. Tears streamed down her face. Her eyes were so tightly shut she felt the sinuses behind her nose begin to bleed. She could not breathe in enough air. Her head started to swim in blanketing dizziness.

Cynderet could feel the Table—confident of its victory over her. She knew it felt her resolve breaking down. It intensified its probing. Cynderet was no longer able to put up a defense. Her equilibrium was failing her; her knees weakened, and her mental strength was collapsing. She knew she was kneeling, yet all she could do was struggle to breathe. Her heart pounding as never before; her lungs crushing under the onslaught of bitter barbs, barbs of scorn, objurgation, and—and hate; the Table hated her.

She felt it as a burning brand. It sizzled against the fragments within her mind; hatred, burning hot, was igniting the tissues within her brain. Cells were felt to burst. She was dying. She could not stop the Table's battering. Blackness was stealing life from her. Only a single iota of coolness, a smallest drip of moisture resistant to the burning could be discerned in a pocket so minuscule Cynderet had only discovered it now. Realizing within its coolness lay her last hope for life;. She drove her life force to it as sunlight drives its warmth through the vastness of space.

The capsule began to grow as her life rushed to it. "No!" it was saying from the deepest welling of a loving heart. "No," it repeated as the coolness began to grow. "No, it is not death for you; but life!"

Cynderet saw waves of water within her mind, waves washing against a rocky seacoast, crashing waves beating upon the rocks of the burning firebrands of the Table. The waves burst high upon the cliffs and misted into the air, continuing to squelch the intense heat of the Table's hate. The steam of combat between fire and water obscured all sight even within her mind. And with the growing mist came a breeze, clearing the steam and ash away. She was able to see the fires within immersed in the coolness of the waters. The fires of hate boiled in effort to repel this newly found power—this power intruding upon the Table's efforts to destroy the Mind Child. Cynderet and the Table noted the source in unison. A third presence was aiding Cynderet— someone who knew of oceans and mists of earth, someone who dared attempt to thwart the Table's power, someone who would die!

The Table picked up the direction of the sends to Cynderet.

It took Cynderet a moment longer to finish putting out the remaining fires within her mind. Then she sent out to find her benefactor.

The Table was already clasped upon the mind of the newcomer. The

Table was a python squeezing upon the life source of sends. It was so intent upon killing; it did not heed what was being sent. It sought only to kill.

The sends did not stop coming to Cynderet. She shared in other pictures of beauty and peace. Other scenes of places, thoughts, trainings, and lives she had never even known existed. They washed over her and sequestered themselves in places new even to her. They were ceded to her mind so fast she could not keep pace with them in their effort to deposit themselves safely away. The sends were a continuous ribbon of images blurred in haste: flashing colors, scents aromatic, and sounds literally thundering in the rush to enter her mind, each with its own sense of purpose. Their speed was heightened by the impetus of desperation. It was as if each vision had its own intelligence, desperate to penetrate, desperate to be a part of her.

"You have purpose, Cynderet. I charge you to find and fulfill it. My knowledge and wisdom are yours. They will be with you always."

She felt the sends cease then. She felt the physical gasps for air that could not fill lungs and blood system with enough oxygen to stay alive. She also felt a spiritual sense of dignity and rest in knowing its service had been well met. She felt the sacrifice willingly surrendered in exchange for her life. There was a feeling of giving Cynderet had never known before. The feeling of unselfish desire to help someone deeply loved. She felt Reht's gift of self and his good-bye.

With the realization of what Reht had done, Cynderet finally burst out in anguish. She heard her own cry of denial as she collapsed upon the floor in total despair.

The Table gloated in its winning. It had broken the Mind Child. The only one to have ever known its workings, to know it was alive, except for the Eldresses. It had made her pliable enough to be taught.

The Table relished its destruction of the Hert for his petty attempt to save his ward before the Table totally destroyed her. It knew it sought to kill her, but it was satisfied with the death of the intruding Hert instead. "I will destroy her later. For now, I will allow her to become an apprentice. The feeding upon her will be that much better later. She shall be taught by the best—and the worst—her own mother."

CHAPTER THREE

For two days, Cynderet lay in the peace of a coma. Luanta attempted to stay with her during this time, allowing her body to heal. By the third day, Cynderet was experiencing periods of semi-consciousness; however, she remained unaware of where or who she was. Her mother saw the improvement and felt a sense of relief, having feared the ordeal of the initiation would leave further scars, impairing Cynderet's ability to fulfill the Society's expectations. She looked down at her daughter resting quietly and smiled. "Soon," she spoke, "We will begin the training. You will see, Cynderet, under my guidance, you can become the greatest Energy Feeder." Luanta took a moment's pleasure in envisioning the training and the many things Cynderet would learn through her.

Cynderet jerked in violent, sudden movement. Luanta could recognize a healing in Cynderet's better color and increased physical motion as she lay in her nest. It was good to be mothering an apprentice. "It has been a long wait for me," she mouthed. Cynderet moved again; an arm twitched to come to rest over Cynderet's eyes.

Reliving the ordeal of initiation, Cynderet again saw Linnet striking her head on the edge of the Table. She watched helplessly as Linnet's jerking body fell to the ground. The Table had killed her; the Table had deliberately dragged her into itself and killed her. Cynderet remembered her own battle with the Table. She remembered her feelings of utter despair. The Table taunted Cynderet by showing how it killed Linnet. It was all to antagonize her into submission. When she fought to prevent the Table from succeeding, it gave up its pursuit of submission and tried to destroy her. Cynderet's renewed visions brought her to the ultimate cost of Reht offering his life for hers. She felt again his passing. She moaned in the realization there was nothing she could do to stop it. Once again, the Table savored its conquest as Reht died and she succumbed.

The visions continued within her. They became jumbled with repetition. She was unable to keep each incident separate, and the scenes within her mind's eye were interwoven in a continuous replaying of pain, terror, and death in an already tortured mind.

Cynderet's body began to shake. A scream escaped, muffled in her blankets. Cynderet clearly called out Reht's name followed by a hoarse; "Not you!" She thrashed upon her bed. She was bound by the images. She fought to free herself of them, crying bitter tears of loss. Her body exhausted, ceased to struggle as she collapsed into whimpers and dried tears. Exhaustion brought her to a quiet sleep.

Witnessing Cynderet's struggle, Luanta felt something break inside. Still stunned at hearing Reht's name with its accompanied denial, she burped and swallowed quickly, feeling the bile burn her throat. She washed it down with further swallows. A twisted snarl drew across her lips as a hardening shudder closed about her heart. "These pathetic emotions and sentiment for a Hert. A Hert! I should have known. I should have seen it coming" she gritted out through tight teeth. She continued, "This will not be tolerated. I will see to it!" Looking again at Cynderet, Luanta mouthed, "He was an unforgivable failure. He failed me." Luanta recalled how she had chosen him specifically for Cynderet. From the Council Guard, she had drawn the best. He died when he should have lived to aid in Cynderet's training. "And she weeps for him! Uuwaahh! It will end here. No such sniveling weakness will be allowed to prevent you from becoming an Energy Feeder!"

Luanta leaned wearily against the back of her chair she was sitting in. She held hands to her head in frustration. How had such an impaired creature passed the initiation? She felt an unbidden twinge of conscience, almost a touch of remorse crossed her thoughts. The image of the Table came to her, and in a form of reverence, she placed her hands out in front of her, palms down. The Table knows what it is doing, she reasoned. Maybe, she thought, Cynderet will get over this forsaken endearment soon.

Cynderet began to thrash in her nest again. There was another scream. Luanta recognized another whimpering cycle beginning. She felt her reasoning shatter, her resolve crack. Her jaw set in hard lines of ridged anger; hate rose within her when an old thought crossed her mind anew, "He did this. He brought about this deformity of being in her. If not for him, I never would have been settled and burdened with this ingrate! He will pay. They all will pay!"

Luanta allowed herself to become overwhelmed by a sudden need to feel the surging energy waves of stolen life swelling within her. She drowned her moment's fear with thoughts of pleasure gained draining a vicarious male of his life's force. "I will drain him to a powdery shell and treasure each sensation. I shall bathe in his dying!"

She pushed from her seat, turning towards the door. Just then, another sobbing series streamed from Cynderet. Luanta grasped the handle and pulled. Her hand failed to turn the latch before she attempted to open it. Her wrist jerked in pain as her hand slipped its grasp. She grabbed anew, turned, and threw the door open. It banged the wall and slammed back, hitting her in the shoulder. With an ugly snarl on her lips, she flung it open again and kicked it behind her as she lunged through the portal.

Luanta descended the stairs bellowing orders; there was no room for question. "Get in there and watch!" she shouted. All restraint lost to bitter anger, she added, "Hopefully, she will just die!"

She did not wait to see if she was heard or if the recipient was responding. She extended her arms straight out from her sides and dragged them quickly to her front. Her fingertips joined together, arms forming an arch in front of her. There was a wavering in the air around her. It started just outside her arms and imploded upon her; she disappeared in her Energy Web.

On the fifth day, Cynderet opened her eyes and tried to see where she was. She recognized her room and drew comfort, knowing she was in her own nest. A Hert sat in the chair close to the door. His head was slowly rolling down the wall to his shoulder as he dozed.

Cynderet's head reverberated with a dull throbbing at each beat of her heart. Her eyes had difficulty staying focused on the details within her room. Her chest felt heavy. Her breathing came in quick, shallow gasps. Determined, she tried to move. She stopped mid-motion as tiny knives of pain raked her rib cage while she tried to roll her body to the edge of the nest. She collapsed into the hollow her body had made lying for days in the nest.

Knowing the sharp pains would return if she moved bodily, she struggled to awaken more fully. She forced herself to roll her head to one side to better examine the Hert. She knew Reht was gone. She could remember the incident with a clarity her eyes could not achieve now as she strove to fully awaken. This Hert looked rather familiar though; she was not certain how or why. Seeking greater acuity, she carefully drew herself up into a ball using the thighs of her legs to put pressure on her ribs, and by leaning slightly to the side, she allowed her body to slowly roll. The pains did not come. Reassured, she worked her elbow deep into the hollow; and using it as a lever, she raised her body up into an almost huddled position. Dizziness struck;. She closed her eyes. She refused to succumb and waited instead. The spinning lessened;. Keeping her eyes closed, she dared to extend her legs to the nest's edge. Her feet and legs felt the coolness of the room when they escaped the covers. She let them drop at the knees and bodily drew herself to a full sitting position on the edge of the nest. She attempted to open her eyes once again. She felt the disquiet of nausea and shook her head. She regretted it immediately as the resulting pounding drove throbs of painful barbs into her temples and sinuses. Keeping her eyes closed and pushing gently with her hands now flat on the nest, she felt her feet touch the cold of the flooring. She drew on the chilling sensation, letting it settle the nausea and waited. It worked. After a few minutes, she was able to reopen her eyes. Yes, she was sitting up.

The Hert must have heard something. With an awakening spasm, he opened his own eyes and smiled. He spoke, "I have awaited this moment for two days now. I must admit exhaustion drew me into slumber, but I am able to assist you now as you need."

He added motion to words and came to her at the edge of the bed.

Cynderet recognized him now. He was Linnet's Hert. The memory opened the door to an immediate reliving of those horrible few minutes of loss and anguish. If he cared for Linnet only a little bit as she cared for Reht, then he must feel pain also.

She asked him.

His response was a slow, eye lowered, "Yes." Then they both looked at each other in realization that neither had spoken a word.

Cynderet remembered Reht's warning too late. Her secret was now clear to Linnet's Hert. Cynderet felt confused and ashamed at the same time. She looked quickly to right and left. She was buying time trying to think. How could she remedy this situation?

"Fear not, Child. I sense your fear of what I will do now with this bit of knowledge gained. I will not betray your secret. I had seen you on occasion look to Reht as if speaking to him, and he to you; but never did I see your lips move. I felt there had to be some kind of connection."

Looking away for a moment, the Hert seemed to have decided a course and continued, "The Hert may speak this way to each other. You also are able to so, though how this is possible, I do not understand." The question remained in his eyes as he continued, "Reht was my friend. We were both called to serve our wards in the same season. He and I were both Council Guards before our call. I have lost Linnet and you Reht. We both share in loss. I am pleased to be with you."

Cynderet was not so quick to feel the same, but she knew he was sincere. "My loss will remain a void forever. I know you mean well, and I trust in your good faith towards my secret. He warned me to keep it only between us. If you are to be my protector now, then perhaps I am glad you know, for it was a very important part of our relationship."

"I will honor your confidence as I honor his memory, Child. I am Serenten. I am your Hert now." He thumped his chest with his clawed hand held in a fist.

Cynderet recognized the sign of respect among the Hert.

Serenten then placed his arms where Cynderet could grasp them to help herself stand up.

She looked up to his face and knew she would be well cared for by him. She sent her thanks and grasped hold of his arms.

It was another two days before Cynderet finally saw her mother again. Luanta had come back late the night before. Cynderet had heard her open and close the door to her own nest. Serenten had acknowledged her questioning send that it was indeed her mother home from Energy Feeding.

That next morning, Cynderet was downstairs preparing something to eat when Luanta came down to the gathering area. She too was hungry. She had that hyperactive feeling common just after feeding. It was difficult for her to keep her hands from shaking. She wanted something to fill the emptiness of her stomach, hoping it would settle the shakes. Energy Feeding gave vitality and power;. But offered no nourishment to the body.

Cynderet was not really interested in eating. She knew she must have something to regain lost strength and help the healing process. She prepared herself a little fruit. It was difficult to think about eating. Her heart still felt heavy. It dimmed her appetite. She gave an occasional deep sigh, each time pausing in effort to regroup her thoughts.

Luanta overheard the sighs and finally could stand it no longer. Softly, she said, "It has been seven days. Reht is dead. I selected him personally for his perfection in training. He was supposed to have been a well-tuned tool. But he could not take the strain of the council meeting. I never knew him to be so weak. He must have had a failing inside he did not show. Now, he is gone. We do not spend days mourning the loss of a tool." Her voice had risen in conclusion both in volume and tempo.

Cynderet was stunned and quiet.

Her mother continued, "We are the Supreme Beings. All others are simply for our use and purpose. You have been initiated to become a member of the Society of Energy Feeders. You must lose all the frailty. No more weakness will be tolerated. You must be strong and purposeful."

Building irritation grew to anger as Luanta concluded, "Now, cease this noise and fix my meal!" She bit back adding, "You freak of nature", because of a sudden aversion to offending the Table.

Cynderet read it. Shaken, she realized how different their feelings were regarding Reht. She also knew she had to change the current direction of things. It was time to begin training. Reht would want her to. She struggled to pull herself up straight and settled her shoulders. She looked to her mother, gave her the food, and said, "I am ready, Mother. I will put my loss behind me and begin my training." Inside, she knew she would never forget Reht. He was her closest friend. Suddenly, she understood: her mother knew nothing of how Reht died. She thought it was because of a physical complication due to the tension of the initiation!

"Good! Go get dressed for a walk. Your first lesson begins today. We will be leaving the city for the bulk of the day. Now, hurry!

"Besides, I have to get out and moving before these shakes drive me insane."

Luanta took Cynderet up into the surrounding hills of the city, areas Cynderet had never been in before. She and Reht had traveled the lower reaches, but had not gone out of sight of the city itself. Here, Luanta said they would find things different and not so protected. Cynderet did not understand her meaning at first;. It did not take long before she realized some of what her mother meant.

They had been following a path leading over the first ridge of hills and then dropped down into a canyon behind. Below the ridge, a thick canopy of large, broad-leafed trees shaded the forest floor from the haze of light above. Only thin slivers of light penetrated directly; ,most light was diffused and lost in deep shadows of heavy foliage. There was little underbrush beneath the large trees though massive trunks blocked the view of the path after only a few yards. Where several trunks amassed together, there was often no visibility at all. The direction Luanta was taking became twisted and turned frequently. Shortly after dropping into the canyon, Cynderet gave up trying to see ahead at all.

Watching her mother, Cynderet noted she seemed to be looking for something. Cynderet could not determine what it might be other than it was alive. She followed and opened herself up to the emotions of the area. Her mother continued to look for the illusive life form. The sensations of the forest were new to Cynderet and hard to comprehend. She could feel the calm of the trees and the tenacious determination of the local molds and mosses to their purposes. There were many insects around busy about their lives, constantly on the watch for predators. The birds here were few, most were in other more open areas feeding.

Cynderet began to feel eyes watching them walk. She looked to her mother still searching for something. Cynderet could feel her determination to find it. She could also tell that whatever watched them was larger and more intelligent than the other life forms she had been feeling so far.

Cynderet focused her attention upon the creature. It was new to her, one she had never encountered before or heard of. Its thoughts and emotions she found interesting and foreign. It was concerned for something. In fear of them, it kept something hidden, not wanting it to be found. This creature seemed to recognize what Cynderet and her mother were. It thought to pick something up for attack, any kind of a weapon.

She felt it move away from what it was protecting;. It was providing a diversion. Cynderet could read its commitment to its purpose. It had little hope, but it had to try.

Cynderet had slowed down in her study of this new being, and Luanta had moved ahead a few steps. Luanta followed the path around a tree, bringing her into a facing position of where the creature was hiding. Cynderet read the creature's thought of attack as it leapt in front of her mother.

Her mother never hesitated. In the same moment the creature tried to throw the stick it had found, Luanta took a step to her side and in fluid motion lifted her arm and hand to point towards the creature.

Cynderet sensed her mother's feelings of pleasure. There was a feeling of release, a feeling of exhilaration for being able to strike out at something and inflict pain. Cynderet read her mother's almost gloating in that she deserved this satisfaction for having to deal with a helpless initiate like Cynderet. Luanta was reveling in the grace of motion, almost as a step sequence in a dance.

For Cynderet, it was as if each step was in slow motion. She saw each aspect of the encounter. Her mother's fingers were joined together in an open palm and the tips of her fingers were brought to face the creature in an upward arch. As the hand rose from her side; , darkness extended in length from her fingertips;. The blackness became a severing blade that took the creature under the raised arm and smote the arm off at the shoulder, searing the wound as it did so.

Cynderet felt the world around her go black from the outside in. She remembered the sense of blackness from the other day and knew she was fainting. She turned from the sight;. She could not hide from what she had just witnessed, nor could she hide from the subsequent happenings as they occurred to the creature. She was too deeply in tune with it.

The creature screamed in pain. It turned to bolt away in a futile attempt to divert and flee.

Luanta sent a searing lance of night through the creature's back, piercing its heart.

Through the creature's last thoughts, Cynderet read a heart-rending concern before it settled to the floor of the forest and died. The air remained heavy with the pungent odor of burned flesh and hair.

Cynderet held her hands to her face in disbelief, fighting an acrid burning to her nostrils and to control her threatening nausea.

Luanta turned to Cynderet, saw her repulsion, and laughed. "Normally, I would only have been able to send a blunt force field against it. Because I have just returned from feeding, my powers are much greater."

Luanta took Cynderet's shoulder in a firm grasp and drew her around to face the path again. "Come, I am anxious for you to learn a little more of what we can do when empowered." Luanta walked around the creature, expecting Cynderet to follow.

Cynderet sensed another life. There was something still out there: something that was being protected. What could be so important that the creature was willing to die for it? She followed the impulse around the tree to her left. In a hidden hollow was a tiny version of the creature still lying dead on the path. Cynderet was sure it was a baby. It was frightened and huddling deep into the heart of the hollow, watching her closely with large eyes, unmoving. Cynderet could feel its mixed messages of fear and despair. Cynderet felt empathy for it.

Cynderet heard her mother coming up behind her.

"Oh, good! A second lesson today. And so timely."

Cynderet felt a change in her mother's attitude. It was foreign to anything she had ever felt of her mother before. No, there were actually two attitudes— two thought processes going on at the same time. One was, was what? A lie. The other was a deeper cunning—motivating the first.

Cynderet turned to look at her mother to see what she was doing. She was unprepared for the superficial change in her mother's appearance and demeanor. It was so opposite to what she read in her mother's mind.

Luanta pushed by towards the hollow and told Cynderet to watch. Luanta exuded kindness and friendship as she positioned herself in front of the youngling. A powerful bond of trust and acceptance took place within the youngling towards Luanta. It came out of the hole as if to a long-lost friend. Luanta collected the youngling in her arms and cooed. She turned to Cynderet.

"It is called a Charm Spell. It is an important tool in the hunt and feeding. This, along with the taking of our human form, is how we lure the human male to us." She gave the youngling a tender squeeze while making clucking noises to it. She continued in Cynderet's lesson, "This little creature thinks I am its closest friend. It will do anything for me. Watch."

Luanta told it to climb high up into the tree. It went up with a struggle at first, and then more easily as it found a better grip in the cracks of the tree's upper bark and thicker branches. When it reached the outstretched limbs of the tree blending into the upper canopy, it turned to look down to Luanta.

She smiled up to it.

At the same time, Cynderet felt a change in Luanta's façade. She knew what was going to happen even as her mother spoke the words up to the youngling. Luanta extended her arms up towards the creature saying, "Now jump to me."

Without hesitation, the youngling let go of the limb and jumped to Luanta's waiting arms. It descended quickly. Cynderet felt its confusion when Luanta dropped her arms and took a step backwards. She heard its intake of breath in alarm and could only watch it reach out with arms and legs seeking any kind of hold while it plummeted downward. Luanta had dropped the entrapment of the Charm Spell from its mind. The youngling tried in desperation to grab anything to stop the free fall. There was only air. It died on impact with the ground.

Cynderet looked at the crumpled form;. A barrage of heart-rending emotions smothered her; constricting in her throat. She felt tears brimming in her eyes and turned her head away from her mother's view. She could feel Luanta watching her and struggled desperately to regain control.

Luanta's anger was mounting;. Cynderet knew at any moment Luanta would explode in a tirade. She turned back to her mother, forcing herself to look into her eyes. For the next several seconds, Cynderet fought her reactions to the wanton slaughter. She tried not to give any cause for her mother to objurgate her.

Luanta stood staring at Cynderet. The scrutiny was intense in her determination to understand what her daughter's true disposition was. *Surely, Cynderet would now have a firm grasp on the powers of Energy Feeding and the Charm Spell. These are such critical parts of the Society's being.*

Cynderet knew she had failed in her efforts when she read Luanta's recognition of the tears still welling in the troughs of Cynderet's eyes. What happened next would remain imprinted in Cynderet's heart for the rest of her life.

Luanta spoke not a word, and the tension creases of her forehead melded into the gnashing of jaw and curl of lips. Anger transformed through fury to settle deeply within as loathing. Everything suddenly changed.

Cynderet felt her stomach drop away and experienced an emptiness matched with sickening rejection. She was alone. She was vulnerable. She was no longer wanted and yet trapped. They were both trapped in a societal bond, bound to the Table's purpose. Luanta was trapped with the most despicable of beings, and Cynderet was trapped with her mother—a mentor who vehemently hated all that Cynderet was. She realized her mother would do far worse things and force Cynderet to be a part of it as an initiate. She also knew her mother would no longer be doing it to help her succeed. Luanta was set on one thing: destroying Cynderet in such a way that the Table would not hold her accountable.

That night Cynderet's mind rehearsed her mother's last remark before they left towards home: "We are done here." Luanta then turned her back on Cynderet. Without looking at her again, Luanta walked the path to the city in conspicuous silence.

They had not talked since.

At one point, later in the day, Luanta was sitting at the table just staring off into space. Cynderet tried to appease her mother by sending a suggestion of her working to conform. Her mother slammed her hands on the table and strode out the door without a backwards glance. Cynderet was still waiting her mother's return as she retired.

Serenten witnessed the display and shared a questioning look with Cynderet. She shrugged her shoulders and ran upstairs before tears overtook her.

Into the wee hours of early morning, sleep had proven elusive. A frustrating many hours passed in rolling back-and-forth, tossing and turning to find even the simplest of positions to ease the aggravation experienced in both body and mind. The dampness of tears remained evident on her pillow and in the corners of her eyes. Gone was Reht, for whom she wept his loss. Now even her mother was gone, though still alive and within the city. Cynderet tried to sense her presence but was unable to locate her anywhere within the house. She had not returned. Serenten was fast asleep in his nest. Loneliness dominated Cynderet's deepest thoughts. In a desperate effort to find solace in sleep, she forced herself to lay quiet. Systematically, she drove from her mind any thoughts intruding in her valiant determination to stay blank of mind and find sleep. A fantasy of finding someplace where she was wanted played at her attempts of control. It swirled about the vestiges of dimness as sleep finally came.

Her sleep was not restful. Instead, she fought dreams of what had happened during the day intermixed with anguished distortions of the initiation ceremony, though none of Linnet. Cynderet sought to run from the agony of her dreaming—agony of loss so poignant these past wakeful hours—her loneliness, the creature and its youngling's horrid death, and the vanished care of her mother. She envisioned herself running through the hills among the thick tree trunks huddled within the canyon. The path she followed led through new places of shadow, darkness, and mist. The mists came swirling around massive trunks and lingered over open surfaces of dampness and leaves. Here, the ground was soft and silent in her passing. She continued to run, seeing her way along the path only a few steps ahead in the mists. At least it was away from the broken forms of death behind. Her breath became more labored in her prolonged run. Being fatigued, she slowed her steps and tried to peer more closely ahead. Could she see a little further? Was the path opening up and her vision clearing?

The path began to widen. Grass, sparse at first, interceded in the regions between the trunks now not quite as massive yet majestic in their growth and foliage. The leaves were no longer broad and expansive. These leaves were longer though narrow and pointed at their ends. They looked like long pins or needles. Brushing up close to a bough, the points jabbed her skin pricking with scraping tips. The dense canopy of foliage no longer blocked sunlight. The mist was burning away, allowing her to see that the trees separated a distance beyond either side of the path, now a road. A stream gurgled along to the right of which the road seemed to be following.

Cynderet was standing, catching her breath just to the side of the road opposite the stream. Up ahead, she heard voices. There followed a harsh command for silence.

She could not see where the voices came from. Instead, she saw an older man in the weathered and worn clothes of a farmer. He was leading an empty farm cart with two children sitting on the rein bench. The single horse, sway backed and head down, plodded along the road with a dusty shuffle. They all appeared to be in the listless state of a hot day.

They had just come around a bend in the road ahead and were reaching the area where Cynderet thought the voices came from. The voices remained quiet.

The family and horse looked so tired in the heat. *It must have been a long hard day,* Cynderet thought. Realization sank in: it was mid-afternoon and not night as when she ran in the mists. She was contemplating this awareness and its meaning when things began to happen quickly.

Suddenly, a large, burly man came rushing out of the trees. He grabbed the unprepared farmer by the throat literally lifting him up off his feet from his position alongside the cart. The burly fellow began shaking him, yelling and cursing in the stunned farmer's face. The children sat motionless with mouths agape, their minds struggling to comprehend what was happening.

Simultaneously, two more ruffians came running out of the trees. They rushed to the cart, attempting to grab the children. The young girl was the first to rouse from surprise. Noting the two approaching, she jabbed her brother in the arm, trying to get him to follow her off the cart. They got to the ground just as the two reached the cart. The girl had strategically placed the cart between themselves and the attackers. The boy remained confused and slow to act, but the girl grabbed a horsewhip and turned to face the assailants coming around the cart's back.

Cynderet's yell for them to run into the trees was stayed when a stranger rushed right past her. He was hunched over slightly, taking advantage of the cover of the perimeter trees.

He paused for an instant at her thought. He looked in her direction. His eyes did not seem to register anything. He shook his head continuing his hurried assault along the trees. He was well hidden in the shadows, his woodsman clothes blending in. He was armed. His sword remained in its leather scabbard.

There were now five brigands near or at the cart. Two had taken a stand beyond to watch the road. The burly one had thrown the farmer to the ground and was searching him for something as the other two continued in efforts to corral the children.

The boy was physically encouraged by a push to get beneath the cart by his sister. In her effort to get him to safety, she dropped her focus on the brigands she was slapping at with the whip. Instantly, she was caught up in one's arms. His back was now to Cynderet, but she saw him shake the young girl's wrist wickedly, forcing her to drop the whip.

The stranger saw it also and became a whir of motion.

A knife suddenly embedded itself deeply in the brigand's back. He dropped the girl in a futile effort to grasp the fatal blade. Two paces of the stranger later, a second knife was in the ribs of the bully searching the farmer.

The bully looked blankly into the stranger's face;. The stranger made a strong upward heave of his knife arm and the bully simply lifted up a step and slid off the blade to the ground, dead.

The stranger then rolled low into the path of the third and unsuspecting brigand who was coming at a run around the backside of the cart to get at the boy. The motion bowled the thief over. Not sure what just happened, the thief sought to get up. From a kneeling position behind, the stranger pummeled the heel of his knife into the back of the brigand's neck. He went down with a thud, lifting a cloud of dust from the road.

The last two brigands watching the road realized something was wrong. They turned and saw what was happening to their accomplices. Drawing their weapons, they rushed towards the stranger with battle-ax and sword.

With a hefty upward pull, the stranger raised the unconscious bandit and pushed the bulk into the first on-comer, allowing the body to take the cleaving blow of the battle-ax. The stranger ducked to the right, going under the sword swing of the second attacker. As he did so, he slashed deeply with his backwards held dagger, now in his left hand. The move sliced the brigand's sword arm tendons just under the back of his wrist. The sword sailed in an uncontrolled horizontal arc of momentum as grip was lost.

The thief watched his blade fly several feet into the road. His dumbfounded look went to his useless arm now held mid-belly while he sank to his knees on the ground in shock. He passed out in that position, the severed arteries pulsing his life away.

The last remaining brigand took a quick look at his fallen comrades. He looked into the stranger's face and saw death for him also. He let go of his battle-ax still deep set in the shoulder and neck of his dead companion;. Backing a few quick steps, he turned and ran.

The stranger mercifully slit the throat of the kneeling brigand now unconscious. He wiped his dagger off on the brigand's cloak and retrieved his other as he turned to the family.

The farmer was still lying on the ground. The girl had lifted his head into her lap and was talking to him in a comforting manner. She looked up to the approaching stranger, unsure what to do.

The stranger smiled to her, "You have done well. Let us get him over into the shade of the trees, out of the dust and sun."

The farmer began moaning, coming back into consciousness as they worked to lift him. The stranger helped him into a sitting position and then to his feet. Together, they walked in short steps to a shady spot beneath a tree.

The girl hurried back to the cart and took up a water bucket. Heading off to the stream, she called to the boy still hiding beneath the cart. She instructed him to get the cart and horse to the grass off the road.

She returned with the cool water and bathed the farmer's face with a cloth pulled from her skirt pocket. The stranger seemed pleased with her spunk. He gave her a pat on the shoulder and walked back to the cart to help the boy.

They unhitched the horse and he told the boy to take the horse for water at the stream. He checked the thieves, taking what little was of value and returned to the farmer. He handed the farmer back his coin purse retrieved from the bully. The battle-ax and sword he wrapped in a dead man's cloak and put behind the rein bench. Turning to the young girl, he gave her a small boot knife and sheath he found on the thief who had caught her.

Cynderet noted a reflected shine of a gold medallion impressed into the heft of the knife and its sheath. She could not see any inscription on them from where she remained observing. She did note that the matching medallions were not perfectly round. They were oblong with a niche, like a wedge of cheese, cut from the bottom. Cynderet heard the stranger say something to the girl about having shown a lot of good sense and courage.

Cynderet asked herself how she would have reacted in a similar situation. This was all so foreign to her.

The stranger suddenly looked in Cynderet's direction. He seemed to sense something. He started to walk back in her direction though he did not seem clear as to where she was because his eyes kept traveling to either side of her as he came.

Cynderet was touched by his obvious care for the family; he was getting too close! His finesse of battle was too practiced. She felt a sense of panic welling up inside. He was now only a step or two away. This dream is too real! she thought; ,her body set to run. The mist was there, closing in from beyond the cart and family. Instantly, it drew in upon herself, erasing the scene from the outside in. The last thing she saw was the green of the stranger's eyes piercing into hers. She was in the mist and gone.

CHAPTER FOUR

The forest and road were still there behind him. He could hear the soft chatter of the girl to the farmer in front of him. He continued to stare, sure that he had seen something—sure of the eyes looking hauntingly into his own. He had finally located the essence of the questions he had sensed only to have that essence vanish. The questions had been like voices in his head, spoken clearly. It had been human. It had been—?

Yes. It was female.

Perplexed and uncomfortable, unable to learn more, his eyes took one last look around—nothing. He knew it was simply to satisfy a gnawing hunger, something missing, something sought for years and still missing.

He shook his head in the familiar attempt to clear it.

Razon turned back to the family behind him.

The farm girl was dipping the cloth back into the bucket of water to reapply to the farmer's brow. With a toss of her head, she threw her long brown hair from her face over her shoulder. She showed a natural grace in her movement as she methodically went about her business. The boy evidenced a youthful spring in his lanky form, pulling on the lead line to bring the worn plow horse back from the stream; water was still dripping from its muzzle. The dead remained where they had fallen. Death and life—the scene evoked a sudden pull upon his heart.

Unbidden, he was reminded of family. Guilt washed over him in a cold sweat. At twenty, he had succumbed; now he was thirty-four. Few of his kind ever lived to this age. Death had become so familiar to him. "How much time before it is my turn?" he asked himself again, for an eternal instant.

He shook his head. One more time, he drove the memories away.

"Boy," he called, "help me get these bodies into the trees." He walked back into the present. It was time to get these people moving.

After they had disposed of the bodies, Razon took a look at the family and the surrounding area. It would be dark in a few hours. He walked to the old farmer still being tended by the girl. "It is time we left. It will be dark soon; there may be others."

The farmer spoke in a hoarse whisper to the girl. She nodded, yes.

She turned and looked squarely to Razon. "Sir, earlier we were afraid you were walking away and leaving us. We are grateful you did not. Rather, you have remained to assist us. I am Ashley. My brother is Patrick. This is our grandfather. We are all very thankful for your aid." She continued undaunted, "My grandfather has asked if you would not remain with us home. His throat is so sore he can only whisper or he would ask you himself. We would be pleased to provide you a meal and a place to sleep this night." And, as if to ensure his acceptance, she added, "The closest inn is still several days away in the village. However, it is only a bit up the road to our home."

"So? You know me to be a stranger here?"

"Recently, there have been many strangers about, sir. Though, none have been of your character, rather as these who attacked us. It is very dangerous of late. The nights are worse than the daylight. It is not safe to wander after dark, even for one as capable as you. Will you not please join us?"

It took only a moment for Razon to answer, "I would be pleased. It is true I am a stranger and I have several days yet to travel. There have been no inns for me for many days. I welcome the invitation. I tire of my own cooking and the sound of voices besides my own will be refreshing."

Arriving in the front yard of the family's home, Razon viewed a humble cottage with a small clearing around it. A large oak stood behind the cottage offering shade in the last hours of the day's heat. Predominant of the sunny side was a well-tended garden. Razon gave the farmer credit for his healthy vegetables visible. Out of the meager forest clearing, he was able to raise enough for his family; and a little extra to sell in the village marketplace.

"We wus jus' com'n home when we wus, wus, ah…" Patrick struggled to find a word still foreign to his experiences of life.

"Assaulted," Ashley aided, a subtle tone of contempt all but hidden.

"Yep. That wha' we wus," he finished matter-of-factly, his mind seeming bent in a new direction the next moment.

"We be runn'n' late, kids. Get on with yer chores," the farmer rasped out.

"I will join you, if you will permit me," Razon said.

"Welcome, fo' sure," he graveled out. He failed to control a fit of coughing and hunched over struggling to ease the strain on his chest.

All watched him for a couple moments before Razon caught Ashley's eye and tossed his head for her to get going.

She responded immediately, grabbing Patrick's hand and stepping off to the cottage. Nearing the steps, Patrick got a gentle shove towards the plow horse still standing in the traces of the cart.

The farmer worked to slow his breathing and control his coughing. When he could breathe without coughing, he stood up straight and, without looking right or left, went to his chores.

Razon followed.

Patrick put the horse in its stall and brushed it down with straw. He then fed the few chickens and the pig in a pen beyond the cottage. Ashley filled and washed at the porch basin and disappeared inside.

Razon worked at the side of the farmer, noting the whole time how labored and halting the man's actions were now that the children were about their own chores and not paying him any mind. Razon recognized a lessening in the old gentleman's guard.

Feeling Razon's eyes upon him, the farmer turned while the last of his pretense faded. "I regret you see me so this eve. I fear I be weak and tired after this day's foul happen'ns. Thanks be to ye we be any still alive," the farmer's voice rasped as a gnarled hand stroked his throat. He made a noble effort to smile; he coughed instead.

Razon saw the pale color, the deep-seated shadows in the creases of time upon his face. There was a stubborn blue tint to the lips visible now that the light was fading into dusk.

With torn feelings, Razon answered, "I have been late too many times to the endings of the work of such brigands. I am relieved that this once I was somewhat timely in my arrival. We were very fortunate the band was not larger."

"Ye be a good fellow, sir. I see much pain behind yer eyes, but yer heart is kind to the need'n."

There was a sudden, determined clatter on wood. Both turned their heads towards the sound and cottage. Running across the yard, Patrick made a purposeful dash to the water basin on the corner of the small porch.

"Ashley calls us to eat," the farmer rejoined. "We best be head'n in our own selves afo' that Patrick gets to help'n his self to the eat'n." He concluded giving Razon a friendly nudge towards the cottage.

Razon was thankful for the change of subject and did as bidden. The smells of a tasty meal wafted from within, ending any hesitation still lingering. There was a rasping chuckle behind. Razon did not turn to acknowledge it; the washbasin was close at hand.

That evening, after the children had climbed the ladder to the loft and bed, the old farmer pulled out two pipes and a small sack of tobacco he had stashed in an earthen jar on the fireplace mantle. He gave a pipe and the tobacco to

Razon and accepted it back when Razon finished the filling of his pipe. The farmer lit both solicitously with a glowing tip from the fire. They both settled into their chairs opposite each other where both could continue to share in the fire's warmth.

The farmer's first pull on the pipe brought on a coughing fit. He took the pipe from his mouth and bent head and shoulders down to help ease the strain. He regained control and sat up again. Tears were evident in the corners of his eyes. He wiped them with the hem of his cotton tunic. "Is softer than the sleeve," he answered Razon's glance, finishing with a smile and rubbing his throat with a callused palm.

Razon noted with concern the continuing pallor of his face and neck. His lips were still with a blue cast to them. There was a beading of sweat on his forehead.

"I no be me self this night. My chest is heavy and troubled in breath'n." The farmer tried his pipe again. This time, only a slight cough escaped. He pointed the mouthpiece of his pipe at Razon. "Ye be an accomplished fighter, sir. No wandr'n lackey, ye, rather a man with a place. Ye do not appear like a court courier nor behave as one in a hurry to get somewhere." The farmer hesitated a meaningful moment then continued, "Yer face tells a story of time and search'n. I know not yer affairs, sir, but I thank ye from my heart for not turn'n away when needed. I am certain all would've been lost save yer arrival."

He took a ragged breath and pointed his pipe to the loft. "These be me only kin; an' me, all theirs. Parents be buried beyond the tree in back as be me wife." The old man paused a reflective moment. He looked to Razon as if to say more, then changed his mind. Instead, he gave a hoarse sigh. "Times be change'n for sure. These brigands be the new scourge of the forest. Be no longer safe up here. We'll be need'n for word to reach the Lord of Skon's Hall."

Noting the truth and timing, Razon said, "I am headed there. I will let them know."

The old man gave a nod like he had figured out a bit of a puzzle but said no more.

Shortly after, the farmer retired to a cot Razon had just refused.

Deep into the night Razon was still sitting by the fire. He could hear no sound of the children sleeping in the loft above. The old farmer was offering a hoarse, painful snoring through his own repose on the cot against the wall. Razon looked into the dying embers. He felt a warmth inside beyond the fire's;. It was good to be in the midst of a family again, if only for a night. He felt a satisfaction in knowing that there would be four less to harm the simple folk of Skon's lands.

The Eyes returned to his mind. The questions asked behind those eyes had been clear to his senses. There was panic behind those eyes. When he finally could focus on their location, the Eyes vanished into a haunting vision lingering just beyond clarity. What was it that perplexed him—just beyond his ken? He shook his head to clear it. *No sense dwelling on it now,* he thought. *In three more days, I will be able to talk to Skon and Laura about it.* He chuckled within himself, remembering pleasant times spent there. He fell asleep in the chair with a smile pulling at the corners of his mouth.

Razon woke up to the cold in the room. His back was sore and his legs were numb. Stiffly, he unfolded from the chair, trying to stand up. Quickly, he sat back down as the waves of nerve impulses hammered him;. His legs were asleep and he knew it would be several moments before the heightening crescendo of tingling needles passed. He kept his legs as still as possible hoping to hasten their passing.

The room was silent. He listened intently. He could hear the children breathing above, but the snoring had ceased. In fact, no breathing at all.

Razon felt a coldness settle around his heart. He forgot about his legs and stood up. The first step sent little coruscations to his brain. He walked stiff-legged to the cot.

The old farmer was absolutely quiet, no rhythmic sign of breathing. Razon touched his neck below the ear and found it cold and still.

Razon tucked the blankets around the old farmer and patted him on the shoulder. "You rest, my friend. You have worked hard for it." It would be a while before sunup. Razon stoked the fire again and returned to his chair.

He stared into the slowly building flames and watched the fire take hold of the new wood. *Like life itself,* he thought watching the flames lap up the new wood, *it grows in heat, in strength, into its adulthood. Soon, it will reach its maturity and begin to weaken until it dies or is allowed to kindle new flame upon the next generation of wood.* He was uncomfortable with where these thoughts were leading. He sought a distraction.

Razon looked at the cot with its bundle of blankets and faded life. He looked away around the cottage. He was not a farmer, nor a family man. He was a warrior, an adventurer. He had chosen to live alone most of his adult life; there had been a brief moment when thoughts had been otherwise, but the search had proven futile. Even at home—or at Skon's Hall—he eventually left to meander alone. He did not know what to do; he did not know what to do here and now. "I cannot just up and leave," he said to himself. "There is responsibility here." Once again, he felt the loops of life tie him from his own appointed direction. Always trying to get to the next step only to be caught in the twists of life's happenings with others. He thought back to a time with his own father.

*****

They were riding between forest villages on business of state in the Light Forest. Razon was in a hurry to get to the next village. They would have their noon meal there, and he was already hungry. Rather like Patrick, he thought. They had come upon a woodcutter with a broken leg. His morning's cuttings were tied in a bundle he was resting against. He was dressed in the rags of a poor man and smelled already of a day's labor. Razon had looked the other way pretending he did not notice. He heard the woodcutter giving thanks behind him as he rode by. Confused, he looked back to see his father dismounted, giving aid. Razon moaned in frustration. The woodcutter heard him though his father showed no sign as he knelt beside the injured man.

"The sire be a good lord to one and all," he said. "I be broken and poor and him, the lord, fix'n to my needs. Shows why the common folks love the lord and his lady. I be sorry if'n I interfere with yer plans, Young Master."

Razon dismounted in shame. He had ended up on foot leading the unconscious woodcutter and his bundle on his own horse. His father had walked beside him instead of riding above him.

"If we show not the example, whom then will truly lead, my son?" his father had asked him. "It is true duty calls, but duty does not exist without those in need. Our journey today allows us some time. We shall still eat, just a little later."

They had. A simple meal prepared by the woodcutter's wife. Yet Razon had been satisfied from the inside out. He had placed two silver pieces under his plate. Still ashamed, he also knew it would be some time before the wood cutter would be up and about to labor again.

Two days later, the whole kingdom knew how the lord and his son had helped the woodcutter.

His father's words returned: "If we do not set the example, whom then will truly lead?"

"I understand your lesson, Father, though I do not think you meant for me to be this long away in your counsels of learning," Razon said to a memory before the fire. "I run out of time and never seem to run out of someone in need."

CHAPTER FIVE

They buried the old farmer beside his family at the base of the old oak tree in the back. Ashley was quiet and, for the first time, appeared at a loss. She had remained the stalwart during the entire ordeal. It was she that stated where and how her grandfather should be buried. She had assisted Razon in seeing it through. Now she sat alone, looking off into the distance. Razon was sure she was seeing the emptiness inside instead.

Razon allowed her room and time to mourn. He looked for Patrick.

Patrick had cried at first when his grandfather was buried, then vanished, Razon guessed to go play. "He does not understand everything," Ashley had commented when Razon mentioned it to her. "He is older than I, but Grandfather says…" a break, pause, and correction passed. Then with renewed determination, she finished with, "…said he is blessed with a simple mind." She had then quickly turned away to hide renewing tears.

Razon saw Patrick slinging rocks from the porch. He hit a crow just landing near the garden. Razon noted his accuracy. It was a glancing blow, but the bird jumped, cawing in alarm and flew away. "Patrick, help me with the chores," Razon called. "I do not know what all needs to be done."

"Yep, I be com'n. 'S lots to do. You do Gran'fa'r's part. I be sho'n ya the way."

Later, in the early afternoon, the wooden clatter started up again announcing a meal.

"Fo'got! We missed our break-of-fast. Ya be finish'n here. I be hun'ry!" Patrick said as he dropped the leather satchel of seed for the chickens into Razon's hand and rushed off.

Razon laughed a bit watching the boy's antics. Realizing he was hungry too, he looked at the bag in his hand then at the chickens gathering around him, pecking at his toes in impatience. Quickly, he tossed the contents to the birds rushing off as well. He did stop to rinse his hands. Patrick was not pleased when Razon made him leave his plate and do the same.

"Ya no be me Gran'fa'r," he mumbled.

"No. However, I know he trained you well. Now be 'ya' gone," he imitated.

Razon saw a small play across Ashley's lips. *Her first step back to normal,* he thought. He gained a little reassurance that he was doing all right in a totally foreign domain. *I am a warrior, a son, a lord by my own right, he thought, but I know nothing of children.*

Patrick stomped back in, hands dripping until he wiped them on his dirty jersey. With no further thought at all, he ate.

Ashley joined them at the table and served herself from the common bowls of vegetables. She did not look up when she asked, "You will be leaving us soon?"

"I will stay to see you settled. Are there others to whom you can go?"

"No. All we have is here in this cottage. The people around us in the mountains struggle just to feed themselves. Grandfather tried to teach them better growing methods, but they turned on him. They told him his ways were not "natural." That is why we travel to the village to sell our produce. The local people will not buy from us."

"We be stay'n here. I be Gran'fa'r now," Patrick said with his attempt at a determined look on his face. He looked to both of them anticipating a response. He saw their mutual hesitation and patient looks. "Well, wha' we go'nn' do?" he shrugged, nonplused.

There followed a contemplative silence while they all ate. A thought came to Razon, "What of the brigands?"

"Ya done for 'em," was the matter-of-fact reply. Patrick sucked a cooked carrot.

"There are more," Ashley reminded him. She turned to Razon. "There seem to be more strangers all the time. This will take time to figure out. Thank you for staying, again, to help." She got up from the table and started to pick up. She stopped, took a breath, and looked again to Razon. "Please, give us thought. We are quite alone."

Razon eased her concern with a smile and a nod of his head. They shared a mutual understanding. She knew he, just like her grandfather, would not desert them. Tears of relief welled in her eyes.

Razon watched her quickly glide out the door and heard her footsteps go around to the backside of the cottage then fade away. He felt a reaction of his own. The stirring of thoughts buried for many years: children, a family of his own. He became lost in his own thoughts.

"Ya jus' sitt'n there ta look out the window or ya go'n ta eat more? I be eye'n the carrots if'n ya no wan' 'em," a voice said, bringing him back to the moment.

Razon moved his plate to Patrick and watched him suck the carrots down. "I like the way they slip inta me mawf."

Razon was amused watching him finish whatever was left. When Patrick was done, Razon said, "You need to finish the chores outside." After a moment, he added, "I will join you in a bit."

Patrick double-checked their plates—still empty. He shrugged his way out the door.

Razon watched Patrick leave. *How easily he takes to the changes of life*, Razon thought. *So accepting of the new roles and place, at peace with it all, none of the internal conflicts that lie just below the surface of both Ashley and myself.* Razon could not deny the building tide of affection for these two. It was quite foreign and yet—he allowed himself to open a deep wound and reflect on a brief but catastrophic moment from his past, a moment of deceitful passion and peace, a false affection, which almost cost his life. For years, he searched, never able to fill the emptiness in his being it left behind. He swore he would never give way to such emotions again. Yet, now, his heart was opening again, opening to children orphaned and with virtually nothing. This time, it seemed different, real, and natural, an opening to a deeper sense of what his father had raised him to be.

The weight of noble reason settled upon his heart. Questions, feelings, overwhelming tides of emotions, they were new, renewed, and yet the ancient essences of being.

"What…?" he asked aloud with hands and face to the heavens. Razon closed his eyes and shook his head.

He went out to help Patrick.

*****

That evening, Razon sat in the chair by the fire. The children had eaten and gone to bed. He was trying to sort things out in his mind when he heard soft padding of bare feet descending the ladder.

Except for her feet, Ashley was still dressed. She saw Razon looking and said, "I did not wish to wake Patrick."

She had something in her hand as she walked to him. In a hushed yet forced voice, she said, "Sir, I cannot sleep." She hesitated, as if taking one last moment before jumping into something of which she was uncertain, yet knew would change her life forever.

Watching her, Razon realized just how old this young lady was. Life had been none too easy for her. She lost her parents early in life, and now her last relative, outside her simple brother, was gone;, yet she met it straight on without complaint. He had great respect for her. She was of a finer character than most people he met;. He guessed she could only be twelve or thirteen years old. He became curious why she was up, obviously not wanting to wake her brother.

"Times are very bad now. When you leave, there will be no one to protect us." A deep determined breath followed, "I want you to teach me how to use this."

There was no question. It was a request. Razon could see an apprehensive look fortified by desperation. In her hand was the throwing knife he had given her.

"You are a brave young lady, Ashley. You are a thoughtful person as well. In many ways, you remind me of, in fact, you are better than myself." He took the knife still in its scabbard from her hand. "This could have been used against you, Ashley. Now, it is yours; you seek to learn its power." Razon looked intently at her, judging her eyes and spirit.

"It is one thing to defend yourself. It is another, entirely, to attack. This weapon can be used for both. It is well balanced to feel light in your hand and still strong enough to be thrown with force and agility. I will teach you its mysteries, but first answer me. Who are you?"

"I do not understand, sir." She spoke softly, unsure of what Razon was asking.

"A weapon such as this has only one real purpose. It is designed to inflict damage and kill another. That is a great responsibility. Death of another, at your hands. It never washes off. You must know who you are to deal with that kind of responsibility—that guilt."

"Then why did you give it to me?"

Razon noted there was no confusion in this question. She was already sure of the answer.

"You were attacked. You were meant to die or worse. You handled yourself well. I saw who you are. But now I ask of you. Who are you?"

Catching on to his meaning, she answered, "I am the only member of a simple brother's family. We are alone. We have seen death to those who would have killed us. I have seen you, sir. I would be as you, to defend my family and myself. I overheard your comment to Grandfather about being 'timely' to our aid." Her voice hardened, "There are more of these brigands around, sir.

I would be ready." The staccato of each word was driven by unquestionable faith.

Razon did not answer. Instead, he looked down at the blade in its scabbard still held in his open hand. He noticed the strange markings on the scabbard and heft. They indicated some kind of allegiance but none he recognized. He perfunctorily withdrew the blade. It was one of the finest he had ever seen in a throwing knife. The knife was perfect in balance and in craftsmanship. All these aspects he noted instantly, a matter of habit for one highly tuned in the skill of blades.

He handed the blade to Ashley—handle first. The blade rested flat on the palm of his hand.

Ashley reached out for it.

In the moment it took her to scream, Razon had reversed the blade and carved invisible lacerations in the air just in front of her face, chest, arms, and legs. So fast, so sure each stroke. His eyes were flames of battle, intent upon one purpose only. The wickedly dancing knife ended its rhythm embedded in the dirt floor between her feet. No quiver, no vibration, motion stopped so suddenly her mind continued to see movement when none existed.

Razon did not laugh. He stared into her eyes.

She felt the hoarseness of her throat and the backwards motion of her body as it sat heavily upon the floor: her mouth open and her eyes staring back in unbelief, in awe.

Speechless and numb inside, she did not know what he would do next. He remained as he was, staring at her. Her mind began to awaken again. She dragged a breath into the hollowness that was her lungs. She felt the heat of tears burning down her cheeks. He had tricked her. Her pride fumed in its raging fire, prickling the very roots of her scalp—indignant.

"How dare you deceive me thus," she ground out through lips barely moving. Her jaws hurt, muscles contracted.

Emotions so foreign to her welled up within like magma seeking vent to the surface. She swallowed and felt the burning heat about her heart as it went down her throat. *This is not right*, her mind raced. *He saved you. You asked him for help. He did not touch you.* Yet, there were strange feelings from deep within that were screaming in pandemonium!

Razon witnessed the many faces of change in her eyes, lips, and jaw. He did not claim to understand women or even people, but he knew blood and death. He knew the killing art. Realizing she was still in shock, he said, "At close quarters, a blade such as this is a thousand deaths. I wanted to make an impression upon you of just how such a weapon may be used. You think tonight. Tomorrow we will see more of who you really are."

Ashley did not pick up the knife. She did not speak. She turned and went up the ladder. Later Razon heard the tiny whimpers of emotion in the release of shock. It had been a hard day for all.

He picked up the blade and smiled. "She will be ready to learn more tomorrow," he said to himself. He had no way of knowing the many hurdles and emotions to be crossed before she would be ready to trust him again.

CHAPTER SIX

When Razon awoke the next morning, he understood what to do: two decisions were clear. The first, it would take a day to get ready, but he would take the children with him to Skon's Hall. Razon had seen too much of the harshness of life. "If I leave these children here, they will starve or be forced to sell themselves out to others as servants or worse. I cannot allow that to happen."

He went outside in the early cold. He walked to the oak and reflected upon the new grave beneath it. "There is much to do," he said in quiet respect. "The children are young and alone. You have done well by them, sir." Razon drew his sword and, in a sign of respect, raised it and pointed to the sky. "I salute you and pray you understand if I take them with me. I have wandered away from my own home for too many years. You have brought back thoughts of family and home. I will see to the needs of these children with friends who will continue as you would have, if able." He paused and looked off into the distance.

A long time ago, he had left home. He had succumbed to a driving desire to see what lay beyond the next ridge. And the next. And the next. It was not uncommon for youths to leave home. A farm could only support so many and work in the city was often hard to find for the more ignorant. Some left by force. It was either that or face starvation, prison, or execution.

Razon knew none of these applied to him. He had talked about it many times with his father. He remembered one time. It was after his fifteenth birthday celebration. His father had given him a long sword of keen edge and fine balance. He was holding it in his lap as he sat, just staring into the fire. His father had pulled a chair up beside him and sat there alongside without a word. He just waited for Razon to speak first.

Finally, Razon turned and faced him. "Father, I cannot shake the feeling. I need to be away from the Light Forest—it is so protected and good here. You have brought the kingdom order and with it, peace. I have to experience how life is elsewhere, or I will never be able to lead in your stead. I am too sheltered here."

"Not everything here is as it seems, my son," he had answered. After a reflective several minutes, he continued, "We, the House of Radiant, have a mission, a charge. It is true things are peaceful now—enjoy it. It will not last."

His father had seen the question in his eyes. "Life is change, my son. The people will grow restless for one reason or another and seek change. It will bring an unsettled period. All things will be subject to question. Perhaps, even our authority to rule will be challenged, but none of that will alter our true purpose. We are the Guardians of the Light Forest—first, foremost, and always."

Razon's father had put his hand upon his shoulder then. "You will leave. It is a part of your growing and learning." Razon's father then turned his shoulder, forcing him to look again at his father's face. "You must remember who you are. You will experience life. You will see how things are away from here and be better able to rule for it but never forsake your true purpose. You are a guardian of this realm. Should we be driven from the Hall of Radiant and forced to live in hiding by the petty whims of the people, there remains the greater purpose. It has been centuries since the last time we were called to defend light. The Lions of Light have been quiet for many generations. But when called, the House of Radiant will arise. my son, you will take my place here. And someday, your heir will take yours. The charge remains with us always."

Razon looked from the grave in front to the sword in his hand. It was the same one he had been given when fifteen. His father and experience had taught him well in its use and in knowing when not to use it. He recalled his last training with his father. He had been the victor after four hours of fight-and-run tactics. His father had placed a proud hand upon his shoulder as they walked back to the castle. Just before leaving the forest's edge into the gate clearing, his father had given wise council that Razon had not wanted to hear, "For many years, I have seen the look of distant lands growing within your eyes. You will leave soon. You know much of hand-to-hand combat. You have been trained well but not fully. Beware, my son, there will always be one who knows more or the unusual. Learn to look and reason first: death is final.

"Be wise in your use of arms. Show peace and justices to all. When you have met yourself, come home. It is not enough for you to return merely to rule in my shadow. Go, Razon, learn what you must, then return to accept your call and station."

Two days later, Razon was gone. That was fourteen years ago. He reflected on how young he had been then. Now standing beneath the old oak tree, he could see his father standing there. "You have met yourself. Make ready. Come home, my son."

The second decision: to return home.

Razon went back to the cottage with a short-lived sense of peace within himself. As he entered the cottage, Ashley and Patrick were just coming down the ladder.

He was just opening his mouth to greet them when Patrick cut him off, "Wha's go'n on? Ashley's face be all puffed up and red. I finck she's sick or sump'n."

Razon looked to her and could tell last night was a rough one. Before he could respond at all, she swatted Patrick a tap to the back of the head and thrust herself away into the cooking area with a hard set to her eyes and a firm turning away from Razon. He felt the fist of cold rejection jab his insides with confusion and uncertainty. He walked over to Ashley. "I am saddened you had a difficult time sleeping last night. It was my desire to——"

"Do not bother yourself over me, sir. I will feed you both soon. May I suggest that you prepare for your journey?"

"Yes, we do need to prepare." He caught the singular pronoun. He thought he understood, "No, we will go together. I would not leave you alone."

"We will do well to stay, sir," she answered coldly.

"I do not understand. Are you suggesting I leave while you two remain here alone?" Razon's dismay proved difficult to hide as it began to shift to anger, none of this made sense. She was just a child. Where was the reason of before? Where was the respect for elders?

"Forgive me, sir. You have been of great help to us. However, I am sure you have important matters awaiting your attention. You have been delayed by us long enough."

Razon recoiled from another inner blow to the midsection. He never even saw this turn of events coming. He knew no way to respond. "Important matters?" he stuttered. "Of course, I have important matters. The first of which is to get you and Patrick safely away to someone who can care for you. Just what is about here?"

She turned like a cat. That was the only way he could describe her lithe movement of body. She faced him directly. "It is true we are alone now. You have aided us beyond what any other would have done. However, sir, we must be about putting our lives back together. You, on the other hand, have other matters you must also return to. I will feed you and then you should be away."

"I do not believe this change!" It was Razon's turn to be entirely out of sorts. He had never been in such a predicament before. He forbade himself from treating children roughly, and she was not threatening him in any way, except disallowing him to care for the needs of these children. But why? he asked himself. *What could have happened in just one night? What happened to the young girl, witty and pleasant? And where did this hissing she-cat come from?*

"Well…" he thought hard trying to find that illusive, ego-saving response. He found none. "So be it. I do need to report the malicious activity to Lord Skon. I will return to see how you fare in a few days."

"You need not return, sir. We shall be fine. Patrick is quite capable of handling Grandfather's duties." She turned away, preventing him from seeing a sudden weakening of spirit now that Razon was actually going to leave.

*****

The next morning, Razon left early. Still torn inside, he had waited several minutes after packing before he turned to leave. Neither Patrick nor Ashley had made an appearance. Now a mile or so from the cottage, he walked resolutely as a mist hung over some of the hills to right and left of him. It matched his mood. "I have no right to force my will upon those children," he muttered to himself as he continued walking the next couple miles. He remained mentally and physically recoiling from a sleepless, bitter night of confused self-arguing. "Yet it is an uncaring heart which would allow them to remain alone in such futile circumstances. These are lethal times and those children are defenseless." His mind tore reason apart trying to determine what to do.

Razon was coming over a rise that opened up to the vale below and saw a small trading caravan in a crook of trees along the road. A couple of early risers were beginning the morning's cook fires. A lazy gray column of smoke rose from one fire with a pot's A-frame being set. He watched as one of the perimeter guards walked towards the cook. He greeted the cook and started to settle into conversation when both jerked as if hit.

The cook fell to the ground unmoving; the guard had an arrow's shaft in his leather armor. He broke the shaft, calling a warning to the other two perimeter guards. Razon could see one was already down and the other was slain by an assailant from the trees.

It all happened so fast that Razon could not follow each confrontation. It was only a matter of moments before the whole caravan was overwhelmed by at least twenty brigands coming from the protection of the trees.

Razon, his mind working as a military strategist, watched the scene below for a few minutes to assure his evaluation of combat capability and strength of force. He could not believe the size or the finesse of these brigands. *Whomever leads them knows what they are doing, he thought. The entire attack was well timed and carried out. A force like that is a threat to this whole region. Skon needs to know about this,* Razon mused. *The common folk here have not a chance.*

He turned and began a paced run back to the cottage. "Too many have died. I will not allow you to be among them," he said to the children he was returning for. This time, there would be no argument!

CHAPTER SEVEN

Serenten sat in the same chair he had occupied for endless hours during Cynderet's recovery. He watched the child as she tossed and turned in a fit of dreams. It was a restless night;. At one point, she screamed, bringing him rushing up the stairs from his own quarters on the gathering floor. His Council Guard training had been keen and he continued to live by that training. Even in sleep, he remained acutely aware of his ward;. He did not know what caused the scream, but he was ready. He had paused just outside the portal for a moment to sense what was within. Sensing she was alone and not in physical danger, he had entered quietly. Timorously, he sat in the chair, even now undecided if he should stay or go.

Cynderet began to moan and mumble in her sleep. She appeared agitated in her dreaming. Watching her restlessness and still unsure of her sincerity led him to reflecting about her: she confused him. Reht, his closest comrade, once said she was special, different than the rest. Serenten remained unsure. The Energy Feeders were very deceitful and cruel, even Linnet, who was a coward, had a venomous streak in her.

Linnet never would attack him personally; she enjoyed setting him up only to lie about the circumstances. He remembered the last time. She had been visiting friends late into the night well beyond her curfew. When Serenten reminded her it was late, she became angry at his questioning her, saying he had no right. Arriving home even later, she told her mother Serenten deliberately led her a new way and got her lost, "He said it was important for me to learn my way around." The tears followed, always pitting Linnet's mother and her anger at Serenten. His beating was minor compared to some, but he understood well he was just a pawn in a power game of control and lies.

Serenten felt the old anger growing inside. He tried to bury it only to have other thoughts rekindled. He knew other Hert who had been killed for less offense than Linnet's suggestion. They died at the whim of an enraged Energy Feeder just back from feeding. Others were gated away to defend an Energy Feeder in trouble and never returned. The Hert were merely tools. Even if we could read an Energy Feeder's mind and see it coming, we would still be helpless against them. They have powers beyond anything we can comprehend, he mused. He remembered his first communication with Cynderet: "I do not know how it is possible with this child. I certainly could not do so with Linnet," he muttered. Initially, after her death, there had been a brief feeling of loss. There had followed a hopeful sense of freedom believing he would be returned to the Council Guard and to the association of other Hert. That too was denied him by Luanta and her ordering his continued servile existence as Cynderet's Hert. What remained deep inside was a bitter hopelessness.

Feeling guilty and knowing Cynderet could read his mind, he quickly looked at her to assure she was still asleep: she was. Perhaps it is one of her kinds of tricks? he questioned himself. Somehow that did not feel right. And Rhet was never critical of her—never. Yet Cynderet was Luanta's daughter. She was in training to become an Energy Feeder, but she did not lie. Rather, she met him straight on with a disconcerting forwardness. She did not follow the patterns of the others. She was unable to assume their bat-like form—was that why she was different? "I do not think so," he answered his own question. "There was great tension between Cynderet and Luanta when they returned." His musing was interrupted as Cynderet began to awaken.

Well aware she could read his mood even, if he did seal off his mind, he turned and quietly left the room. He closed the portal and descended the stairs. Questions continued to assail him. Was her sincerity real? Could he trust her? Or, was she a deeper, more cleverly hidden lie, a façade he would someday rue and even forsake?

Cynderet woke in her nest. As she arose, sitting on the edge, she remembered her dream of the attack on the family vividly. She felt chagrin at not having stayed to see what the stranger would have done when he approached her. *He certainly did not appear threatening. But, death has come so easily to so many in the last many hours*—even in my dreams, she reasoned.

Cynderet thought of the girl. *So young—much like me in form and size, and yet she was so quick to react. She showed no hesitation. Her mind worked well. She did not let fear hold her back. She acted quickly, even to help her brother.* "I wonder how she came to be in my dreams?" Cynderet asked herself. "I have never seen anyone like her, not even in a dream.

I should be able to face my trials as she did."

Cynderet thought about the youngling her mother killed yesterday. "I will never become an Energy Feeder if I cannot endure my lessons. My mother was right to become so angry with me. I will never pass my Last Rites if I cannot be strong in my training."

She rehearsed the lesson in her mind, even when forcing herself to watch and learn of the Energy Feeder's power of charm her body shook, unable to accept the death of the youngling. "What is wrong with me?" she whispered to herself. "An Energy Feeder must be able to kill in order to enhance her magic from the energy gained by feeding! A 'cripple of the Society,' the other girls call me. I am not like the others. They all know it. Even the Table knows it!". Seeking to build her bravado, she sat straight. "I must be strong! I must become as Luanta!" The decision felt firm with resolve in her heart. "I will model myself after the girl. We looked very close in age." Cynderet felt there was much she could learn from her dream. A confidence grew as she mulled her resolve over in her mind.

"So? The Mind Child pretends a renewed sense of self?" a now familiar and malign being hissed within her thoughts. "An identity beyond what I will allow," it continued. "I wonder. How is it that you have such interesting ideas?"

Cynderet felt the twisting fingers of fear enter her heart; her moment's confidence shattered. "How can this be?" she whispered, the surprising intrusion driving reason from her. Her body shook as blood pooled in her stomach. She felt light-headed.

The voice preened pleasure at her response. It resounded powerfully within the chambers of her mind. "Surely, you do not think yourself capable of escaping my power, Mind Child?" it mocked. "It is I who will make you, or," a thoughtful pause followed by measured words, "I who shall destroy you: my choice, my whim. Either way, a sweet treat to feed upon. Your moment of enrichment shall be short-lived. It truly is pathetic." The Table laughed, "Dream about your moment of purpose. It is nothing but a fantasy. You cannot escape me. Remember?"

There flashed before Cynderet's mind echoes of her initiation. She realized suddenly, she had been unconscious when she had been appointed an apprentice. She saw herself being carried home incoherent, a blubbering mass of raw anguish, the Table having proved its mastery over her.

"You may look to your mockery of a training. Try to become an Energy Feeder. I may even let you pass your Last Rites. I shall see." The Table gloried in her anguish. It continued purposefully in its twisted words, "Fear not, Mind Child." It cooed, "I will be with you always to assist in your learning." It released its hold—its caustic laughter resounding amid the broken shards of Cynderet's hope.

Cynderet was left holding her hands tightly to her head. The Table was gone, but how had it come to be in her mind? What did it mean a "mockery" of her training? She realized then how vulnerable she was—not just Luanta's change towards her, but of the Table's twisted hate as well. "I cannot escape its wrath or its continued rape of my mind. It can come and go as it pleases!" she realized. "Is it watching me all the time?" she asked as she turned to the window and looked out into the city towards Council Peak. "Is there no haven from its vile tainting of my hopes, of me? I have to get free! All is wrong here: Luanta, the Table, my deformities, my hopelessness…" In sobs, she fell to her nest again.

"No!" she clamored, wiping a damp face on her sheets. "The girl did not cease fighting, not until he came, not until it was all over. I will not either!"

Cynderet rushed out of her room. She needed someone to care. She knocked on Luanta's chamber portal: no answer. She ran down to the gathering floor. Serenten was there. She ran to him.

Taken by surprise, he looked down on her for only a moment before he felt of her anguish. Torn between his cautious distance and her need for solace, he simply held her.

When settled enough, Cynderet asked, "Have you seen Luanta?"

"No. She left quite a while ago, not saying where or when as to her leaving or return."

"I must get somewhere, somewhere I can think!" she exclaimed. "I want to leave," she added quickly, "to go for a walk."

"It would please me to go as well. Where?"

Pulling away from him only enough to see his face, she answered pensively, "Beyond the city. Into the mountains where it is quiet and far away."

"We should prepare a bit. We will be gone awhile if that is your wish," Serenten counseled. He was encouraged by her acquiescing with a simple nod.

They put together packs of food and water to last the day. Cynderet was careful to leave a note for Luanta. One was never sure when she would be back, but Cynderet wanted to avoid fueling her anger if possible.

Cynderet and Serenten were just leaving the city when Harriant saw them from above. She flew down for a closer look, wanting to be sure that it was Cynderet she saw. Closing in, she said, "So Cynderet. You are finally up and walking again. I had thought you might never get up from your nap. However, are you feeling?"

Cynderet recognized Harriant's voice and taunting thoughts without looking. The whining twang of her squeaky, deceitful voice was like none other in the city. She carefully hid the groan inside, "Thank you for your concern, Harriant. Yes, I am able to get around quite well now." Cynderet knew the best way to deal with Harriant was to ignore the verbal jabs. Most of them were petty and pointless. "How is your training going?" Cynderet asked, attempting to be polite.

"Oh! Quite well. Being trained by Ermentrude. The Senior Eldress is so wonderful," her voice oozed. "I am sure to be the best ever. You must be just dying to begin your training. However, will you be able to start with Luanta being so ill?"

"What do you mean 'ill?'" Cynderet asked, taken completely by surprise.

"Oh! You know. She rarely feeds anymore. I overheard Ermentrude telling her just this morning she has not been well for a long time. She told Luanta she needs to overcome her weaknesses and that the best way to do that is to strike out at what is ailing her. Ermentrude is so wise."

Cynderet let the cooing go unnoticed as she tried to piece together what Harriant was really saying. She realized her adversary's simple mind and words agreed. She had to shut Harriant up to prevent this gossip spreading rumors of Luanta. "Well, thank you again for your concern. My mother is quite fine, actually; I assure you. In fact, we were just out yesterday, and my training is proceeding well. She has already demonstrated the Charm Spell to me." Cynderet knew neither creature had been human, but Harriant could think what she wanted.

"You mean, you saw her charm someone?" Harriant was plainly envious. Apparently, Ermentrude was not as quick to display her powers for Harriant.

"I witnessed absolute obedience to her wishes." She carefully avoided saying more; she saw a way to keep Harriant's chatter about her mother from spreading. "I am sure when you are ready, Ermentrude will demonstrate the Charm Spell for you."

Cynderet knew she had succeeded as she watched Harriant's face go from jealous to livid.

"I am ready!" she screeched. "I am apprentice to the Senior Eldress. I will be the best!" Harriant hissed through clenched teeth.

Cynderet could see her lower lip turn white where her fangs pushed tightly against it. Cynderet realized she was glad she did not have to worry about that distorted body form. She quietly endured Harriant's glare waiting for her to decide what she would do next. Harriant was desperate to lash back, but she was not sure where the insult actually was. She could think of nothing else to say. A long silent glare followed, and then with vicious strokes of her wings, she banked herself sharply and flew back to the city.

"Cynderet, beware. That one is dangerous. She will strike back one day with more than words," Serenten sent.

Cynderet simply nodded, knowing he was right.

Cynderet and Serenten were going down the same backside of the mountain ridge she and Luanta had walked—had it only been yesterday? She could see the heavily forested canopy about to embrace them in arms of shadow as they walked.

Cynderet stopped short. Serenten knew she had something on her mind. He waited patiently for her to bring it out.

"Serenten, coming down from the ridge, I looked out over the forest. It all looks the same. All the trees have big flat leaves. Where do the trees with the needle-like leaves begin?"

Serenten was confused at first, unsure if he had heard her correctly. She repeated the question.

He took a moment to consider. He had seen most of the land around the city while on patrol for the Eldress Council. He knew of no needle-leaf forests anywhere near the city. In fact, none anywhere on the Shadow Plane. "Of which forest do you speak, Child?" he asked.

"Where the mists gather and obscure sight. Where the forests change from these trees before us to tall slender ones that point like bird beaks to the sky. Where the path becomes a well-traveled road." She paused for a minute as she recalled the horse and cart. She had never seen a horse before, or a cart, or a human, for that matter; yet she knew what they were on sight.

She saw Serenten's patient, if confused, look. They continued walking. She felt unsure if she should tell him about the girl and the stranger. Except for her walk with her mother, she had never been anywhere beyond the city or in the hills immediately overlooking it. Though not having seen humans before, she was certain that was what they were. The whole setting was complete, even the conflict—again, something she had never seen—was completely clear to her understanding. Had it been just a dream? Or something not a dream: something real? She had to know.

They continued deeper into the forest. The thoughts of familiarity continued to perplex her. "Serenten?" She whispered the question, feeling that would make it less difficult to ask, "Is it possible to travel in one's dreams to places that have never been seen before and yet seem so familiar?"

"Dreams can take you anywhere," he said matter-of-factly. "They can take you to places both known and unknown. Why do you ask such an interesting question? Have you a dream you wish to share with me?"

Still not ready to open up completely, she asked, "Have you ever seen trees with leaves like needles?"

"Yes, but none upon the Shadow Plane. Reht and I saw them on the Plane of Humans while serving the Eldress Council. They were much as you describe them." He was still speaking casually, but his look showed greater interest. He asked telepathically if he could see what she was speaking of.

She shut him out, still not ready to open up. Cynderet made sure he was not listening to her inner thoughts before she continued remembering the encounter with the stranger. Serenten was respecting her privacy. She thought about the young girl. They seemed about the same age. They were about the same height with similar hair coloring. Cynderet had not considered it before but realized they shared a lot of similarities. She considered her own form, the one she could not change. It was the form the Society used to attract the male human. Did that mean she looked human? "Do I look like a human to you, Serenten?"

"You are in your human form now. All Energy Feeders have such a form. You look very much like the female human." His tone implied it was common knowledge.

"Do humans have children who change in size as they grow…younger and older?"

"Yes. The same as you have grown." He looked at Cynderet quizzically. "What is it you have seen?" he asked with more interest than he intended.

Cynderet noted his interest; she understood that it was either tell him all or drop the subject. Without having enough answers and no one else to turn to, the dropping of the experience was not an option. She was still hesitant; she studied him and read that he too was hesitant about letting her in. He did not close his mind to her; he swallowed his fears and let her feel safety.

She opened her mind's door to her dream and allowed him to see it in detail. They studied the stranger's ability to fight with a blade together.

"For just a dream, you know a great deal about melee combat in close quarters. You have even envisioned the weapons and their variations well," Serenten noted, impressed by the accuracy of the short sword, battle-ax, and the stranger's throwing knives and dagger. How could it be that Cynderet should know so much? he asked himself. Thinking he knew the answer, he asked her, "Did Reht speak of these things to you?"

"No. Reht was very quiet about his life prior to his becoming my Hert. He taught me ideas and wisdom, never of his life before nor of weapons."

"That may have been to protect you," he muttered, still rather perplexed by the acute degree of subtle variations in the weapons and the techniques used by the stranger.

"What do you mean?" Cynderet interrupted.

"What?"

"You said Reht may have kept quiet about his past to protect me. What did you mean by that?"

"There are many secrets about us. Things we do not even know. Reht was older than the rest of us. He was already…" Serenten dropped the thought suddenly. He closed his mind.

Cynderet caught his closing thought of having said too much.

Something, some nebulous thought began opening in Cynderet's mind. She looked again into Serenten's face. She spoke to his mind, afraid to even utter the words lest the least bit be heard, except between the two of them. "He was already what? What do you mean he was older? He was older than whom?"

She felt his fear grow. She noted the twinges of distrust. Not of her, he could have shut her out at the very beginning. No, it was distrust of what opening-up would mean. "You cannot deny me these answers, Serenten. I have no one to turn to. My mother refuses to acknowledge or even want me. Reht was the one to save me from certain death. I am at the very brink again, and if you do not confide in me, if you do not share what you know with me, I may very well be dead very soon!" Cynderet realized that though it was a passionate moment, she was telling the truth. The Table had all but said so. "Serenten, look within me. I am telling the truth and you are all I have!"

Serenten saw her truth. He knew it even before he looked. "You require a step of me I am not sure I can take."

She saw the wounds poorly healed. She could sense the vibrations of tender nerves. Serenten shook inside. He was battling memories and emotions private to himself, a war of traumas from the past. He finally smiled a wry grin asking for understanding.

He shut her out of his thoughts as his mind battled in just what he should tell her. A long pause followed. Deep searching looks to her, into her mind and heart. He took a long time to respond, ready to deny her plea. Then he remembered how she had placed her trust in him regarding her being telepathic. He knew he would never divulge her secret to another. He recognized the same sense of loyalty within her to him. She was different.

"The Hert are not native to the Shadow Plane, Cynderet. We are traded by the interplane traveling Wherants who bring Hert here as slaves from our own place. The Energy Feeders, your Society, only take the very young. That way, we have little memory of home to get in the way of our training here."

Cynderet's eyes searched Serenten's face intently. She saw the myriad of changes in that moment as long suppressed thoughts and memories flashed by just behind his eyes. The buried bits of home in his heart still held in the deepest parts of his being. They were feelings, sensations, no scenes, just the heavy depth of belonging—and then: loss.

"Serenten, tell me more. Who are the Hert, really?"

"I do not think it wise to continue this discussion, Child. There are some things that should not be said."

"Why not?"

"Do you not understand? The Hert are slaves to the Energy Feeders. Why do you think other Hert are treated so badly?"

Cynderet suddenly remembered the horrible scars on Harriant's Hert. There were others she had seen injured as well. She felt overwhelming shame. She could not believe how inattentive, no, how blind, she had been. She saw only the superficial; she never even suspected the true depths of humiliation the Hert were subjected to.

Reht had protected her. She saw it then; her relationship with Reht had been different in so many ways to those of other Hert and the Society. "I am so sorry, Serenten. I never even realized what was happening. All along, Reht and my mother kept me from seeing how others treated their Hert." She stopped; a new thought became clear. "No! I see now—not my mother—it was Reht, alone, who protected me, even from my mother. That is why she has changed towards me. Reht is gone and now she must…" her voice broke as she felt the weight of full understanding.

It was Serenten's turn to see the heartrending emotions upon her face.

"That is why my mother hates me so. All the time before, Reht had been between us, protecting me from what my mother really was." She lowered her head and with glazed eyes looked at the path. "Oh, Reht!" she moaned. "We truly were more the same then even my mother and I are."

She looked to Serenten. "Why? Why is it this way, Serenten? Why am I not as my mother? She loathes me and yet the more I learn, the more surely I know I can never be as she is—as they are."

Serenten took Cynderet into the shelter of his massive, scaled arms as she broke down in waves of despairing sobs.

Serenten looked down upon her head as she wept. He felt waves of empathy wash over him. He knew. He could no longer doubt it. "Reht," he said inside, "I understand now why you feel so strongly about this child." He called upon the image of his mentor in his mind. "I will do all in my power to protect her and emulate your care for her." He knew, in that most sacred part of his soul, he could never turn away from this radiant jewel of the heart.

As Cynderet quieted, she heard rich wisdom come to her mind, "You must be who you are, Cynderet. You must be at peace within, for if you try to be anything else, you will be only a shell: a lie."

"Thank you for your kind thought, Serenten."

"Child, it did not come from me. But I heard it as well, for it was in your mind and you were open to me."

Serenten knew, but he waited for the impact of his words to settle within Cynderet.

"It was something Reht would tell me when I was troubled as now, but it was different this time. It came from within me, did it not?"

"Yes, it did."

"How is this possible? It is like he is right here inside me!"

"It is called Dream Sight," Serenten said in a hushed voice. "It is the gift of knowledge passed on to the one most dear to a Hert when he dies. It is a breath of one's collected wisdom given to another. I have only heard of it as a mystic tale of home."

Serenten paused, struggling to remember what he could of the legends. "Reht must have known much more of our ways then I imagined. You have his wisdom within you. His memories and knowledge he gifted to you."

"How does it work, Serenten?"

"I do not know, Child. I know of it only as a legend, as a tale shared among the Hert here as a lingering memory, a hope of homes, lives we little remember."

Cynderet tried to hear more within to listen for the sound of Reht's voice. Nothing. With reluctance, she finally stopped.

It was getting late and time to head back to the city.

Serenten and Cynderet were just leaving the edge of the forest proceeding up the path to the top of the ridge where the city below would be open to view. It was then the thought stirred Cynderet to a moment's panic: the Table! She had forgotten about the Table during their walk and subsequent discoveries. Fear and apprehension closed an iron grip around her heart. What would the Table do if it found out about the Dream Sight? Stopping cold, she reached to hold Serenten from his forward progress. At her touch, he felt her fear.

"Serenten, I forgot all about the Table during our walk and discussions. It has such reign in my mind I do not know what thoughts are safe—if any!" Intensity of concern encompassed on her face as she continued, "It even listens to my dreams. It may know of our conversations!"

"I can feel the power of the Table throughout the city, though only as a sensation, a hum in the background of life in the city. It has no power over me as it does you. It is only a sound. I do not feel it here, Child. I do not think its powers reach this far."

Serenten took a moment and just listened, turning his head about to allow what sounds were there to clearly reach his ears. "I hear and feel nothing of the Table. It searches the minds of the Energy Feeders just like creatures in the wild will lift their heads periodically to ensure there is no danger about. You are an initiate. It does have power in your mind as it does in all the rest, including the Eldresses. However, they are not as attuned to it as are you. I do not think they even know of its being unless it is when they are in council."

Feeling relieved, "Then I do not think it knows of the Dream Sight. I must keep it a secret. I believe the Table seeks to destroy me. I must keep Reht safe until I learn how and why he entrusted me with his knowledge. Hidden within his Dream Sight, he may have left answers to help us both."

Serenten remembered his first days with Cynderet and her turmoil of mind and heart. An idea came, "Reht has been with you since he died. If the Table does not know about the Dream Sight gift to you by now, then there must be a reason. Perhaps it is hidden such that even the Table cannot find it." Another thought occurred to him, sending a pulse of hope through him, "It may even be that Reht purposefully hid the Dream Sight so that the Table could not find it. Remember he is—was so much wiser than I."

"How do I find it?" Cynderet questioned, believing in the truth of Serenten's understanding. "His thoughts have only come to me once, here in the forest." She began to feel a certain frustration growing. Serenten would not confide in her what he knew of the Hert, and now Reht seemed to have given her a gift that she could not use or find.

Unaware of Cynderet's concerns, inspiration opened to Serenten, "Child, how did you know of the things you saw in the domain of the humans?"

"I do not know. They were just there. I did not even think about it."

"Dream Sight must be hidden beyond your conscious levels. It comes to you from within like something you have learned so well you no longer have to think about it. The Dream Sight is every bit a part of you. Search within, Child. It is you who holds the key. The lock seems to open upon your need and ability to listen. The Table does not share in these things. That is why the Table cannot see it. It does not have the key as Reht determined it to be." Excitement growing as understanding came; Serenten pushed further, "Let us return to the forest for a while longer. We will find a place for you to be at ease, then you look to find the secrets."

Putting words to action, it was only a moment before Cynderet had turned Serenten around by grabbing his arm and both were retreating back down the path into the forest.

Within a half-hour's search, they found what they were looking for: a downed log off the trail covered with comforting moss. A small stream trickled by providing a rhythmic melody humming away anxieties. Beyond the stream, it opened up to a small glade before forest encroached to close all off from sight.

Cynderet sat down comfortably against the far side of the log. She looked about at the pleasant surroundings. She sensed Serenten taking a seat above her. Feeling secure, she closed her mind to everything but the sound of the trickle of the stream. She allowed no other thought to enter her mind, just as Reht had taught her.

"First, relax the body. Be at peace. Next, clear the mind of wandering and intruding thoughts or tensions. Then, when all is quiet within, look inside. Look deeply, you will see the innermost places. They will be you, yours," he had said. "Look."

She followed each step perfunctorily as taught. She felt at oneness with her surroundings and within. Her mind cleared more quickly than ever before, though unbeknownst to her until much later. She passed by the conscious thoughts, having driven them from her mind to reach deeply inside. She came to a place of stone walls and floor. Here, the floor stones were worn smooth from use. Against the far walls, she saw several portals, each with a stone alcove defining its entrance. Each portal was of wood—heavy, massive doors held by bands of iron. Each was unique; some she knew by sight while others were new to her. She reached the securing latch of a new one. As she examined the door, a mist and stream appeared surrounded by trunks of trees. As she touched the metal fixtures, the mist began to stir. Without opening the portal, she looked far into the mist and recognized the beginnings of the road she had walked when she saw the stranger. Satisfied, she knew what was beyond this portal. She went to another, and another, each time looking upon the respective portal's surface vision. They would appear blank until she looked on them, then something would show itself to her acquainting her with what was behind. Once each door had been identified, the vision returned immediately upon her gaze at it. She would easily know each when needed.

There was no vision or sign when she looked upon the last one. It was set deeply into a dark corner. There was no light here. She walked over to the alcove it sat in. As she reached its arching passage, a feeling of peace and welcome washed over her. Tears welled up in her eyes. She found it difficult to put a name to the feeling, but it felt warm. A glow surrounded her heart. She felt as if she had returned home, but to a home she never knew before. She felt Reht's presence everywhere; he was so close. She believed that with a little effort she would be able to see him here in the shadows. With confidence of what she would find, she entered the alcove. She took the portal's latch into her hand and tried to open it. It would not.

She could not understand. She tried it again.

It remained locked to her.

"Reht? Why do you not open to me?" She fought back sudden despair. How could she be so wrong? This had to be the place; there were no other places to look. She tried to force the latch open.

It held tight.

Tension built within her. She was desperate. She felt hope waning for the last time. She sat down on the floor, looking at the portal with questioning eyes. "Reht, why do you shut me out?"

The voice returned: "Be patient, Little One. It is not time for you to enter here. Do not despair. This portal opens both ways. It will continue to open, providing aid when you need it. However, for you to open it, you must first be ready. You must be strong in who you are or what lies within will overwhelm you."

Cynderet knew simultaneous joy and disappointment. She knew the voice. She felt the familiar power and wisdom of her mentor and guardian. "Reht, what if the Table finds out?" she asked.

"Fear not, Little One. Place before the door the things you want kept safe and they will be drawn within. They will be yours and with you when you need them. It is best this way: until you are ready."

"Reht, I miss you so. Why do you hide from me? But for Serenten, I have no one." Cynderet felt the tears trail down her cheeks and settle into the grooves at the corners of her lips. They flowed freely and washed down her chin, pooling upon the stones of the alcove's floor. They christened the sanctuary;. It became her place of security and self-assurance.

"All that I may give you is here, Cynderet. This is our place. However," the voice warned in wisdom, "now that you know where this place is, do not allow yourself to linger here overly much. It would be unhealthy. One day you will hold the key to this portal. For now, allow this archway and alcove to cleanse your anguish away. Now place what you wish hidden before the portal."

Cynderet had difficulty seeing through her tears, but had no puncheon to dry them. It was as if each washed away some part of her fear and loneliness. Through the resulting hazy mist, she placed each part of her discussion with Serenten in little baskets before the portal. It was difficult to see clearly, but she viewed enough to know each was received within.

When the last basket had been taken, Cynderet's tears had also ceased. There was a renewed peace of mind and a hope she had not felt in days. She did not understand much at all but knew that the Table had no power here. There was a different sense of strength growing inside her. She realized she never would be alone. Reht was with her always: in love, in faith, and in what she would come to know later as purpose.

Shaded by the tall trees in perimeter around the glade, Serenten stood watch over Cynderet. He saw the tears bathing her cheeks. His immediate concern lasted only an instant as he noted the calm smile upon her face. She had not closed her mind to him. He remained outside in respect for her. He did not know what Reht had done; he did know it was for Cynderet only. The fact that Reht had bequeathed this child his Dream Sight was sufficient for him. It meant his memories of home—so few and confused—were of some place real. It meant he also had an identity beyond that of *slave*.

He considered what that meant. It replaced some of the bitterness he had felt for so long. It meant he could choose to give of himself to another. Reht had given him a gift also. The gift of knowing he belonged somewhere. He truly did have a home. Now of his own will, he chose his place to be with this gifted child. His guardianship of Cynderet was his self-proclaimed purpose: one he would not—he remembered an earlier thought—forsake.

CHAPTER EIGHT

Luanta felt her resolve slipping away as she stood before the open passage into the rocky heart of darkness. The lack of any light within played tricks on her vision. There was motion beyond. She could see slight variants of heat moving deep inside the cavern. The creatures reminded her of wavering shades of blackness. She could see one standing inside, just within the passage's entrance. It was waiting for her to either enter or leave. All reminded her of why she was here, and now she stood once again questioning her presence of mind to even be here. The powers within this darkness were without equal in their cruelty. They loathed anything capable of living in all but the deepest shadows of daylight. She knew they tolerated the Energy Feeders for reasons of their own. She also knew they kept their own confidences. Their treachery exceeded even her imagination.

She had her own purposes as well, so here she was. Ermentrude had assured her that she was in a position to bargain. The remedy of her endangered spirit and the potential culmination of her hate were in line with what these cunning beasts, these Wherants, also sought. "You both share a course of mutual purpose," she had stated.

Luanta was not so sure. It had been thirteen years since she entered this passage last. She did not like the way she could feel the powers of the vile presence within. It irritated her nakedness beneath her sheer gossamer robe with tiny barbs of perversion. She was in her human appearance. She was sure her seductive prowess had helped in the initial bargaining last time. However, the ultimate cost had been high. She had paid dearly. The cost, almost her very life. She remained uncertain as to what really had saved her then. Whatever it was, it was of the Wherant's choice and not hers. This uncertainty added to her present perplexity. It was only the desperation for revenge that brought her here now.

"He knows your mind, Luanta," a voice from just in front of her said.

Luanta jumped back impulsively as the creature stepped from the wall. She had thought the shape to be a mere rock at the mouth of the passage. Even her infravision had been unable to detect its presence.

"You seek his aid once again to shore up your ineptitude." It laughed, a merciless laugh of belittlement at the panic just fading from her eyes. "You will find his temper cooled at present. There have been recent changes that you may find to your advantage."

His statement, his clarity in understanding her purpose, his very awareness caught her off guard. *How is it possible for him to know my purpose?* she asked herself. Still, she did not doubt its truth. Luanta suffered a continuation of self-doubt. These *Wherants are devious and self-serving like no other creature I know, yet if his temper is cooled at present*—it meant only greater threat to her—of that she was certain.

"Enter. I will insure his audience with you, Luanta. He knows you linger without. Do not tempt his benevolence further," the warmth less gargoyle whispered with harshness, penetrating her body and irking her nerves. "I am Stone's Throw and Strike. You may call me Strike." Without further attention to her, Strike turned and shuffled inside.

Luanta followed a hesitant step behind him. She still could not see any warmth emanating from his body; he was as cold as the very stone of the tunnels they began to travel. Within, there was absolutely no light. She followed his shadow cast only by the warmth of the torch he gathered for her benefit of infravision. The torch's light of flame was virtually swallowed in the darkness of the tunnels.

Luanta knew from her last visit that the tunnels were chiseled right out of the mountain stone itself. There was no thought of aesthetics, only function. A large enough passage to allow free movement of the creatures who dwelled here was all that was sought. As they walked deeper inside, Luanta felt the caressing stares from the side passages upon her form. Her stomach pitched nervously. She remembered too well their personal forms of pleasure. She mentally reproached her weakness. She fought her fear by allowing anger to swell within her. An arm reached out to touch her;. She side-stepped and shot a bolt of electricity into the appendage. The body's warmth allowed her to see it. The resultant light from the charge lit the tunnel for an instant. It allowed her to see the Cretan's pain before the light was swallowed up into the very walls. There was keening laughter of other observers. She was forced to walk faster to catch up to her unhesitating guide. He never once looked back nor to either side. Luanta knew it was stay up with him or become lost within these halls, a victim of the whims of whoever found her first.

She could only see differing degrees of heat but realized they had entered a huge hall by the change of sound and dispersion of the warmth from her guide's torch. There remained no light. She could see the surrounding creatures by the warmth their bodies radiated. An enormous single mass radiated in front of her. She shuddered in the chill of realization; there was no way out now, except by their will and guidance. She felt a fool.

"You are right, Luanta," a voice said from before and slightly above her. "It is foolish of you to tempt me again so soon."

She knew that voice, recognized it from years ago. She began to shake uncontrollably, remembering what that visit cost her. A quiver went through her. She hissed spontaneously. It was instinctive. Her reflexive posturing helped revive her spirit a little. She determined to continue this posture if only to preserve what little was left of her resolve.

Visions of her first visit overplayed the darkness surrounding her. She was uncertain what was real. She knew she had been used last time. It angered her further. Although the Society viewed all other life as objects for their personal use, here, before this massive, vile presence, even her own malign evil was dwarfed.

"You would form a pact with me and mine that meets your own purposes," the giant patronized her. "Do not trifle with me. Your charms of creamy skin and full endowments have no interest to me this time. I would eat you as if mutton from a spit."

She felt some of her fear leave her. He had his own purposes that kept her safe. He would have acted instead of talking if it were not so.

"However," he continued, "your being an Eldress has slightly more sway. For we have a minor respect for the Eldress Council in that our trade with you has proven valuable in the past. Soon, we will demand payment for the goods, the lives, traded with you over the centuries. We await our time."

Luanta felt an ominous wave of apprehension to root-out of what that day would bring.

"You would have us support your effort and destroy a mere human," he said. "How interesting that one such as you should find this paltry being of such significance. Again, you turn to us for help. It is for our own wants that I attend your groveling petition." He was patronizing her again. His tone softened to almost a whisper, "You see, there remains something we want."

She could imagine him toying with his fingers as he spoke. "A mere trifle, really, but one that is of petty interest to me: a ring." His soft tone rose in crescendo to a ground shaking bellow, "One you failed to acquire previously when you fed upon Lord Radiant!" The creature swelled in rage, his massive body seemed to fill the end of the hall. The crack of a whip sent flames from the floor of the hall. They dissipated instantly into the darkness.

Although Luanta could not see clearly, his mass radiated tremendous heat in anger. She broke out in a body sweat. She was not sure if it was because of the sudden heat or the remembering of her previous failure.

He hissed, slowly, each bitter word: "You were most fortunate I did not smother you in endless blackness and the forever anguish of the prison nests of the Lightless Plane," his voice rose in volume, "but for your daughter's conception, I would have!" He roared, slapping the tails of the whip he wielded on the floor again. Flames shot high from the impact, lighting the crags of face and heightening the glaring glow of sanguinary eyes as the flames vanished.

Luanta felt a sharp pain strike deep inside. What did Cynderet have to do with anything? She promised herself to find out.

The demon waited, allowing the tension of the silence to draw Luanta's full attention. "Fail me again, Eldress, and I shall take the greatest pleasure in watching your slow, painful obliteration as you are forced into the propagation of my minions!" His mass settled down perceptibly.

Luanta felt a change of demeanor. She waited to see what would happen.

There was a clap; she thought of hand. A red glow arose between her and the Lord Wherant. In front of her, highlighted within the glow, stood a small table she was sure was not there a moment ago. On top of the table rested a box with its curious markings glistening of the reflected red light. Beside the box rested two crystalline figurines: one mounted on a winged serpent-like creature, the other standing alone. Luanta looked at them and then up to the Lord Wherant. She noted his rare patience in watching her. His sanguine eyes held hers for what seemed like hours. He looked deep into her. She knew he was measuring her strength of will.

He broke off the stare and said, "See and learn."

In her mind, she saw the box removed from a leather pouch with a familiar seal upon it. The box was placed in the light of day. It opened. Immediately, the day's light began gathering into it. The box seemed to swallow the light causing a wave of darkness to wash over her from behind. All was becoming totally dark. In its darkness, she felt movement around her but could see nothing. Her mind's vision closed.

"When all is ready, open the box in the light of day near your adversary's hall. You will be able to destroy him in the darkness. No light can penetrate it. He and his people will be blind. Your conquest of this petty man will be assured."

"And these?" she asked of the two crystalline figurines, their shapes void of fine detail beyond rudimentary shape. Except for the wings, arms, and legs, it was impossible to tell what they represented.

"They are shape-changers," he answered. Again, in patience, Lord Wherant showed her mind how they were to be used and then closed the vision. His lordship continued to study Luanta.

She became uncomfortable in his perusal. His patience with her was at odds with what she knew of him. Why? she asked herself silently.

Without preamble, the perusal ended. Lord Wherant clapped his massive hands again, and Strike opened a leather pouch, the same one she had seen in her vision. She recognized the medallion on the leather's side. He placed the box in the pouch and folded the end over itself. He finished securing the bag closed with the leather strings attached. Strike placed the two figurines each in a separate box. He placed the several containers carefully into a black bag, a bag that seemed to swallow them up without any evidence of weight or bulk. He handed the black bag to Luanta and disappeared back into the darkness.

Lord Wherant broke the resulting silence, "When you have acquired the ring, give it to my servant, Strike. You may then remove the box from its pouch. To do so before would be disastrous for you," he warned.

Luanta suddenly understood that Strike was to remain with her. She was not pleased having to keep company with the gargoyle. She wanted to object, but stopped. *There must be more behind all this, she thought. Lord Wherant is being too placating. I would be a fool again to tempt him.* She knew his demeanor could change instantly, bringing about her swift destruction, or, as she remembered his warning, it could come very slowly. She chose to ask instead, "How is Strike to travel with me? Is he able to Force Field Web?"

"It will be your responsibility to gate him with you," was the reply. "Once given the ring, he has the power to leave the Plane of Humans, but not go there. You must see he gets there if you wish to succeed."

She thought she saw a way out of his company: "His presence will be easily noted by humans. Is he able to take on another form?" Luanta was certain he could not. She waited, almost daring to be smug.

Lord Wherant began to radiate a slow growing intense heat in his anger.

Luanta knew her grave mistake: she went too far.

"You dare question my wisdom in this matter?" he fumed. "You shall come to know your place."

Before she could move or dodge, the thongs of his whip slapped flame and encircled tightly about her. The heat of the cords burned her flesh. She tried to worm out of their hold only to have them fasten around her more tightly. She began screaming in pain. He drew her closely into his chest. He laughed in vicious snorts, watching her squirm.

The whipcords cooled and began to fall from her one by one. As they did so, he began licking her wounds. The sounds and the touch of his attentions where beyond her endurance; she knew she was in hysterics. She could feel the uncontrollable sobbing and rasps for air. She begged him to let her go.

He did.

She fell from his chest and tongue to the floor in a whimpering mass: her pride shattered. Her wings patted the floor involuntarily. Unconsciously, she had reverted back to her normal form. The coldness of the stone was soothing to the burning of her skin.

Lord Wherant let go of her mind.

It took a few minutes to realize she was not burned nor even physically damaged. The whip had entangled her. She knew she had changed forms. Beyond that, all had been only in her mind. Anger and a horrible sense of betrayal began building inside her. She had succumbed to his will in her own mind. That was what he was doing while he stared at her. The truth tore at her like a rupturing organ. He had planted in her brain his own form of mind-control. She screamed bitterly as she realized she was now his slave. He had gained a master's power over her. Robbed from her was the sanctity of her own mind.

"You will do my bidding, Luanta. You will, or I will show you even greater pleasure," he laughed derisively.

Luanta's bowels writhed inside her. "This never would have happened, but for the violation of my plans by that man in the blue cape, my adversary will die for this! I will wallow in the destruction of Blue Skon and all of his hall!" She clenched her fists tightly. A scraping curse ripped from deep within as she turned and fled Lord Wherant's mocking laughter.

CHAPTER NINE

The battlements of Skon's Hall rose high into the flaming hues of dusk. On each tower's pole waved the Golden Pegasus, flying with wings extended across a field of deep blue. Razon had been with Blue Skon when the wondrous creature's effigy and background color were conferred upon him by the king: "For valiant efforts in defense of King and Kingdom." He was made Lord Skon of Skon's Hall that day. Below; his colors flew the pendant of de Faire, his wife's family heraldry. Razon recalled that inside, over the hall's central hearth, hung similar adornments. There the vestiges of the two houses were joined into a single flag: "For our son, a marriage of two families, two lives," Skon was known to say to all who questioned it.

It was a long ten years with only intermittent visits of short duration since Razon was last here. Razon could not settle down, always looking for the illusive companion of heart. Still, Blue Skon remained his best friend and Skon's Hall, his home base. He always felt more at ease here than anywhere else, including the Light Forest. Here, he had worked hard. He had fought hard, shed sweat and blood, and built this estate side-by-side with Laura and Skon. He had earned the right to sit in this hall. The difference meant a lot to him. It was not just the reward of birth into the ruling family. It was labor, cost, and earning.

Once again, he was returning to his friend; he felt a difference this time. He was bringing the children—his pledge. He was providing them a chance to become something. He was not sure what. "Skon will understand. He will see through this morass of feelings I suffer and know the way of it," Razon mused to himself.

He renewed his grip as he pulled the lead line on the horse. He leaned his body forwards, aligning action with his heading. He looked again at the rising battlements and to the waning afternoon light. It matched his feelings. "It is the setting of a wandering life and the beginnings of my readiness to return to the home of my father. Soon, I shall accept the responsibilities my father would have of me."

He trudged on, hardly acknowledging the cheers of those who recognized him and called out, "Lord Radiant!" *The salutation is a little grandiose for this cavalcade,* he thought. He tugged at the lead of the plow horse pulling the cart of household belongings, the two children ambling at his side. And Patrick dragging his pig. The heads of the children were continuously bobbing from sight to sight as they passed through the village.

Razon looked at Ashley. "I usually plan my arrivals at less conspicuous times," he felt he had to say as another hailing came from a merchant's door. "Today I wanted to arrive during daylight so you and Patrick would have a chance to see Skon's Hall and the village." He decided not to add his wanting them to have some sense of security and knowledge of the lay of things. He recalled their responses when he told them they had to leave the cottage; that he was taking them with him to Skon's Hall.

"Ya say we be go'n to the Lord's castle?" Patrick had asked with an enthusiastic gleam in his eye. Ashley had been more reserved, more silent. Razon had expected her to balk at having to leave. There was a tense moment as she considered his report of the massacre below the mountain. Finally, searching Razon's face, she answered, "It is for the best. Our time here is past." There had been no further hesitation about packing.

Later, after the cart was packed, Patrick was seen in the shade of the porch practicing light whip snaps with a long willow stick. Ashley was not in sight. Razon went through the cottage only to find it empty. He was just passing a rear window, closing the shutters, when he caught a movement at the trunk of the old oak tree. Ashley was there in the shadow of its limbs. Razon watched her almost prayer-like good-bye to her family buried in rest. His heart went out to her. He dried the tears in the corners of his eyes, remembering her hard words earlier. He did not go to her. "There is a barrier raised between us now. I would not rob you your moment of farewell with my awkwardness nor chance sparking your ire. But, know this: you are wise beyond your years. Well, have you met your trials of life. To you, I pledge my sword and life, if so needed, to see your sorrow healed." He had turned from the window in time to see Patrick's homespun pant leg vanishing back outside from the doorway.

✶✶✶✶✶

The man had been sitting in the same seat of the tavern for the greater part of three days. Out on the street, he could hear the excitement. At last, Razon the Radiant had returned. He felt like his backside had permanently conformed to the shape of the chair. His instructions had been clear: to watch and wait until the Lord Radiant returned to Skon's Hall. He was relieved the return had not been longer in coming.

The tavern master was curious why he lingered, even the souses left for a while each day. This one stayed from morn until eve. He left only to go upstairs to his room at night. The master received plenty of coin for his tavern's services and the fellow was social enough to mingle with the patrons. The man seldom spoke though, except an occasional grunt or nod of understanding. The master had not seen him in the village before. The master even asked around, after the first day. The whole affair did not feel quite right. The fellow was no disturbance and he always seemed pleasant. His coin was easily taken.

The man stood up; curling his nondescript cloak around him. He pulled his hood over his head; it shaded all but his mouth and chin. He tossed two additional silver coins to the tavern master. "Thanks," he muttered as he stepped outside.

He saw Razon's cart-parade ambling down the street with its spattering of followers. He stepped in behind, following to insure himself Razon was indeed going to Skon's Hall and not stopping in the village. He noted the two children with the least bit of interest. Satisfied that it was indeed Lord Radiant, he went to the tavern stable and had his horse saddled. He gathered his pack from his room, mounted, and headed out of the village. The sun's light was fading quickly into night.

Once out of sight of the village, the shape of the man and beast became soft and ethereal. There was movement within the encasement of the two bodies as of maggots wriggling just below the skin's surface of a cadaver. The horse developed wings as it metamorphosed into a flying, serpentine creature. Its calciferous body bore the shapely form of what had just a few moments before been a man—a woman now. She sat near the creature's neck with the ease of one well accustomed to its undulating pattern of flight.

She flew along the forest edge away from the road. Her mount's spear-like tip of a tail waved up and down in an opposing rhythm to the strokes of its wings. Her report would be made by midnight.

*****

Everard separated himself from the very obliging, passionate vixen that had given him such pleasure. He walked over to the washbasin and rinsed his face. He had found her rather helpless by the road just a few days earlier. He had found it unnecessary to force himself on her. Rather, she seemed willing, even eager, to please him, perhaps out of gratitude. The irony tickled him to a quick chuckle. He turned to look again on the responsive beauty. She was up and walking to him. He warmed watching how her breasts bounced seductively with her every step closer to him.

"Did I please you, milord?" she asked, her hands working a massaging caress from his chest around to his back.

Everard's answer was lost in heavy breathing of renewing pleasure.

She snuggled her breasts into the matted hair of his chest. Her lips drew a moist path from the base of his neck to his lips as she drew his mouth to hers. She felt the heat return to his loins as her tongue played about his lips.

"Ply your fingers more deeply," he moaned through her kisses.

She moved one hand down his spine subtly working her fingers on the muscles along his back. Her other hand left his neck.

He moaned again in anticipation of both hands kneading his muscles.

He hardly felt the prick of the narrow blade. It slipped easily between his ribs. The heart stroke was clean, no blood, as the skin and muscle sealed around the mortal puncture wound.

She took pleasure in his silent scream of surprise and death. She continued her kiss of his open mouth, penetrating her tongue deeply. She lavished in the last breath of his collapsing body as it folded upon itself still in her arms. She allowed it to slowly slide to the floor.

The murderess gathered his clothes and weapons belt. Then, she hefted the body to her shoulder with a strength her body belied and walked out the door. She stashed the corpse in a cleft of the creek bed. With Everard's own sword, she partially caved in the upper ledge to cover the body. She climbed back up the bank and donned his britches, chain mail, and tunic. She belted his sword about her waist and cinched it to meet the swelling of her belly. Her body took on Everard's visage and shape. She assumed his personality just as she had studied it for the past three days.

One of Everard's sentries noted his return to camp.

"Just letting the worm rest a little," Everard said to the sentry's challenge. "Too bad though, about the girl, I mean. I should have known she was too good to be true. She tried to steal my purse and stick me with my dagger. Hated to slit her throat." Almost as an afterthought, he added, "I would not go down wind of the creek for a few days. She will start to stink by morning. You might pass the word. Truly, I had planned on sharing her."

The sentry felt disappointment in his guts. He had been looking forward to his turn after hearing Everard's heavy groans of pleasure for the past nights.

Everard went back to the cottage and began making his plans.

Everard's changeling wasted no time. Early the morning after her taking on his form, she called a conference with his lieutenants. The meeting had only been in progress a short while when one of the forward sentries raised an alarm to camp. Three strangers were coming towards the hideout.

"Two women, one riding, and a burly looking fellow?" Everard asked.

"Ya, that be them, exactly."

"Let them in. I have been waiting for them. Bring them to my cottage."

"Aye, sir."

"My fellows, I ask you to go about your duties now, but not too far, mind you. There will be much to discuss when I conclude with our guests." There was an obvious lit to Everard's voice, a known preamble to adventure and renewed wealth. They left the cottage with eyes searching the hideout's entrance for a look at these new arrivals.

It was not long until they appeared. The woman in front was beautiful— beyond any they had ever seen before. Even dressed for the morning's cold, her charms could not go unnoticed. Their hearts warmed immediately as did their bellies. The second woman was riding a winged lizard, a creature new to them;. The two seemed as one in synchronized motion. The third of the party looked like a hump of drab clothing with a rounded appendage where the head should be. All identity was hidden within the folds of clothing and the low setting hood. His walk was like a shuffle with little puffs of dust lifting with each step.

His smell affected the horses. They began to mill around the holding corral with increasing agitation. A section of the rear fencing broke down and the horses filed out at a near run. Several of the nearer brigands rushed to check the horses' escape. Two were run down before others could get there in time to help. It was several minutes before the brigands had the horses back in the corral. By then, the threesome were in the cottage.

"The sooner I can be rid of you, the better," Luanta said angrily to the huddled mass of clothing. She ignored Strike's cold answering stare from below the hood's hem.

"My time will soon be accomplished here, providing you get about the business at hand and cease trying to anger me, Luanta. Remember this adventure does not work without me." Strike turned to set on a trunk in the darker corner, joining two windowless walls. He took an observing view of the rest.

Luanta held back the retorts that came instantly to mind. She decided to wait her time. She turned to Everard, "Berenice has seen Lord Razon arrive at Skon's Hall. She did not see the ring, though I am sure it remains around his neck the way he wore it before."

Everard nodded. "I have met with my lieutenants. None even suspect that I have experienced a change." The threesome smiled. "Your small army awaits outside," the Everard changeling concluded, sweeping an arm to indicate the area of the hideout beyond the cottage door.

"Good! Strike says we must send Berenice back to the village." Luanta felt a mixture of distrust and frustration, having to wait even a little longer now that she was so close to her goal. "I have been carefully informed that I must wait until Strike has Lord Razon's ring of the House of Radiant before we can destroy Skon and his memory from this life." Luanta's face twisted into a quivering snarl of upturned lips. She turned away from the others. Over her shoulder, she said, "Go, Berenice. Return to us with the message we may proceed. Study Lord Razon and learn where and how to best acquire his ring. Now go."

It only took a moment for Berenice to mount and fly out of the hidden vale into the tributary canyons.

Luanta turned to Strike to see what he was doing. He was visibly asleep on the trunk. Luanta felt like sending a verbal jab his way but held back.

Strike took in her inclinations and subsequent change of mind. He smiled deep in his folds. "You learn quickly, Luanta," he whispered to himself. He closed his eyes and went to sleep. The brightness of the morning was beginning to irritate his eyes.

Everard studied Luanta's back waiting for her to continue with instructions.

Turning sideways to Everard and still having a peripheral view of Strike, Luanta said, "It would be best to keep an eye on Skon's Hall and their movements. I want to know exactly what they are doing. Send out several small parties to watch. Also, keep up the raids. I want Skon to be aware that peace will never be his again." A wicked gleam of anticipation flickered in her eyes. "Now I would like to clean up and rest a bit."

"There is a room here," Everard answered, showing Luanta the door.

Everard started outside to instruct his army. He stopped at the door to see what the bundle of cloth was doing. He appeared asleep. Everard went out, closing the door behind him.

✲✲✲✲✲

Though Razon was always forced to look up into the bearded face of his towering friend and felt dwarfed by the broad, massive shoulders haloed by shoulder-length straw blonde hair, he gladly accepted Blue Skon's solid welcoming handclasp. It had been over a year since they had been together. With Skon's first words of welcome, it was all as if only yesterday. Razon watched Laura take instant charge of Patrick and Ashley.

Laura de Faire, the cherished sister of the wandering Wolfgang the Meek of Wizzard, Razon recalled. They were the last of their line as well. Razon and she were equal in height, and though her feminine form was curvaceous, it never ceased to amaze him what a lethal weapon she could be, both with sword and without. Her beauty of golden hair and hazel eyes was complemented by her form, grace, and poise. Blue Skon's wife was a gracious hostess with intelligence that seemed to note everything and yet made her guests always feel at home. "If I could have found a woman like her, my years of searching would have been over long ago," he mused out loud. He watched her as she led the two awed children, mouths open and eyes alive with excitement into the hall's main chamber.

Razon realized Skon was still at his side. He looked up the eight inches Skon had over him and saw his gentle blue eyes studying him.

"Still you search, aye, my friend? This time, to bring back children and yet the elusive lady is as absent as ever."

"How is it that I cannot find an end to this burning hunger inside? I can never be whole until there is…is a woman, the right woman, to fill the void inside?"

"My friend, you seek what does not exist. For over twelve years, you have traversed the king's realm and those of seven others to find the one to meet your self-imagined ideals of another: another who was a lie. She was intent only upon your death. When you come to grips with this fact, you will find the search is no longer for the One. Rather, a one to provide fruition in purpose. And a return home."

"I know you are right, Skon. There has been a change in me. I feel it. I think it is because of these two children. While in their cottage of poverty,

I realized they were the ones whole and I, with so much, the one suffering infirmity. They lost their grandfather and sole parental figure. Yet, they remain fast in knowing who they are. Me, I still search and find myself empty."

"So, the children have won your heart. I thought as much in the proud display of horse and carriage bespeaking your daylight arrival. No hesitancy for fan-fare this time." Skon smiled his jest upon his friend's face.

"Right," Razon followed. "Hale! Lord Radiant. He and his entourage of ladies and squires, each nobly mounted upon plow horse and hay cart, piggy in tow.

They both laughed. They followed Laura and the children while patting each other's backs with renewed bonds of ken and kin.

CHAPTER TEN

Cynderet arrived back in the city with two things clear. She knew her mother's feelings for her had altered radically because she knew her daughter and apprentice would never become an Energy Feeder. Why, this was so remained unknown. So was what she would do about it. Cynderet also understood that Reht had worked out a way to be with her, and she must protect this knowledge from her mother and the Table.

On the return trip through the forest, Serenten had tested her without warning and tried to find access to the chambers he knew were there in her mind, only to be thwarted each time. The Table did not know these places existed. She hoped this would keep Reht's sanctuary safe. The nagging question was if Serenten's attempts were headed off because she expected them. He had tried to make them random, to come at times he felt she was unprepared. Would it be enough? She did not fool herself about how powerful the Table really was.

Cynderet went to bed the third night with a sense of relief. Her mother had not come home, and she did not feel the Table was aware of what all had happened. She no longer felt totally alone, knowing Reht had bequeathed her his Dream Sight.

Cynderet woke up feeling fresh and clearheaded. She spent a few minutes just lying in her nest, reflecting on the past several days. She knew things would never be as they were. Her mother and the Table both sought to deny her progress in the Society. "In fact, I could never allow myself to become as my mother," she mused. "So what am I to do?" She thought about the stranger and the children. "How did I come to be there? It was not really a dream. Even Serenten says it was too real. It was not of—" she stopped the thought instantly. She knew exactly what to do before she could continue this kind of thinking. She had to get back out of the city.

She dressed quickly and sought Serenten. "We need to go back into the mountains. There is so much that I need to think out, and it is no longer safe to even daydream here."

Serenten knew she was right. "Allow me to get some things and a food sack prepared. We will leave then."

It did not take them long to be back into the mountains. As soon as they were over the first ridge, Serenten said, "I do not feel the hum of the Table within my mind. Still, let us go deeper into the forest;. We will be out of sight of wandering eyes as well."

"I have been reaching out with my mind and find no thoughts near us," Cynderet said. "There is no one near or aware we have left the city. I agree it would be better to be deep inside the forest. There, I may concentrate on our thoughts and discussions and not have to worry about others coming near."

They traveled beyond the mossy log and the curve in the trail where Luanta had illustrated her power of charm. They went further than Cynderet had ever gone. She was looking for just the right place. She was actively aware of the life forms as they walked. She was not satisfied until they came to a thickly forested turn in the path. She felt a feeling of contentment below and to the right of them. There was a pleasant feeling of warmth upon the backs of the birds there. She motioned to Serenten and sent that she wanted to get off the path and into the trees to see this place of warmth. The feelings there were of solitude and security.

They stepped into the trees, walking for several yards. The trees opened up, showing sunshine beyond. They were actually on a knoll of the forest. Below them, it opened up into a small clearing with a running stream, gurgling proudly at the far side. It was not very large, but the sun was shining upon most of it.

They found a small game trail to follow down into the vale. Cynderet felt the birds and other creatures watch them descend into the openness of the vale. Then seeing no threat, the creatures went back to feeding or lying in the morning's sun.

"This is a good place," she said as they sat on a rock at the base of the knoll. "The only sensations here are of peace." She felt a quiver of pleasure that there should be such a spot. She knew her mother would never have brought her to such a place unless to prove how powerful she was somehow. Cynderet pondered how different she and her mother were for a few moments. "Serenten," she said, "I am not what Mother or the others would have me to be if it means seeking to destroy things. If Luanta was here, she would try to attack or charm something just to show how dominating she could be."

Serenten remained quiet knowing this was the beginning of the contemplating Cynderet had come here to do. He looked to her and nodded instead, allowing her to continue. He did not want to intrude with his own thoughts until she asked or needed them.

"The Table seeks to destroy me. Luanta hates what I am, and I could never be as she is. There is no place for me in the Society, and I have no way of living anywhere else. I feel like I am walking a path that leads nowhere. Yet Reht always told me to be what I am. To be otherwise would be a "lie," he said. I feel closer to the Hert than my own kind. Tell me about the Hert. Tell me what you remember of your youth. How did you come to be here?"

"Ah, Child. I remember so little. I remember feelings more than anything."

Cynderet felt his attempt to put her off. She saw his reluctance to open wounds long closed. He was unsure about looking at the past of his youth. He changed his mind; he allowed her to see within. He understood what it was she sought. Strength came as a result of his knowing they were both seeking a sanctuary from the egocentric ways of the Society. Finally, he was able to open up.

"I was so very young. I remember playing. The light of day is clear and I can see just fine. Then I feel fear—fear as I have never felt it before. Everything goes black. There is no light at all. It is so dark I cannot see to move. Suddenly, before my eyes adjust to the infrared spectrum, something grabs me, lifting me up. It holds me bound to its chest by its arms as it rushes out of my home. There are many of us taken. I can see the heat of dark shapes hunched over moving down a deep passage carrying us away from our homes."

Cynderet saw in his mind the visions coming back to him. They were both there, seeing together. "Others are screaming. I can hear my own. There is the smell of straw and dampness in the dark. We are huddling close together to keep warm. The sends of others are all jumbled in fear and anguish. It seems to go on endlessly. I do not remember much more for a while. I think I passed out from shock and exhaustion."

Cynderet allowed him time to continue. She could feel his pain as if her own.

"The next thing I remember is waking up deep in a cavern. Reht is there holding his hand out to me. He takes me to food and clean clothes. Then, he is gone. I do not see him again for a long time."

Serenten stopped and looked at Cynderet. "I had forgotten that Reht was there. He did not come with us. He was already there. I did not see him again until I was old enough to begin training as a Council Guard. The rest of us stayed in that cavern a long time. Years I am sure, but how many, I do not know." Serenten was quiet for several minutes.

Cynderet felt his emotional fatigue. He had reopened scenes he had closed tightly to his mind since that time. She knew there was much more. She waited as long as she dared before she asked her next question. She was afraid he might close down his thoughts completely.

"Do you know where this cavern is or how you got there?"

"I think so," he said as he looked to her. "It is very difficult to tell, really."

Cynderet felt the oppression of the cavern set upon his thoughts. She knew he spent a long time there. She saw how, over time, memory of home and family became buried inside by the struggle just to survive day-to-day. She cried silent tears with him as she experienced his realization that he was only a slave. He had been so young and so alone. He had been much younger than she was now, but the devastation was the same. Cynderet also felt the deeper, stronger pull of his determination to live. Others did not make it. They died from broken hearts.

He continued, "There was no light or indications of day or night, just the cavern. We did everything using infravision. I think it is deep inside Council Peak. When we were finally allowed out, we walked up many flights of stairs. We came out at the lower chambers of the Council Hert barracks.

"I remember not being able to see. Everything was misty because of the brightness of the day's light hurting my eyes. We were tested and assigned different tasks by the Eldresses. I and seven others were chosen to become Council Hert."

Cynderet felt empathy for his heaviness of heart.

His shoulders shook as he finished, "Most of the others I have never seen since."

She gave him time to ponder. He had drawn upon memories and emotions he had not allowed himself to experience for decades. "I am glad we found this spot, my friend," she sent. "At least here we are safe to look at things we dare not examine in the city."

He did not answer her send, but she felt the touch of kinship in his receiving it.

They ate their midday meal. Serenten kept to himself for a long period after they were done eating. It was not until Cynderet noticed that the vale was in the shadow of the forest that she playfully attacked his thoughts about how he had driven away the sun with his gloomy state of mind.

"Me?" he countered. He threw at her the visions of thunder and storm, rain pounding in the wind blasting her mind's inner walls.

Not to be outdone, she changed his pounding rain to soft feathery snow.

She stopped the fun with a mouth-opened stare. She gaped at the uniqueness of every flake she could focus on.

Serenten ceased the winds, allowing Cynderet to watch, spellbound, as each snowflake descended in small pendulum arcs, falling gracefully, like a feather on a calm day.

"I have never seen such a thing as these intricate bits of crystal. Where do they come from?" she asked.

"I do not know for sure," Serenten answered, a little befuddled himself. "I believe they are a type of rain from the Plane of Humans. They are not from this plane. I have never experienced them, myself. They must be of Reht."

She twisted towards Serenten. "Tell me about the land where humans dwell!" she demanded, anxious to know more.

"I know so little, Child." Serenten admitted. "My times there were always brief and restricted in purpose."

"Then just tell me what you remember. What you saw and did," she pleaded.

"None was ever pleasant. I do remember one time well. I should have died then, I think." Serenten's voice dropped into a softness Cynderet knew to be apologetic, as well as informative. He was hesitant to speak at first. He was not pleased with his part. She could read it as he prepared to tell the account. "I remember being gated by Luanta to a place of cells with people, humans, locked up within. I and two other Council Guards were guarding the entrance to the area where she and a man in black robes talked with humans. At first, she was just talking to them, asking them questions.

"Luanta was determined to gain information none seemed to have. When no one would tell her what she wanted to know, she became angry. She turned to torture, each time was the same. She tied a human to the table and asked a question, something about where someone was.

"When they did not answer, she picked out another who was forced to watch the horrid death of the first, only to have the routine repeated. She was fanatical about getting some bit of information they did not have. The screaming went on and on.

"After many had suffered and died, we heard activity outside the portals to the dungeon. Those outside the portals, who were in league with the man in black robes, were having difficulty with intruders. We could hear the clash of weapons and sounds of the dying.

"Luanta became infuriated and killed three prisoners instantly. She dragged a fourth out of a cell, an older man. I did not have time to see what happened after that. The intruders burst through the portals. My companions and I were armed, all being Council Guards.

"We were positioned just inside. The intruders must have expected us, because they came in quickly and ready to fight. But instead of fighting when they saw us, the first two turned and bolted back in fear. They ran into the next rank of intruders causing great confusion, which we used to our benefit. We attacked, slaying three. The fourth, I will never forget.

"He seemed a bearded giant who stood alone in front of a few others still disorganized. He did not run. Instead, he saluted us with his sword. His blue cloak shimmered as he did so. One of my comrades made a step-thrust-parry-and-slice maneuver perfectly executed, only to find he missed the man in blue entirely. He never got a second chance." Serenten continued, "The man drove his sword deep into the guard's chest. He stepped in towards my comrade's body as he heaved his sword upward, hefting him off the ground. This blocked my attack. Behind him, arrows were being loosed into the two of us left by one of a forest green cloak, and another I never saw clearly. I was hit thrice.

"I turned to avoid further arrows. I saw Luanta circle her arms in front of her beginning to Force Field Web away when I was propelled towards her by a solid hit to my head. All went black for me. I know not what happened after for I awoke within my quarters being attended to by Reht. He said I was the only one to return with Luanta.

"Luanta was livid for several days about it. She even sought my execution for failing to protect her. The rest of the Eldress Council denied her petition, saying I had fulfilled my duty by defending her long enough for her to return safely to the Shadow Plane.

"I do not think she even remembers my involvement now. Shortly thereafter, she had another brush with danger. I was told it almost cost her life. I believe it unnerved her. She has seldom gone to feed since. It was several days before I saw her again. That was just before we all knew you had been conceived."

"So what Harriant said may be true. My mother has not been herself. Is that why she is gone now?" Cynderet asked.

"There is a change: just a feeling I have," Serenten said, "but you know it as well. Let yourself remember how things have altered. Now Luanta is gone. Things are altered more than ever before. Harriant said Luanta had been to see Ermentrude. She has not been seen since. None of this bodes well."

Cynderet took time to ponder what Serenten said. It was true. She knew it was. She took a closer look at the last several days, and how her mother had changed. "The last time I saw my mother, she sought only to punish me for being unable to share in her oppressive pleasures. She has anger burning as I have never seen it. Inside, she is harboring hate, and the need for vengeance against a human."

Serenten added, "She must be seeking to resolve that hate. That has to be what Ermentrude was talking about in the conversation Harriant overheard."

"But who is this human? Who is he? Why is he so important to bring my mother to such an all-encompassing state of hate, and yet go years doing nothing about it? Why the sudden change? There has to be more to this!"

Cynderet stood up and started to pace. Shaking her head, she tried to think it all through. It did not make sense. "My mother never waits. Patience is not in her. There must be another reason. It must be fear that has held her back all these years." Cynderet knew she was right. It was the only thing that fit. It opened to more understanding. "That is why she seldom fed, because she was afraid to." Cynderet felt something click into place. "My mother is no longer afraid! What could happen to take her fear away? She has gained the advantage somehow but how?" Cynderet sat back down. She looked at Serenten.

"You have come to see much, Child. There are parts still missing. Perhaps we should talk to Harriant again," Serenten said with an adventuresome gleam in his eye.

"We will have to make it look like her idea to tell us what she knows," Cynderet followed.

"Could you plant such a thought in her mind? She is quite simple," Serenten suggested with a grin.

Smiling back, Cynderet nodded. "I think so. I have never tried before. Wait, I have to—whenever my mother was becoming angry with me, I would suggest to her that I was desirous to be an Energy Feeder like her. It usually worked. That is until lately. Yes, I will plant a thought of how she could belittle me with the information we want. That should be easy with her disposition."

Cynderet felt a unique feeling, one of being in control. It was new to her. She liked it.

CHAPTER ELEVEN

Harriant went to bed bitter again. Ever since Cynderet had challenged her about not being ready to learn about the Charm Spell she had sought a way to get back at her. She could not think of a way yet, but when she did, it would hurt Cynderet so much she would never dare shame her again.

Her determined pursuit was affecting her dreams. She saw herself talking to Cynderet. Shenet was there, looking with admiration at Cynderet who had just finished one of her smart answers that always made Harriant look stupid and immature in front of the other girls. Harriant hated the smug look Cynderet gave her and that tilt of her head, just daring Harriant to try something else.

Harriant got an idea. It made her entire body tingle with delight. There was no way Cynderet could get out of this one! She would prove how weak Cynderet's mother was. She had heard the whole conversation between Ermentrude and Luanta. She could destroy Cynderet with the other girls because she knew why Luanta was gone.

Harriant woke up anxious to confront that impaired discredit to the Society. "This time, I will show the others just how groveling Cynderet really is. She is nothing but a crippled defect to the Society," Harriant pledged to herself. It took another hour of winding down in excitement before she returned to sleep.

Harriant got up that morning with a feeling of elation she had not felt since passing her encounter with the Table and her initiation. She finished her duties early and asked Ermentrude if she could go out for the rest of the morning. She would be back in time for afternoon training.

Ermentrude had studies of her own she wanted to do. Welcoming the possibility of time away from her pesky apprentice, she let her go.

Harriant sought out Shenet first. She wanted to make sure others witnessed her moment of triumph over that prattling bit of Hert dung!

They found Cynderet just where Harriant's dream had shown her to be. She was sitting under a tree all alone. Her Hert was nowhere around.

Cynderet continued looking up into the tree watching the antics of the birds while she read Harriant's thoughts and excited state of mind. Shenet was with her, though not really sure what was to happen.

"Hello, Cynderet," Harriant said as if she could milk sweetness from a bitter tree. "I see you are bird watching all alone again. It is too bad you cannot train, what with Luanta gone and all."

Cynderet read Harriant's mind for every inflection and layered thought. It was easy to pretend to be attentive to her voice, for she missed nothing. She sought to get everything that Harriant's simple mind could offer.

"Hello, Harriant. I see you are up early this morning," she said to insure a good baiting.

"Oh, yes, I will train hard today. Ermentrude gave me time off this morning for doing so well already. I am so sorry it is not the same with you. You look so forlorn without your mentor here," Harriant responded. She was feeling wonderful in her knowledge of what Luanta was doing and Cynderet not having any idea.

"I know my mother will have much to teach me when she returns. She is the best mentor I could have. The Council made it so," Cynderet continued in her guise. She was careful not to let Harriant know that the Table was the real decision-maker of the Eldress Council.

"It is true the Council of Eldresses knows what is best for us all. That is why I am apprenticed to the Senior Eldress and you to Luanta." Harriant beamed in her belief she had set Cynderet up for her wicked stab. "Luanta is the sick one. Just like you, Cynderet. You are both cripples in the Society—it is known to the whole Council."

"How can you say that of the second greatest Eldress of the Council?" Cynderet challenged.

"She is second, but shall never be first. She has not the strength needed to lead. Even now, she must turn to the Wherants for the power to destroy a paltry human." Harriant was smug and confident. She unleashed all she knew in mind and voice. Her bitterness was allowing Cynderet to see it all. Harriant finished with what she felt would be the end of Cynderet, "She has proven too afraid to even Energy Feed without help!" Harriant laughed a vicious gloating laugh. It rang high, grating on the nerves. Cynderet read Shenet's internal shrug of shoulders at the pain of the sound.

Cynderet also read Harriant's memory of the visit between Luanta and Ermentrude. Much of what she voiced was indeed true, which wrenched Cynderet's heart for her mother. But greater was the pain of finding Luanta had gone to the Wherants to work out somekind of a bargain, allowing her to destroy a human she feared and his entire family. Knowing Luanta's penchant for killing and the history Serenten had just related the day before, Cynderet was not so sure the man had not simply been defending his own way of life and self. The Wherants were known to the Society to be most self-serving and devious demons.

It was not necessary for Cynderet to play at tears of shame. They came naturally, flowing all to the pleasure of Harriant. Harriant's laughter continued to soil the air for long moments after she and Shenet had left.

Serenten came to her from around the corner where he had been hiding. "I too saw it all through your mind, Cynderet. I feel a return of the bitterness I knew as a youth. I am so sorry this is yours to feel."

"We must leave. The Table will feel these thoughts for sure. I will run away. Harriant is right. I am crippled—beyond anything she would inflict me with."

Cynderet turned to flee. It was too late.

"You would know of your mother's doings?" the Table asked within her mind. "See what she is about. You will die in the viewing!" The visions of dying humans were forced into her mind. Scenes beyond anything she could imagine: men, women, and children slain in the most awful ways. The burning of entire villages, the smell of smoldering flesh was driven into her. She felt herself giving way as children were skewered on the lances of fiendish armies. She slipped into unconsciousness as the young girl she had seen in the forest was being torn apart by a huge winged creature. Its racking claws embedded in her chest and stomach, pulling. All went black with the girl screaming in her mind.

Serenten closed his mind to the barrage before the Table realized he was witness to its visual assault of Cynderet. Instead, he picked her up as she collapsed to the stone pavement. Her body was quivering from the impact of the scenes the Table was pounding her with. Only by getting her out of the city could he save her from the Table's merciless attack. He ran with her in his arms.

Cynderet was completely unconscious when he got to the edge of the city. The humming of the Table beat upon his senses. He knew the Table continued to drive at Cynderet's mind. He started up the hillside. His fear she was dying forced him to push harder. The climb seemed to never end. His lungs labored to pull in enough air to keep him going. He reached the top of the ridge exhausted and out of breath. His feet were bleeding. He had torn off a toe claw amongst the jagged rock. He limped over the ridge and into the canyon below.

He could see the trees ahead as the intense humming of the Table ceased with distance. Only when he was within the shade of the trees did he slow. He located where Cynderet had come to know the Dream Sight and laid her against the log. He hoped she could feel the coolness of the moss. He walked into the stream and soaked his hands in the cold water. He cupped them and brought water to her brow and face.

Cynderet's breathing was shallow and ragged. There was blood at the corner of her mouth. Serenten felt she must have bit her lip during the Table's murderous assault. There was also a trickle of blood in the canal of one ear.

Serenten tore off Cynderet's sleeve and used it as a cooling cloth. He forced himself to make several trips to the stream. Finally, in exhaustion, he rested her in his arms. It had been several hours since their meeting with Harriant.

"Please do not let yourself die," he begged. "You must be strong, Child. I lived through my pain. You must also."

Serenten collapsed into a stupor's sleep, still holding her close to him.

*****

The Table screamed out its mental waves to the members of the Eldress Council still in the city. It could not believe Cynderet had managed to escape its telepathic blast. No one could have lived through it, yet she had stolen away beyond its range of influence. She must have had help. Who? It had killed that interfering Hert. There must be another. It must be her new Hert. How? Where? Harriant's simple mind had shown no sign of the Hert's presence during her meeting with the Mind Child at the tree.

The Table bellowed its mental call again. It could sense the Eldresses coming. They were too slow! It rushed visions of Cynderet as a traitor to their minds. It showed her violating the Council Peak in an effort to get them to move faster.

By the time they reached the Table and went into their chanting for enlightenment, they had called out the Council Guard and had them stationed at every defensive position in the city watching for Cynderet and Serenten. The Table was furious at the constant delays in getting the Ritual of Enlightenment started. As soon as their hands were placed upon the Table, it began to devour the energy they fed it. It sent out its mind, searching with renewed vigor trying to locate Cynderet. It would not let up. It searched every place in the city it could penetrate. When it could not find her, it went beyond into the surrounding hillsides. Nothing. Wherever she was, it could not find her. She had to be far outside the city.

After a passing of several hours of mental searching, the Table found the Eldresses drained of energy to feed it. They had exhausted themselves. It broke off the chanting ritual as they began to nod into sleep still trying to maintain the feeding chant. In frustration, it had Ermentrude send out scouts into the mountains to find Serenten.

*****

Serenten awoke stiff and cold. He listened to the sounds around him for indications of trouble. The sun's dim light was fading away. It was late afternoon. Cynderet was still unconscious in his arms. Her breathing had slowed. It was so shallow he had to put his ear to her mouth to hear and feel its exhale. She was dying. He knew it. Serenten felt hopeless. He had never intended for time to slip by like it had. One thing he knew for sure, there would be a search party determined to find them. He had to find a safer place to hide.

Serenten gathered Cynderet into his arms and gently carried her further into the forest. He had closed his mind to Cynderet's visions to prevent the Table's attack from affecting him. He did not know if Reht's Dream Sight had come to her aid. Serenten did not want to risk further trauma to Cynderet by looking into her mind now. If there was something Reht could do to help her, Serenten was sure he was doing it. Serenten remembered the vale they had found peace in. Was it just the day before? He headed to the forest glade deep in the midst of the trees.

CHAPTER TWELVE

Laura led Ashley and Patrick into the common room. Here were the great tables for eating and a grand fireplace in the middle of the far wall. Above it hung a huge banner: a field of blue like a clear winter sky. Within its center flew the Golden Pegasus. Its wings were extended as if in a graceful soar. Below the Pegasus, just at the bottom of the flag was a wide white band. It extended side to side with only what looked like a wooden challis standing upright at the right end. Ashley stared at it, trying to remember where she had seen them before. It came to her quickly; it was on the towers outside, only there the white band flew as a separate banner. Here, they were joined together into a single flag.

"It is supposed to be for me," a voice behind her said.

She turned quickly to see a boy a little older than her standing close behind her.

He smiled, "Greetings. My name is Ryan de Faire. I live here."

Ashley recognized the family similarity in his golden hair and facial form with the Lady Laura. "It must be wonderful to live here," she answered.

Ryan gave a funny look with a slight roll of his blue eyes, definitely of his father. "I guess so, for you. I cannot wait to leave." He turned and was gone.

Ashley thought she had said something wrong by his sudden departure. She felt a hand placed gently on her shoulder.

"Do not be overly concerned with Ryan's rudeness," Lady Laura assured her. "He does know better. He feels denied the "adventures of life" because he is expected to live up to his father's standards. It irks him. Do not take his poor manners personally." Noting her need to feel accepted, Lady Laura added, "You are a very pretty young lady with a good head on you. Ryan will come around soon. For now, we better catch up with your brother though."

They turned to the right and entered a comfortable sitting room. Patrick was stuffing a handful of grapes into his mouth.

"You may wish to take them off the stem first," Lady Laura cautioned.

Patrick looked up at her as he began chewing, not fully aware of her meaning. A moment later, he stopped chewing with a crinkled brow. He looked for somewhere to spit out his mouth's contents. In the unfamiliar surroundings, he could find nowhere that would not offend his hostess. His brow sunk deep into the top of his nose as his face began to sour. With a look of desperation, he opened his hand. A bowl was suddenly and deftly placed upon it just in time to collect the juice, peels, and stems. He looked up into a narrow, warm face, resting upon the neck of a man's willowy frame.

"It is the stems which are bitter. The berries are fine with the sweetness in their juices," the man said, a smile formed at the corners of his mouth and creased his hollow cheeks. The man then bowed and taking the bowl, departed the room.

"Who be that?" a wide-eyed Patrick drawled captivated;. He commenced, wiping leftover juice at the corner of his mouth on his sleeve.

"That was Quick the Quiet. We call him Quick. He sees that things run smoothly around here. He is Lord Skon's man."

"Wha's that?" Patrick asked with a slight tilt of his head.

"Someone who helps with the daily chores of a lord. Like a squire would be to a knight," Laura answered. "Let us see about getting you some food and a warm place to rest." She took them to a small table with chairs around and then pointed to the washbasin off to the side against a discreet wall. "Wash your hands and then come here to eat."

As soon as they finished washing, they found that Quick had set two plates of food on the table and was returning with a tray, holding a pitcher and several goblets. They were down and eating within a heartbeat. Ashley turned to Quick and thanked him. He was just going around the corner when he heard it. He stopped, turned, and acknowledged her gratitude. He gave a slight bow of his head and a smile, then left.

It did not take long for Patrick to finish. Ashley was still working on hers as he gave a hearty burp, wiped his mouth with his sleeve, and turned to Lady Laura. "I be tired. Ya wan' me ta sleep with me horse in the hay?"

Ashley wondered what the answer would be but was too embarrassed to speak. She thought about giving Patrick a kick under the table, and then decided against it. She was not sure what his reaction would be.

"No, Patrick. That will not be necessary. We have a place ready for you and your sister. But first, let her finish eating and then Quick will show you where to clean up and sleep. We will let you two share a room tonight to ease the strangeness of this hall. Tomorrow, after you have rested, we will show you around. Will that be all right?"

"Yep, tha' be me think'n too."

Ashley stared. Patrick's ability to speak like he was in control always amazed her. She was relieved as Lady Laura bestowed a knowing smile her way.

Lady Laura turned to leave. "I will see to the men and be right back."

"Patrick! Use that cloth by your plate to wipe your mouth, not your sleeve. And show some respect. These are nice people."

"Yep, they eats good too. Ya fink they got more?"

Ashley heard voices coming and sent Patrick a last look. "Behave," she warned. She finished her last bite and modeled how to use the cloth for him.

Blue Skon entered first. He still had a hand on Razon's shoulder as he turned the corner into the sitting room. Ashley immediately noted the close bond between the two men. Razon seemed to beam a new light just being here in this hall. Laura came just behind finishing an anecdote with Razon.

"You two well cared for?" Skon asked. "I understand you have met Quick, and he has met your brother's appetite." He smiled. It looked natural on his square face. He was tall. Ashley had to look up to see his face as he spoke. He must have noticed, for with no hesitation at all, he squatted down at the table's edge; they were now eye-to-eye.

"Thank you for your kindness, sir. We are very pleased to be in your home. Skon's Hall is most welcoming," Ashley said. She noted how broad his shoulders were as they rose just above the table's edge.

"You are quite a lady. I have seldom seen such wonderful manners in our guests. It is a pleasure to have you grace our home. You show sound training. We shall call you Lady Ashley. It will save trouble in the village and I think it befits you well." With a slight turn of his head, he took in Patrick, "I understand you are very good with horses and their care. Am I correctly informed?"

"Aye, sir. That ya be!" Patrick responded proudly.

Ashley was relieved to see him refer to the lord with a little more respect than shown earlier.

"Good. We shall call you Squire Patrick, and on the morrow, early, Quick will introduce you to our few animals. What say you?" Skon asked in a serious tone. "Think you able to arise early and care for our stock?"

"Aye, sir. I be sho'n ya now if'n ya will?" Patrick's chest was swelling, and Ashley made note of how easily Lord Skon made them both feel important and at ease in the great hall. Inside, she gave thanks to the forces that brought them here. It took her back a moment to realize that those forces had been Razon, no—Lord Razon, as the village had addressed him. Was his title a gift also? Somehow, she did not think so. *I will ask Lady Laura when I can. She will tell me the way of it,* she said to herself.

Shortly thereafter, Quick was back. He led the children to their room for the night. Razon watched as they said good-night to all, including himself. Had

Ashley's face almost shown a smile for him? He could not be sure. She had been so distant since the knife display. She had not spoken in conversation with him since they left the cottage. Only responses to questions and discussions about things needed as they traveled did she voice. He still could feel the bite of her bitter words the other morning. He decided he was wrong about the smile just as Skon broke the thought.

"You said there was trouble in the mountains?"

Razon noted the serious tone. Skon could do that, one instant be the pleasant host, and the next, firm and in command. He took seriously any threat to his holdings. It was not so long ago, Skon too had been poor and alone. He knew what it meant and cared greatly for the welfare of his people.

Razon waved his hand towards the chairs in the sitting room. He waited for Laura and Skon to sit before he began. It was so natural. Here, he was an equal, and he felt it. "I came upon the children and their grandfather in a bandit attack. Their grandfather died that night. Then two days later, I was coming out of the forest towards the vale at the base of the mountains when I came upon a trade caravan under attack. It was early morning. The traders were just getting up when hit. The bandit force was about twenty in number and well-armed. They knew what they were doing. It was well-planned and executed.

"I went back for the children. That was four days ago. We had no trouble coming here." Razon waited for the information to sink in.

Laura caught the slight inflection of Razon's voice at his going "back for the children." She studied him closely. There was something going on between Razon and Ashley that made them both very uncomfortable. *I will watch and see,* she decided.

"Tomorrow morn, we will take a patrol and go see the vale. Let us go speak with Captain Hamilton now. Quick, you come also."

Without even turning, Razon knew Quick was there. He was not called Quick the Quiet without reason. Razon knew no one who could disappear within shadow or remain as silent as Quick. Even with his tall frame.

"Excuse us, milady," Skon said to Laura. Then, the threesome left to see the captain of the hall guards. Laura would know what was said. Razon did not know how, but Laura and Skon had no secrets between them. And the knowledge was shared too fast for waiting to be told.

The next morning, Ashley woke up to Patrick's pushing her shoulder. "Ya should see the horse stock wha' Lord Skon's gots!" Patrick said excitedly. "If'n ya hurry ta the window, ya can see the Lord leav'n. I was help'n 'em saddle up."

"You mean, Lord Skon is riding away?" Ashley asked, still fighting to wake up.

"Yep, and Lord Razon be go'n wif 'im," Patrick added as he went back out the door.

Ashley jumped out of bed and ran to the window. It looked out to the side of the hall where Lord Skon and the patrol were just passing into the main street of the village. She saw Razon in a forest green cloak riding at Skon's side. Both were fully armored. Her heart sank to her stomach. There were eight soldiers with them. Just behind Skon, one carried his flag: the Golden Pegasus soaring in its field of blue. Ashley noted Skon wore a cloak of the same blue. It shimmered in the morning's light.

Ashley quickly changed into her clothes and rushed out to find Lady Laura.

*****

Patrick saw a shadow slip away off to his left. It had looked to be his size. It was too much of an adventure for him to walk away from. "I be think'n ya wus listen'n at our door. I be find'n ya," he said as he followed.

In a few quick steps, Patrick reached a large stairway leading down. He did not see any movement. He looked quickly to his left just as a door in the far wall shut. He ran to it. He listened at the narrow door before rushing in. He felt excitement inside;. His heart was beginning to pound heavily. He liked it. There was the sound of soft footsteps moving away echoing off the walls of what seemed to be a narrow passageway on the other side. The steps sounded like they were going up. Curious beyond tolerance, Patrick opened the door. It opened on a small cubical with narrow stairs going up. He saw a shadow of shape turn on the stair landing above him. He took off at a run going two stairs at a step. He heard a door clang shut.

Patrick reached the upper door and pulled it open. Outside, it was full daylight and at first, the reflective glare of the morning sun shining off the stone battlements blinded him. He backed into the portal. Squinting allowed him to look around. It was an outer tower of the Hall. There was a large platform in the middle with three steps leading to its upper platform. A strange wooden contraption loomed above with a bow lying horizontally across its front. Just on the far side was a figure standing near the battlements looking towards the village. Patrick had only seen him briefly last night, but knew who it was. "Wha' ya be watch'n?" Patrick asked, sure already of the answer.

Ryan turned around quickly. "How did you get up here?" he asked rather sharply.

"I be follow'n ya. Ya make so much noise it be easy." Patrick ignored the glare and walked to Ryan, taking a position beside him to also look at the village. The last of the patrol was passing into the village and out of sight. "So ya be watch'n 'em leave, aye?" he asked.

"Yes. Someday I am going to ride off just like that and maybe never come back," Ryan responded.

Patrick noted a touch of bitterness in Ryan's voice.

"Why do ya no go wif 'em?" he asked as he made a slight leap up to sit on the rampart. Then he looked down.

"My father says it would be too dangerous," Ryan answered, surprising himself even responding to this stranger's questions. The boy seemed completely open and honest. "I think my father is afraid I might like the real world outside this prison. So, he keeps me locked up here."

Patrick looked quizzically at Ryan. He took his time as he studied his face. "Yep," he said, "Gran'f'ar would say ya's got a rock set'n sour on yar stomach. I be thnk'n ya need some hard work to shake it."

"Oh, really?" Ryan chided with a snicker. "And who are you to figure what I need?"

"I be know'n when I gets a 'poor me' feel'n Gran'f'ar would send me out hunt'n crows in the garden or turn'n soil. Said I needs ta work it off. I gots so I be real good wif a sling an' a stone."

Not to be left talking idle words, Patrick took out his leather sling and a stone to prove it. He placed the stone carefully in its saddle and looked for a target. The hall's outer perimeter was well-cleared for defense. Patrick could not find a suitable target. "Ya gots someth'n to throw?"

"Yeah. How about this?" Ryan asked with a sly grin on his face. He climbed the three steps up the platform and pulled a quarrel from a basket beside the strange bow-like contraption. He smiled at Patrick, indicating he would throw it to see if Patrick could hit it.

Ryan was well-trained in the use of a long sword and had good arm muscling. He threw the quarrel like a spear high, into the air. Up and away from the battlement's outer wall, it climbed like a javelin. Ryan looked at Patrick feeling superior.

Patrick immediately went into motion with his sling, spinning it over his head.

Ryan mocked his whirling with a laugh.

The tip of Patrick's tongue could be seen clenched between his teeth at the side of his mouth. His eyes never left the flight of the quarrel. As it reached the peak of its arc and started back down, Patrick let fly his stone. It took the quarrel in the middle, breaking it in two.

Patrick looked at Ryan. Ryan was turning to him with his mouth opened agape.

"I did not think you could do it," he stammered.

"Easier than a bird. Never know wha' way some birds be turn'n in flight," Patrick answered matter-of-factly.

"Can you teach me to do that?" Ryan asked.

"Sure," Patrick responded with confidence, "if'n ya gots someth'n ta trade."

"I could teach you to use a sword," Ryan offered.

"Yep. That be a good trade ta me." Patrick was pleased with the idea of learning a real weapon. He had been impressed with Razon's skills and wanted to learn some of his own. "We be need'n a place ta practice and a lot o' targets."

"Follow me," Ryan stated with a welcome feeling of being able to do something of an adventure himself.

CHAPTER THIRTEEN

Henry the tavern master looked up as the front door opened. In the bright light of midday, he saw the strange man enter again. Henry had not thought he would see him again so soon, yet here he was. Remembering his coin to be good, Henry showed him his usual seat and made sure all was to his liking. Maybe it would be another profitable three days.

"May I get you anything special?" Henry offered. "Midday's meal will be another hour, but I have bread and cheese to offer with a flagon of mead."

Nodding acceptance, the man said, "Things seem quiet after the arrival of the Lord Radiant fellow. Must not have come back into the village?"

"Oh, no. In fact, he left with the Lord Skon this very morning, early. Have not seen nor heard from them since. Seems there was some trouble in the mountains," Henry answered. He saw the man's surprise. Thinking he might leave, he added quickly, "They should be back anytime."

The man seemed to settle a little. "No matter," he pretended, "I will have the bread and cheese, thanks."

Berenice, back in the male form, settled down to eat. It was up to Everard's group to worry Skon's soldiers. She knew Razon may or may not be back soon, maybe not at all. She would eat and wait out the day here. She had other things to do tonight.

*****

Ashley did not find Lady Laura immediately. She looked in the few areas she had seen the evening before. They were all empty. Only the great hearth offered any sound with its morning fire driving out the night's chill in the great room. Ashley grabbed a small bunch of grapes from the sitting room table and then retraced her steps to her room.

The central area in front of her room's door was well-lit from the day's light. Ashley noted that the shadows she saw last night in the corners were actually plants, indoors. The light came from a great opaque dome over the entire ceiling area. It was so high she could see the walls of two more levels above her. There was a hexagonal water fountain in the middle of the area floor. The water spewed up from the center's tiled pillar. Beyond the fountain, she saw a grand stairway leading down with massive pillars on either side of it. There was enough room on the stairs for several men to walk abreast. She had never seen anything as grand in her life. It amazed her that she had missed so much last night when Quick had taken Patrick and her to their room.

Ashley walked to the stairway head and looked down. It dropped at least twenty feet before it opened into a huge expanse. She thought she heard something, a rhythmic clicking of metal against metal from below and started down the steps quite curious. She stopped about halfway down. The bottom of the stairway opened up to reveal a spacious chamber with supportive columns on either side.

She was amazed at what she saw. Lady Laura, dressed in breeches, was wielding a sword and dagger against the lord's man, Quick. Both were like dancers embracing the heat of contest. Their grace and movement held her spellbound. It went on for a long time. Neither showed the advantage over the other. Quick used a short sword and dagger against Laura's long sword and dagger. Although Laura had a longer reach with her sword, she could not find a breach within Quick's speed and agility. They were equally matched. Laura feigned to the right by dropping her shoulder then rolled a forward somersault to Quick's right. He did a backwards flip to land clear of her dagger strike and parried her long sword.

Using the weapon's impact as a fulcrum, Laura pivoted to his left, drawing her sword free. As she did so, Quick spun fully around to catch her dagger with his and lift up. It allowed his short sword to thrust towards Laura's midsection. Ashley screamed fearing he would make a clean strike just as Laura caught the thrust in the notch of her sword where the pummel meets the blade.

They both heard Ashley's scream and stopped the blade dance. With lowered weapons, they turned as one to look her way.

"I thought he would kill you, Lady Laura!" Ashley came down the stairs too fast to stop.

Quick dropped his weapons and met her fall with open arms and a twist of his willowy frame. It allowed her to brake her fall and yet remain standing when she found her balance.

"You are an awful man!" She beat at him with her fists. "You would have killed her!"

"Lady Ashley, I would never do any such thing," he answered as he took her hands into his, gently restraining her blows. "It was merely practice. If not so, we would never have been doing acrobatics, I assure you."

"Ashley, he is right. You need not fear for me here. Quick is a wonderful Weapons Master, and we were only practicing." Laura took Ashley's hands from Quick and drew her into a hug. "It was very kind of you to be concerned for my welfare. Come, let us sit while I dry off my face."

Laura guided her to a table and chairs at the side of the room where a pitcher of water and glasses were joined by a couple of towels. Laura took one and tossed it to Quick while she dabbed at her face and neck with the other.

Ashley wiped an unwanted tear from her eye as she watched Laura dry off. Feeling a barrage of emotions, Ashley blurted out, "I am sorry if I endangered you in your practice. It was so much like when I asked Lord Razon to teach me how to use a knife. He almost killed me. His eyes turned hard and the blade sliced through the air so fast it was only a blur. The next thing I knew, I was sitting on the floor of the cottage with the knife embedded at my feet. I thought I could tru…" Ashley could say no more as the sobs raked her body.

Thinking she saw an answer to last night's question, Laura asked, "Is that why you are so angry with him?"

Ashley nodded her head, continuing to hide in her hands.

"Ashley." Laura spoke softly. "Lord Razon is the finest sword-and-dagger man I know. If you asked him to show you how to use a dagger, or knife as you say, he would do it the only way he knows how. He is a warrior, one who has battled side by side with my husband to rid this countryside of the evils they found here. He would show you a weapon as it really is," Laura said as she knelt at Ashley's side. "I think you may have misunderstood his intent. If Quick or Lord Skon were asked to teach you, it would have been the same. You see, they are the ones who bring peace and safety to this land. I will share some of their story with you later. For now, understand they are the ones who know what it means to put their hopes and lives aside for the sake of others." Laura gave Ashley a hug about the shoulders and helped her up. "Come, dry your eyes and I will show you."

Ashley stood up expecting Laura to illustrate further how Skon and Razon helped fend off the forces of evil from the land. She was very surprised when, instead, they walked to the other side of the room. There was only a large double-door cabinet at this wall. As they got to it, Quick opened both doors. Inside was a vast array of bladed and bludgeoning hand weapons. "Pick out a blade that looks like the one Lord Razon showed you," Laura instructed gently.

Ashley gave a cursory look at the weapons, thinking she could see them all easily. There were so many. She had to start again and actually search each space and weapon. She looked past the swords positioned against a rack in front of the knives, just behind and higher. There, just outside the swords' shadows, was a narrow blade and unadorned handle. It had two matching mates behind it. She picked one up and looked to Laura and Quick.

Quick asked, "Is this the type of blade you asked Lord Razon to teach you about, Lady Ashley?"

"Yes. It looked every bit like this one, except this one is missing the embedded medallion on the handle and the other had a sheath with it too."

"Lady Ashley, I can understand why Lord Razon would display such a blade to you as he did. This is an assassin's blade. It is meant to kill silently and in many wicked ways."

With that, Quick turned deftly and threw not only one, but four others which seemed to come from nowhere, all into the chest of a straw mannequin across the room. Each blade hit such that a V was formed in the heart marked area of the mannequin. Ashley saw a similar intensity in Quick's eyes as she had seen in Razon's. She held herself steady with Laura's arm still about her.

"I am thinking these may be good for you to learn of, Lady Ashley. They are light and easily hidden in a woman's clothing. It will take much practice to learn their ways. I will teach you. But first, let Lady Laura teach you some of a more honorable weapon."

Ashley looked to Laura. She gave a quirky grin and took out a narrow bladed long sword. "It will teach you balance and poise." She handed it to Ashley with the pommel up and the tip just above touching the floor. Ashley was looking at the ball of the pommel eye to ball.

She reached her right hand out to grasp it single-handed as she had first seen Laura holding hers when Ashley first came down the stairs. Ashley attempted to heft it and immediately found herself dropping it. It was obvious her balance was off, and it was a choice to fall herself or allow the sword to do so. Ashley struggled to regain her balance and some semblance of grace. She looked to Laura and Quick to see their reactions to her poor start. Neither was allowing any hint of their disposition to show through carefully held blank looks.

"Perhaps another try?" was all that Laura said.

Ashley resolutely picked up the sword pommel and stood it back up as Laura had it initially, then she grasped the pommel with both hands, allowing the sword tip to slip out at an angle before she even attempted to lift the blade from the floor.

Laura seemed pleased and showed Ashley how to poise the weapon to parry high, low, and side to side. "Correct handling and learning the sword's balance is essential to learning further techniques. Practice these simple motions until they become habit. It will take a few times, but you will learn well, I think," she said.

By the end of her first ten minutes wielding it slowly side to side then up and down, her arms felt weak and quivered to the point that Laura took the sword from her. Ashley knew her arms would ache for the rest of the day. However, living up to his promise, Quick showed her how to hold the balanced assassin's blades and throw them. They were much lighter after working with the sword.

Ashley was startled to see he had replaced the straw mannequin with a stack of hay, three bales high. He must have done it while I was trying to use the sword. I did not even notice, she thought.

Her aim was good the first time; the blade hit the bottom bale near the top. The rest missed, bouncing off the bale clumsily each time after that.

Quick went to retrieve the blades.

After several series of throwing the blades, he brought the blades back again where Ashley and Laura stood. "Lady Laura will teach you the ways of the long sword. You will grow into it," he said. "Only after your training with the sword are you to practice with these." He gave her the three blades. He took a sheath for each from the cabinet. "For you, they must be used in self-defense only, of yourself or a comrade. That is what separates a warrior from an assassin."

Ashley noted his seriousness and agreed. She just finished putting the blades up when Patrick and Ryan came in. Ryan was much broader of build than the lanky Patrick, yet Patrick seemed so natural in his almost swagger of an ambling stride. He went right up to Quick. "If'n ya be done, I be teach'n Ryan here the ways of a sling. Be it okay wif ya and the lady?"

Quick looked to Laura with an amused nod and received her similar approval, though turning quickly to hide a growing humor. Both had noted the gleam in Ryan's face. His blue eyes seemed to shine with excitement. It had been a while since either had seen that degree of enthusiasm in him for anything.

"Aye. If you do not mind, I will watch and learn myself," Quick said. "From the master himself, I am sure." Somehow, Quick felt he was not patronizing the boy when he said it either.

Ashley and Laura moved to a group of chairs against the far wall and sat to watch the display.

Laura was very pleased that the two children were making a smooth adjustment to being at the hall. That was good, she felt, because their recent days had not been so pleasant. "Things are building up to something. I can feel it."

She put back on her smile and took pleasure in the moment's joy.

CHAPTER FOURTEEN

Razon and Blue Skon were making good time. They would be at the mountain vale about midday the day after tomorrow. The horses were fresh and well-rested. The troops were pleased to be out of Skon's Hall. Everything seemed to be going well. "Then why this heaviness of feeling inside me?" Razon asked himself.

Blue Skon noted that Razon seemed distant. He had been disinterested in the antics of the troops during their nooning. Skon watched but said nothing; thinking it was due to concern for Ashley and Patrick. By evening, Razon seemed pale and almost edgy of temperament. Skon knew him well enough to recognize that something was really troubling him. "What is it that eats away at you, my friend? I am sure the children are fine. Laura and Quick will have no difficulty in making both feel at home at Skon's Hall."

"Aye, to be sure," Razon answered. "No. That is not what affects me. There is a growing weight upon my soul that belabors my disposition. I feel that something is not right. Yet, it is impossible to determine what." Razon turned in his saddle to look up at Skon. "I actually feel ill inside."

"We will be at a good night-camp soon. We will get you off that horse and back on the ground. It just may be that you have become so used to walking that you are uncomfortable riding the animal. Mayhap we should get a hay cart for you to lead, aye?" Skon jested in an effort to bring Razon out of his somber mood. It worked. Razon laughed. In short order, he was withdrawn back into himself again.

The patrol was coming out of a hillock of trees when Razon felt a painful burning of his chest. He loosened the upper straps of his breastplate and pulled it a few inches from his body. He pulled at the strings of his shirt neck, and looking down to his chest, he saw a redness developing where his ring rested against his breast. The ring was hot to his touch.

"Skon! Something is terribly wrong. I know it. My signet about my neck is burning me. Look!" Razon showed Skon the redness at the center of his chest just beneath the resting of his ring on its chain.

Skon took the ring in his hand and felt its warmth. "Why would it do this?" he asked.

"I know not for sure. It is the signet of the Family Radiant. It has powers of its own, which I do not know or understand. This much I know: its powers bind the family. My father often said the Family Radiant had a purpose for being in the Light Forest and a charge. This ring, of which my father has the only other mate, seeks to keep us ever mindful of that charge." After a meaningful pause, he added, "I left home before Father told me what the charge was."

They made camp and set the perimeter guards out. Things were quieting down from the bustle and dust of making ready for the night and the next morning's journey. Razon remained ill-tempered and restless. The burning of the ring grew so painful he was forced to take the chain off from around his neck. It was now in a purse he carried just inside his armor's breastplate.

Skon joined him at the fire where he was gazing into the embers remaining after the evening meal's fire burned down. Skon sat down beside him. Rather than speak, he too gazed into the fire. They sat together for a long period with not a word shared. At the next changing of the guard, Skon got up and took a tour of the perimeter to make sure all was well. Coming back, Razon was still sitting at the fire. He was holding the Ring of Radiant at arm's length, just letting it hang by its chain. He was looking at it with the fire's embers lighting the backside of it. Its emerald jewel glistened in a halo of red and orange reflecting the light of the embers. There was a light of its own beginning to emanate from within the emerald set just above the signet portion of the ring. It changed the embers' red glow on Razon's face to a lighter shade giving his face a fuller radiance. "It is awakening of its own, Razon?" Skon asked.

"Aye. I am beginning to see something deep within the heart of it. Come, look within it yourself."

Skon sat down beside him again. It was true. There was a scene opening up to both of them. A forest glade dimly lit in early afternoon. There was a thick backdrop of trees and a strange reptilian creature sitting at its edge holding something close in its arms. As the vision clarified, they could see it was a girl. Skon jerked with recognition of the creature's type. It was familiar enough to him having fought its like twice on differing occasions. The last time had been to save Razon's life. He was drawing his sword as Razon took his arm and pulled him back down.

"We fought the like of these when we saved those few prisoners from the Wizzard in black, remember?" Razon thought a bit more, "What? That was more than twelve years ago? But this one does not seem to be a threat to us, nor to this maid. In fact, he seems to be protecting her," Razon said as he realized what was wrong with her. "Look, she is not sleeping. She is unconscious!"

Razon and Skon looked deep trying to figure out where and why the scene was visible to them. They did not notice the wraith forming within what little smoke curled from the dying coals of the fire. The figure was almost complete when they saw it. This time, Skon did draw his sword Blue's Song. However, he learned long ago to hold until the situation was well ascertained as to its danger. Things were not always as they seemed.

The wraith offered no threat. Both watched as the last tendrils of smoke gathered into her form. It was a girl. Although only in hues of gray and shadow, it was evident she was alive. Her eyes opened and she looked to each of them. Her scrutiny came to rest on Razon. She lifted her hands up in supplication to him. "Help me, I plead. I am dying. I know you to be a friend to those in need. We have nowhere else to turn." Her voice was calm, almost distant.

The figure began to vanish as the smoke tendrils drifted apart, fading into the night. Her hands continued to beckon to them as its apparition dissolved in the night's air; soon, there was nothing left. The scene was still visible in the ring's stone.

The reptilian creature seemed to look more closely at the girl, as if listening to her. Then it made eye contact. There was no lip movement, but the words came clearly, "She has called you. Her pain is beyond what little I can do. Please give heed to her call. If not, she will die soon."

Razon turned to Skon. "I feel like I know her. I have to go but how?"

"Come, my friend, hold onto my arm. I know how to go."

Skon turned to his patrol leader. "If we are not back by dawn, go back to Skon's Hall." He then lifted Blue's Song into the air and they walked into the fire.

They never touched it. Instead, they stepped into the glade's afternoon shadow. In front of them was the creature. The girl, still unmoving, was lying in his arms just as they had seen it. "Greetings," Skon said, as he placed Blue's Song in its scabbard.

Razon knelt beside the girl opposite the creature. He studied her pain-racked face. "She is dying," he said, as if answering a question in his own mind. He was still holding the ring upon its chain. There was a faint green radiance issuing from it that highlighted the girl's face. Both Razon and Skon felt a twinge of disbelief as they thought they recognized her.

"It cannot possibly be her. She is too young!" Razon stated.

"Nor is she of the same temperament," Skon added, "Although the facsimile is unnerving in its degree." He turned to the creature. "Who is this child?"

"She is Cynderet. I am her guardian. Serenten is what I am called. Her wounds are in her mind. They are real."

"Skon! She is the one I saw when I found Ashley and Patrick. I am sure." Razon asked of the creature, "She has green eyes, right?"

"Aye, that is true."

They each turned to look at Cynderet. The ring's radiance had been growing in intensity and now all three saw its illumination upon her. It seemed to cast her face and neck in a shadowless glow. The hues of green grew in intensity. The radiance took an ethereal form and began to encircle her head and neck with wavering tendrils of light. The tendrils split into three prongs as they contacted her face. Two circled around to the back of her head and the third took a course over the top and behind. The tendrils circumvolved her head in continuous courses of light. The beauty of Cynderet's face was enhanced as Serenten had never seen it. All saw great peace within the slowly relaxing features.

Feeling concern for Cynderet as the ring started its radiance and the alien tendrils began to emanate, Serenten looked inside her mind. He witnessed a green radiance enter her mind and surround what remained of her life's glow deep in the chambers of her mind. The radiance began to swell outward, driving back the gnawing emptiness of death eating away her life. Death slithered away from the light as if a myriad of worms undulating back to their slimy burrows of earth. The light seemed to wash the chambers of her mind clean of all death's vestiges. Serenten followed the growing life through halls of Cynderet's mind. Everywhere was the glow of Cynderet's life, filling the void left in death's retreating wake. The walls of her mind took on their natural hues of color and life in the power of the green radiance.

Serenten returned quickly to the chamber where the last glimmers of Cynderet's life glow had death at bay before the ring's power came to her aid. He noted the pearl of life still rested outside the portals of Reht's alcove. Cynderet now sat there, no longer a mere pearl but in full form. She was sitting with legs crossed, her head bowed. She turned her head and smiled to him. Tears swept vision from him as joy's elation flooded him. She was alive, even if only in this special place. He withdrew to watch the transition with confidence all was being healed. Serenten saw the transformation of life open again in other chambers as he withdrew. He was not surprised at the sight of birds singing to the brightening of her thoughts. *She loves the birds so much,* he thought.

She was reaching consciousness as he left. He was looking into her face again, answering a question of Razon as she opened her eyes.

Cynderet felt the peace she was feeling in every part of her soul. She reached out with her mind and senses. She heard voices around her. She recognized Serenten's. He was speaking to others she did not know. She opened her eyes.

"She is waking," Razon said as he continued looking into her face. "Aye. She does have the same green eyes I saw." He smiled at her. "Hello, Child. Be not alarmed. We are friends," he said.

Serenten gave her a little hug of his arms still holding her. "I do not know how, but these men heard our call and came to us."

Cynderet took a moment to find words and actually speak. She looked at Razon. This time, she had no fear of him. She remained weak. She whispered, "It is you. You came."

She turned to Blue Skon. "I remember you were both sitting, staring into a dying fire. I called to you. You heard me."

"Aye, we did," he nodded back.

Cynderet added softly, "Just now, I felt a warm glow within my mind. It seemed to melt away the horrible pain I felt. I still feel so weak of body. I do not think I can move yet, but, Serenten, I feel to be healing."

Razon noted the ring on its chain. It was no longer glowing or even warm. He placed its chain back around his neck and dropped the ring within his jersey. Thoughts connected for him; he looked back at Cynderet. "It would seem there are powers many that join us together. We have met before, have we not?"

"Yes. I saw you help a farmer and his children when attacked by brigands. After, you came towards me—you were so deadly—I am afraid I panicked and fled. I am sorry."

"Be not apologizing for turning from this scoundrel," Skon offered. "I have seen even famed warriors turn from nothing but his smile and run."

Although Cynderet was too weak to laugh, she did manage a smile with the laughter of the others. It helped break the distance between each of them.

"We need to get this child someplace where she can rest," Razon said.

Serenten shook his head. "It will be impossible here. There will be many looking for us, if not already doing so. She is not safe here."

"Skon's Hall," Skon said. "It would appear the ring's power has aided her greatly, but Laura can do much to help," Skon pointed out. Turning to Serenten, "And you come also," he added, "I feel no need to fear you, though I must say, it is different for me to be speaking to you instead of communicating in a more bodily language."

"Aye, I understand. I do not understand all things, but I know we all care for this child well."

Razon and Cynderet spoke almost at the same time. "They are coming." They looked at each other for a moment in wonder.

All lay low in the shade of the trees. They looked to the forest to see if there was movement close by. It seemed to be quiet. Serenten sent his search into the trees to see if he noted any Hert close by. Whatever Razon and Cynderet heard, he could find no Hert in the vicinity. He rolled to his side and spoke to Skon. "You need to get her out of here. If she is found, they will finish what was started."

"Aye." Skon reached out to Razon. "Razon, give me your sword. Take Blue's Song and allow your mind to see our campfire. Take the girl's hand and when you see the campfire clearly, step into the scene in your mind. You will be there. Come back for Serenten and me."

Refusing Skon's sword, Razon whispered hoarsely, "No! You must be the one to do it. Only you must take her directly to Skon's Hall. Nothing then can go wrong. I will stay with our new friend here."

"So be it," Skon admitted. "Hold the sword while I lift the child. I will be back soon. Try not to move from here, or I may not be able to find you again." With that, Skon took Cynderet's arm and helped her stand up. Lifting her in his arms, he received his sword back from Razon. He took a step into the glade and they both were gone.

Razon and Serenten watched them disappear. They shared a sense of relief knowing she would be safe with Lord Blue Skon. They looked back into the forest watching for whatever was coming. Suddenly, there was a sound from behind them.

They turned in unison.

Ermentrude and two other Eldresses stood there. It was too late to try anything. They did anyway.

*****

Berenice watched as Razon and Blue Skon disappeared into the fire. She had been stalking the patrol since dusk. Her winged mount had no trouble following the scent of the horses. It made excellent time catching up to the patrol.

Now Razon had vanished. Berenice decided to wait and see what developed. It had not been necessary to kill anyone so there would be no alarm. She and her mount metamorphosed into rock-like material similar to that surrounding the camp.

When dawn started to threaten the night's darkness, she felt it was time to move. Razon had not come back nor had Blue Skon. Berenice had overheard Skon's orders. "They will head back to the Hall. It is time for us to leave," she said to her mount. It nodded in accord. They did not want to be found out in the open by the patrol on its return march. It was time to report back to Luanta.

CHAPTER FIFTEEN

Luanta felt tired after her arrival at Everard's hideout. Glad of the moment alone and away from the company of Strike, she smiled remembering the horses running away in fear. "He reeks so badly, even the dimwitted animals of this earth cannot stand his smell." She made a mental note. This information may prove useful later.

She sat on the bed and reached into a deep pocket of the leather traveling pack she brought with her and currently sat beside her. She pulled out the black bag, opened it, and looked inside. She saw nothing. It looked like an empty bag. She put her hand into it, and by feel, she found and drew out the box in its own pouch. The medallion holding the ties was familiar to her.

It was the same she had seen on a dagger she had gifted to a Wizzard many years ago as a gift for his several occasions of aid in trying to locate Lord Razon of Radiant. The last time she was with the Wizzard ended in a bazaar twist. They were questioning captured prisoners about the lord's whereabouts; the prisoners knew nothing. She and the Wizzard had just decided to kill them all when they were interrupted, ironically, by the very one they sought: Lord Razon. And his menace of a comrade Lord Blue Skon had shown up at the very dungeon they were using to question the prisoners. She was forced to leave quickly. The Wizzard was killed shortly after her departure, but she had found Razon later without him: "Only to lose Razon again because of that bastard, Blue Skon. I will laugh in glee as he dies, and his precious hall crumbles to dust!"

She untied the bag. Carefully, she placed the closed box on the bed. She knew better than to open it. She felt an incredible sense of power course through her, knowing that the box would allow her to destroy her nemesis. She would not fail this time. She would acquire the signet ring of the House of Radiant, destroy Blue Skon, and corrupt his memory to one of failure and death; and pay her debt to the Wherants. She would be rewarded greatly she knew, but more importantly, she would never fear a human again!

Luanta put the box back in its carrier and closed the black bag. She lay down to sleep with dreams of humans dying in battle. A particular male would die most horribly, she promised herself.

Luanta woke up ready. She did not like having to wait so close to the end of her suffering. I will go check on my small army, she decided. There is still much to do here to get ready for the attack of Skon's Hall. She left her room to go find Everard.

She saw Strike still sitting like a bundle of rags in the windowless corner. She decided to leave him there and wasted no further time leaving the cottage. She was walking with a purpose for the first time in months, no, in years.

Luanta walked into the open air outside. The sun was shining brightly above her, putting the whole vale in light. At first it hurt her eyes, but they quickly adjusted. It was a minor price to pay for the satisfaction to come. She saw that the corral had been easily repaired and the horses were quietly resting in the afternoon warmth. Everard was speaking with a couple of his lieutenants as Luanta approached.

"Aye, and here be the lady to lead us to riches like we have never seen." Everard pointed to Luanta and all eyes turned her way. The men could not help but experience a melting feeling in the pit of their stomachs. Luanta sensed they would do anything for her. It was a delicious feeling to know she had such control over them and yet could purposely deny herself the pleasure of feeding on any of them. That could wait until later. She smiled. "Everard, what a handsome display of manhood in your officers," she toyed, setting the tone of her waiting period.

*****

Lady Laura found the day's proceedings enjoyable. It seemed each of the children, including Ryan, had found growth and purpose. Now all were in bed. She nervously paced her room, still waiting some word of her husband and Lord Razon. Skon was nowhere to be found. Normally, she could follow his activities with her skrying. The magic they shared allowed them to communicate easily when close together and sense feelings when further apart. Right now, there was nothing—no feelings at all. Skon was somehow sealed off from her.

She skried the camp and its night arrangement. All appeared quiet—quiet except for Razon and Skon both being absent. Growing impatient, she waited with feelings things were happening beyond any of their control. There had been bandit raids before. There had been other reports of a growing band of brigands in the mountain areas. This did not feel like a loose band of thieves. "I can feel a much greater menace growing. Like none I have felt for years.

There is evil growing."

Laura drew her night robe about her shapely form and went to stand before an inner wall of her room. Waiting was not the problem; it was the not knowing that ate at her. A wave of her hand and a mark glowed in the dark as a hidden portal silently opened to admit her. With the familiarity of a welcoming friend, she took the steep steps down to find a vent for her frustration. A pale green phosphorescent glow preceded her into the deeper reaches of Skon's Hall: her places.

Within the deep bowels of the underground chambers beneath the Hall, Laura entered her work chambers. She went immediately through the main room and into a much smaller room in which four covered frames stood, each in a corner. She went to the first one and carefully pulled back the cloth covering. The emptiness of the glass within the freestanding frame was void of any reflection. Not even the phosphorescent light about Laura could be seen in it. Laura waved her hand in front of it. Slowly, a swirling began to build within. The emptiness converged upon itself and began to offer its perspective. Not a reflection of Laura or the small chamber but of a cave.

The cave was dark and obscure. As it clarified, Laura's green light shown off its walls. There were boxes and casks stacked in order against the far wall. Closer to a passage into the cave's darkness, there was a table and several simple wooden chairs. There were no signs of anyone having been there since Skon had last visited it.

Laura covered the first glass again and went to the second. It opened up to a grove of trees at the edge of Skon's lands overlooking the main road and bridge leading to the king's citadel. She shuddered, remembering the major battle fought there when they had first cleared the region of the forces of evil. Tonight, all was quiet and calm. Laura did not go to the other two mirrors—if Skon were in their locations, she would know already.

Something was wrong. She could not shake the feeling, yet as she listened to her heart, she knew Blue Skon was well. Why could she not find him? She ensured all was covered again and left the small room.

She entered the main chamber and took a seat among her stacks of books. She opened one of her tomes to read then stopped. In her mind just behind her eyes, she saw Blue Skon return home. He took a step into their personal chambers from thin air. He carried something in his arms, forcing him to hold his sword loosely in front of him. She watched him look quickly about the room for her. Seeing her absence, he took his burden through a door into an adjoining room.

Laura ascended the steep stairs quickly. As she climbed, her mind's eye followed Skon laying his burden, a young girl, gently upon the bed in the room.

"She needs your help, Laura. Come quickly," he said as if Laura were in their own room.

Laura was there as he placed a blanket about the girl.

"I have brought another ward to Skon's Hall, milady," Skon smiled. He watched her with a caring concern, knowing she astutely took everything in. "She called to Razon and me from some distant place. Razon remains there, he…and another. I must bring them back as well."

"Who is she, Skon?" Laura asked, as she took control of her care.

"I am not sure. She called to us through our fire." Skon could not hold back the rather helpless look his wife knew so well to play on his face when he felt a bit embarrassed by circumstances, he either could not explain or could not help. "She was near death," Skon continued. "Razon and I went to her aid. This young lady has suffered wounds of the mind. She experienced a most marvelous healing by Razon's family ring. She said she was healing inside. There is much to this story I do not know, and a lot more I do not understand. It will have to wait. This I do know: There are strange things going on and I must get back to Razon. I will return soon."

Skon took a step from the bed and formally saluted his bride. A thought passed between them as Skon turned and walked through the emptiness of the room and disappeared.

Laura reflected on the meaning of that thought. Together, they had faced and forged so much. They felt responsible for the people of the hall and the village below, for all the lands Lord Blue Skon had jurisdiction over. There were many times, as now, when they had to be apart. The one solidifying factor, above it all, was their union. Everything else could be lost. Their faith and love in each other would endure.

Laura looked to the young girl in the bed beside her. The girl was in a restless sleep. Laura pulled the bed blankets about her shoulders.

Cynderet began to moan with an agitated, faltering voice. It sounded similar to Laura's son, Ryan, when he was having nightmares. Pulled by a mother's compassion for all children, Laura sat on the edge of the bed and spoke soothing words as she stroked Cynderet's hair with her fingers. Carefully, she listened to the child's being: listening with her heart as her brother Wolfie had taught her years ago while she studied the healing arts. She perceived the anguish and pain Cynderet held deep inside. She could see the Ring of Radiant had healed the wounds of mental conflict; Cynderet's mind was well-repaired.

The wounds of heart were not. This girl felt alone and rejected. It tore at Laura's own heart.

It had been many years ago now, but the wounds of a broken heart Laura knew well. Her parents were slain before her very eyes while she hid helplessly locked in a chamber of protection. That loss left her alone in a burned shell of their home. The memory remained vivid and stark to this day. If Wolfie had not come to her from his own travels, she would have been thrust out into a harsh land with no one to turn to. Wolfie took her in, cared for her, and helped heal the loss of parents. She and her elder brother, so much older than she, became close family. Then one day, a meek young warrior showed up at her door. He said he was called Blue Skon. He held a note from Wolfie, asking him to escort Laura to Wisshard: The City of Learning. The family had grown after that—first: her marriage to the soon-to-become Lord Blue Skon and, two years later, Ryan.

Laura listened to Cynderet's heart again. "Child, you may feel welcome here. Have peace," she said as she began the healing ways she had learned so well.

Laura knew they would bind her wounds. She knew because within her own soul, she knew she would never allow this precious child to face the harsh world alone.

*****

Skon arrived back at the forest glade. It was quiet and empty. There were no signs of the other two or any other life in the immediate area. He went to the rise that offered Serenten and Cynderet protection from being found. There were signs of activity here. Several sets of new footprints marred the ground. The markings were unusual in shape and form to Serenten's bare feet and Razon's boots, both prints clearly evident. So, where were they? Skon carefully avoided making any decisions until further search was completed. He stepped five paces from where he and Cynderet departed. Then he made a careful circle scrutinizing the ground closely. The footprints of all were evident. Taking another five paces out and circling, he found the tracks disappeared. Only Serenten's showed the path from the forest to the glade. None leaving, and no tracks of the new arrivals coming either, that meant only one thing to Skon: arrival by flight.

"Any other option requires specific knowledge of specific details to arrive safely or serious consequences could be incurred," he muttered to himself. He did not think these new arrivals had such knowledge because the newest tracks appeared almost side-by-side, not single file as the other options necessitated. "It has to be by air," he mused.

To make sure, he took another five paces and circled. This time, it brought him to the edge of the trees at one point. He was just circumventing a large tree when he noted a glint of light to his side just beyond the tree's massive trunk. He walked towards it and found Razon's sword protruding from the soil like a small javelin. Skon did not touch it. Instead, he looked for further signs of why and how it was there. There was no damage to the tree or to any of the plant life on either side of the tree. The sword had to have come from directly in front of the tree. Making a straight line to where Skon started his concentric circling, he found only his own track. *The sword was not lost in conflict, or it would not have come in as a straight shot like this. Razon had to have deliberately speared it there. It is a message: he is still alive or at least was alive and thinking when he left.* Scratching his beard, Skon realized it was a hollow relief; he had no idea where Razon was now.

Skon searched longer with nothing else found. Muttering to himself, he said, "How they left or why is not clear. Once again, it has to have been by air. Even the newer tracks just disappear. To confirm his thoughts, he walked the path in the forest a way in either direction. Only Serenten's prints of arrival were found. He was carrying Cynderet at the time and deeper impressions were clear."I do not know this region. I know not friend from foe or where to go. Perhaps the girl can shed some understanding on what happened to them," he reasoned with himself. If not, he would come back with Quick and do some serious looking along the path. "Razon will be found!"

*****

Laura knew Blue Skon was back. He was just putting his sword back into its scabbard as she rolled over in bed to greet him.

Despite his frustration at not finding Razon, he could not help but to acknowledge how special this lady was to him. He sat upon the bed beside her. He did not answer her questioning look at first. Instead, he coaxed her into his arms and drew the covers up to shelter her from the early morning coolness. Brushing his face in her shoulder, he breathed in the smell of her. This was his favorite spot;. The comfort of this woman and her inner strength set him at ease.

"I cannot find them, milady. Razon and the creature have just disappeared. There were no tracks beyond the small area that included my steps. I thought I would ask and see what the girl could tell me." He gently pulled a finger through a night's curl, stroking her hair. "It is a strange land there, to be sure."

Laura lifted herself to see Skon's face more clearly. Smuggling into the warmth of him, she said, "I feel there is much more to all this than just the rescuing of a child." Remembering Ashley and Patrick, she added, "Several children, in fact. Too many things are happening for each to be an isolated occurrence. Think of the children here, now three, all about the same age. The brigands in the mountains are highly organized, and Razon is well involved in each." Laura pondered, "What is really happening?"

"It goes deeper yet, milady," Skon realized. "It was Razon's ring which showed us the child and her creature guardian, Serenten. Razon and the child had met before when Ashley and Patrick were attacked by the brigands. You are right. They are all connected somehow. For whatever reason, Razon is being singled out." Skon suddenly realized something, "I have to find him. He has disappeared and all speaks of nothing good for it. We must speak with Cynderet."

Laura put on her robe and the two walked quietly into Cynderet's room.

CHAPTER SIXTEEN

Blue Skon and Laura entered Cynderet's room to find her sitting up in bed waiting for them. Laura noted she was still pale and weak from her ordeal. Laura remembered the feelings of despair and rejection she had found deep within this child. Laura looked again at Cynderet with her wide, anxious green eyes and cascading copper hair currently sleep-crumpled. She was a beautiful girl. Her youthful innocence still rang clear. "You are not alone nor are you without hope if I can help it," Laura said to herself.

Cynderet gazed up at her and smiled. There was trust there and something else. It would be a while before Laura could identify it, but it filled her heart warmly.

Blue Skon's greeting broke the thought, "Good morning. How do you fair today?"

Laura went up to Cynderet and placed a side blanket about her shoulders.

Looking away from Laura to Skon, Cynderet answered, "I feel shaken from my ordeal and uncertain of the future. Yet, I had a restful night." Cynderet paused and looked back to Laura. "I have not actually met you, though I know you to have cared for me most kindly. I feel like we have known each other for a long time."

"Aye, Cynderet. I spent much time with you while you slept. To your mind, I spoke peace and hope. It is a part of the healing art I learned from my brother," Laura responded. "You are safe here in Skon's Hall. When you are able, we will go visit with the others who dwell here."

"This is Skon's Hall?" Cynderet's voice cracked as recognition of the name brought Harriant's thoughts again, "Your mother has sought an alliance with the Wherants to destroy a paltry human and his hall."

"Aye, you are a guest in our home," Skon said, not realizing the cause of her alarm. He continued, "Do not be fearful. There is none to hurt you here."

"You are Lord Blue Skon. I remember now. I did not realize of whom you were when I called to you. How I was led to Lord Razon again, I do not know. However, his powers allowed my healing in the forest glade. Now your lady continues to see to my care." Cynderet experienced a mixing of Emotions:. Hope and relief to be alive were at odds with the washing of guilt and fear as she recalled these caring people were soon to be attacked by her own mother. She was so confused she closed her eyes and shook her head to clear her thoughts.

Laura watched the conflict of emotions in Cynderet's eyes. Laura placed her palm upon the girl's head and spoke words Cynderet had never heard before. She did not jerk from nor fight off the words. Instead, she felt her scattered thoughts fall into order in her mind. Gentle tears began to well and course down her cheeks. She nestled into Laura's comforting arms; a warmth was shared between them. There was no effort to move with either one as emotions were battled out.

These people are not enemies. I am among friends. They are caring people. Why would my mother want to do them any harm? Cynderet pondered.

She felt herself walking the corridors of her mind. Reht was there. He was walking beside her. "Reht, where have you been? I thought you had left me."

Reht took a moment to study her. "I was always with you. You were badly hurt." He started to say something more, but stopped. Instead, he said, "Lord Razon and Lord Blue Skon responded to your call for help."

"How? Why am I here?" Cynderet felt the circle of questions starting again. "Everything is so confused and jumbled. Yet, here I am within the home of my mother's enemies. I remember now so clearly the name she would curse when angered with me. And here, I find peace and solace as never before. Why?"

Reht continued to face her. He waved his outside arm in a huge arch. Within its passing, Cynderet found herself and Reht standing on the height of a large hillock, ending in a cliff overlooking a vast forest. There was a sole oak with its limbs gracefully shading a spring of clear bubbling water. They went to it and sat down looking out over the forest. Reht took his time before answering her question, allowing them both to take in the vista.

Cynderet felt a great comfort fill her heart. "I feel so at peace here. Where are we?" she asked.

"This is a place of my Dream Sight. I will explain its history to you some day." Reht took Cynderet's hand gently in his massive claws. "For now, I will try and help with your first question. You have found and met a part of your purpose. These are Lord Razon's friends. They are your friends. You must meet this trial and do so equal to your own sense of right. All things here are tied together. There appears to be much contradiction in your life. There is a reason, a purpose to it all. You will see the way in time." Reading her question, he added, "No. I do not have all the answers. I only have what my Dream Sight can show. You have a purpose. It is not for me to tell you or for me to even know it. That is why you are here. For now, look within yourself for truth and direction. It is here." Reht wiped a remaining tear from her cheek, smiled at her, and turned, walking away.

Cynderet watched as Reht walked down the face of the hillock fading into the forest. She stared in the direction for a long time, thinking about his strange answer. Inside, she knew he was right. She closed her eyes and looked for the truth he spoke of.

She thought about home. She had always felt more at ease when alone or with Reht. They had often gone walking or sat in the shade of the tree at her window talking. She felt uncomfortable around the others her age. Harriant had been so spiteful and bitter towards her. The others had been more tolerant, but that was all. Cynderet had read their thoughts. *It was because Luanta was a Council Eldress, they had been careful around her. They may have been able to change body form. They never could change the way they were,* she thought. *I was never a part of them.* Cynderet stood up. "Then, who am I?" she called to the forest having swallowed up Reht. She looked for a long time waiting for a response. There was none.

Turning again to look from the cliff into the distance, she could see the bounds of the forest. The mountains there were tall and jagged. Heavy, dark gray clouds hung in the air around them. She felt the weight of them, like sorrow on a sunny, bright day.

She turned away. In her mind, she could see the inviting arms of Laura reaching to her. She went to them. Cynderet's eyes opened to find Laura still sitting beside her with arms around her. The hand upon her head had dropped to her waist. Cynderet knew. She knew that Lady Laura had left when Reht had come to her in her mind and then returned when he had gone again. Cynderet realized Laura knew she was telepathic and had given her privacy. Cynderet went to Laura's mind. The door was open to her question.

"No, Child. I am not telepathic in the same way as you. I only have a few spells of magic to allow me some measure of seeing."

"Do you know why I am here?"

"No. I do not know. I only know that there are forces at play that go beyond the normal. I do know that you are caught in the middle of these forces." After a pause, she added, "As is Lord Razon. The why and what of it, I do not know. Will you enlighten us?"

"I do not know that I can. So much remains unclear to me as well. I will tell you what little I do know," she said aloud.

Lady Laura smiled. Lord Skon had taken a waiting stance at the foot of the bed. His eyes did not show any knowledge of what had happened, only the patient confidence that soon some order would be brought to the moment.

"Lord Blue Skon," Cynderet started, sitting up with a sense of urgency, "Skon's Hall and all who dwell here are in horrible danger. You have an enemy," Cynderet could not bring herself to admit it was her mother, "who has formed an alliance with demons to destroy you."

Cynderet studied each face. The announcement took the lady and lord by surprise. Laura stood up immediately and looked to Skon. Cynderet read that Laura had no doubt as to the truth of her message. The two shared a long look. Laura was the first to recover.

"That is why I feel like there is more to all this than simple banditry."

Cynderet realized Lord Razon was not there. "Where is Lord Razon? I must warn him also. In fact, where is Serenten?" she asked, somehow knowing the answer.

It was Skon's turn to bow under the weight of guilt. "I do not know. I went back to get them after bringing you here. They were gone. No tracks, no signs, they had just vanished. I came to ask you what you might know."

Cynderet shuddered involuntarily. A crushing fear settled in her heart. "They are prisoners, I just know it!" she cried. "Because of me!" Her composure collapsed. "It is all because of me," she repeated.

"What is because of you, Child?" Skon asked with an obvious attempt to hold back his own agitation.

Laura responded for her with another question as greater insight came to her. "Cynderet?" Laura asked. "Those you have warned us of, are they the same as those who tried to kill you?"

"No!" Cynderet responded too quickly. "That is, I could not think so." She held her breath as she considered the question from different angles. Her body began to shake uncontrollably, comprehension sinking in. Her mother may not have tried to kill her outright, but she never had done anything to prevent the Table from doing so. And, she remembered, in the forest, her mother's affection had suddenly turned to loathing because Cynderet would not, could not, become an Energy Feeder. She collapsed into sobs as she discerned the Table and her mother were equally opposed to her surviving. She whispered in staccato, "It must be because of me."

Again, holding her, Laura said soothingly, "No, Child. You are caught in a maze of the doings of others. In all this, you…" seeing the situation more clearly, she continued, "and others are innocent. You must not carry this burden. It belongs to those forcing you into this position.”

Skon ceased his renewed pacing with an idea, “How did you find Razon and me the other night? You came to us, remember?”

“Yes,” she sobbed, “twice I have found Lord Razon. I do not know how.” After struggling for breath, she added, “Each time I was asleep or unconscious. I was in a place deep within myself. The visits were as dreams.”

“Can you get there while awake?” Skon asked.

Managing some control of her emotions, Cynderet answered, “I have never tried before.”

“Go ahead and try now,” Laura urged. “I think I know what my husband wants. I will join you if it helps. We will go together.”

“Yes. I would like that, Lady Laura.”

Cynderet took Laura’s hand, glad to have her in this attempt. Cynderet looked into Laura’s hazel eyes and entered her own mind, opening it to Laura, letting her see and share in what Cynderet did. They went straight to the foyer of portals becoming so familiar to her now. They entered the foyer before the great doors, securing her dreams of Razon. The portal of the misty trees was well-defined by repeated visits. There was a new door beside it with dying embers of a fire giving up its last wisps of smoke. “This is the one, I am sure of it,” Cynderet said with confidence. “It is new and looks exactly like when I called to the lords.”

She reached the latch and opened it. The door gave them entrance and they went in together. It was early morning at the camp sight. A small trail of dust was lifting as Skon’s soldiers were just leaving the clearing heading into the trees on their return to Skon’s Hall.

“This is amazing,” Laura whispered, unsure if she should hail the soldiers or just let them go. She decided on the latter. If there was any trouble, she felt confident she could get back to Blue Skon easily. She reached down with her hand to the covered fire-bed. The soldiers had finished with it and covered it with dirt. “It is still warm.” She looked up to see what Cynderet was doing. She was watching the soldiers leave completely unaware of Laura’s examination of the fire. “Cynderet, I have a strong feeling that if we followed Lord Skon’s men, we would soon be back at Skon’s Hall. I have been through various kinds of dreams before. This is not one of them. This is no dream, my young friend. This is real.”

Cynderet just stared while contemplating exactly what it was Laura said. If she should feel surprise, it was not happening. “I think I already knew the fight at the farmer’s cart was real. I was not sure and did not know how to test such an idea. But it was very different from a dream."

Cynderet took a casual look around the surrounding perimeter. All was exquisite in its finest detail. "I should not be able to do this. I should not be able to travel like this," Cynderet mused aloud. "This ability to travel from one place to another by the power of the mind, this, this is Energy Webbing. I have not received the Last Rights—I am not even an apprentice anymore."

"An apprentice of what, Cynderet?" Laura asked.

Cynderet gave an embarrassed smirk. She had forgotten Lady Laura was even there in her musing. She was not sure how to answer, "I do not know how to answer your question, or even if I should." Cynderet could not look Lady Laura in the face. She hung her head down with guilt, remembering her mother would soon try to destroy these people.

Her mother! The only parent she knew. The only life she knew. As much as I can never be as her, I am still one of her kind. Cynderet turned back to Laura and finished, "You would not like me if I were to tell you who I really am."

Daunted not in the least, Laura put an arm around the slender form. "Oh, I believe there are many things I would not like going on about us, but I am certain you are not one of them, nor even the cause or an enemy to us." Laura gave Cynderet a motherly squeeze and then let go. "Can you take us home?"

"All I have to do is go back through the portal. I think."

"Well, we will learn nothing more here. Take us home, please."

Looking back into her mind, Cynderet took Lady Laura's hand. They walked easily back through the portal and into its foyer.

Cynderet opened her eyes. They were back in the room they had left. Lord Skon looked expectantly from one to the other. "You both disappeared. Something must have happened," he said a bit edgy.

Lady Laura saved Cynderet from having to explain what she did not understand. "Cynderet has discovered that she can go to a few special places simply by walking through doors in her mind. However, we still do not know how she located Lord Razon to begin with. There remain a few details still not understood."

Blue Skon struggled to hide his frustration. He could not help thinking time was running out—especially after Cynderet's warning of the demons' pending assault on the hall.

Laura read his concern, "We need to let Cynderet rest a bit longer while we all consider what we know and what we must do next."

"Aye, milady." He had understood the message. Turning to Cynderet, he said, "It has been a rough go for you these past several hours. Your healing is well along, but rest is needed for you now." After a moment, he added, "Fear not, my young Cynderet. We will find Lord Razon and your friend. Let me stir the stew pot a bit in my mind while you sleep." Lord Skon gave her a warm smile and left the room.

Lady Laura helped her lay down and tucked her in with the covers. She sat beside her a moment and, looking into the child's eyes, said a simple command: "Sleep."

Cynderet closed her eyes. She did not see or feel Lady Laura get up. She knew only what sleep offered her.

Laura joined Skon in their room. Skon was already pacing his rhythmic pattern back-and-forth. It was normal for him when he could not see the answer to a problem. Laura noted the wearing of the throw rug about midway between the window and door that defined his course. "You must remain patient, my husband. She has abilities foreign, it is true, though she remains a child," Laura said quietly.

"Aye, to be sure," Skon answered as he passed her to the door. "The power to teleport is a magical thing. I do not understand how magic works." Skon was adjacent to her on his return path. "That is your domain." Skon reached the window and reversed in a military two-step. "I do know she uses not spells. Her power is a part of her."

"I agree. Perhaps…" here, she hesitated, not sure she wanted to finish the thought. It was a delicate issue between them, "perhaps we should discuss this with Missive?

She knew how uncomfortable Skon felt about magic theory and use. She also knew how he felt about the brownie. Skon was a warrior. He was comfortable only with magical items of combat. He led men well. He was even becoming a good statesman for the region with the king. He did not do well with creatures of pure magic. Missive was not only such a creature; he was also Laura's familiar. When it came to magic, he knew more about Laura than Blue Skon did. Laura felt sure that was the real rub. Laura expected him to hold off on the idea. She was surprised at his quick acceptance.

"Aye. We should meet with the little Fire Fly," Skon answered. "I think there is magic everywhere in these matters. Cynderet may be a child, but her home is not of this earth." Skon grew silent again. His pace resumed from the door. "Razon is still there. I must get him home!" Skon stopped and looked to his wife with a facial front of shear determination. Inside him, Laura knew he worried for his friend.

"Let us go to my chambers. Missive will help us understand, I am sure." Laura led the way back down into the bowels of Skon's Hall.

Once in the main chamber, Skon sat in his familiar stuffed chair. Often, he would sit there when Laura was about her studies. He would sit quietly watching her or doing studies of his own. Laura's brother Wolfie had taught him how to read. He had come to enjoy it. It gave him broader understanding and ideas to help with running of the lands and their populace.

This time, he remained sitting upright and encouraged Laura to summon her familiar. She nodded her compliance with a moment's questioning glance to make sure he was all right with this. Skon returned the nod.

Skon saw no change or action of Laura. Suddenly, on the arm of his chair, a little, four-inch man creature sat scrutinizing Skon's face. Skon jerked in surprise, having expected him to take his normal perch on Laura's shoulder.

"It is intriguing you should be so ready to discuss this child with me, Lord Blue Skon, Master of Skon's Hall and all its fief. I am flattered you sought my wisdom so early." In a quick fluid movement, he leapt upon Skon's shoulder and whispered in his ear, "There is magic here. Are you able to handle what you do not understand?" Missive teased.

"Aye, Little Wonder," Skon answered with a hint of temper. "If it be that you get off my shoulder. To speak I came, not to get camaraderie!" Skon's hand instantly shot up to sweep Missive from his shoulder. Before he even got his hand in motion, a tiny, brilliant light burst from where Missive had been into the air and, in a lazy, wandering manner, flew to Laura's shoulder.

"'Fire Fly', 'Little Wonder'? Such sweet nothings to be called by," Missive teased, undaunted by Skon's frown. "Yet, you seek to dust me from my perch. I could have been hurt!" In mock weeping, Missive turned to Laura. "Hold me, my sweet, lest my heart be broken beyond all repair."

"You are fine where you are," Laura replied, not allowing herself to be drawn into the male conflict of personalities. "My husband Lord Blue Skon and I need answers in order to save Lord Razon of Radiant." Laura brought seriousness to the moment with her tone and by using formal titles of people Missive knew only too well.

"So be it, milady!" Missive mimicked. "I already know your thoughts. Let the master of our small fiefdom share his with me."

Laura suspected a touch of mockery in the studious posture Missive took as he sat down on her shoulder and crossed a leg over his knee. He looked to Blue Skon patiently waiting, hand supporting cheek and head.

Blue Skon started to say something, then held his tongue. With the restraint of the statesman he was becoming, he started again. He explained how he and Razon had come to find Cynderet. He talked of Serenten and the forest of dim-light. He left nothing out knowing that although Missive was a pesky magical tease, he was, beyond anything else, devoted to Laura and, therefore, to him as her husband—or at least he hoped so.

"Cynderet is of the Shadow Plane," Missive answered with perfect assuredness. In a majestic pose of indifference, he looked at his fingernails as he answered, "I do not know of her personality, nor do I know why she came to you and Lord Razon," Missive paused dramatically. "I do know that nothing good comes to Earth from the Shadow Plane. Their magic is strong," after another pause for effect, he continued, "and full of lies. The Energy Feeders dwell there. You have encountered them before." With a look to both Skon and Laura, he added, "And their reptilian slaves. Those who rule in the Shadow Plane are in league with the Wherants, demons of the dark."

Skon considered what Missive said. He remained silent, looking to the floor. Laura held her questions waiting to see what Skon would say or do next.

"Cynderet is different," he said confidently, looking up at Missive. "She has powers unique to her, it is true. Her creature is of the same look as those I have fought and slain. But, she is not an Energy Feeder. I put my oath upon it!" Skon said with finality.

Laura nodded her agreement, feeling pride in her husband. She knew how difficult it was for him to have any kind of serious discussion with Missive.

"You are correct, Lord Skon," Missive agreed. "She is too young. And she is not of the same temperament. That much is certain."

"Then why the creature Serenten? Who is he, if not one of the creatures Skon has fought before?" Laura asked.

"Neither you nor I have met him. It is impossible to know his character without meeting him personally," Missive reminded her. "Just the same though, there is the rare one of differing mind. It is possible he is not as those we have encountered before."

Missive took in a deep breath as he remembered something. "You know, the reptilian creatures are not native to the Shadow Plane. They are traded as slaves by the Wherants. It is possible her creature is loyal to her and not to her Society."

Skon brought them back to Razon. "How does this allow us to help Razon?"

"She travels through doors in her mind. That is what Lady Laura saw when she and this child arrived at the camp of your men this morning."

"They did what?" Skon asked, totally confused. He looked to Missive and then to his wife.

"Oh, you missed that part, Lord Skon. I forgot," Missive baited.

"That was the door Cynderet chose to show me when explaining how she found Razon," Laura hurried. "Your troops are safely on their return by the way," Laura smiled at him. Laura gave Skon the full account by the magic they shared.

"How quaint," Missive said as it ended. "I heard every bit."

Skon and Laura both turned to Missive with looks of "so" and looked to Missive to continue.

Not to be patronized, Missive milked the moment for all he could. It was not every day he had Lord Blue Skon's attention. He reversed his crossed legs, then looking at each slowly, he continued, "Energy Feeders teleport to the Human Plane easily. This child can teleport also. She just has to learn how it is done." Missive pretended to pick his teeth, waiting for a reaction to his wisdom.

"You mean other than by doors?" Laura asked.

"Yes. She did not start out with doors. That was simply her way of 'cataloguing' if you will," Missive answered.

"She thinks she does it in dreams. I heard her say so," Skon interjected.

"Only to find Lord Razon," Missive corrected. "For some reason, she has actually found him just by needing him." Missive paused a moment, "She must seek him specifically, I think. It is magic that allows this. Each type of magic is somewhat different. But all creatures, which are capable of teleporting in any way, must first visualize where they are going. Otherwise, they may end up stuck in a wall, buried in the earth, or falling from the sky. I saw a griffin one time stuck in a tree by his hind leg. He was not happy!"

"It is the same with Blue's Song, my sword," Skon enjoined. "I must first see where I am to go, then command for it to happen." Skon felt good coming to understand what Missive was saying.

Missive gave him a quick, uncharacteristic smile while he flicked the air just above his ear indicating enlightenment.

"We need to ask Cynderet to search for Lord Razon in her mind," Laura said. "Then when she has located him, ask her if she can go there. If she was able to take me to your camp, she can take us to Razon."

"Or, at least, allow me to see where he is so Blue's Song can take me," Skon added.

"Why not use a mirror?" Missive asked, resuming his superior demeanor.

"They are easily adjusted if a clear vision is gained."

"It would mean a possible back-trail an enemy could use into Skon's Hall," Skon said. "Should something go wrong before the mirror passage was closed," Skon reminded all.

"True, my husband," Laura joined. "However, it would allow us to take Quick and bring everyone back at once. Missive could remain at the mirror, to close it, should someone follow us."

Skon looked at Missive, trying to decide if that was a good idea or not.

"Fear not! Oh, Mighty Lord Blue Skon of the Golden Pegasus," Missive said as he took a noble stance on Laura's shoulder. "You will have the light of my life with you on the other side," Missive continued. "How could I possibly let you down?" Then as an afterthought, he added, "Do not yourself be the last to come back, you are thinking, or I may shut it on you." Missive gave a quick chuckle, and then cooed, "Knowest thou not my undying love of thee?" Missive placed folded hands to his cheek.

Laura laughed. "Fear not, fine husband, once apart, rest I never will know 'til joined we are again," she said, carrying the poetics further.

"Aye, it would be good to have Quick by my side. The two of you would be too lovesick to protect my back, I think," Skon countered. "Let us be talking with the child when she awakes. For now, I will be for my bed."

CHAPTER SEVENTEEN

Berenice flew into the hideout just as dawn was opening to the morning's sun. She did not bother to wake the snoring lookout. *Luanta can take care of him later, she thought. Now she had to make her report.*

She dismounted and entered the cottage. Spike remained seated in the corner—to all the world still asleep. Berenice went directly to Luanta's door and knocked. Luanta immediately allowed her in and called to Everard to join them. She had heard the horses stirring as Berenice returned and was waiting.

Close behind in Berenice's wake shuffled the gargoyle amazing her how, at his dust-raising saunter, he could move so fast. Luanta did not acknowledge the gargoyle, knowing his penchant for vague answers. Once the door was closed, she turned to Berenice and said, "Well?"

"Lords Razon and Skon vanished within the dying embers of their night's campfire last night enroute to the mountains. I waited until almost dawn to see if they would return. They did not. They communed with a wraith in the smoke of the fire that pleaded for their help. That was when they disappeared," Berenice stated flatly.

From a single drop of acid in the pit of her, Luanta felt a slow burning anger begin to engulf her with a bitter heat radiating into every part of her body. She fought to control it, to find reason before she exploded in rage.

"What of the troops with Lord Skon?" Spike asked the changeling. It caught Luanta off guard and brought a moment's sanity to her.

"They were instructed to go back to Skon's Hall should the two not return by morning's dawn," Berenice responded.

"When Lord Skon and Lord Razon do return, they will go back to the Hall as well," Spike said with just enough disdain to catch Luanta's attention. "Perhaps you should send the changeling back to the Hall to wait for their return," he concluded with an air of dismissing anything further as beneath him. He shuffled back to the main room and resumed his post-pile posture in the corner.

Luanta watched him settle. "One day I will see you…" Luanta started in her mind.

"You will see me what, Luanta?" Spike sent back. "See me crushed into a mound of sand?" He looked up from his perch, and with eyes glowing from beneath his hood, he extended his tongue. Slowly, he licked his lips imitating the manner of the Wherant lord licking Luanta's burning flesh.

Luanta lunged at him; she flew through the door at a sprint with only one thought—to smash Spike's sneer. She felt the impact of the wall without ever seeing it. Spike was sealed within a stonewall.

Luanta felt the impact with her left knee and right arm first, drawing a grunting scream while the rest of her collided smartly with the wall. Her face took a hard hit, twisting her neck painfully.

Having heard Luanta's scream, the door guard rushed in from outside to see what was happening.

Impassioned to kill something, anything, her anger overwhelmed all sense in reason; Luanta turned and blasted the brigand with a powerful bolt that slammed him back into the now closing door.

He crashed through its thin planks, thrown to the ground outside. His legs and arms quivered spasmodically as his mouth uttered strange groans. His head lay at an awkward angle with a large plank splinter protruding through his throat. He died before others got to him.

Luanta slapped her hands together in a stinging mix of discomposure and yet to be vented rage. She turned on her heel and faced Berenice. "Get back to Skon's Hall and bring me that ring!" she bellowed. She waited the moment it took for Berenice to exit her room. Everard remained quiet, already in the central room. Daring any to speak, she entered her room, slamming the door behind her.

Luanta heard the voices of men removing the dead guard. She felt the unseen glances cast in the direction of her room. "Let them stare," she hissed. "It will only make the slow torturing of Blue Skon that much sweeter."

Suddenly, Luanta had a thought: Lord Skon and Lord Razon had disappeared after seeing a wraith. What if there were other factions in the quest of vengeance she did not know about? What if she was being used as a pawn in a larger Wherant game? There was someone who would know. Luanta threw her arms around herself, forming the familiar circle and vanished.

Once back on the Shadow Plane, Luanta wasted no time seeking out Ermentrude, the Senior Eldress. Ermentrude's Hert recognized her. He did not mistake the determined look about the Eldress who strode towards the gathering floor. He felt her eyes search him out. The gaze of fire she sent him was perfectly clear. "I seek the Senior Eldress." Tolerating no delay, she added, "At once!"

"I will inform her you are here, Eldress Luanta." He turned to leave. He did not care for this Eldress. She was trouble and totally unpredictable. He went up the stairs to a small chamber off from the nest rooms. He knocked on the portal and then entered the room.

Ermentrude was scouring a large book, sitting at a small table. "What is it?" she asked. "I am not in a mood to be bothered."

"Eldress Luanta is here to see you, Senior Eldress."

"Ah, yes. Her timing is impeccable. Maybe she can shed a little light on how a human was found among us." Ermentrude thought for a moment, If Luanta is involved in this, and I am certain she is, I do not want to appear too concerned. "Let her sit for a while. Tell her I am very busy and will be down in a few minutes."

The Hert was very pleased with the message. It will be good to see this one have to wait, he grinned. He turned and went down the stairs.

Luanta looked up as the Hert came down. She impatiently stood up and walked towards the Hert. "You may show me up."

"Eldress Luanta," he answered, waiting a moment feeling good about the situation, "I must ask your patience. The Senior Eldress is very busy and will be down to see you in a few minutes. She asks you to wait here."

Did she sense a feeling of smugness in this Hert? "Everywhere, I am surrounded by fools." She was worn-out with the continuous delays. Vestiges of anger seethed just below the surface. She looked back at Ermentrude's servile Hert. She was sure he was looking down at her. She had an idea. This will be a sweet repast for today, she thought to herself, a plan forming firmly in mind. "Go tell the Senior Eldress that my message is urgent and cannot wait. I will follow you up." Putting action to words, Luanta started walking briskly to the stairs. She knew he would not let her be first.

The Hert was caught by surprise at first then realized she would go up without him. He rushed ahead of her and proceeded up the stairs. He managed to get several steps in front of her and immediately opened the door. He entered. He knew his mistake instantly.

Luanta heard a startled scream from the room, immediately followed by a slamming of a flat object on a table inside. "You dare enter without knocking!" Ermentrude screamed.

Luanta was careful to stay clear of the portal's open frame as a flash of light and the sharp smell of magic filled the air. The Hert bellowed in pain. He came flying backwards through the opening and over the banister into the open air above the gathering floor. He fell with arms flailing the air, a smoldering hole in his chest where the firebolt had hit him. He was dead as his body crashed into the floor below.

With a smile tickling the corners of her mouth, Luanta entered the small room. "I am sorry to rush in on you, Senior Eldress. I heard a scream. Are you all right?"

Embarrassed at the show of a moment's weakness, Ermentrude quickly rose to greet Luanta, "You are so kind. It would be so welcome to find a Hert who was teachable." Quickly finding her composure, she added, "Come, Luanta, sit down with me. What is it you want?"

Luanta was back in charge. She sat down and waited a moment before speaking, "I have followed your wise guidance. I met with Lord Wherant. He has agreed to assist me…" Luanta gave a slight shudder as she remembered what it cost her for that aid. "…in destroying my enemies." She studied Ermentrude's face for its reaction. *Is it possible you are in league with others behind my back?* Luanta asked herself. *No. I think not. You would have nothing to gain.* Luanta continued, "However, it appears there are others involved in this that I am not aware of. The yester-night, my enemies were seen to entertain an ethereal guest. Their guest was seen to beckon to them. No words were heard, but suddenly, they all disappeared. That was a full day ago. They have not been seen since."

Ermentrude's face pinched slightly at the eyes. She knew something, Luanta was sure of it. Watching Ermentrude closely, she said, "I have come to seek your wisdom in knowing if there are others against me in my quest, others I do not know of yet."

Ermentrude thought she understood what was happening; it all began to make more sense. "Yes, I believe you are correct. I do not know how a wraith fits into it all. That is a new twist." Thinking it out, she asked, "Do you know where your daughter is?"

Luanta was taken off guard by the question. She noted that Ermentrude's face became blank and secretive. An alien feeling of dread went through her. "No, I have been gone several days, as you know. What has happened to Cynderet?"

Ermentrude sensed truth in Luanta's response. She felt urged to continue, "Cynderet is at the heart of a conspiracy against the Society."

Luanta's mind raced in confusion. She started to laugh at first then somehow realized it was not a joke. "I do not understand. Cynderet is the leader of a conspiracy? Here?" Luanta sought some indication or glimmer of comprehension as to the truth of the allegation. Nothing came to her. "How?" she finally asked. "She is only a child and incapable of such an idea. She cannot even be trained as an initiate!" Luanta's statement reminded her of the last time they had been together. She had shown Cynderet the Charm Spell and Cynderet became sick and weepy—a total coward. "No, it is impossible that such a spineless bit of spittle could be as you say. Where is her Hert? He would be more likely."

"Luanta, in the few days you have been gone, much has happened. In sacred ritual, the Eldress Council was warned to find and destroy your daughter. In our search for her, we found Cynderet's Hert in the company of a human. They are both in the dungeon." Waiting for the information to sink in, Ermentrude paused. Seeing understanding by the look of new questions in Luanta's eyes, she continued, "We have not found your daughter. She has disappeared."

"Humans?" Luanta asked in shock. *First a wraith then Cynderet is a supposed conspirator. Now her Hert is captured with a human on the Shadow Plane. What is going on?* Luanta felt the drop of anger begin to build within again. Everything was too close to be unrelated. "Who is this human?" she demanded.

Ermentrude noted Luanta's anger. It seemed to clear Luanta of any implication in the conspiracy. *Besides,* she thought, *it is not directed at me. We will see if Luanta knows anything more.* "We do not know," Ermentrude answered. "I will show you his things. He was well of armor, but had no sword. Come, I will show you."

The two went down to the gathering floor. Stepping around the dead Hert, they entered a side chamber. On the table was the human's gear. Luanta thought she recognized the surcoat. She passed her hand over the whole pile uttering a word. A brightness radiated from beneath the human's breastplate. She reached for it quickly and lifted. Lying just below it was a ring bound by a heavy chain necklace. The ring radiated a pearl iridescent of light to her Magic Seeking Spell. She took the necklace up in her hand, examining the ring without touching it. A slow smile lit her face. "I know this ring," she said softly as she turned to Ermentrude.

"Then you know where your daughter is?"

"Cynderet? No," she answered, her own train of thought broken. After a moment, she continued, "No. She is not gone. She is too close to her Hert. If he is still here, she must be also. Take me to this human and the Hert. We will get some answers." There was a warm confidence inside for the first time since meeting with the Wherants. Looking back at the ring, she said, "I will hold onto this for a while." She turned and followed Ermentrude to the dungeon.

Two Council Guards joined them at the portals to Council Peak. They accompanied the Eldresses into the heart of the mount and the dungeon chamber within. Ermentrude gave the order and one of the guards hefted Serenten to his feet, facing him to the Eldresses. The other slapped him twice severely across the face to wake him. Serenten's eyes began to open with a disoriented blur.

"Where is my daughter?" Luanta demanded.

Serenten struggled to clear his mind. He had been unconscious since the Eldresses had blasted him. He and he remembered someone else had been with him, the human, Lord Razon.

Impatient with Serenten's not answering her, Luanta stepped up to him. Without touching him, she lifted his head up in an upward motion of her hand. "Answer me and I will make your death quick," she hissed.

Serenten was surprised to see Luanta. When did she get here? He asked himself still trying to get a sense of things. He could think of nothing to say.

Luanta hit him with a magic bolt from her hand. She blasted him, slamming the back of his head into the wall.

"I do not know!" he breathed in a mix of alarm and anger.

Luanta hit him again. This time, with a charge to his chest. His whole body slammed against the wall. His shoulder pounded into one of the chain-binding retainers of the wall. Serenten felt a driving pain shoot through his back.

"You think to get angry with me!" Luanta gritted quietly through clenched teeth. Instead of letting him fall, she kept her hand just off his chest, forcing his body to grind on the chain's binding.

Serenten groaned with pain. He looked pleadingly to the two guards standing on either side of him. One turned his eyes away;. The other, the Captain of the Council Guard, stared back at him. He smiled wickedly.

Luanta let go her magic hold on Serenten. He slumped to the floor as his knees gave way.

Luanta prepared to ask him again where her daughter was when she saw the second form still unconscious on the floor. "I will ask this human," she said to Ermentrude. Luanta reached to roll Razon over for a better look.

With strength renewed in desperation to protect Razon, Serenten struck out at Luanta with his arm. He missed her as the chains pulled the shackle deeply into his wrist, forcing his arm to swing wide of its mark.

The smiling captain jammed the blunt end of his weapon into Serenten's mid-section, driving the air from his lungs. Luanta slammed another bolt of magic into him as well. He impacted the wall again;. This time all went black.

He never felt his body bounce off the wall and twist wildly against the chains as he fell to the ground.

Luanta watched Serenten collapse. She thought about killing him and decided against it until more was known about her daughter.

She looked back to the human before her. Luanta rolled him over for a better look at his face. It was Razon. She turned to Ermentrude. "This is the human you were talking about?"

"Yes. We captured these two together in the forests beyond the city."

"This is an unexpected gift," Luanta said. She turned suddenly to the Council Guards and commanded, "Leave us."

The two looked at each other and left with a quick nod of the head.

Luanta waited until she was sure they were gone. She turned back to Ermentrude. "Do you know who this human is?"

Ermentrude noted a hint of excitement in Luanta's voice, "No. Only what I have already said. What is it you know?"

Luanta looked back to Razon. He was fully unconscious. She slapped him. His body responded like a rag doll. She knew it would be a while before he would wake up.

Ermentrude waited a moment longer for Luanta to explain who he was. When she did not, Ermentrude finally asked with obvious irritation, "Who is he then?"

"My apologies, Senior Eldress. I should have spoken while I examined him." Luanta stood to speak. "He is the one I sought when I encountered Lord Blue Skon. In point-of-fact, I was feeding on this human when Blue Skon attacked me."

Serenten heard voices in the deep murk of semi-consciousness. His whole body hurt. He opened his eyes carefully as his cheek pressed into the cold floor. He thought he recognized who was speaking. Everything felt fuzzy and disoriented.

The voices continued: "His sudden appearance interrupted my feeding. It also forced my leaving before I could perform the body-cleansing phase. Instead of warding off pregnancy, I had to defend myself." She gave a bitter laugh.

The laugh was familiar to Serenten. He recognized Luanta's voice. He remembered where he was and remained perfectly still.

"Somehow, this human must have lived through the feeding. He is Lord Razon." Giving a strange smile to Ermentrude, she finished, "This human intruder is Cynderet's father."

Serenten's mind walked a thin line between reality and dreaming. He felt his ability to focus on what was said waver in and out.

Luanta looked back at Razon on the floor, then to Serenten, "Whatever is going on, I do not think all the Hert are involved in it. There is no way they could be. In the meantime, we will wait until these two wake-up for further questioning."

Luanta took a few moments to think things through, "When we are done with them, these two will make great sacrifice to the Table."

Serenten heard nothing more as the mists of dreams swallowed reality up, sending him back into unconsciousness.

CHAPTER EIGHTEEN

Razon lay still while trying to get his bearings. Other than knowing he was still alive, nothing was familiar. All was black. Panic struck instantly as he found he was blind. He forced himself to remain calm. Although he could not see his hand, he felt it under his cheek. With a gentle finger, he messaged his closest eye. There was no evidence of damage or pain, except the throbbing behind both his eyes. It seemed lodged about the middle of his brain. He tried to roll over and found his chest throbbed as if several ribs were bruised or broken. His head pounded too much to even try and lift it. So, he remained lying on the smooth surface supporting him. Unable to see anything at all, he guessed it to be a floor. His arms bore this out as he gently moved them out from his body. There was a familiar clanking of trace chain;. When he found and reached the limit of the shackle length, he realized he was the one chained. Lying perfectly still, *which is the most comfortable pace to move at, or not move rather,* He found a moments amusement in the thought. He forced himself to remain calm and tried to discern any aspects of his surroundings. All was sealed in darkness without a breath of breeze. Sound gave him his greatest sense of bearing. There was someone else in here. He could hear the regular breathing of sleep.

Once again, Razon set about seeing how much movement he was capable of. He stretched his right arm first then his left. He could almost touch his knees before the shackles bound him. He attempted to roll on his back again, and while holding his breath, he used his backside as a fulcrum to roll over. It worked—he was on his back. He carefully lifted one leg by pulling up the knee and found it shackled at the ankle, so was the other. Finding his calm demeanor slipping quickly, Razon pivoted against his chains by lifting his arms and legs to spin against the pull of his chains and spin on his backside, reversing his position somewhat. His head landed on something softer than the floor.

Razon felt the slow rise and fall of a massive chest. His head was resting on someone's body. Clarity of thought was slow to come. A vague vision of three bat-like creatures with wicked canines hung like a heavy curtain his mind fought to part. There had been someone else. He and a reptilian man-creature had united in a futile effort to fend off the bats. They were big bats. Full-sized and female, he mused as their physical form became more defined in his mind.

They smashed us with magical bolts of energy. They must have knocked us unconscious—I mean really unconscious. How did I get here and where is the other fellow? He had a name, what was it? Serenten, that was his name!

Memory of the situation became clear, There was a girl. And Blue Skon was there. They just got away when those flying, fanged females arrived. They did not try to kill us, at least I do not think so, though I feel mangled inside my chest. Another memory returned, Aye, I threw my sword as a warning to Skon. He was coming back to get us. How long ago was that?

Razon tried to lift himself up and instantly thought it a bad idea. The crushing throb of his head forced him to leave it, resting on the breathing cushion of the one beneath him. Traversing his hands from his shoulders out to get an idea of size and, maybe, who his companion was, he felt the body beneath him. The skin was finely scaled at what he thought was an arm. It must be Serenten, he thought. "Serenten? Can you hear me?" Razon whispered harshly in the direction he thought would be the head. There was no response.

Razon tried prodding the body. There was no sound, but the body did budge some. Razon was about to try it again when a massive arm wrapped around him. It was stopped suddenly, reaching the end of its chain and sparing Razon a crushing grip about his torso. There was a violent pull of the arm. Razon felt it moving above him in what he thought was another attempt. The chain crackled again;. The body roared in anger.

"Serenten! If it is you, do not hit me. I think I may be blind, and I hurt too much to move yet. I cannot see a thing. Be careful!"

"Aye. Everything is dark, but I can see. And I like not what is here. My head hurts." Serenten looked at Razon trying to clear his own mind. "I think I remember who you are now. How did we get here?" Serenten barked groggily.

It was clear to Razon that Serenten was not thinking clearly yet. He tried to explain what little he remembered in an effort to get the reptilian coherent again.

Serenten started to speak. He hesitated as orientation settled in. He started again, "Aye. I remember now. It was Ermentrude and the Eldresses who came on us. They used their magic when we resisted." A thought stopped him for a moment. "Wait!" Serenten struggled with confusing contradictions. As it became clear, he said, "I remember them questioning me later—here. It was about Cynderet. I did not answer them so Luanta—Luanta was here, how strange," he said questioning. "She blasted me again. Everything went black after that."

After a pause, he continued, "We should be dead. They are without mercy.

There must be something they still want from us. They must still be looking for Cynderet." Anger swelled in him. Serenten pulled violently on both of his arm chains. They cracked as they were pulled taut. They did not give beyond that. Razon, forgotten, was thrown to the end of his chains by Serenten's force.

"You are going to crush me yourself if you do not stop banging those chains!" Razon yelled. "Take a minute to think this out!" He was in pain. He was very familiar with blows to the body taken during combat;. Nothing he could recall was like the crushed feeling in his chest now. He knew there were too many disadvantages in this dark for him. He had to take more time to figure things out. If he truly were blind, it would make things even worse. "Are you able to see anything, Serenten? Is this blindness permanent?" he asked, concern growing again.

"Blind? No, I do not think so. It is the dark we are in. Oh! I have figured it out. I know where we are!" Serenten countered. "We are in the deep chambers beneath Council Peak." Serenten roared in anger, and this time only gave a powerful jerk on his far arm's chain. "They will not let us live, you know. They will torture us until we tell of Cynderet. Then they will kill us."

"We must think and work together," Razon encouraged.

"You know not this place or its purpose."

"It is true, this place is new to me, as is the situation with bosomed bats dressed only with magic." Razon pondered on what he could understand. All was still vague to his mind. In an effort to lighten the growing apprehension, he drew upon his experiences of the past. He remembered something Skon said just before leaving him and Serenten to take Cynderet to safety. He had said he would be back. Razon chuckled, remembering a time before. "This much I do know: no matter how difficult the situation or dire the straits we face, if Blue Skon is still out there, he will not let up until we are found. Ha! I know more. This is the type of situation when an old friend named Elfgon would relate some meaningful story to instill faith and grit. Let me try doing the same. It may help us both to find our aplomb.

"Blue Skon and I had only met a short time before this story, and on opposite sides of weapons, I might add. Well, we came to understand our differences and started working side by side for the king and the Six Realm Alliance. Three others were with us at the time on a mission assigned us by Wolfgang the Meek, a kind of emissary for the king."

Serenten could tell Razon was seeing the story in his mind as he recited it;. There was growing excitement in his voice. Serenten could sense the truth in what Razon was telling.

"Landsfall, a Rover; Quick, a skinny rascal and dangerous with a blade; and I were trapped in this realm of an ancient evil warlord. Although the warlord had been dead for a long while; his fortress was being used by other enemies of the realm. It was quite a dismal place with magical traps and secret passages everywhere. We had made it in with Skon, and then the three of us were suddenly separated from him," Razon gave a low chuckle before continuing. "The story goes, we made a wrong turn. Skon was in front, and when all went black, the three of us moved as a group while he continued ahead. Next thing we know, we have fallen into some kind of cell with no way out. None of us were hurt, but we would be in this cell for days, all the time thinking it was all over for us."

"What was Lord Skon doing then?" Serenten asked, finding interest in the story.

"Well, you have seen Skon. He is rather a giant fellow. Not knowing where we were, or how to find us, he only had one choice: keep going. He meets up with this giant snake-like creature called a Navasu that has been waiting for him. It was a drawn-out battle, and when he was done, we were still all gone." Razon gave a chuckle remembering the next part. "Now Skon does not give up on his friends. He garnered light enough to see where we were last all together;. From there he back-tracked us on our wrong turn. He comes to a solid wall and cannot find a way through it or around it, so he does the next best thing.

"He goes into the mountains, hires a dwarf-mining crew, and digs us out. It took five days of hard work. He never quit. When he was done, the whole labyrinth was torn up. One could walk a straight line from beginning to end. We had gone through some kind of secret trap passage and were held as a group with only our rations and what water we had to sustain us."

Razon patted Serenten's arm close beside him. "As it turned out, Skon started with seventy-five miners. Whatever of value was found was shared equally with them when we were found. They dug. He defended them as needed. Last I heard, Skon is still not welcome in those mountain mines. It seems the share those miners earned after the dig let them retire!"

Razon slowed his reciting then, and in a quiet voice, added, "He would have stayed there if it had taken months and we were found dead. You see, Skon holds loyalty as the greatest of all virtues. It was something I could never fully understand, but even though we met under less than friendly terms, he took me in and taught me the very lessons in day-to-day example that my father tried to teach me when I was younger. I can only see it now—why I considered Skon's Hall as home." Razon was quiet in reflection for several moments.

Serenten found himself spellbound by the idea that someone could be that devoted to his friends. Serenten had never had a friend, unless it was Reht. And that was only marginal as Hert had no other purpose here than to obey the Energy Feeders. It was a slave's existence.

Razon breathed a sigh, then finished his thought. "Skon allowed me to live what my father sought to teach. For that, I owe Skon my life."

In the dark, Razon turned to where he knew Serenten was. "Loyalty, that is what I pledge to you here and now. I have been taught at the feet of two of the greatest, my father and Lord Blue Skon. We will see this through together. That counts for much I have come to learn." After a brief pause, he added: "though I may actually be blind."

"I have never had the luxury of an ally;. Here in the very most dreaded place of my existence I find a comrade worth dying with;. So be it! We will face life and death together!" Serenten pledged.

The silence lasted only for a poignant minute, but it was enough. A bond was formed between these two, Serenten and Razon.

"Can you see, Serenten?" Razon asked.

"Aye, I can see. We are beneath the most important structure of the Energy Feeders. I am sure they think we can tell them where Cynderet is. We are going to die most horribly, and we have little time," Serenten said as if counting on his fingers.

"All that and I forgot to dress for the occasion," Razon jested.

Serenten was caught off guard at first, then catching the humor, chuckled deep within his massive chest, "Aye, and I have a headache." Serenten added, "So, lest we have to entertain, what do you suggest we do?"

"I like your attitude now much better. First, we have to find a way to get free of these chains."

"I tried for years as a young one. Even now the chains remain firm."

"Let us both try on the same one. Say yours, between us?" Razon took hold of Serenten's arm and followed it to the shackle on his wrist. "Shall we?"

"Aye, why not?" Serenten agreed and took the chain in his two powerful arms.

Together, they pulled. Their backs bowed in the darkness as they put their power into the pull. Razon, having more chain length because of his smaller frame, planted his feet squarely on the wall and pulled back with his legs as well. At first it seemed impossible. Serenten's head pounded with pain. He began to give up just as there was a squeal of metal. A pop of stone followed.

There was the slightest give. Renewed hope came to him.

Together, they began to pace their breathing, taking in huge gulps of air. They locked the air in their chests and pulled. In marked unison, they breathed and pulled again. Hope remained in their hearts from the earlier pop. They gave their every bit to the work.

Serenten saw heat build where the chain was bound to the wall. This was where the metal was worked the most and so the most brittle. The metal was heating up as it weakened. He reached deeper within himself and found power to match the all that Razon was giving. Greater power came as Serenten realized he was working side by side with Razon for the same purpose. He was not alone. It was together that they would beat this chain. That brought the strength needed to pop the bindings from the wall.

Serenten had an arm's length of chain still attached to him by a shackle;. The other end was now free of the wall. He patted Razon on the back as they sat to catch their breath and handed him the free end. "When you are ready, we will give you one of these also," he promised.

"That would be nice. A matched set between us, I mean. Just give me a moment. I will be right with you." Razon worked to get his breath.

It took several tries;. They knew they had freed one. It was this confidence which allowed them to eventually free the second. It broke at a link just above where they had their grip. Then their hope took a dive.

"We cannot reach the other chains together. We are too far apart," Razon said as he realized he could not reach Serenten's outer arm's chain.

"Aye, and our legs are chained as well," Serenten joined.

"We need to think this through a little." Razon sat down and began to think. He could not see anything. He still could not tell if he was blind or not. He did have a good idea of the set up though. "This is going to take a while," he said, as he sat down leaning his back against the wall.

"I swore I would never allow myself to be here again. What a mockery I am," Serenten said sitting down as well.

Razon could sense the disappointment in his new friend. They had done so well on the chains initially only to be outdone by distance in the end. "You cannot allow yourself to give in. Stay strong in yourself. You do not want to end up as I am. I know what it is to be a mockery. I have been there a long time."

Serenten was surprised by the open confession. "How is it that you are so? I have seen you fight, sir. I have seen you slay my comrades and live."

It was Razon's turn to be stunned. "What do you mean you have seen me fight?"

"The Eldress Luanta had taken prisoners on your earth. She was torturing them for information. My duty was to protect the doors to the chamber where she worked."

Razon could see nothing of Serenten's face; only his tone showed Serenten's remorse in his involvement.

"You and the other warrior, Lord Blue Skon, were with several others. You attacked at the door." Remembering those the Hert had killed, Serenten felt uncomfortable talking more. After a pause and change of direction, he added, "Anyway, Lord Blue Skon fought with sword while you and another slew us with arrows. Someone almost killed me with a war hammer."

"Aye, that would have been Wolfie. I remember the battle now. It ended quickly. There was a bat woman that got away and one of the reptilian creatures was thrown into her as she disappeared. That must have been you. You looked rather as a pincushion as I remember because a comment was made about you not lasting long wherever you went. We finished off the Wizzard in league with the bat and set the prisoners free." Razon chuckled a moment at the irony. "You fought well yourself. You killed the overzealous magistrate and his two guards. We had been telling him to slow down. He was the one who had his men rush the door.

"A week later, Skon fought two others of your kind. He was trying to save my life." Razon reflected a moment, "Neither would have been you, though."

Razon went silent as he remembered what happened to him. In a hushed voice, he began a tale: "Skon and I, along with the usual comrades: Landsfall, Elfgon, and Quick had just returned from a very difficult campaign for the king, although no miners were required," he jested. "We were in a tavern sharing a few pints when the most beautiful woman I ever saw walked down the stairs from above. She was supple and sure in her grace. I remember how her hair shimmered and her skirts swished as she descended.

"It was like music in motion. She smiled right at me. Now that was a first—I can tell you. There were not many whose attention I gleaned. It was usually Landsfall or Elfgon who earned the attention. Well, following what I had seen them do before, I got up and invited her to join me at a second tavern table away from my friends. I was captivated. I hardly remember anything from that point on.

"The next thing I know, I am in a bed stark naked and she is in the throws of combat with Skon. Two of your kind appear out of nowhere and she is gone. After that, all I know is what Skon says happened. It was several days before I was even conscious again." His tone changed slightly, "I almost died, you know. If it had not been for Skon and my ring, I would have. I was slipping into a deep coma. Skon says it was the ring that saved my life."

"What is this ring of yours?" Serenten asked. "A ring of healing of some kind?"

"I do not think so, though it has powers I know not of. It is the Ring of Radiant. It belongs to the House of Radiant as a symbol of authority to rule the Light Forest. The king wears its mate."

Razon grew silent again.

Serenten could see the look on his face through his ability to see infrared. There was pain there. "What is it that hurts you so?"

Razon looked in his direction though he could not see anything. "My duty was to return to the Light Forest. I have spent, no, wasted, the last twelve-plus years searching for the woman. I could never accept the idea she was trying to kill me. I mean why? I had never seen her before nor did I have anything she could want." After a prolonged pause, he continued, "Anyway, that is my shame. I forsook my duty to find her. I kept telling myself if I could find her, I could save her. I have not seen her since. And yet, even to this day, all I have to do is think about her and her vision comes clearly to mind." Razon turned away then and became recluse.

The confession affected Serenten in a strange way. He could not quite put his finger on it. It just seemed like there was more to the story. Some part which he knew, which eluded him. He watched Lord Razon as he sat on the floor with his head down and his wrists, bound in chain, resting over his knees. His hands hung limply.

Razon finished, "Skon says I was never meant to live through the ordeal. He says it was my ring that saved me. I was unconscious on the bed. He said I was fading away fast when the ring started to emanate a green glow. It worked its way about me rather like what happened to Cynderet. I started to gain strength several days after that. It was very close, I am told. You know those are the only two times I have ever seen or heard of that happening and I have carried the ring with me since I was eight years old."

Razon turned to Serenten. "Would you like to see it, as much as your vision in this dark will allow?"

"Aye, to be sure," Serenten answered.

Razon reached inside his jersey to retrieve it. Serenten watched as Razon's demeanor went from willingness, to confusion, and then to loss.

"It is gone. They must have taken it from me!" Razon looked to Serenten.

"It is the only possession I have left of home. That and my sword left as a warning for Skon. It was my charge."

Serenten thought the comment was rather childish at first. Then he began to consider its implications. The Lord Razon was a great warrior, he was sure. There was a deeper problem. It had to be what Razon meant about being a "mockery." He had fallen short of his own purpose and now even his token of lineage, for that was what it was Serenten was sure, was now gone.

Serenten could see the beginnings of a broken man. It was so familiar to those whom he had seen fade away into death as a youth in these very dungeons.

"You must not give up on yourself, Lord Razon," Serenten encouraged. "You have known me not at all, yet we have struggled together as long seasoned friends. Do not give up now. I do not know how, but it will work out. Remember what you said of Lord Blue Skon. He is still out there somewhere and as the Eldresses have not found Cynderet, we can be sure he is thinking as you said.

"He will not stop until he finds you, finds us. He gave us his word to return for us. You are too much a man of greatness to quit or lose yourself from your purpose. Trust now in those who…" Serenten felt a warmth of faith inside, "those who are loyal to you."

Serenten watched as Razon's eyes turned his way. Although he knew Razon could not see in the dark, there was a small smile that lit his face. Serenten was sure his blindness of eye was only due to the dark within Council Peak. And he was sure his blindness of being was only as temporary. "Aye, even now you are noble enough to acknowledge me even if you believe not in my words as yet," Serenten said to his again head-lowered companion.

*****

Cynderet woke up to the midmorning sounds of life. There were voices outside her room and the smell of food. Cynderet's stomach rolled inside. "How long have I been asleep?" she asked herself.

She sat up and looked around her. She found a bowl of strange fruit on a small table beside her. Beyond the table, a slight breeze blew fine curtains away from her window allowing them to billow in gentle waves just caressing the floor. There was a strange yet hauntingly familiar calling from outside her window.

Cynderet climbed out of her bed and wrapped a light blanket about her form. She went quietly to the window being torn between enjoying the gentle sway of the curtain ends against the floor and the call from outside. She stood just far enough from the curtains to allow them to move but also permit her to see outside as they did so.

There were grain fields below her in the near distance;. Farther away, she could see the mountains. Looking to the fields again, she saw the stalks of grain rippling in the wind. There were several black objects almost floating on the uppermost stocks where the grain tassels hung in the breeze swaying gently. One of the forms took off in flight and flashed bright red on the shoulder of its wings. Another called out to it and took flight as well. Cynderet recognized the birds;. They were the same kind as the one she had seen at home. It had died shortly after being inadvertently brought by an Energy Feeder returning home from feeding.

Cynderet was delighted to watch the birds' antics until she heard renewed voices coming from beyond her door. She turned and, drawing the blanket firmly about her shoulders, she listened at the door. The voices were of children discussing body maneuvers of dodging and attack.

Cynderet was unfamiliar with the latch to her door. She tried to open it but could not find the release. Suddenly, everything was quiet outside her door. Cynderet backed from the door a step as she listened intently. She opened her mind and read the thoughts of the children. They had a plan. Two children were sneaking up on the door. They were going to pull it suddenly open into the passageway outside. They thought someone named Quick was behind it. Cynderet read the children, thinking they were playing a game. She looked around her room for an idea on how she could play too.

She took off her blanket and standing just to the side of the door decided what her part would be.

The door latch moved with barely a click and suddenly burst open into the passageway. This allowed Cynderet a free view and room to work while the other two were limited by the bulk of the door. As two tried to tip toe in, Cynderet dropped her blanket on those attempting surprise and stepped into the doorway behind them.

The two groaned in alarm and then in frustration at having been found out. An additional squeal of mixed laughter and surprise arose from the third person standing just outside the door as Cynderet cleared her way back into the center of the room. The two in the blanket struggled a moment before they could cooperate enough to get the blanket free of their heads.

In a brief moment, all went quiet with a feeling of embarrassment floating like a cloud in the room. "I am sorry," the girl said standing alone. "We had no idea it would be you in there. I mean, we thought it was someone else." The girl ended with her voice failing in confusion, not knowing what to say.

"I be think'n ya be a trap set by tha' fella Quick," a shorter boy with an end of the blanket still in his hands said. "Who ya be? I no seen ya afore," he said bluntly.

Cynderet read instantly that this one was open and honest. She went from face-to-face with her own sense of confusion. The game had been fun, but she had no idea what to do now. She had never been in the company of boys before. And the girl—Cynderet knew the girl;. She stared for a long moment with mouth partially open. "I know you," Cynderet said finally. She looked to the shorter boy. "I know you too. You have a horse and cart," she managed to finish, no less aware of how to proceed.

"Yep, but ya no be answer'n me question what I asked first," Patrick said, not to be ignored.

Ashley was next to throw off her embarrassment. She took control of the situation, "Yes we do." Turning to her brother, she added, "Patrick, show some manners and be patient. You have not even introduced yourself."

Turning back to Cynderet, Ashley pointed to each child and introduced them. I am Ashley. This is my brother Patrick. The silent tall one is Ryan. This is his home."

Cynderet looked at each as they were introduced. Ryan remained silent. He was a wide mix of emotions difficult for Cynderet to read clearly. He was embarrassed but also caught by Cynderet's beauty. She felt her cheeks grow warm at that. And angry, angry that his parents had another guest. Again, one he knew nothing about.

Ryan looked around the room. He then looked to the inner door leading to his parents' room. He interrupted Cynderet identifying herself in answer to Patrick's question, "Where are my parents?" He looked at her and, not waiting for an answer, asked, "Why are you in my old room?"

"I am sorry," Cynderet managed. Thinking that Lady Laura and Lord Skon had to be his parents, she added, "I do not know where your parents are. They left me to rest earlier this morning."

Moving from the rather confrontational stance of all standing facing one another, Ashley moved to the small table. "Well, you must be hungry if you got in last night. Come sit here with me. Do you mind if I have a couple of your grapes?"

Finishing her own introduction, the newcomer said, "I am Cynderet and I would love to eat, but I know nothing of what grapes are."

"Ya mean ya never ate grapes afore?" Patrick asked in open amazement.

Ashley smiled, knowing he had just learned about it two days ago himself.

"I be show'n ya the way." He took up a small handful and plucked a berry off. "Ya no want ta be eat'n the stubby wood thin'." Patrick popped the berry in his mouth and chewed. While demonstrating each step clearly, he added, "And the seeds be bitter, so spit 'em out." Again, he showed her the process applying a bowl at the side of the plate as his receptacle.

Ashley started to laugh. Cynderet found it contagious and soon all three were laughing.

Cynderet was confident these two would easily become friends. She looked to find Ryan. He was shutting the door to her room after having gone into his parents' room. He would be a different matter. He was too caught up in himself.

Ryan left the room without further word to anyone. Patrick looked to the girls, then back to Ryan's vanishing shadow. "If'n he be train'n, I no be want'n to miss mine!" Patrick looked to Ashley expecting some nod. She gave him only a toss of her head towards Cynderet. He looked to Cynderet and, in an infrequent remembrance of manners said, "I be pleased ta meet ya. If'n ya excuse me, I be gone now."

Cynderet was not sure how to respond, so she just smiled. That was enough for Patrick. He was gone before she turned back to Ashley.

"Your brother is pleasant enough. What is the problem with the other? I do not think he likes me."

"Do not let him bother you. Lady Laura says he feels caged in and takes it out on everyone else," a smile crossed her face as she added. "So you see, it is nothing personal towards you. Let us finish eating here. And I see Lady Laura has provided you with clothing. It is there on top of the chest at the foot of your bed. Once you are dressed for the day, I will show you around."

CHAPTER NINETEEN

Blue Skon and Laura found the children in the training room. They watched from the steps for a few minutes.

Ashley finished her daily struggle to control the long sword. The difficulty was evidenced by the pearling sweat on her forehead. She was getting better and was following the council given as accurately as she could. She put the long sword away and picked up her throwing daggers. They were in a belt she had placed on the table with the towels. This part she enjoyed. Quick had said to practice with them only after working with the sword. *These are like desert after the main meal,* she thought having readily adapted to the manner of sweets after the main meal in Skon's Hall.

Ashley wore the daggers and belt around her thigh, either when in pants or in skirts. Quick had rigged the belt for her and shown her where to slit the seam of her skirt to allow her hand access to the blades. When wearing britches, as now, she wore the belt exposed on her right thigh. Quick had instructed her to wear them whenever she was up. "In order to get the feel of them," he had said. Ashley figured it was part of being a warrior. The thought sent an exhilarating pulse through her body. It felt good. She had been rather embarrassed wearing them at first—until she remembered Lord Razon's prowess when so desperately needed by her family that day. Only his skill with these very types of blades had saved them. He never even drew his sword.

She stopped a moment to reflect on his prowess with weapons. She would be dead if not for him—she and Patrick as well. She knew she should apologize to him for her display of bad manners that last morning in the cottage. *He did not deserve the way I treated him. Where is he? I have not seen him for two days. Not since he and Lord Skon rode away.* Ashley thought a bit longer, *Cynderet says Lord Skon is back. Where is Lord Razon? I will ask as soon as I finish my training,* she resolved.

Laura watched Patrick reprimanding Ryan for poor form in the use of his sling.

"If'n ya no put the stone in the saddle right, the shot be go'n wide on ya!"

It intrigued her that this farm boy could speak so plainly to Ryan and Ryan accepted it. She noted Cynderet in the corner where Quick stood watching the entire proceedings with a careful eye. From his hand hung the trail-cords of his sling. *Patrick has definitely made himself welcome among the males of the Hall,* Laura thought. *No,* she chided herself, *even the women of the hall enjoy his antics. And certainly his appetite.*

"Cynderet looks to have fared well from a full day and night of sleep. She has even made a friend or two already," Skon said, watching as Ashley looked to Cynderet, then Quick before throwing her daggers. The third hit then bounced off. "Ashley's talent for the throwing blade improves everyday," Skon noted to Laura. "How is her sword training progressing?"

"She can lift the blade well enough now. Her parries are slow, but well placed. In time, she will develop muscle enough to wield the weapon." Laura watched as Ashley collected and threw her blades again. One hit center. "She does have the knack for throwing though."

"Aye. I am pleased she is learning to wear them all the time." Skon looked to his wife and finished the thought with their magic, "She may need them, and I know not how soon."

"Yes, my husband. And Ryan, his weapons as well. Have you alerted Quick and the troops?"

"Aye. There are two patrols out and one in the village letting key folk know. Word has also been sent to our friends asking for their aid."

"Would you that I should contact Wolfie?" Laura asked him.

"No. Not as yet. His work is great at Wisshard," Skon answered. He thought again as he had several times in the past two days of how he would like his brother-in-law at his side. And again, he remembered how important the work he did was for the Six Realm Alliance. "It is difficult for me to call on him, not knowing what we truly face."

Changing the subject, Skon asked, "Let us get Cynderet as soon as the training is done. I am getting anxious. It has been a full day and some already."

When the training had ended, Lady Laura collected the children and told them they would be going to the village with Captain Hamilton. There were things needed for the Hall. She would take Cynderet with her. They too had things yet to be done.

"The real adventure is here, is it not, Mother?" Ryan asked tersely, confident of the answer. "Once again, I am being pushed away like a child." He looked in anger at his father talking quietly with Quick in the corner.

"Yes, Ryan," Laura answered. "Your father and I will be on an adventure as you put it. We may be gone for a while. We are not pushing you away, though. It is that we do not know what we will find. Your turn will come." Then recalling the eminent attack, she added, "And sooner than your father and I would like."

With a strange premonition, she turned to Skon with a question. He read it and nodded.

He excused himself from Quick and strode over to join his wife and son.

"Ryan," he started as soon as he got to them, "the fact is, danger is coming from many directions. Captain Hamilton will need your training as an escort for our guests. We must prepare the Hall and the village for a possible siege. You know as much of what is needed here as does he. Together, you make a team. Do not fight him. Render your aid to him and to our guests."

Looking at her son in a strange new light brought on by Skon's words, Laura added, "The time for protecting you as a child has ended, I think, my son. And well before I would have it if my ways were allowed."

Ryan felt the reality of what his mother was saying, not by her words, but by his father's signing in the finger language shared only with Quick and Skon's closest allies. "Watch your back," he signed. A simple movement of his fingers brought home the true gravity of the situation. Whatever was going on, he was no longer being completely hidden from it.

Ryan turned and saw Ashley coming towards them. He also saw Captain Hamilton coming down the stairs. Ryan turned to his father. "If you will excuse me, I will go arm myself for our trip to the village."

"His tone is new to me, milady," Skon said with a smile at the respectful manner Ryan used in addressing him.

Laura smiled her hope as she turned to meet an eager looking Ashley.

"Lady Laura, Lord Blue Skon," she greeted them. "Have you seen Lord Razon? I must speak with him."

"We have not seen Lord Razon for over a day," Skon said seeking to hide his concern from her. "We go now to get him. Why? Have you a message for him?"

Ashley thought a moment, but disappointment denied her quick thinking. "No. I guess it can wait until I see him again. Thank you." With that, she excused herself and went to join the others. They watched as she tucked her knife belt a bit lower on her thigh. She made an imaginary grab at a blade as she walked.

"That child has the gift of weapon awareness about her already," Skon said. "I am thinking she is a natural for the dagger."

He looked to his wife for a response and saw her pensive look. "What are you thinking, milady?" he asked.

"I be think'n Quick be needed here more'n wif us," she mimicked Patrick in an attempt at levity. "I fear he will be needed here the more so."

"Aye, My Wife. I will inform him to follow the children."

"No," Laura said pleading with her husband, "if Ryan found out Quick was following, he would feel we were giving him words only and no faith in sending him to the village as we did."

"Do not worry. Ryan will never even know Quick the Quiet is there."

Laura looked to her husband. His decision was made based in part on her concern. She had already changed Quick's role in the day's activities. *I fear you are wrong about Ryan knowing, my husband. These are dangerous times, and Quick being with the children will ease my heart much. I will hold my tongue,* she thought, holding herself silent and stoic lest he perceive via their magic.

After setting the children on their trip to the village with Captain Hamilton, Laura, Skon, and Cynderet went back to Cynderet's room. "My man Quick will be joining us in a bit," Skon said. "In the meantime, Lady Laura would like to introduce you to a friend of hers. He is very small, so do not be surprised, all right?"

Cynderet nodded trusting in the two of them knowing full well they would never do anything to hurt her.

"His name is Missive," Laura joined. "He is going to help us try and find Lord Razon and your guardian, Serenten. Are you ready?"

"Yes. I am ready." She turned and looked directly at Blue Skon. "It has been many hours since you last saw them, has it not?" she asked with a touch of concern for him that only Laura could see.

"Aye, Child. And I grow concerned for them with the delay."

"I know. I can read your fear for them. Lord Skon, thank you for all you have and will do. I am so sorry I have brought this to your home."

Skon gave her a rare bow, deep and polite. Before he could say anything, a new voice spoke up.

"Child, you have brought none of this," a little man sitting on Laura's shoulder said. "You brought us timely warning. Now, let us be about our friends." With a similar deep and courtly bow as Skon's, Missive introduced himself, "I am Missive, Lady Laura's agent, if you will. I am going to help you locate Lord Razon and your guardian, Serenten."

Cynderet read the confidence of the little man. She could not read his mind. When she realized his mind was closed to her, she looked at him in surprise.

"Yes, Child. I know you are telepathic. I am afraid what is in my head is a bit much for your tender years."

In a flash, she saw hundreds of years slip as one intense blur before her mind's eye. It was there and gone. It was his history. None of it stuck. It was only a sample of him and a warning. "You have your own Dream Sight. You do not need mine as well, aye?" he asked, smiling and a glint of chastisement in his eye.

"I apologize for intruding, sir," Cynderet said in her mind. "I am ready to begin," she said aloud for all to hear.

"Good. Lady Laura will join us, if it is all right with you?"

"Yes. I have already traveled with Lady Laura. She would be welcome again. What about Lord Skon?"

"He will remain here until we know where we are going," Missive answered. "Besides, right now he is in conversation with his man Quick. I think we will proceed within our world of magic while he visits those more of his understanding."

Cynderet was not sure, but she thought she noted a hint of mockery in the response. Instead of feeling alienated by it, she felt a sense of the familiar. *At least the many levels of subtleties in the Society remain the same even here,* she mused.

Together all sat in the Foyer of Doors within Cynderet's mind. "Close your eyes, Child," Missive said. "Do not look to any of the doors. Instead, look to Lord Razon. Find him where you last saw him," Missive instructed. "See him as everything was at that time. Then follow him, not yourself."

Cynderet found it relatively easy with Missive's coaching. She saw Razon standing as last time in the glade of the forest. He was leaning over her with his ring losing the last of its green aura. She was lying against Serenten in his arms. Skon stood at her feet looking in all directions then back to her. Cynderet could feel Missive and Laura with her now even though it was as if they were all three looking down upon a scene in a painting.

The trio watched as Cynderet and Skon disappeared in their return to Skon's Hall. Now only Razon and Serenten remained. The two turned in their huddle to watch the forest. Razon slowly, quietly drew his sword from its scabbard. Suddenly, they both looked behind. Shadows were falling from the sky. Three bat-like women, Cynderet recognized them immediately, landed at the feet of the two men. Razon and Serenten jumped up, both knowing it was a futile effort. Razon took a magical blow to the chest. He kept his senses long enough to turn his back on the Eldresses and throw his sword into the forest brush. He turned back quickly to find all the Eldresses focused on Serenten as he made a desperate effort to protect Razon. Cynderet screamed. She was only too familiar with what the magic of the Eldresses could do. "They are dead!"

she cried aloud.

"No, Child. Just watch," Missive said quietly.

The Eldresses searched the area for any sign of others; there were none as Cynderet had remained in someone's arms the whole time, so no evidence of her presence was to be found. The Eldresses bodily carried Razon and Serenten into a chamber of darkness unfamiliar to Cynderet.

"I cannot see anything," Lady Laura said after a long pause.

"Our young friend and I can," Missive replied. "They have been chained to the wall of a dungeon. It is kept in total darkness of a magical origin. I can see them only in the infrared spectrum. This darkness is of the Lightless Plane." Missive turned to Cynderet, "Do you know this place?"

"It must be deep within Council Peak. I have only been to the peak once. For my…" Cynderet stopped, ashamed to go on.

"For your initiation as an Energy Feeder, correct?" Missive pressed.

Cynderet began to shake as shame and fear took her. "Yes."

She looked to Lady Laura pleading for understanding.

Missive chortled a slight cynical laugh, "I knew it."

Lady Laura only looked into Cynderet's eyes. "It did not take you long to realize your mistake, did it, Cynderet?" she asked calmly.

"No, Lady Laura. The first five days, I spent in a semi coma. When I did recover, I was in training only two days before my mother came to loath me." Cynderet shook with tearless emotions. So much loss, so much pain. She felt numb as she looked from Lady Laura to Missive. "I was not cruel enough to complete even my first week of training. It took one day to learn I could never be as my mother or my Society."

Cynderet drew quiet for a long time. "I no longer have a home or family. I am an outcast. The only friend I have is in that dungeon with Lord Razon."

"Then let us be about getting them out!" Missive pushed. "I know what you are. And I know what you are not. An Energy Feeder you will never be. I just like knowing I am right." Missive smiled, "It is my turn to say I am sorry. Please forgive me."

Without waiting for an answer, Missive turned to Lady Laura. "You cannot see to alter the mirror for rescue, but I can. Shall we proceed?"

"Yes."

*****

Razon had been asleep for several hours. Serenten continued to contemplate what Razon had told him about the Ring of Radiant and his family charge. *To have family and purpose must be the greatest joy of all, he reflected. I know, until Cynderet, my life was of little worth to anyone, except for my ability with the Council Guard weapons. Only Reht was better than I. Interesting that both of us should be released from that duty and assigned as guardians of Cynderet. Perhaps the Eldresses did not want us carrying weapons because we were so good,* he thought.

He considered what else Razon had said about the woman, *He carries a great burden. He is ashamed of his actions in searching for the woman because it has delayed his return home, yet I think it is because of his unrelenting search he has become the man he is. There was no hesitancy in helping either Cynderet or me. It was he who organized our effort at these chains.*

Serenten began to whisper as he continued looking at the sleeping form. "It actually felt good to combine muscle with his, even if we did not get free. He is a man of good character. I have never heard of a human surviving the Death Feed of an Energy Feeder;. Who is to say what impact that has had on his being." Serenten thought of Razon's comments about himself. "I would say you have done very well in meeting the trials set before you. It runs deep within you, my friend. I have no shame in dying at your side. It is only a matter of time before they come for that. If Lord Blue Skon is as tenacious as you say, he will need to come soon." Serenten chuckled at a thought. Musing aloud, he said, "You are a warrior. You will not go easily to your death, I think. Given the chance, you will fight. Well, we shall both fight united. We will take others with us, no?"

"Well, battle is always more fun with two or more on a side," Razon acknowledged, surprising Serenten that he was awake.

"How long have you been listening to my ramblings?"

"I think it was the thought of fighting I woke up to. With the high level of self-belittling I am bathing myself in, a fight would be a welcome diversion right now."

"We each have almost a weapon apiece with these free lengths of chain. When they come again, I assure you, it will not be for our health." Serenten grew quiet for a moment. "The Eldresses will seek to sacrifice us to their

Table. It is the usual end to things foreign or not understood."

"That is a common practice almost everywhere. I was hoping for something less predictable."

"You could suggest they just letting us free for observation."

"If not that, escape would be nice."

They both laughed. "It is good to laugh. And strange to do so here in this dungeon," Serenten said. "When I was captured as a youngling and forced into slavery here, I thought I would never laugh again."

"My father taught that no matter how deep the well life has thrown you in, a laugh will lift you higher than any tear of self-pity or curse of anger."

Razon looked down in the darkness to where he imagined the floor was. "I would like to have returned home to make him proud of what his son has become."

Serenten touched Razon softly on the shoulder. In a whisper, he said, "My friend, make him proud now. It is time to get angry. I hear them coming."

There was a sound of a door opening, and after a long moment, it closed again. They waited anxiously for further sounds or signs. The door at the far end of their cellblock opened. Razon could see several armed Council Guards in the dim light behind them. Then the door shut, robbing the chamber of its momentary light. Razon was blind again. But this time, he knew it was not his eyes.

Serenten spoke a quick plan to him in a whisper.

Razon gave only a nod. *This will be a real test of a warrior's mettle. I fight blind,* he thought. He quietly gripped his loose end of chain in his hand and reached towards its binding, pretending it was still attached to the wall.

The Council Guards approached closer. He would follow Serenten's plan as best he could. He waited, listening intently struggling to find his bearings by sound.

There were three guards. Two came towards them carrying walking shackles. One stayed back. Serenten recognized him as the Captain of the Council Guard who had hit him. "You will be coming with us for questioning," he announced. "It seems the Eldresses want you before the Table." He gave a slight chuckle, "It is too bad I will not be stating your lineage, but your initiation will be short-lived, I think."

He laughed at his joke while the other two put their weapons aside, out of reach, and laid out the walking shackles. They began to undo the chains about the prisoners' feet. The guards did not notice the loosened arm chains.

Razon felt a Council Guard at his feet. He was pretty sure how the guard was kneeling by the way he checked his foot shackles. Razon gripped his one secured arm chain. When he heard the click free of the shackles, he heaved himself up, catching the guard in a headlock with his legs. Razon twisted forcefully to get the guard off-balance and down before the guard was able to bring his greater bulk into play.

At the same time, Serenten wrapped his free chain around the neck of the second guard. He lifted him up by the chain and crossed his arms behind the guard's neck. The guard turned in an effort to free himself. The chain cut deeply into his throat.

The captain struck out at Serenten with the dual blades of his pole weapon.

Serenten rotated his body as the keen edges sliced a long gash across his chest. The movement saved his life.

Immediately, the blades were coming at him again.

Serenten hefted the struggling guard into the path of the weapon. The blades cleaved deeply into the guard's rib cage. Serenten rolled the dying body down and away from him locking the weapon's blades in the body.

The captain lost his grip of the weapon.

He turned to give the alarm when he ran right into the pommel blow of Skon's sword. "That will be enough from you," Skon said, as the captain fell flat at Serenten's feet. Skon turned to greet Serenten's surprise, "I am back as I promised."

Skon proceeded to dispatch the guard at Razon's feet, then returned to release Serenten's last arm chain.

"When did you get here?" Serenten asked in grateful amazement, as Skon began to release him from the shackle. "Your timing could not have been better!"

"Sorry I did not get back in time to help in the forest glade. When I got there, you were gone. It took a couple days for Cynderet to figure out how to find you. I am very glad you stuck around here so she could."

"Cynderet? You did not bring Cynderet here?" Serenten asked in alarm, looking for her in the chamber.

"No. She is fine. And safe, for now," Skon assured him.

Serenten took up the three pole arms. "I will be keeping these for now." He smiled his thanks to Skon. He went to help Laura release Razon. "How is it you two see so well in the darkness?" he asked over his shoulder.

"A friend gave us a small gift of seeing into the infra-red spectrum," she answered with a smile. "Shall we go?"

The Captain of Council Guard was chained to the wall in place of Serenten. "A parting gift for the Eldresses. You know I will not be welcome here again," he said most casually.

"Aye. They may think you ungrateful," Razon chided. He was grappling for polite yet firm contact with Laura in his continued blindness, as the security of the chains was missed. She took his hand and placed it in her own.

"Come. I am thinking this has been all too easy," Skon said. "Let us hurry on our way." He turned and walked towards the middle of the room. He motioned for Laura and Razon to go before him. Skon handed Razon back his sword as he went past.

"Thanks. I have felt off-balance without it."

Skon gave him an encouraging pat on the shoulder.

To Skon's side, Serenten noticed a slight difference in the air of the chamber. A shallow haze, almost like double vision in a mirror, except beyond it, Serenten could still see the deeper dungeon walls clearly.

Skon ushered Laura and Razon through, then turned to Serenten. "Let us leave this place quickly!" He took Serenten's arm to lessen any delay, and both walked into the haze.

A small sarcastic voice chortled in the empty air. "I must be growing soft, Lord Skon. Welcome home."

Then the haze was gone.

*****

Luanta waited a few moments longer;. It had been some time since the Council Guard left to get the prisoners. After several more minutes, she signaled Ermentrude and the two descended into the dungeon again. Except for the two bodies and the chained captain, the dungeon was empty.

"Where have they gone?" Ermentrude asked.

"They will be returning to Skon's Hall."

Ermentrude was perplexed at Luanta's lack of concern. "What will you do now? We still do not know where your daughter is."

"Cynderet? She is not a worry to us. She will come sniveling when she finds her Hert is gone. Come, let us go back into the light."

Together, they walked the corridors of the dungeon to the stairs leading out onto the Table level. There were Council Guards waiting for them. "Go and release your captain from his chains," Ermentrude instructed.

Luanta and Ermentrude walked out into the light. Luanta stopped and looked at the ring she stroked in her hand. She smiled as the possibilities it presented raced through her mind. She held the chain, allowing her a closer look at the ring dangling at its end. She enjoyed the feeling of control she felt. The Lord Wherant had said she was to wait until the ring was away from Lord Razon before unleashing the power of the black box. The wait was over. It was all up to her now. She had only to give the ring to Strike and she could attack Skon's Hall.

An idea tickled her *mind: Why do I have to give the ring to that smelly rock?* She asked herself, *Why not sacrifice it before the Table as a gift to the Wherants—without any help from Strike?*

"Ermentrude, you are the Senior Eldress. How would you like to be the one who presents this gift to the Lord Wherant? I am sure he will be most pleased to receive it," Luanta cooed.

Ermentrude smiled back, "I shall see that it is done with much ceremony. Why not deliver it yourself?"

"There are a couple pebbles in my shoe I wish to rid myself of."

"So, having begun the quest to rid yourself of a nuisance to your feeding, you will not stop until it is done," Ermentrude reasoned, pleased for Luanta and not fully understanding Luanta's reasons.

Luanta decided to let her remain a little off in her understanding. It may prove helpful later, she thought. Luanta smiled as if Ermentrude had hit on her purposes and bowed politely. "I will be to my work. I will let you know when to begin the ceremony. I will return, myself, with word. Until then, keep the ring well away from danger."

The two nodded their shared realization that Blue Skon and Razon had come to the Shadow Plane once. They could do it again.

Luanta smiled, "I will be off to my little war now." She vanished in her Energy Web, leaving Ermentrude to find a secure place for the Ring of Radiant until Luanta brought word to proceed with the ceremony.

CHAPTER TWENTY

Captain Hamilton and the children were just getting into the village from Skon's Hall when a loud outburst of growing excitement could be heard from the market-place ahead. The din was well above the usual level in the hacking of goods;. There was the unmistakable ring of alarm in the noise. "Come children, let us hurry to see what is about," Hamilton urged. No further prompting was needed as the group picked up the pace to a solid hustle.

They came around the corner and stopped short. Before them was a display few would ever forget. At the forefront of a dispersing line of pack animals, of a kind none in the village had ever seen before, rode two horsemen in total contrast to each other. The first appeared to be a man in the finest flowing silks seen. The colors were layered to match the sequence of a rainbow. The blues of head and shoulders bled through the spectrum to the reds of leg and boots. The second was a tall powerful fellow of forest greens and earthy browns. Neither displayed any armor save the weapons worn at their side or on their back.

"I have not seen a spectacle of such magnitude since the last time Elfgon was here," Hamilton chuckled to the children. Turning to Ryan, he added, "Remember you the merchant elf from your early youth, Master Ryan?"

"I remember only a thin being of sharp features and pointed ears who traveled with my father for a season. Surely, this cannot be the same?" he said unbelieving.

"Aye, young master. The same and then some. Hearest ye the textile merchants rave in jealousy and lost revenue?"

Hamilton looked for a moment longer;. His arms were folded across his chest, fingers tapping an amused staccato on his forearms. "I had better make my presence known in the square lest there be trouble. I pray you will await me here."

With that, Captain Hamilton walked away from the children. As he progressed into the market square, he noticed and called to his side, two of Skon's soldiers in town on patrol.

"Ryan? Who are those people?" Ashley asked having never seen such flaunting of color on a person before.

"The colorful Bird of Paradise is an old accomplice and friend of my father's. His name is Elfgon, the Merchant of Hamwell," Ryan said, rather quickly. "The other," spoken in a quieter voice of awe and respect, "is Landsfall Far. He was with my father and Lord Razon during the cleansing of the land prior to Father becoming Lord of Skon's Hall. He is a Rover, a wandering wilderness and forest warrior. Come on,; let us get a little closer to see what happens." Putting action to words, Ryan went into a brisk jog down the street.

The others were granted no choice except to follow. Ashley finished only a few steps when she found herself alone. Patrick still stood behind just staring at the pair. Ashley returned, grabbing his shoulder and dragging him along. "What is it? It is not like you to linger behind so."

"Be ya see'n the look o' that man in green and leather? Never be I see'n one o' his like afore," Patrick's voice was intense in its wonder of what he saw. "And his horse like I never seen—a wondrous animal!"

"Do you see the pack animals?"

"Yep. Wha' be they?"

"I do not know. I intend to find out though."

Ashley and Patrick joined Ryan on the veranda of the village tavern. It was only a few yards from where Captain Hamilton greeted the two visitors.

"Hamilton Harm, you old soldier you. Looks like easy duty suits you well here," Elfgon teased loudly, waving his arms like a thespian on stage.

"Aye, and I be thinking you lost your magic mirror and need for common folk to be granting you your oohs and aahs," Hamilton responded. Turning to Landsfall, he added, "How is it the Lonely Rover finds himself beside the Flower of the North?"

"Greetings, Ham," a quiet, deep voice said. "It be good ta lay eyes on a more sober soul, it be true. This Humming Bird of Pointed Ears is so bright my horse and I woke up twice in the night thinking the sun was up!"

By this time, several of the textile merchants had managed to catch up with the visiting friends. An obnoxiously large merchant pushed his way forwards and faced the two on horseback while bleating to Captain Hamilton. "You allowing these new-comers to the market to be driving away buyers from the locals what been working so hard for the lord and all to produce fine cloth?"

"Jason of Cotton Creek, you be full well-known the Lord allows Elfgon free trade on his lands," Hamilton reminded him firmly, expecting this. He knew he had to meet it fully and well. "You be remembering it was the ideas and learn'ns of this same one which taught you the ways of new patterns to your material and a tighter weave. Since your learn'n, you have acquired a small fortune holding the secret as your own. Now take your following back to your stalls and see what else you may learn."

Feeling disarmed and bowing not only to Hamilton's counsel but also to the building public number anxious to see what Elfgon brought, Jason turned to leave casting a last defiant look at Elfgon. In return, he received Elfgon's wink of the eye, and a patronizing, sweeping motion of his hand ushering him away.

Jason strode away from the two newcomers. His turn of body did not hide his look and suppressed fury from Ashley. "That one will be trouble, I think," she said, pointing him out to Ryan.

"Aye. He usually is. Father tolerates him because he is a free man, owning, by right of title, a bit of Cotton Creek."

Elfgon took no hesitation in redirecting the interest of the crowd, "Look ye, my fellow traders and buyers to the goods being unloaded from the backs of my modest animals. Come, see, and handle the wares of far off lands and peoples."

Once the crowds were dispersing in generally the direction of his wares, he turned to Hamilton "I have a not-so pleasant surprise for you, sir. Look ye to that coming quietly out of sight behind the village."

Hamilton knew instantly the subject had changed and not for the better. "Aye. What is it?" he asked, turning.

"This morning, we rescued what be left of one of yer patrols com'n ta Skon's Hall," the quiet voice said. "Of the eight ye sent, three be still alive to ride. Be we mov'n ourselves from the center of attention?"

Landsfall extended his arm down to double-mount Hamilton on the back of his stallion. The three rode back the way Hamilton and the children had come.

"I be sorry, children. We be calling our visit to the village short. Come, return along behind me to the Hall," a pained yet dutiful Captain of the Guard said.

As the small party rounded the corner back to Skon's Hall, they were joined by ten others. Two were Elfgon's riders riding wide. Three, in surcoats of Skon's Hall, led four horses with rolled tarps laid horizontally across their saddles. A fourth rider in surcoat was struggling to stay in the saddle.

Ryan knew then that all his parents had warned of earlier that morning had been true: and worse. He knew well these silent soldiers and those rolled in the tarps. He had trained with them and had shared stories. Now four were dead. In a strange mood, he gripped the hilt of his long sword tightly. Somehow, this did not feel like an isolated incident. He vowed he would come to wield his sword on something other than straw. And soon.

However, it was Patrick's sharp eyes that picked out the strange shadow against the outer wall of Skon's Hall. "Be that your father's man Quick standing there?" he asked Ryan.

He looked towards the shadow. He could not see Quick as plainly as Patrick seemed to; it did not matter. There was no question his parents had sent Quick to watch out for him. They had not really trusted him at all. It was a baleful realization to bear, intensified by the loss of friends now being borne silent and gone to Skon's Hall. A sneer crossed his face at the irony of the analogy.

*****

The stranger sitting in the tavern, alone again, did not need to see the patrol return to know the dead had passed by. Berenice, in a man's guise again, could smell them. She also knew they would be the patrol she had followed three days ago when the lords had vanished in the embers of their fire. Razon was not with them.

It was time she went into the Hall and see if he had returned some other way: Tonight would be fine. There would be no moon to possibly illuminate her or her mount as they flew in.

*****

Laura finished wrapping Serenten's chest. "The healing balm will have you well on the way by this time tomorrow. I will leave you and Cynderet alone now."

"My thanks to you, Lady Laura. To you and your lord for being of such kindness to care for Cynderet as you have, and now me." Serenten squeezed Cynderet's hand still holding his with its own solid grip.

"Aye. It is good to have you with me again," Cynderet agreed. "Now I do not feel so all alone, though I think we have many new friends here." Cynderet turned to Laura, no words came to mind, so she simply smiled and sent the emotions of gratitude to Laura's open heart. They shared a brief moment of understanding.

Suddenly, Lady Laura's demeanor changed. "There are others who need my help. I must hurry. Please excuse me. I will check upon you later, friend Serenten." With that, she left at a quick pace, leaving the two in concerned wonder what the problem could be.

"What has happened, my husband?" Laura asked anxiously as she entered the guards' dispensary. "I heard you call and came as quickly as I could."

"The patrol," Skon started trying to contain his anger. "Razon and I left them several days ago. They were ambushed by those brigands Razon spoke of. We lost four of the eight. Please attend this fellow lest we loose another. He is in a bad way with arrow wounds."

Laura looked to the fellow lying on the table. He was quiet with steady breathing. She looked at the blood on his surcoat. "How is it he is still alive?" she asked as she removed the coat. His armor had already been stripped away. The surcoat was acting as a warming blanket. "Someone knew what they were doing in keeping him alive this long," she said, beginning to get beyond the makeshift bandages to the actual wounds.

Not getting any answers, she turned to her husband. He had the strangest look on his face. "I do not remember the last time I saw tears threatening and a smile broadening your face at the same time wounded were being cared for. It is in marked contrast to the anger in you just a moment ago."

"Elfgon and Landsfall arrived just in time to save him and the other three." Skon spoke in quiet thanks. "They answered my call. As we speak, they are with Razon getting a briefing. Elfgon brought ten of his own troops to help as well. Eight of them have taken position in the market square as merchants bolstering my six-man patrol."

"Ah! That is good. Once again, we are in the midst of our friends, Companions of the Blade, to confront an unknown evil. I am sorry Wolfie could not be here with us as well."

"He trusts in our ability to handle this. He is about the tutoring of others more in need I am sure, milady. Your brother is the most nurturing of any monk I know. The King and the Six Realm Alliance are in good hands."

"Yes. Now I plead you, leave me." Laura turned her head slightly to look at him. Her hair had been tucked neatly into the collar of her coat, a stray curl spun on her forehead.

Skon looked at her that way for a growing moment. "Aye. I will send someone in to assist you as needed," he said, about to leave.

Turning again, he spoke his thoughts sharing with the one he trusted most implicitly. "You know, demons are not an everyday encounter. We will be well-tested. They do not take this kind of activity lightly. Why us? What is there to gain? There must be something they want badly. Cynderet indicated it was revenge. Well, perhaps for some but not demons. We are not that important."

Laura watched Skon walk out and quietly close the door. "I must speak with Cynderet and Serenten again," she mused, "for you are right, my husband. We are not that important, except to each other."

*****

Ashley found Razon just as the briefing of Elfgon and Landsfall was breaking up. All bore firm faces and hard eyes. She felt very small and uncomfortable in the dispersing midst. It was not easy to apologize, and the temperament of these men did not make it any easier. Still, she did not want to put it off any longer. The weight was heavy to bear, and she wanted this behind her. Razon had a way of disappearing and this was a duty of responsibility.

Fortune smiled on her. Patrick came bolstering into the room with no hesitation at all and approached the Bird of Paradise fellow in bright colors. "I be wonder'n wha' those beasts of labor ya gots be?" he asked straight out.

It caught Elfgon by surprise for only an instant. As a master of the stage, he took Patrick aside with a wink to his friends; his face became a glowing mask of amusement. "Well, you are an astute fellow. You are the first to ask of them here. Come and I will tell you about the Camel of the High Mountains."

Ashley turned back to Razon and saw him looking at her with a gentler eye as Landsfall patted him on the shoulder and turned to leave.

"Greetings, Lady Ashley," Razon said formally, "I had hoped to see you. I have heard of your training. You are doing well, I am told."

"Lord Razon," she started. The pause growing longer and more unsure as she fought for the words to say, "I, I—"

"Aye, it is you. We both agree on that account, I believe."

"Sir, this is a most difficult circumstance for me. Please do not mock me as well."

"Ashley, I do not mock you. You obviously have something you wish to say and find it difficult putting it to word," Razon smiled at a quick thought of humor from the past. "In combat, we have found that humor often lightens the mind, allowing clear thought and vision. I only sought to employ the same for you. Forgive me."

"See? That is the problem. You are always so sure of yourself. So, so…" In frustration at not being able to talk, Ashley lifted her hands in front of her as if holding a bowl. "You always have the answer!" she boomed louder than intended. She ignored Patrick's hard stare and Elfgon's look of question. Seeing nothing further, they returned to their conversation. Feeling color warming her cheeks, Ashley turned her back to Razon.

Gently grasping Ashley by the shoulders, he turned her to face him again. "Oh, Ashley, believe me, I am rarely in possession of the answer. And as far as being sure of myself, well, your opinion will change with time, certainly."

Not understanding his intent, Ashley felt further embarrassed and put-off. Taking a firm stance and determined voice, she said, "Lord Razon, I have come to say I am sorry. I am sorry for the way I treated you when you tried to teach me of the knife and its ways. That said, let me add, I do not appreciate your belittlement of me!"

In grand elegance, Ashley turned on her heel and stalked proudly from the room.

Razon was caught completely off guard.

"Ah, you do have the way about you, aye?" a rich tenor voice said. "You know," a pause for effect, "the child is in love with you."

Razon turned an angry eye to Elfgon. "What are you talking about? She is a child. And, besides that, she is angry at me all the time!"

"Aye. This is the man I know so well. A Master of Combat, always a hand to those in need, and the hind end of a…a camel, when it comes to the ladies. It is all a mask, my friend. Women do that."

Elfgon's parting laughter forced Razon deeper into his newly-found chair. Ashley was not the only one hiding behind a mask: "I think I will go visit Serenten. At least I can talk with him."

Razon got up and walked to his room. There was something he wanted to get first.

CHAPTER TWENTY ONE

Ryan rumbled about his room in an agitated humor, "It is not right, the way my parents treat me. I have been training in weapons since I was old enough to lift a short sword. I have worked the horses, tended the wounded with Mother, and challenged even Quick and Captain Hamilton with the long sword. My father is stifling me! He was out on his own at my age and knew hardly anything of a warrior's trade." Ryan kicked the bedpost. It hurt. He gritted his teeth at the pain. Closing his fist tightly, he sought some way to vent his anger.

Ryan did not hear the quiet knock on his door. He did not know Quick had been there and now retreated.

"Lord Skon?" Quick said as he joined his lord and friend in the armory.

At the formal tone, Skon stopped the examination and recount of weapons to listen to his man. In a flash, Skon recalled how Quick had been the first person he had ever hired to work for him. Skon had been under Wolfie's tutelage. They had been doing some traveling and needed another hand. Skon had accumulated a small cache of gold by then and hired Quick at Wolfie's suggestion. The roles had been reversed almost immediately as the older Quick taught Skon lessons in the various blades and in wisdom in moving unseen. The three developed the sign language they used in combat. Later they taught a few others, including Elfgon and Landsfall. Laura and Ryan also knew the code.

With time and through shared encounters, the relationship between Skon and Quick grew much beyond hired wages. Skon trusted all that he had to Quick the Quiet. In return, Quick had come to devote his life to the care and defense of this his family.

"What is it, Quick? Why the formal tone? We are alone."

"Skon, I was found out this morning by the young squire Patrick. His sharp eyes picked me out against the wall of the Hall when the patrol was discovered. They came back early. I had little place to hide." Quick paused for a few moments to find the right way to say what he came for. "The squire pointed me out to Ryan. Ryan suspects you do not trust him alone yet. He is very hurt and will do something rash. He reminds me a mite of a youngster I knew once."

"Aye. Were it not for you and Wolfie, I would have died long ago." Skon searched the face of his friend. "There is more to this, I be thinking."

"Aye, Skon. Your son is going to run. If not today, then soon. He is not of the temperament to let this settle and be forgotten."

"And you want my release to follow him." Skon knew he was right. The confirmation came in Quick's silent single nod.

"I will stay as long as Ryan does. When he leaves, I will leave also." Quick read Skon's look. Skon felt bound to both son and duty. Quick knew which Skon would choose if it came to that. He continued, "You would do the same and you cannot. Too many need you. You are their servant just as they are yours, even more so. This is because you know what would happen if they had no Lord of Skon's Hall."

"Aye," was all Skon said. Too well, he remembered the efforts, blood, and lives lost to cleanse this region and make it safe again. Had it not been for Quick and the others, it may well have ended differently.

"You never knew that you saved me, did you?"

The comment caught Skon by surprise. "What is this? How?"

"When Wolfie encouraged you to hire me. You never asked anything about me. On his recommendation alone, you opened yourself to me. Now, I know this place and your affairs better even than you."

"Aye. I depend upon you as my right hand, perhaps more. And I thank you."

"Do not thank me. It was that blind trust which bound me to you. You never asked about my past, my qualities, my reasons. You simply trusted me and that trust only grew more with time and turmoil shared." Quick never let his gaze drop from Skon. There were things never said until now. And now was the time to say them. "You never knew I was the greatest thief in all the Six Realms and beyond. You never even questioned my worthiness. You gave me the greatest gift: trust. I will return it to you by being your man for Ryan."

"Aye, Quick. I could ask for no one better. When all is done, remember this is home to you both. Never forget it. And, when the time comes, tell Ryan."

The two men shook hands and embraced. Both knew Ryan would leave. The question was, when?

*****

Ashley walked a self-belittling course down the hall towards her room. She could not stop the flaying of her conscience. "Every time I try to talk to him, something goes wrong. Why is it so hard to stay civil?" she mumbled.

"I think you are a little young to be talking to yourself," said a gentle voice just coming to her side said.

"Lady Laura, you surprised me!" She stopped and waited the moment it took for her to join her. Embarrassed, Ashley tried to explain, "I used to talk to my mother when I was younger. She was my mentor and the only female I had to learn from. That is one reason why Patrick and I almost speak a different language. You see, she was an educated woman who fell in love with a gentle but poor farmer. After she died, there was only Patrick and Grandfather. They never could understand me, so I began talking to myself."

"I am sorry about your mother. You two must have had a special relationship. I am a bit envious, I am afraid. I am pretty solo here. At least until you and Cynderet arrived." Noting Ashley's questioning look, Laura continued, "Oh, yes, there are women here in the Hall, and even some good people in the village. The servant women rather avoid me, and the towns-folk, well, as good as they are, 'Ignorance does still abound among the masses' as my brother puts it." In a mock whisper, she continued, "You see, they all think I am a witch." She stressed her point with silent nods of her head. Laura waited to see Ashley's reaction. When she did not shy away from the thought, Laura added, "I prefer to be called a healer or mage."

"My mother was a mage, though not a very powerful one. That is why she was able to teach me so well. She was the only one in our family who could read and write. Father did not understand what that meant, but he loved her anyway. She taught me how to read and write. I guess she thought I might become a mage too someday."

"And do you have such interests?"

"I do not know. I do know I love working with the blades, though. When I get strong enough, I want to practice with you, just like I saw you and Quick doing that first morning."

"Oh! That reminds me," Laura interjected. "Lord Razon asked that I give this to you. He said he gave it to you once already. Maybe if I gave it to you, it would stick, he said."

In Laura's hand was the sheath and dagger from the cottage. The medallion, an oblong disk with a wedge removed, shone in the reflected light.

"Thank you, Lady Laura. When did he give it to you?"

"Just this afternoon. He said you two had talked and it was important to him that this go to you."

Taking it from Laura's hand, Ashley felt its balanced weight in her hand. Even in the sheath, its quality could be felt. "I will see that it does 'stick' this time."

"Good. I think it means a lot to him." After a few renewed steps of silence, Laura asked, "Would you like to go to the village with me? I am going with Elfgon and Landsfall. Razon will be going as well, though," she added with an inquisitive look.

"Yes, I would love to go. And I will behave before Lord Razon. I will just ignore him!"

"I think you are going to be a dangerous woman someday, Ashley."

"Not yet?"

"Do not rush it," Laura said with a firm tone. After a brief pause, she gave Ashley a knowing wink. "You and Cynderet have both grown beyond your years in the trials life has brought you. I am afraid I also had to meet similar trials. You both remind me of myself at your age. I wish I could allow you a little more time as children."

"You are very kind, Lady Laura. Will Cynderet be going with us?"

"I think not. The shock of Skon's Hall is great enough. The village may overwhelm her!"

Ashley and Laura, with the rest of the party, arrived at the village in early afternoon. Immediately, Elfgon introduced the ladies to his traders of silk. Lady Laura had instructed him that she wanted a bit of time so Ashley could just be a girl. Elfgon, always ready for a show, made it his personal responsibility to see a good start before catching up with the others.

The others went to check the village for defense. They sought out Henry the Tavern Master, one of the key people of the village defense. He turned to his older son. "Ye be watch'n o'r the place in me absence," he instructed.

The changeling, Berenice, heard the instructions and noted Razon instantly. She was still in the tavern, patiently waiting for nightfall. The appearance of Razon in the village was a welcome gift. It gave her a chance to study him before she entered Skon's Hall tonight. Still disguised as the stranger, she got up and followed the group out the tavern door.

Ashley also saw Razon enter the tavern with the group of men.

"Has he come out yet? Or is this your idea of 'ignoring him?'" Laura asked.

"Oh! I am sorry. I must be rude staring off into space like this."

"Ashley. Do not spoil the day by being coy with me. I already know the lines."

"You are right, Lady Laura. Truly, I am sorry. Yes, they are just coming out now."

Laura turned to see the men as well. Razon was the shortest in the group, although the tavern master had them all for girth.

"I wonder who the onlooker is?" Laura queried.

Ashley followed her gaze to the stranger. As she looked at him, she sensed a warmth about her thigh. She reached down and readjusted her knife belt. As she did so, she touched each blade as a methodical check Quick had taught her. "Never forget they are there. Learn to feel each as a part of your body," he had instructed.

She found the hilt of the outermost blade warm to the touch. She looked down in curiosity;. It was the new one from Razon. Intrigued at this development, she kept her hand on the hilt, lifting and settling the blade in short, quick, and gentle lifts. She heard voices crossing the way. Looking, she easily found Razon;. He was giving instructions to the group. They were heading towards a side street up and away from her. She watched the others follow Razon. The stranger, straggling behind, seemed to stop and just watch. Ashley found him to be an enigma as he shimmered in the afternoon light. It was like shadows mixing together, not clearly defined yet still present. She closed her eyes to look anew. Just as she opened again, Laura called to her. The shimmering still remained, but a new quest was presented.

"Look at this colorful jersey, Ashley. Feel how soft it is. It has more fibers to the strand, allowing it to be very soft to the touch. This gentleman says it is Angora."

Ashley complied and released her hold of her blade to caress the soft cloth.

"It is beautiful. May I hold it to my face?" Ashley asked, doing so as the merchant nodded yes.

That evening as things quieted down, Razon stood outside Serenten's door, waiting for him to respond to his knock. He heard light footsteps coming. The latch clicked open. Razon stepped back in a momentary surprise.

"Are you all right, Lord Razon?" Cynderet asked, holding the door open.

"Aye, to be sure. You reminded me of someone else—from another time is all."

"Well, it is me 'to be sure'." She emulated, a grin on her face. "Please enter. Serenten will be glad of your company. I am afraid I grow quite tired and keep falling asleep in the chair. I will leave you two in search of my own nest."

"I believe they call them a bed here," a resonating voice said from his own bed. The massive Serenten struggled to sit up to greet Razon.

"It is good to see you again. Help me up so I may sit for a while. This being confined to a bed reminds me of chains yet."

"Good night. Do not keep him talking all night," Cynderet said as she left for her room.

"Good night," the other two answered in chorus.

"So? What was that stumble at the door, Lord Razon? Still afraid of the dark, are you?"

"Serenten, just call me Razon, please. I am a lord of nothing, and you are just as lordly as I, so just Razon please. And as for my little doorway dance step, well, it is that Cynderet reminds me of another so perfectly, except in age. That was a long time ago."

Changing the subject, he added, "It is good she is your caretaker. She is very protective of you."

"My very guardian," Serenten answered, "she is yours also." In answer to Razon's questioning brow, he continued, "It was her ability to find you that allowed Skon and Laura to free us. She is your guardian as well. Your guide-and-girl, so to speak."

Serenten saw a mental connection. Suddenly, he grew quiet, just staring at Razon.

Growing uncomfortable, Razon asked, "What? Why are you staring at me so?"

"Tell me about this 'other' from so long ago. Tell me all about her, Razon."

"I am not sure what your mind is thinking. Perhaps you just need a good story. Aye. I will tell you the tale." Razon went to sit in the chair Cynderet recently vacated. After a short reflective pause, he started, "Well, she was the one I told you I wasted so many years searching for. Skon and I were with some friends in a tavern. We had just returned to the borders of what is now Skon's lands from one of many 'cleansing campaigns' and sought to relax." Razon's face took on a reminiscing glow with a smile tugging at his lips. "We were all just getting settled when the most beautiful woman I have ever seen walked in the room from above. All she did was smile and I was totally captivated by her.

I do not really know what happened from that point, except what Skon tells me. And, as I recall, I told this story to you when we were both chained to the wall in the darkness. It is the same woman."

"Humor me. I have my reasons."

"Humor you I shall then," Razon went on to tell Serenten the whole story of how Skon burst into the room he and the woman shared to find them together in bed. It was still difficult to think of her as actually trying to kill him. Finally, Skon saved his life by killing two reptilian creatures. During the battle, the woman disappeared. "She just vanished, Skon says."

Serenten listened to every word, asking no questions until Razon was done.

"Earlier, when we were still chained, you thought these reptilian creatures Skon fought were of my kind. Were they?"

Razon felt uncomfortable having to answer.

"Oh, come now. Do not hedge on me! They either were or they were not. Which is it?"

"Aye. Blue Skon said they looked just like you."

"Aye. Now we are getting somewhere." Serenten rubbed his hands together in an infrequent show of excitement.

"What? Where? Where are we going?"

"Back into the past," Serenten cut; in not wanting to lose momentum. "This woman, she was not real, was she?"

"She has always been real to me," Razon hedged with his own truth.

"Aye, of course. What does Skon say?"

"He says she changed into a human-sized bat and then vanished."

"And when you saw her, she looked just like Cynderet. Except for the green eyes, right?"

"Well, I think so. It was so long ago."

"Aye," Serenten countered with a hint of mocking, "so long ago that even now all you have to do is close your eyes and 'she is there'," Serenten reminded him of his earlier telling of this tale.

"Aye. Even now," Razon admitted, remembering also.

Serenten changed his tone. He became almost casual, no longer prodding for answers, "Do you know who Cynderet is?"

"Only what I saw when Skon and I found the two of you. And what little we talked about in the dark."

"Who else do you know that has green eyes?"

"Outside of my family, very few. No one around here."

"Cynderet does. I think she got them from her father. Her mother has black eyes."

Rather whimsically, Razon joined, "So did the other woman."

"Interesting—that." Serenten waited.

Razon took a while to realize Serenten was not smiling.

"What is it you are saying, Serenten? I grow tired of this game."

"When we were in the dungeon, the 'Darkness', as you call it, we were visited by two of the highest members of that plane's society. They came to question us. You were still unconscious, so they questioned me about where Cynderet was. I did not answer.

"As a result, I was beaten by one of them with more magical bolts. One of them, these Eldresses, recognized you. Just as I began to lose consciousness, she said something very interesting about you. I had forgotten all about it until you mentioned my 'guardian'."

Serenten looked sternly at Razon. He wanted to make sure Razon heard what he said, "This Eldress turned to her companion and asked, 'Do you know who this human is?' The other said, 'No.' Then she, the first one, said, 'He is Cynderet's father…'"

Razon sat back in his chair. After a long pause, he said, "You are not making this up; are you? We have not known each other long, but it is as if we had been friends forever. Please assure me, you are not making this up."

"My Friend, I feel the same bond about you. And my oath is to Cynderet. I am not making this up. The Eldress said you are Cynderet's father."

"Who was this 'Eldress' that she would know me?" Razon asked, actually afraid of the answer.

"Luanta, the second highest of the Society. The same one I defended against you and Lord Skon years ago. She is Cynderet's mother—your lover from the tavern so long ago."

Razon just stared at the wall beyond Serenten.

Serenten could not read his thoughts, but the confusion and uncertainty were both plain in his look.

After a period of several quiet minutes, Serenten said, "Think about it, Razon. The Ring of Radiant has only done its magic of healing twice you said: Once for you, and once for Cynderet. Further, she should not be able to Energy Web, that is travel from the Shadow Plane by magic, or in her case, by mind only. Yet to you, she has done it twice. Never to another. No, she has done it three times counting her first dream of you helping the children. All these things between you two—like family."

"That was her in the forest there? I had forgotten," Razon said, remembering more. "I only saw her eyes, green they were. I felt strong kinship for whoever was there. When Skon and I joined you in the glade, her eyes were closed. I knew they would be green."

Razon asked Serenten, "What does this all mean? What do I do now?"

"It means your search is over, for one thing. Lord Skon is right about Luanta. Cynderet's mother is beyond saving. In a way, you have saved Cynderet, your daughter, instead. She is not like the rest of them."

"Skon says she came here with a message to save Skon's Hall. She was instrumental in helping us escape from the Darkness. If what you say is true about her mother, Cynderet and I are a much better family match, to be sure."

"Aye, to be sure. Cynderet's temperament is more like yours. As is her sense of duty."

"Aye. This is going to take some thinking. Please do not speak of this to anyone as yet. There is so much to put into place. I go to my own room to think this out."

"Wait not too long," Serenten said, thinking of Cynderet. Then he remembered where he was. "Besides, I need company now also. I am freed of chains, only to find confinement in a bed." Extending a theatric reach to Razon, Serenten raised himself up on the other arm, "Oh! Save me too, Lord Razon!"

Razon gave his characteristic shake of head. And, in a chuckling stupor, stumbled to the door and out, saying over a shoulder, "Aye. Chains and the dark do strange things to us all, aye?"

Ashley found Lady Laura having a conversation with a woman she recognized as the cook. As she drew closer, she felt the warming of her thigh again. She did not respond immediately as the two ladies looked to her.

Lady Laura greeted her while the other quickly turned away and left. The warmth at Ashley's thigh became uncomfortable as she returned the greeting. She reached down and found the gift blade hot to the touch. She disengaged it from the holster belt. As she put the knife and its sheath into her jersey pocket, she noted the cook seemed to shimmer as she walked away into the kitchen.

"What is all that about?" Lady Laura asked.

"Nothing. The new blade gets uncomfortable sometimes. Have you seen Patrick?"

"The last I saw of Patrick was when Landsfall left for the training chamber. I am afraid Landsfall has found a shadow."

"I am glad. Landsfall seems like a wonderful person. You and Lord Skon have some fine friends."

"Yes, we do."

"Where are you going now?"

"I thought I would check in on Cynderet. I was going to take her a little meal. She must be hungry and tired caring for Serenten as she does."

"I will join you, if I may. She said Serenten took special care of her on several occasions. It is the least she can do. I will put a plate together for Serenten as well. I wonder what he likes?"

"If he is like any of the other men here, he will eat almost anything."

Once the plates where fixed, the two went to Serenten's room, thinking to find Cynderet there. As they went past Razon's room, they could hear the footfalls of pacing.

"It is a man's thing," Laura said to Ashley's questioning look. "Lord Skon does it whenever he has trouble putting thoughts together. Razon has a lot on his mind as well, I think."

"And I am afraid I have not helped him much," Ashley said in a humbled hush.

"Well, let us shake off our somber thoughts. Here we are."

The two knocked and were asked in.

CHAPTER TWENTY TWO

Berenice had no trouble subduing the cook woman. She found the unexpected meeting with Laura an exciting interplay to her real purpose. If it had gone wrong, the lady would have died. Then the girl arrived;. It was time Berenice got about her business. She could fool one in a superficial conversation; two was risky—not to herself. It was just harder to hide two bodies before others came—there was not a lot of room left in the salt meat barrel.

Berenice sniffed the air, having been in Razon's company earlier in the day helped tremendously. She had an idea of how he moved, what his stature was, and his fitness level: and his smell. She could find any living creature within a hundred feet just by smell. Her mount could do the same within a quarter mile. Her fashioner had dedicated much time and power to her creation. She knew her skills well. There was no hindering problem with a memory of what life was like before her crystalline being.

She located Razon's scent. He was up-stairs in the guest wing. She walked boldly as she had seen the cook do while being stalked. She entered the wing seeing no one. *This will only take a moment,* she thought. It was time to move quietly.

Berenice was outside Razon's door without a sound. She listened to the sound of his pacing within. She could tell by his pace he was agitated; that would make her work so much easier—he would be preoccupied and totally unsuspecting—until too late.

She knocked on the door. There was an impatient response. "I am the cook, Lord Razon. Lady Laura asked me to fix you a plate, thinking you may yet be hungry," she replied.

"I will be there in a moment."

Berenice heard a shuffling inside of weaponry being moved from the table to the bed. She could tell by the soft pat as it landed on the bed, he was unarmed. She smiled to herself.

Razon reached the door. *Mayhap, she will have a little wine as well,* he hoped. It only took an instant to open the door wide, allowing the cook in with her tray of food.

There was no tray.

Razon looked to the cook's face with his own question and saw, instead, killing eyes. His weapons training allowed him to see a full circle of peripheral vision. He saw the cook's hand, coming from her waist, transform into a stiletto blade. Razon lost only a second before slamming the door on the arm of the blade. The door bounced back from its frame. Somehow, the arm did not give as flesh would. He did not feel the blade pierce his side. Razon shoved the door closed again, this time, locking it against the arm with his body. He wedged his foot at the base of the door to further secure it. Desperately, he reached for his sword on the bed. It was too far!

Suddenly, there was a crash of a fist against the middle of the door. The door planks gave way. Razon felt the splinters jab his skin. He tried to dodge while trying to hold the door closed. He felt the second piercing of a blade into his rib cage.

The door shattered with the next blow. The cook grabbed Razon around his neck and drew him into the hallway. Razon felt helpless against the immense strength of the cook-now-creature. His feet slipped from under him in his own blood. It bought him a precious moment.

Laura and Ashley were told Cynderet had gone to her room. They left Serenten to his food and headed for Cynderet's room. They were just reaching the end of the hallway when they heard a crashing sound of a blow against wood. They gave each other quick, questioning looks when a second blow sounded louder than the first and an aftersound of wood giving way. Laura dropped her tray on a hall table and, drawing her long sword, took off at a run. "Get help!" she called behind her to Ashley.

"Who? Where?" Ashley called after her. Uncertain of her location or the nearest help, Ashley decisively ran after Laura.

Laura stopped just around the corner of the adjoining hallway. She tried frantically to decipher what she saw. The cook seemed to be wrestling with Razon. It did not make sense.

In the instant it took to determine Razon's danger, Ashley was there. She saw the cook drag Razon from his room through a destroyed door. "Not the cook?" she said, questioning what she saw. Her side felt on fire.

Preoccupied, she brushed at the irritation. The burning grew more intense, forcing her to reflexively reach for the source of her irritation. It was in her deep skirt pocket. The knife hilt slipped into her hand as if of its own power—the burning pain was gone. Simultaneously, the cook's image dissipated before her eyes to reform as an opaque blackness in the shape of a human. Razon was being attacked!

Ashley reacted without hesitation. The impetus to her arm and coordination were as never before. She had no thought but to kill Razon's assailant. The blade was cool and exacting in its purpose. It felt alive as it left with the power of her arm's under-sided heave and ending flick of the wrist. The motion was fluid. Ashley knew her control was different this time—it was perfect in technique.

In slow motion, she watched Razon impaled a third time by the creature. He tried to twist, avoiding a deathblow. As he did so, the creature turned with him, exposing its back and side to the precise passage of Ashley's knife through the air. It slid deeply into the creature's body, slightly above the midribs of its back. The blade was sideways and to the left of its backbone just as Quick had taught her.

What happened next imprinted itself in her mind forever. Bright colors of light flashed wildly; in the colorful silhouette, the creature screamed. Its limbs flew from its hold of Razon. The creature began to turn to find its assailant. Its blackness went white as it exploded into fine powder. The rainbow of colors turned pastel in the whiteness of the dust. Razon slipped downward, his head doing a slight second bounce as it hit the stone floor.

Laura was just getting to him with her drawn sword ready for a strike at the creature. She covered her eyes from the explosion of light and dust.

Ashley stood spell-bound as her knife clattered to the floor.

Laura slid to a stop on her knees at Razon's side. Her sword followed beside her on the stone floor. Her lips mouthed unspoken words. She looked Razon over quickly, noting his clothing consisting of britches and cotton shirt only. She tore the shirt away from his body, exposing his wounds. Taking bandages from a small cabinet suddenly appearing, floating in the air at her side, she began administering to the wounds.

"Once again, you must tend my wounds, Laura. I am glad you came when you did," Razon mumbled as he passed out.

"Aye, my friend, but never for such wounds as these."

Laura withdrew a tiny earthen vial and removed the cork. Using her fingers as a swab, she dabbed the liquid on his lips, allowing the dribbles to flow into his mouth, activating his natural swallowing reflex.

Shock shuddered through Ashley's being; an imploding blackness stole her vision away. She was powerless against the feeling of her legs giving way and her crumpling gently to the floor. A name came to her mind and she spoke it just as all coherence faded away.

Laura did not see Ashley faint and fall. She did not see the knife disappear. She did not know how it was once again in its sheath in Ashley's pocket. Neither could tell how it came to be that the oval medallion with a wedge missing was now replaced by the form of a familiar oak tree.

Ashley awoke with her head in Cynderet's lap. Serenten was standing above her with a strange pole weapon in his powerful arms. She had never seen him before. Only from Laura's description did she recognize him. She rolled her head to see Razon. He was still on the ground outside his room. Laura was kneeling beside him, anxiously working on his wounds.

Skon came running into the wing, followed by Elfgon and Landsfall. There was a moment's tension as the two newcomers challenged Serenten.

"No!" Laura hollered. "That is Serenten. The attacker is dead."

Elfgon gave an amused smile, "My humblest apologies, sir. I will ask your forgiveness later."

Landsfall had no chance to do anything as Elfgon grabbed his sword arm.

"Let us check the rest of the Hall and warn Hamilton!"

"What be it we seek?" Landsfall managed.

"Demons, my friend, big fat demons," Elfgon answered, discerning the work of demons with the accuracy of his Elfin heritage. He dragged Landsfall back down the hall.

Ashley tried to get up. Cynderet put a comforting palm on her shoulder and suggested she remain lying down a moment longer.

"You will be well," she said. "Allow yourself time to adjust to what has happened. Once again, you have been of strong heart in face of danger."

"What about Lord Razon? Is he, is he…?" she could not form the words.

"He is not dead. He is badly hurt. Lady Laura has been caring for him. Lord Skon is there now also, so is Lady Laura's little friend."

"Who?"

"Lady Laura's little companion of magic. His name is Missive."

"I do not think I know him."

"Well, you rest now. He will wait until later." Cynderet turned to Serenten standing close by. "Serenten, help me get Ashley to my room. We will do better watching out for each other there."

*****

Luanta returned to Everard's mountain hideout from her visit with Ermentrude. She purposely arrived just outside the canyon entrance, allowing her a moment to examine her small army. She felt things were finally falling into place. It was time to get things started. She felt confident and hungry for an end to Blue Skon. She could not help smiling, knowing the Ring of Radiant was safely in the Senior Eldress' hands. It meant the end was near and with Everard's bandits and the power of the Lord Wherant in her black bag, the goodly folks at Skon's Hall were doomed. Her smile grew; she called Everard and his lieutenants into the cottage. "Now it is my turn!" she congratulated herself as she entered the cottage door.

Strike sat in his corner. The waning afternoon sun shone outside. His corner was darkened in shadow. "You are planning to attack the human," he said without preface. "Has Berenice returned with the Ring of Radiant?"

"No. I have not seen her," Luanta answered testily.

"Then why is it I sense you will be forging ahead with this plan of destruction without it?"

Luanta understood enough of his ability to read her to know if she just answered his questions as given and did not dwell on the ring itself, he would not know she already had it.

"I am tired of waiting. It is taking too long!" she allowed her voice to rise, hoping she could bait him. It worked.

"You fool! The mission will fail without the ring. I must have it and return to my lord before you open the box!" Strike struggled to get down from the shelf: his body sedentary after three days of sitting. "The Ring of Radiant has powers you do not understand. If not away from the family members of the Hall of Radiant, it will neutralize the power of the box!" Strike stared at Luanta, trying to drive home the point.

"Then go get it!" Luanta screamed at him, enjoying the venting of her hate for him. Through clenched teeth, she continued, "Go help Berenice get it from the Lord Razon, because as soon as my troops are readied, I am going to open the box and destroy all those that hold me back!"

Strike did not respond immediately. Instead, his head slowly rocked from shoulder to shoulder as one would to stretch tight muscles. He sensed something was wrong. "There is something going on here. It is not like you to show such bravado, Eldress." Strike studied her now bland face.

Unable to read it, he added, "Whatever it is, know this: if the Lord Wherant does not have the Ring of Radiant when all is done, he will hunt you down. When he finds you, you will never see light again. And if the ring is still at Skon's Hall when you do open that box, there will be a fire display as you have never seen in the clash of Light and Darkness."

Luanta struggled to maintain an uncaring demeanor on the outside. It took great effort. She was sure Strike spoke truth.

Strike finally gave up his efforts to warn her. "It is unfortunate such hopes are placed upon the weak-minded," he said, shuffling his first step towards the door. His body was slow to move at first. With his second step, he moved a little easier.

He was just getting to the door when Everard came in. His three lieutenants were filing in behind him. Everard dodged the stone gargoyle. The others were not able, all four ended up scattered to the floor in disarray.

Strike exploded in rage and threw the other three off him like an erupting magma vent. The men went flying. Strike centered his bulk in an effort to get back up.

"Nice power display," Luanta taunted at him as he finally reached the door alone.

"It was nothing compared to what you will see if you fail to heed my words, Eldress," he hissed.

"Where is the Rock going?" Everard asked, helping his men up.

"On a treasure hunt. Shall we get started with our own?"

*****

Serenten was returning to Razon's room after seeing the girls to Cynderet's. He felt their decision to share the same room for company and mutual care was a good one. Ashley had been pleased, knowing Cynderet would be with her. Ashley's last concern had been for Razon. "Please let me know how he is doing. Tell him I am sorry I have treated him so badly of late." She slipped into sleep shortly after Serenten's assurance he would.

What remained of Razon's door was just being carted off by two guards when Serenten arrived. The white powder lay on the stone floor and traced their steps away. He was not comforted by what he saw and heard as he looked into the room.

"I have never seen such wounds before, Skon," Laura stressed as she continued to dab at the seeping blood from the two chest wounds. "I can only slow the bleeding, not stop it. And he has a punctured lung."

"That creature knew exactly what it was doing," Skon replied, helping her as needed.

"I do not think these are just puncture wounds," she said, shaking her head in frustration. "There seems to be something else in there.

See how the redness of the skin continues to grow? It acts like a poison or a rapid infection."

"The creature did not attack Lord Razon by accident," Serenten said, leaning in the doorway. His weapon gripped in one hand. "He was its target all along. Interesting, that; given it is Lord Blue Skon who is meant to be destroyed according to what Cynderet and I were told."

"Pleasant thought, that," Skon said sarcastically.

"Aye. But why the Lord Razon?"

"I do not know. He is only our guest here. He must be of importance to someone else."

"What of his being heir to the Light Forest?" a small man floating in the air above Razon asked.

Serenten gave a small jerk of alarm at the new voice. Missive was hidden from Serenten's view by Laura as she worked. "Be at peace, our scaled giant. It is only little and old me," Missive said by send.

"Ah, yes, the Gate Keeper. What is this of the Light Forest?" Serenten sent back.

"Lord Razon is more than a lord. We just call him that here for his protection. Some would get upset if they knew a crown prince from outside the Six Realm Alliance was here semi-permanently. Few know he is actually heir to the Light Forest, far to the northeast."

"He mentioned a duty and a charge, but not what it was."

"Now you know." Missive floated higher above Laura's head to see everyone, and to be seen of them. He took his time fluffing the pillow he was floating on. His action drew everyone's attention as he intended. Only Laura ignored him, now dabbing at Razon's lighter wound.

Feeling ready for center stage, Missive turned around ceremoniously and asked aloud, "Would you like to know more?"

"What?" Skon asked, confused at the open, unexpected question.

"Pardon me, oh, Unknowing One," Missive cast over his shoulder. "I was about to explain a possible reason for demons to want Lord Razon dead.”

“What? You know something and have not told us? How kind of you to keep us ignorant instead of insuring we protect him from this!” Skon said testily.

“I could not even have foreseen this, Lord of the Manor!”

“Stop it, you two!” Laura chastised. “Missive, get to the point—now!”

“Aye, milady,” Missive complied, mimicking Skon’s endearment for her. “As I was saying, Lord, no, Prince Razon will be King of the Light Forest one day. King of a realm much older than any of the Six Realms by many hundreds of years.”

“So?”

“Its history predates the driving of demons from our earth.”

“You mean Lord Razon is the reason the Wherants are aiding my mother?” Cynderet asked, having come to the door unseen and unheard.

“Aye, young lady. That is my sight of things. What is yours?”

“My sight is ignorance, Man of Magic. However, I have come to say there is another being without Skon’s Hall. I felt of its anger. It is looking for the creature, now dead, by sending thoughts.”

“How is it you know this, and I do not?” a suddenly cocky Missive asked, arms akimbo. He began to feel threatened by a possible flaw.

“I know not. There is a being though.” She turned to look at Serenten. “It is using thoughts as those of the Table, Serenten. I am sure of it. No other thing I have ever sensed is as vile.”

“Get Captain Hamilton out there with troops,” Skon ordered. “Tell Elfgon and Landsfall also. Have them meet me at the main gate. I will join you as soon as I hear of some possible location.”

“Aye,” a voice from the corner of the room said. Quick stepped into visibility from the dim shadows. He nodded to a surprised Cynderet and Serenten as he left the room. “Beware, you two. They may seek you also,” he warned as he disappeared down the hall.

“There are living things coming from all kinds of places in this Hall!” Serenten said, watching Quick disappear. He turned to Cynderet, saying, “He is right, Cynderet. Let us go to your room. Lady Laura, may I suggest you allow me to carry Razon, and that you follow us there as well?”

“Aye. It is a good place for you, milady,” Skon agreed. “Know you where this creature might be?” he asked Cynderet.

“I do not. I am unable to tell more than that it is close and outside the walls. Its message is calling this crystalline form to it, not knowing where the form is within the hall."

"How is it this, this child, should know these things and not I!" the little man cried, his pillow floating in tight circles, matching his anxiety.

"Well, Fire Fly, we all have room within which to grow," Skon threw out, unable to let go of an opportunity to drill his magical nemesis.

"To the quick, that one hit, Skon of the Manor!" Missive acquiesced.

Skon laughed out loud, rushing from the room. "I grow to like Cynderet more each day!"

CHAPTER TWENTY THREE

Patrick and Ryan heard Quick's question of Captain Hamilton, "Have you seen Elfgon and Landsfall?"

"Only a moment ago. They were headed towards the training chamber."

"Good. I will catch up with them there. Lord Skon has requested you take Hall Guards out the gates and look for any signs of potential enemies. Lord Razon has been attacked. The assailant is dead by the quick actions of the Lady Ashley, but there appears to be at least one other and he, or it, is outside the Hall."

"Aye. I will be out the gates in two minutes. I have a patrol standing ready as we speak."

"Aye. Be careful. These may look human and are not."

Ryan looked to Patrick. "Come on! Let us follow Quick."

Without hesitation, Patrick joined strides with Ryan running for the training chamber.

The boys were at Quick's side when they reached Elfgon and Landsfall. Quick gave Skon's instructions to the men.

"What about us?" Ryan asked angrily. "Is my father to leave me behind again?"

"You shall come with me, Ryan," Quick answered. "Elfgon, inform Skon that Ryan and I stay within to help ensure no others are within the hall proper."

"Aye, and Patrick, you come with us," Elfgon added.

"Why do we stay inside? I thought you said the enemy was without the Hall?" Ryan queried testily.

"Ryan, these are not bales of straw or friends sparing. There is one of us lying hurt beyond your mother's ken to heal. He was attacked within the very walls. Think, Master Ryan, if all blades are without, who will ensure the safety of those within?"

"Aye, Quick. I see the way of it," Ryan acquiesced still unsure, yet seeing the wisdom of Quick's thinking.

"Well, I be ready!" Patrick joined in. He pulled his sling from its belt pouch. "Be it within or without."

"For you, it is without. Be ye at me side and careful, Squire Patrick," Landsfall said.

"Come then, let us be at our places," Elfgon said, ending the chatter. "We go to meet Skon at the gates."

"Our place is to the roof first. We will work our way down," Quick added, taking Ryan with him at a jog to the first tower's stairwell.

Quick and Ryan found the first forward tower untroubled. The guards there had seen nothing. Quick told them of the attack on Razon and encouraged them to stay wary; they then proceeded along the catwalk to the second forward tower.

Ryan was about to hail the tower guards when Quick signaled him silent. Quick pointed to his nose. Ryan was not sure what he meant but held his tongue. Quick lifted his nose high and sniffed. Ryan watched. He was sniffing for something. Ryan recognized the almost panting appearance of Quick's chest contractions.

Quick pointed to his nose again and then to Ryan. Ryan took a deep breath, nothing. He tried the panting action with small quick breathes in rapid succession. Was something there? Did he smell an almost metallic scent, very faint? Ryan tried it again. Yes, there was something. He nodded his head to Quick.

Again, he was told to remain quiet. Quick put his ear to the wall of the tower. He waited like that a long time. Ryan asked in sign if he heard anything. Quick was not sure, maybe. Quick drew his short sword. He slipped to the edge of the tower access hidden in deep shadow. Only the torch of the far wall gave any light here. Quick signaled Ryan to wait a ten-second count before following him. Drawing his dagger as well, he disappeared into the shadows of the tower.

Ryan did his slow ten-count. His heart pounded in his chest, believing if any were close, his heart would be audible to them. Reaching ten, he took a deep breath and held it a moment. Exhaling slowly, he slipped as quietly as he could into the tower access.

He stopped just inside the wall in an effort to imitate Quick's actions of the shadows. Standing perfectly still, he tried to listen. All he could hear was his own breathing and the beats of his heart seeming to pound within his ears. He could not see Quick anywhere.

Ryan entered the tower proper;. Here, the heavy smell was much stronger. It was heady with an almost sweetness to it. Ryan looked again to find Quick. The light of the torch flickered off the wall to his right. The center portion of the wall was blocked from view by the weaponry though the flickering light was present again on the far side. What was lying in the deep shadow at the weapon's base? It looked like large lumps of something connected together. Ryan hunched down into the cover of the shadow. He almost crawled. The smell continued to grow. It seemed so familiar. He raked his brain, trying to remember when or what he had known before to smell that way. Just as he was in position to reach down and touch the deeper shadow, the wind picked up, intensifying the light of the torch slightly. There was a glint on the ground beside the shadow. Ryan was positive it was a sword lying close to the mass. This time, looking into the shadow again, he could make out the form of a body. He touched the confusing sister shadow and found it to be flat to the ground. It felt sticky. He knew what it was and why it was so familiar. It was the same as when slitting the throat of a deer to let it bleed after the hunt.

Ryan looked closer. If it was a man, why did it not look like one? He touched the hump he felt sure was a shoulder; it was. Suddenly, he felt sick as understanding sank in. It was the body of a man—only the head was missing. Ryan was too sick to move.

He rested his back against the stout framework of the tower ballista. He forgot all about Quick and whatever it was they were looking for. All he sought was self-control to keep from vomiting.

He did not see the smooth onslaught of a shadow. The torchlight caught it only for a second. Ryan felt the beading sweat on his forehead and upper lip cool in the faint breeze. He lifted his head to relish its refreshing effect. With closed eyes, he allowed its balming effect to ease his distress. The breeze turned suddenly warm and fetid.

He opened his eyes.

The pair of eyes before and above him blinked. There was a slithering sound as something wet touched either cheek. Ryan was petrified. He did not even breathe. The creature's spilt tongue had tasted his warmth and knew him as flesh. Ryan watched helplessly as it reared up its serpentine head and lunged down to engulf Ryan's head in its mouth. Ryan felt his bladder give.

A second shadow slipped within the distance between Ryan's head and the striking serpent. It was as water between stones, a double glint that repeated itself so fast Ryan thought it was one continuous gleam of the creature's teeth striking him dead.

"Ryan. Ryan, it is done now. Wake up…Ryan."

Ryan could hear his name being called. He felt the splash of cold wet on his face. He felt his body being lifted in one fluid motion from the ground to someone's shoulder.

"What?" he groaned, as the air was partially driven from his lungs in the landing on the supporting shoulder. It was bony yet so strong.

He felt himself lowered again to the ground.

"Good! You are waking up. We almost lost you," a now familiar voice said.

"Quick?" Ryan asked. "What happened?"

"You were about to be this flying snake's second meal of the night," Quick said. "Except he got a sudden case of permanent indigestion. His neck got cut."

Ryan tried to see into the shadow. There were so many bumps and humps in the shadows it was hard to distinguish anything clearly.

"Here, look in the light of the torch," Quick said as he grasped up a torch he had brought prior to trying to wake Ryan up.

Illuminated was a winged serpent the size of a horse. Its long tail virtually surrounded the forward portion of the ballista framework. Its head was at a weird angle to its body. Quick reached out and hefted the head up slightly. It was only attached to the body by the muscles behind what was once its throat and neck.

"I be thinking it will make a great wall mount for your room, aye?"

"I thought I died," Ryan said instead. "Is everyone else dead?"

"Aye. This poor guy lost his head in a bite attack. The other two were torn to pieces by the creature's front claws."

Ryan had only taken a cursory look of the creature. Looking now, he noted that just under the wings were two spindly arms with wicked claws. "I have never seen nor heard of such a creature as this snake!"

"Aye," Quick agreed, looking askance at the creature again. "I be thinking its place is not of this earth," turning back to Ryan, he continued, "Come, let us get you back into the hall proper."

"Before we go seeking out my father, please allow me to keep my pride and get me to my room lest anyone else be privy to my cowardice."

"Aye, Ryan. We would not want any to see the dampness of your britches. Come, I will scout the way before you."

*****

Strike stood in the shadows outside the walls of Skon's Hall. His mental call to Berenice was for several minutes. There had only been silence in return. He knew she was gone;. She would have answered his call by now if she were still here. Then he heard the mental death scream of her second half, her mount. It was for sure, she was dead then.

"What a waste of fine craftsmanship," he bemoaned. His lord had wasted a precious gift on Luanta. His moment of reflection was cut short by the sound of horses rounding the outer wall of Skon's Hall.

Horses—he hated horses. Somehow, they could smell him. He slunk to the wall itself. It was of granite blocks. *A fine stone material,* Strike reflected as he melded himself into the wall itself.

The mounted troops rode by, blind to his presence. A couple of horses did a quick jitter-step as they passed him by. The riders did not read the warning.

Strike, remaining a part of the wall, angrily contemplated his plight having to depend on Luanta to get him out of this plane. And yet horses are more astute than these pathetic humans. *How is it such ignorant life forms were able to seal off the Wherants' sole access to this plane so many centuries before?* he pondered. *With Berenice gone, it now falls to me to get the Ring of Radiant. This will take some doing.* He considered his options and the possibilities of getting inside. *I will wait and watch. There is still a little time. It will take Luanta at least a day to get ready and here.* Strike settled into the wall and waited, appearing as nothing but a part of the wall.

*****

Skon joined Elfgon and Landsfall, rushing from his brief warning from Cynderet. "Where is Quick?' he asked as he surveyed the group.

"He and Ryan will be staying within the Hall. They headed to the towers a few moments ago," Elfgon answered.

"We be hav'n Squire Patrick with us," Landsfall added.

"So be it," Skon finished a little more tersely than he intended. Things were now happening. Things he did not understand nor really know how to handle—demons. "Why demons?" he asked himself again, not for the last time.

"Hamilton is without the walls with a troop of mounted men," Landsfall continued. "They be circling the hall to the left of the gates."

"We shall precede the opposing direction starting out twenty paces from the base of the wall. Then with each circling, branch out into larger and larger rounds about the hall until we reach the orchards just outside the village," Skon instructed. "Elfgon, take the front with me. Landsfall, take the outside flank,

193

and Patrick, you stay behind Landsfall ten paces. Have your sling readied and use those sharp eyes I have been informed of." Skon drew his sword. "Let us go."

"He is not going to make it through this, is he?" Cynderet asked.

Laura looked down into Razon's stuporous eyes. He continued in the moaning he had started shortly after being placed on Cynderet's bed.

Ashley dutifully applied the damp cloth to his forehead in an effort to keep him cool.

Laura looked to Cynderet. "It does not look good for him. I cannot stop the poison from penetrating his entire body. Soon, it will have affected his vital organs, and then there will be nothing we can do."

"This is the work of Demon vileness. Not only was he attacked, but once injured, poison was introduced to ensure the kill," Missive said, still floating on his pillow. "Without a power as great or greater than their magic, he will die for sure."

"What of the Ring of Radiant?" Serenten asked from his protective position guarding the door to the room. "I have witnessed it heal Cynderet after an attack by evil magic."

Missive was thoughtful a moment before answering, "The Ring of Radiant has powers none of us understand. Its history is long before our time. Its healing powers for the House of Radiant are most wondrous. It would work against this for sure."

"Where is the ring?" Cynderet asked, thinking she had a good idea.

"Razon has been without the ring since our capture by the Eldresses. I fear it is now in the hands of Luanta. She made us a visit while we were in the dungeon of Council Peak," Serenten answered. "I am thinking it all has to do with the pact she formed with the Wherants."

"The Wherants?" a quiet Ashley asked. "Who are they?"

"They, Child, are the Lords of the Plane of Darkness. They are inter-plane traders who traffic in the souls of living creatures for slavery, or worse," Missive responded.

"A 'worse' being that creature which attacked Razon?" Cynderet asked.

"Aye. That would be one of their creations," Missive agreed. "The Wherants are demons for sure."

"Why the Demons?" Laura asked. "Why are the Demons involved in this at all? Skon's Hall is of no importance to them."

"In this, you are right, milady," Missive answered. "Yet in this, I be thinking we are not seeing the whole plan. The Eldress Luanta seeks the destruction of Skon's Hall as her vendetta." Missive thought for a moment longer then added, "The Wherants care not about the hall. It is Lord Razon they want…" He stopped short as a thought came to mind. "No. It is not Lord Razon they want. His death is only assurance of their real purpose. They want the Ring of Radiant. They want its power under their control."

"Did you know there is a second ring?" Missive looked at his listeners. "Well, actually a first? This ring of Lord Razon's is the second. The first is worn by the King of the Light Forest. Lord Razon's is its mate to be worn by the Crown Prince or Princess."

Missive continued as things began to fit into place with his knowledge of magic's history during his lifetime, "The rings represent the power that originally drove the Wherants from this earth. The House of Radiant is the Keeper of the Lions of Light, men and women of grand strength and magic who overpowered the demons and drove them out. The rings have magic to counteract the magic of the Wherants."

"Is that the 'charge' Lord Razon spoke of?" Serenten asked. "He knew there was a duty of his home, but did not know what it was."

"Aye. That be my sight of it."

"Then we have little chance of stopping my mother." Cynderet spoke her thoughts aloud. "She is doing their bidding all in the purpose of her hateful revenge."

"Aye, my Enlightened One. Without the Ring of Radiant, Razon will die, and we will succumb to the powers the Wherants have gifted her to ensure her victory. If they sought to make sure of Lord Razon's death, they will be equally sure your mother is successful in her objective. For the Wherants, all these things are connected. After that, well, they will only need to acquire the Master Ring of Radiant to allow their return to the Earth freely."

Quick and Ryan were making their second full check of Skon's Hall when they heard voices from the gates.

"My father returns with Elfgon and Landsfall."

"Aye. Let us be joining them and learn what has happened."

The two rushed down the stairs and out into the front open area at the gates. Captain Hamilton and his troops were just arriving also.

"Hale, Quick and Ryan," Elfgon said.

"What did you find?" Ryan asked impatiently.

"Nothing. Whatever was out there is gone now. We found nothing between here and the village."

"Aye. And we found nothing unusual in the village or beyond," Hamilton added.

"Well, Cynderet was not mistaken. We found and killed a serpent creature alien to anything I ever saw before," Quick interjected. Turning to Skon, he added, "We lost three more soldiers, those in the right tower. I took the liberty of having another guard posted to replace them."

Hamilton cursed, "That means we be down seven and with four more wounded counting Lord Razon. We be down a full quarter of our forces!"

"My men are still in the village. That will be ten. They will be aiding the local citizens unless you want them here, Skon?"

"Nay. They will do well in the village." Turning to Hamilton, Skon said, "Take your three best leaders and have them call up the local militia. It will be best we man the village walls. Have the gate guards doubled as well. With the village militia and local guards, we will have an added fifty to our number."

"Counting us, we be near a full one hundred blades," Hamilton counted. "I be about your orders now."

"Landsfall?"

"Aye, Blue Skon?"

"You are the best eyes and knowing the lay of the land. Go out as our forward lookout. Take whom you will and watch. I am asking you."

"Aye, Skon. I be taking the young squire here, Patrick. His eyes be good, and he knows how ta see change in nature's ways."

"It will be dangerous, Patrick," Skon said to him with a hand on his shoulder. "But I am thinking you will do well, and there is none better than Landsfall Far to be in the land with."

"Aye, Lord Skon. It be me lik'n ta go."

"And I will be joining my own," Elfgon said.

"So be it."

CHAPTER TWENTY FOUR

Cynderet sat in a chair idly picking at the food on the table before her. She sat alone. Lady Laura remained with Lord Razon and with Missive floating above them in large circles on his pillow. At some point, he had curled up and fallen to sleep. Ashley was in her room, and Serenten had taken his pole weapon with him to join Skon in patrolling the outer hall defenses. His ability to see in the darkness aided everyone's watchfulness.

Cynderet kept rehearsing in her mind the previous conversation with Missive and Laura about the Ring of Radiant and the demons. She also remembered how sad and torn Lord Razon was inside.

Just before leaving the room, Cynderet had entered his mind for the first time. What she found there was heartbreaking.

Somehow, the demon's attack had injected a poison into his mind and heart. It played upon his own perceived weaknesses and enlarged them to where they literally tore him apart. Over and over, he kept thinking how he had failed his father. His losing the Ring of Radiant meant disaster.

Cynderet did not understand everything he was thinking. She did understand that his feelings of guilt were tormented further by dreams of demons overrunning the earth. They were abducting human spirits into their realm of darkness. Finally she left his mind, unable to find a way to help him.

Now she sat alone at the table in the great hall. She closed her eyes and mentally sat in her usual cross-legged fashion in the Foyer of Doors before Reht's portal. She was going through the entire ordeal again when she felt Reht sit down beside her.

"Little One, you study the words and dreams so closely. What do they really mean?"

"I do not understand your question, Reht," she answered, a bit of a frown forming at the junction of nose and brow. "What I do know is Lord Razon is going to die. All these people will die. My mother will see to that."

"Aye. She will. What will you do?"

"I feel I have to do something, but what?" She looked at Reht beside her. "What can I do?"

Reht remained casual and quiet, waiting for her to continue.

"I would stop my mother from hurting these people if I could. I would try, anyway. Only I do not know how, or even where, my mother is."

Cynderet thought for a moment, putting together what she did know of her mother's last whereabouts. "Serenten said she had returned home. She had even seen him in the dungeon below Council Peak only to leave him there. I dare not go back home. If it had not been for these good people, the Table would have me dead now."

"Little One, I think the Table will soon be met. You are right. It is your mother you need to find, or more fully, the Ring of Radiant. The ring is as the Little Wise Man says. How would you find it?"

"The first question has to be, does my mother have it?"

"How would you answer that?"

"I would have to go to her. If only I knew where she was."

"I believe you are fully capable of determining that."

"How?" Cynderet looked Reht's direction curiously, not sure he understood what she had said before.

Perfectly poised and patient, Reht quietly answered her unspoken question, "Think, Little One. She is your mother. You found Lord Razon several times. How much easier your own mother?"

Cynderet felt hope glimmer in her heart as she realized Reht was right. She had found Lord Razon by starting where she last knew him to be and then followed his activities from there. She could do the same for her mother. She would start at home. If she went there only mentally, the Table may not have power over her;. It may not even know she was there. "I have no way of knowing how long it will take. In my mind's search, I will still be here. When I find my mother, I will have to meet her in person. I will be gone from here."

"Send word to Serenten. He is here in the Hall with Lord Skon even now."

Cynderet nodded her agreement and immediately sent the message to Serenten of what she was doing.

"I will go with you," he answered without hesitation.

"He cannot," Reht said. "You have not the power of the Energy Feeders to gate him with you. It is a spell of magic. Your power is of yourself, your being. Perhaps when you are fully grown and have reached your full power, but not now."

"Serenten, I cannot take you with me. Besides, you are needed here. You are the only one I know of who can see through the darkness of the demons."

"Aye. I hear Reht's wisdom in your voice of counsel. Be careful, Child.

Your mother will not be turned from her course. That, I know surely." Serenten paused, thinking, "Once you are gone from Skon's Hall, none will have a way to find you. You must find your own way back."

"I understand."

"Then go."

Cynderet felt his fear for her.

"I would be by your side if possible. You have not the magic of the Society. Perhaps that is good:. You are not one of them."

"Good-bye, Serenten. I will return with the Ring of Radiant." She felt regret at having to leave Skon's Hall. The not knowing what would happen to her new friends was hard to bear. Would she ever see Serenten and the rest of them again? She sent a thought to Laura, "How is Lord Razon doing?"

"He is failing fast, Cynderet. There seems to be nothing more I can do for him."

"We need the Ring of Radiant," Cynderet sent, knowing full well it was the only possible way to save him from a slow, painful death. "I thank you for your kindness to us all, Lady Laura."

Not understanding the hint of farewell in the thought of gratitude, Laura said a welcome.

Cynderet left her mind to be about her own business. She sat back in the chair and opened her mind. She closed out everything from the outside just as she had done in trying to locate Lord Razon.

Reht sat beside her in the Foyer of Doors. He said nothing. He just looked at her as he would when she did something that impressed him and made him proud of her. He noted her timid smile playing at the corner of her mouth. He agreed with a nod when she tuned him out and focused on finding her mother.

Cynderet let her mind go back to her home. Her mother was not there. She had been there since Cynderet and the others had rescued Lord Razon and Serenten. Cynderet was surprised to find her mother had been pleased with the escape. Why? she asked herself. There was the over-feeling of pride in her mother's pleasure. A feeling of having pulled something over someone her mother did not like. It was neither Lord Blue Skon nor any of his people. It was someone of—of stone? "It was because she had acquired the Ring of Radiant!"

She opened her mind to the vision of her mother further. Luanta held a chain in her hand—a chain with a ring on it. She was talking with the Senior Eldress Ermentrude about a sacrifice. Cynderet read the prompt, saying, "Time to begin."

Cynderet knew her mother had then returned to the plane of humans. She followed her to a band of bandits. *My mother leads these brigands,* she realized. *The leader is under her power.* She could tell it was a different kind of power, something much more malign than the Charm Spell, yet it was of magic. She looked closely into the leader. He was not what he appeared—she could feel that. He was alive, but not as a human. He was different. Cynderet looked into his eyes, trying to see deeper. She saw the crystal figure of him, or her. He was not a man;. He was a shadow of a woman. A female spirit and a black crystal. Suddenly, Cynderet saw the Table as well. Not as a table but as a living substance in a body of crystalline rock. They were the same kind of creation, mutations of living spirits never meant for the kind of existence they now lived. Her being shuddered at the perversion.

Cynderet's mind was overcome by a darkness. It was immense. Though there was no light within this enveloping void of black, she could see varying glimmerings of individual bodies of heat. Each produced wavering colors of red and orange in the dark. Among them, there rose a huge body of heat. Cynderet watched spellbound as these impressions bore down upon her. There was something else here, a feeling. It permeated the void. It was centered in the dominating, obese mass and radiated throughout the rest. It was the power of perversion she sensed in the mangled spirit and crystal of the bandit leader and the Table. This obese creature of darkness was the master—evil lived. It lived and moved of its own purpose. What that purpose was Cynderet was not sure, but anger and hate were to be felt in it all.

A voice beside her spoke hushed but clearly. "It is the Lord Wherant." Reht spoke as if mouthing the name only. "It is its magic that permeates the Table and the crystalline figure."

"The one my mother feels so sure she controls," Cynderet answered. "She fools only herself."

"Your mother controls nothing. Everything is subdued by the power of the creature in darkness. It controls the figure. It controls the Table."

Cynderet broke into a sweat. She felt her face grow hot, and then her whole body went cold as her blood settled in her stomach. "The creature of darkness controls the Table! It controls my mother and the other Eldresses." Cynderet turned to Reht. "It does. All these things are tied together. That is the secret of all this."

"Aye."

Cynderet read something in Reht's voice. She looked up to him as he stood up from beside her. "And you knew," she said as knowledge burst upon her. "That is the 'aye' of it." Anger grew in her. "All this time, you knew?"

Patiently, Reht looked upon the eyes so trusting, so honest. Very quietly, he answered her as he closed his mind to her possible entry, "Aye, Little One. I did."

"You close me out. I can feel it inside me." Confused and hurt, she continued, "All the time you were telling me to be my true self, that I could not live a 'lie'. What about you? How much of a 'lie' are you, Reht? How much do you know?"

Reht did not retreat from Cynderet's onslaught of questioning. He knew this had to be met. He put his personal fears of losing her behind him. He stood his full eight feet in her mind and took a deep breath. With a voice firm in hope, he answered her, "Cynderet, I am not a' lie'. I am everything you thought me to be: and more."

"My portal is closed to you only because there remains much more for you to learn before you may enter. The day will come."

"Cynderet, you hold the Dream Sight of the Hert within you. It is our story—as much as I know. When the time comes, and you have grown, you will share it with Serenten; and any other Hert who will listen."

"The Hert slaves know of the Table, of its purpose to the Wherants. The Table is how the Lord Wherant controls the Society of Energy Feeders. There was a trade made between the Wherants and the Society many centuries ago. The Table allows the Wherants to bring Hert slaves to the Society. In exchange, the Society provides the Wherants with spirits, those of the initiates like Linnet that did not pass the tests, and were Energy Drained. It is the closest they can get to real humans. However, the Table also allows the Wherants to monitor what the Society is doing, and imprint their ideas upon the Society's thinking."

"Somehow, the Ring of Radiant comes into play in the goals of the Wherants. It is they who seek the death of Lord Razon. It is your mother who is to somehow gain for them the Ring of Radiant."

In a quiet voice of comprehension, Cynderet said, "That is why she is doing this. It will gain her the revenge she seeks, and in the process, she is aiding the Wherants in a much larger objective. But, what does the Ring of Radiant have to do with the Society?"

"This is something I do not know. Only that the Wherants are very cunning and devious. They seek only to benefit their own. They care nothing for the Society. It is merely a means to their objectives."

"What has my mother done? She must be warned!"

"Yes, Little One. Only it will do no good," Reht answered quietly. "She will only allow herself to believe it is all her doing. She has sold herself to destroy your friends."

"Then she must be stopped!" Cynderet resumed her search in earnest. She had to change her mother's course. Not only was Skon's Hall in danger, so were so many others—including the Society.

Cynderet saw in her mind the room of the cottage where her mother had returned. She saw her mother sitting upon the bed holding a black bag. It was closed and her mother kept turning it slowly within her hands. Around and around it went, slowly revolving as she stared at it. Cynderet read her thoughts;. The bag was the answer to her problems. It would destroy Lord Blue Skon.

"No, Mother. It will destroy you," Cynderet said quietly to her, standing just at her side by the bed.

Luanta jerked spasmodically in fear and surprise. She protectively put the bag to her opposite side and looked at her intruder. Seeing her daughter, her mouth dropped open for a second. It closed. Anger overcame surprise. "Cynderet. You…" she hissed. "How did you get here? You are a traitor to the Society," she spat. "The entire Eldress Council searches for you even now!"

"I have done nothing wrong, nor have I tried to hurt the Society," Cynderet responded with a quiet poise that surprised herself, and, by the look of her, her mother. "I have come to warn you of your great danger, and that to destroy Skon's Hall is a mistake."

"You are here for what?" Luanta screamed in confused dismay solidifying into instant rage. "So, you are in league with the paltry Lord Blue Skon. How ironic this seems. I do not know how this all comes to be, but you are too late."

"Mother, you must listen to me."

"How dare you presume to be so all-knowing and universally wise!" Luanta lashed. She slowed down her voice to drive home each hateful word, "You are only a pathetic crossbreed who is more a paltry human like your father than of the Society to which you might have been a part of."

It was Cynderet's turn to be caught off guard. She was totally unprepared for what she just heard. "What do you mean 'crossbreed'?" she asked, stunned.

"Crossbreed: one not truly of a pure race. You are a sickening mixture of human and Energy Feeder." Enjoying the confused, then painful expressions across Cynderet's face, Luanta decided to take some time and explain. She cherished each moment feeding on her daughter's suffering. Just as you have made me suffer all these years, she thought to herself.

Cynderet read it as if screamed at her. She was not ready for what followed. It took a few moments to sink in.

"The human male is only used to settle the new female seed of life within an Energy Feeder. A true Feeder will overcome her human weaknesses while in the womb. Somehow, you were too weak to do this. Why? I do not know. It must have been something about Lord Razon. Instead, you were born with only a human body. No wings, no ability to alter your form, and no power." Luanta's lips curled in loathing. "You have always been my greatest shame. I wanted to smother you at birth. It was the Council that stopped me. In vision, they saw you as a great leader." Her laugh was a bitter chortle. "Now look at you, a coward and a traitor."

Luanta expected Cynderet to squirm at her vicious attack. Instead, she found Cynderet standing before her with a dumbfounded look that caused her to laugh derisively. "You are so stupid you do not even know what I am talking about. Look at you!" Luanta screamed, "You make me sick!"

Cynderet did not seem to hear her. When Cynderet did get her voice again, her question caught her mother by surprise, "Lord Razon? You said Lord Razon. Why?"

Not understanding what was behind the question, Luanta answered honestly in effort to deepen the hurt. "Lord Razon is your father. I was to feed off him until he was only a powdered shell then take the Ring of Radiant to…" Luanta did not finish. She watched as Cynderet sat backwards on the edge of the bed. She could not read this new look on Cynderet's face.

"Lord Razon is my father," she mused in a whisper. Over and over again, she repeated it, trying to make sense of it.

Luanta exploded in rage. She converted to her bat-like form as she rushed Cynderet with her talons opened and wings bursting with a powerful stroke.

Cynderet hit her. Not bodily— in her mind. "No!' The word was not a word: it was power. It halted Luanta as no blow or weapon could. She did not see Cynderet stand up, but now both women stood, staring at each other in shock. Cynderet unbelieving what she had just done, and Luanta that her daughter had that kind of power.

"Who are you?" Luanta asked, non-fathoming.

"I do not know, not yet," Cynderet answered the mutual question. There was so much to understand. "But Reht says I am not an Energy Feeder. I know that now. I could never be of such a hateful society. Life is not as you think, Mother. You are wrong."

Cynderet knew this was her only chance to talk to her mother. She would never listen to her again as soon as she recovered. "Do not attack Skon's

Hall. You are wrong in your hate of these good people." Cynderet knew she was right about the creature as well. "You are only a tool of the Beast in the Darkness. He will ruin you. The Creature of Darkness controls everything you think. All that you believe to be your power is really his. You are only his slave. He will destroy you if you do this."

"Reht is dead," Luanta reminded Cynderet. "And now you are in league with my arch enemy and his paltry group of friends." Luanta waved her daughter off, "No matter, you are the one who is wrong. Your Lord Blue Skon will die, and I will laugh at the watching of it. So will Lord Razon. That is my bargain." Luanta patronized Cynderet with a smile, "If I do not do this, then Lord Wherant will destroy me, in that you are right. I am his slave. I sold myself to him twice. And each time, it has been Lord Blue Skon who has interfered. No more! This time, he will be gone. He will die slowly if I have any choice. No matter how slowly, it will never make up for the humiliation he has brought me. It is no longer a question of right or wrong. It is who I have become."

Luanta looked at Cynderet for a moment and then cocked her head to the side. "You will fight me, Cynderet. You will try to oppose me in this battle. I can see it in your eyes." Almost civilly, she added, "Reht was right. You are not one of us. You are different. I will grant that you are not the total coward I thought you to be, but you are a fool to interfere. The Creature of the Darkness is the Lord Wherant, the most powerful creature alive. It is he who wants Lord Razon's power." Something clicked in her thinking. "It must be the ring." She paused a moment and then asked, "Did you know the Lord Wherant wanted you as well? It was he that commanded the Eldress Council that you not be killed. He planted the vision in all our minds."

Luanta looked at Cynderet, pondering, a drawn quiet moment. "It is you he wants. For some reason, he wants you as his slave. If you do not die with your friends, he will continue to seek you out for his own purposes. You will never be safe from his hunting you. Now go from me. Make your futile effort to help your friends." She turned her back on her daughter and laughed, throwing a dismissing slap at Cynderet over her shoulder. "And your father."

Cynderet remembered her purpose for coming with clarity at the mention of Lord Razon. "Mother, I want the Ring of Radiant!" Cynderet said, reaching for her mother.

Luanta turned on Cynderet. "No!" Viciously, her talons struck Cynderet across the face. "The sacrifice of the ring is my only chance to be free of the Wherants. Go, you Human Dog! Go, or I will destroy you here and feed you to my rock!" she hissed.

Cynderet instinctively felt her face. Her hand came away with blood on it.

Luanta laughed a horrible cackle. Any last vestige of her as Cynderet's mother vanished in that instant. Left was the hate-distorted visage that would haunt Cynderet's memory for many years to come.

Cynderet felt tears stream down her face. Within her mind, Reht took her hand and drew her through a portal newly marked with a clawing hand of talons.

CHAPTER TWENTY FIVE

Cynderet returned to Skon's Hall in bitter shame. It proved impossible for her to tell of her visit with her mother verbally. In the end, Missive was her spokesman as she allowed him to bypass her distress and read her thoughts. He related what he learned to the others.

Lady Laura took Cynderet's shuddering form warmly into her arms. "You were very brave to try. Unfortunately, not every brave act ends as we would have it, even if it were for the good of friends. You cannot blame yourself, Cynderet. I know Lord Razon would say the same." She pointed to him on her bed.

"Notice he has slipped into a quiet sleep now. There may yet be hope for his recovery. He has a strong will to live."

Cynderet looked at Razon and allowed herself to see into his sleeping mind. He was dreaming of a great tower overlooking an expansive green glade surrounded by coniferous forests. Mountains, clear and stark in their jagged peaks, could be seen way off in the distance. There was a man and a woman standing beside him looking into the distance. The man stood tall and lean, his face resembled Razon's though with age and wisdom about the eyes and brow. The woman was regal in her appearance and clothing, her eyes shown with pride and confidence. Although fuller with time about the waist, it was clear she remained a beautiful woman. Cynderet needed no introduction to be certain these were his parents. His father's arm rested on Razon's shoulder. His mother's arm wrapped around his waist. They looked so caring and so close; like a family Cynderet realized. Razon was at peace. "Is that what it means to be of a human family?" she asked herself. She tried to memorize the scene and then left his mind, afraid if she lingered longer, he may wake up.

"Yes, he is resting quietly," she told the others. "He is dreaming of home, I think." She looked around her at the others in the room. Ashley and Patrick were orphans; Laura had been an orphan, raised by her older brother. She knew nothing of Missive. She remembered Serenten and Reht;. They had been abducted from home at early ages, forced into slavery by the Wherants and her mother's society. All bore scars of broken families. "Even me," she muttered in reflection. She did not notice Laura's glance down at her.

Laura still held her close and barely heard her comment. Laura also looked around the room perceiving Cynderet's thoughts with perfect clarity. "Cynderet, you and all these others are welcome here. We are all as family. I believe that is why Elfgon and Landsfall returned to us so quickly at Skon's call. Elfgon is the last of his kind here. Landsfall is a natural loner, yet they too feel home here. Even my brother Wolfie comes often. Sometimes, he comes in disguise just to see how we are doing. He does not want to interfere in Skon's leadership. He is a very humble, quiet man, yet many know how powerful he is in the Six Realm Alliance. You will like him, I am sure."

Neither stated the obvious of Luanta's coming. Both knew they might never live to see Wolfgang the Meek. Still, Cynderet knew Laura's sincerity of her home. She gave her a hug, and, as a child will, laid her head on Laura's breast.

*****

Landsfall and Patrick saw the band of brigands enter the vale at the same time. Landsfall put a proud hand on Patrick's head and tousled his hair a bit. "Ye be hav'n the eyes of the hawk, to be sure. See how the big fellow rides off to the side? He be the one Elfgon and I saw on a hill overlooking the skirmish what killed Skon's men. That will be our man." As a follow-up thought, "Be ye seeing the woman? She may be looking like a large bat?"

"Nay, I be see'n no woman, bat or no. If she be a bat, mayhap she be fly'n," Patrick suggested.

"Aye. Watch our zenith. I be remember'n these bat women surprised Serenten and Razon from above."

"Aye." Without further instruction, Patrick rolled over on his back and scrunched into the hollow he had prepared earlier to watch the vale from.

Landsfall took a moment to notice the ease Patrick had in the wild. It was second nature to him. He was not burdened with a lot of people's rules and etiquette. He went about his duties with full concentration and clarity. *Ye may be hav'n some less education than the others, but yer mind works clear and fine,* Landsfall thought to himself. *Be ye as accepting of learn'n from another? I be thinking, aye.* He turned back to watch the brigands. He had a thought beyond this conflict. If Patrick were willing, he might be a good one to teach the ways of a Rover. *I be forty-two years alive and nary a one ta carry on the ways. It be about time I took me a junior ta teach what I know.* A movement below stopped his musings, but the idea was well-planted.

The band passed through the vale without further stop. After a few minutes, Landsfall and Patrick mounted and followed them keeping just beyond the ridgeline of the hills. They would periodically pop up to the ridge just enough for their eyes to confirm their prey stayed in view and along the suspected route. Patrick developed a surveillance routine of the sky above them, ensuring they were not surprised from above. They never saw the bat woman. They decided the brigands were headed straight towards Skon's Hall. At their pace, they would be there tomorrow mid-afternoon.

"Come, we be reporting ta Skon and then circle back behind these. They be not hard ta find or follow."

*****

Luanta kept thinking about Cynderet finding her. "How is it possible?" she kept asking herself. "She did not walk here, I know. And only a full-fledged Energy Feeder can Energy Web from one place to another. She must have power of her own or help, but how?"

Luanta unconsciously walked a tight circle in her room. She knew she was alone, having sent Everard and the brigands to Skon's Hall early this morning. After Cynderet's visit last night, she did not want any other surprises thwarting her attack and victory. "There is too much at risk," Luanta tried to consider the possible implications. "Cynderet is conspiring with Blue Skon. I must warn Ermentrude. She will want to know Cynderet found me, especially as she is after the ring. That impudent child may prove more dangerous than any of us thought possible. She should have been drained at birth. What could the Wherants possibly see in her?"

Luanta formed her arms around her and webbed to Ermentrude. As soon as she arrived, Ermentrude called her into the room they met in before.

"You have returned early. By your look, you are not done with your nemesis. What is it you are about?"

"Cynderet found me at the hideout. She actually tried to get me to abandon my plans—can you imagine? That worthless cripple found me!"

"When? What happened?"

"Last night, human time. She has power, Ermentrude. She has power to Energy Web. She told me not to attack Skon's Hall. She said they are her 'friends'." Luanta threw her arms out from her sides, still in unbelief. "Then she asked me for the Ring of Radiant—as if I would just hand it over to her!" Luanta gave a forced laugh. "She is a fool yet unpredictable, Ermentrude. She could even come here. You must watch out for her."

"We begin the sacrificial ceremony tomorrow. It will coincide with your work at Skon's Hall, I think," Ermentrude responded. "The Wherants have demanded their payment of spirits held here. It is all to be done at once, the ring and the payment of spirits."

Luanta shuddered. No one knew exactly what the Wherants did with the spirits drained of the initiates who died at initiation or did not pass the Last Rites. It was the payment demanded of the Wherants for the trade of Hert as slaves. The Society carefully preserved these spirits on Council Peak. The Wherants had kept their part of the bargain, now they wanted their payment. *Why now?* Luanta wondered. Why at the same time as her work? Was it coincidental? Somehow, she did not think so. The Wherants were of their own purposes and devices.

Luanta felt a heaviness settle around her heart. Suddenly, she knew Strike had been right. If she failed at this, she would never see light again. The Lord Wherant had made her consequences for failure very clear. Her body broke out in a cold sweat. *What is it really like in the pits of Wherant minions?* She dared wonder a moment. She had been used most perversely by the Lord Wherant when she had failed to bring Razon's Ring of Radiant to him thirteen years ago. "I must not fail this time," she whispered aloud.

"What is that, Luanta?" Ermentrude asked.

Luanta looked at the Senior Eldress. Ermentrude had been her mentor— Luanta's only better in the Society. Could she trust her to ensure the ring was delivered? Luanta knew she had no other choice. "There must be no delay of the Ring of Radiant being delivered to the Wherants. It is my only hope of freedom, Senior Eldress." Luanta's eyes never left Ermentrude's face.

"Fear not, Luanta. You will be free. The ring will be delivered as planned. To ensure this, we will allow no Hert, except the Council Guard Captain on Council Peak tomorrow—just in case." She gave Luanta a nod of determination. "We will enlist the aid of the Table's power to ensure all is done right. You were my apprentice. Now you sit beside me as Second Eldress. You, Luanta, will be Senior Eldress after me."

Luanta knew Ermentrude meant every word she said. It was a comfort to know the Hert would not be allowed near. It was possible for a Hert rebellion, especially from the bitter slave Serenten. If he was with Cynderet at Skon's Hall, and she was sure he was, his death would be certain.

"My thanks, Senior Eldress," Luanta said formally. "I find peace in your words. I will go to lead my armies now." Luanta found herself forcing a confidence she somehow did not fully feel. She bowed to Ermentrude and webbed back to the brigand hideout. She would fly from here to her forces in the field. "I will be bringing my real army in a little black box."

*****

Cynderet volunteered to stay with Lord Razon, allowing the others to find rest in their own rooms. Quick brought in a cot for Ashley and Cynderet to use;. Neither were interested in sleeping anywhere else. Ashley occupied the cot first and was instantly in the depths of an exhausted slumber. Cynderet sat in a stuffed armchair near the door. Her eyes were closed though sleep was far from her.

She pondered Lady Laura's declaration she and Serenten both had a home here. Even knowing Luanta, she could no longer think of her as Mother, would soon be here in force;. There remained a sense of welcome, of being a part of something wonderful. Mayhap it was because they all knew something of the loss of parents—in her case, the death of Reht. Together, they made up a body of friends—no, of something much grander than friends—they made up a family. And lying in her bed was her father. Cynderet did not question this. It all fit. "Will I ever come to know you? Will the next few days rob me of learning all you can teach me of who I am?" Twin tears traversed quiet paths down her cheeks. She realized her sitting alone in the chair was so opposite the needs of these friends and family surrounding her. "I have no idea what I can do further to help these people I care for, I love. I will do whatever I can to stop Luanta from vanquishing Skon's Hall and all it has come to mean."

"Reht? Where can I go to find the Ring of Radiant? Luanta says it is to be sacrificed. It will have to be with the Eldresses for that to happen."

"Aye. And once it is with the Wherants in the Lightless Plane, it will be lost."

"I must get it back."

"It will mean returning to the Society."

Cynderet thought about her last encounter with the Table. If it had not been for the Ring of Radiant, she would not have lived. "I am scared, Reht. Afraid if I go, I will die. The Table will not let me get away again. It seeks to destroy me as much as Luanta would destroy Lord Blue Skon. Yet if I do not try, our friends, our new family, will all die."

"Fear is a good thing, Little One. It teaches us caution. It helps us weigh the importance of choices we make. You see clearly the choices before you. Soon, you will have to make the choice."

Reht paused and let his statement sink in. Then he spoke his heart. "You have grown much in the past few weeks. You are no longer a child, Cynderet. That time has been robbed of you. You do not mourn its passing. Instead, you turn to face each new trial and circumstance as it comes. You are like your father, I think. You seek for goodness and offer kindness to others. You are ready to defend these things as well."

Reht put his arm around Cynderet as they sat together in the Foyer of Doors. "You have faced openly the reality of the choices you have made. You have chosen rightly. You will make the right choice again. That is my trust in you."

*****

The next afternoon, Landsfall and Patrick stopped and watched the brigands settle into day camp below them. The brigands had moved off the road into the dense forest outside the village. They picketed their horses and built cook fires.

"Be looking like they plan to spend some time here," Landsfall shared with Patrick. "Notice the two heading back ta the road? They be hav'n a purpose, ta be sure."

"Mayhap we should be after 'em?" Patrick asked, watching them slip away.

"Nay. The real happen's be when the big guy gets up and moves. Our best learn'n be right here. Let us settle in for the wait. Be wantin' a bit more dried apple or bread?"

"Aye. But I be think'n o' grapes. I be miss'n 'em a lot."

"Here then, try some dried grapes. Be callin' them raisins."

After an hour's wait, the two brigands reappeared. They were not alone.

"Landsfall, be look'n at the new fella. I be think'n it be that Jason what was mad wif Elfgon." Patrick pointed, allowing Landsfall to pick them out from the trees.

"Aye, Jason of Cotton Creek. And he looks pleased with himself too. This be the start of things ta be sure. See the pack mules com'n in with him?"

Landsfall took time to explain as he watched below, "Cotton Creek lies just outside the village wall on the other side of this forest. It feeds into the river right at the bridge to the front gates of the village. I be think'n our Jason fellow be aid'n these brigands into the village."

"Wha' we be do'n?'

"For now, we be just watch'n. Our time comes when they get up and move again."

Patrick resumed his ongoing zenith watch. It was hard to really see any distance, except right overhead due to the trees, yet he persisted. Landsfall recounted what was happening below as things changed. It was because of this shared watching that Patrick was able to see a flying shadow skim the trees towards the brigands' camp. "I be see'n sumfin' fly'n' in," he reported as he turned over to see it land.

"Aye. That be our bat-woman. See her com'n out of the trees ta the right. She be all pretty now though."

The two watched as a beautiful woman left the trees and walked boldly towards the brigand leader.

As Luanta arrived at Everard's side, he pointed towards Jason. Luanta smiled at him, enjoying the effect of her Charm Spell. "You have been so kind to keep us informed of Lord Skon's patrol movements for the past several days. I look to your continued aid in our current efforts," she cooed.

"Aye, to be sure, milady," Jason answered with wondering eyes. He found his mouth salivating and swallowed before continuing. "It be an easy thing to get you into the village. I always bring me fabrics in on the evening before I sell them. All your men have to do is lead my animals as if working for me."

"Oh, and clever as well. I like that about you, Jason of Cotton Creek." Luanta stroked his cheek with her open palm. "How many will be needed to lead your animals?"

"The full three what Everard requested, milady. The rest will be placed about the forest waiting for the gates to open."

"We will be ready to take position in four hours, Luanta," Everard said.

"Good. I will be leaving for my own part as it gets dark. Go and feed our friend here. I will join you in a moment."

Landsfall and Patrick saw the conversation. They were too far away to hear. The answer to some of their questions came an hour later as Jason began showing three brigands how the packs were untied and the market square pavilion setup.

"They be planning ta enter the village as Jason's men, I be thinking. We best be getting back ta Skon's Hall."

It took Strike the most of the night and next day to learn to distinguish the different sounds within Skon's Hall. He had finally been able to recognize the voices of authority from those of servants and soldiers. He heard none he thought to be Lord Razon. Still, Strike persisted, feeling certain Lord Razon was within the hall. Berenice would not have entered and died if not positive he was here. She was not created for that kind of waste. *I must listen in on only one voice. Perhaps then, I will hear of his location through its conversations.* He listened to several for a few minutes to decide which voice to focus on. Strike chose a girl's voice. She seemed to speak to many different people on a wide range of subjects. *Just the kind of voice I need. Sooner or later, she will be speaking to or of this Lord Razon. Then I will locate him within. It was only a matter of time.* Time he had. It was the Ring of Radiant that was needed.

Landsfall and Patrick took over an hour to circle around Everard's band. They made a wide circle to ensure they came into the village from the rear gate. They found Skon, Hamilton, and Elfgon reviewing the troop positions in front of the tavern.

"They be com'n," Patrick joined in as they walked up to the small group.

"Aye, that they be," Landsfall seconded. "The bat be with them also."

Turning to Elfgon, Landsfall added, "So is yer local fabric competitor. It be Jason of Cotton Creek we saw showing the brigands how ta get in the gates. They be com'n as his animal drivers."

"Yup, tha' be the way of it. We see 'em learn'n how ta act normal and all," Patrick summarized.

"Well, it would seem my place is at the front gates to welcome my friend of the cloth, aye?" Elfgon said, rubbing his hands together as if cold. "I have been too tolerant of the greedy small guy."

"Aye, and I be thinking his group will be trying to open the gates tonight and let the others in," Hamilton said.

"What are you two going to do now?" Skon asked.

Landsfall put a hand on Patrick's shoulder. "Patrick and I be returning ta the trees. I be a much better aid ta ye in the woods than in the village or on the walls. And this young squire shows good promise in the forest as well."

"Be watch'n for the bat," Patrick warned. "She be fly'n in the night be me guess. All bats do."

"To be sure, though there will be no moon tonight. That will make it easy for her and hard for us," Skon responded. "Hamilton, you better let the troops know about the 'bat'. Elfgon, you take the main gates. I am thinking Jason of Cotton Creek will be glad to see you. Myself, I will be to the hall with Quick and Serenten."

"How be Lord Razon?" Patrick asked.

Skon looked at both Landsfall and Patrick. "He was doing well until about midday. Last word was, he was having nightmares and squirming a lot. Lady Laura said the inflammation was getting worse. Ashley and Cynderet are at his side constantly, taking turns as needed."

"Aye. We be getting back ta the forest," Landsfall closed with a serious purse to his lips. His eyes sparked the anger he was finally allowing himself to feel. "It be time for payback."

"Be not worried about saving any for me, Landsfall," Elfgon joined. "I get the fat cotton picker."

"Remember the bat. She has eluded us before and it will be her that is bringing the demons," Skon reminded them all.

*****

The sun was beginning to set behind the mountains when Jason of Cotton Creek rode to the main gates. He led a procession of six mules. Every two were led by one of his men. Captain Hamilton greeted him from the gate ramparts.

"Hale, Jason. I be thinking ye might not make it in tonight. Ye be later then normal."

"Aye. It be a heavier load this trip. It took longer to pack."

"Well, be bringing yourself and mules in."

Jason signaled his men to proceed through the gate. He was very pleased things were going so well. *Hamilton will soon be cursing this moment,* he thought. *Too long, he and Lord Skon have been letting outsiders in on my trade. And that Elfgon is going to pay for cutting my profits!*

Jason gave no thought to the closing of the outer gates behind him. It was the normal procedure at sundown. It was the inner gates closing in on him as well that alerted him that something was wrong.

Elfgon stepped from the shadows into the inner court as the inside gates finished securing Jason and his drivers within the court. "Good even'n', fine Jason of Cotton Creek," the hated elf chortled.

"What is the meaning of my being closed in by the gates?" Jason challenged, trying to sound important. He could not shake the sudden feeling he was found out.

"It would seem you have hired a new crew of mule headers, Jason," Elfgon answered. "It seems they are well-armed for local cotton pickers. They look like brigands to me."

Jason's men all reached for their weapons as the trap became evident to them.

There followed a chorus of opening crossbow portals on both sides of the inner gate walls. Jason and his men looked around at the sound. They were open targets, easy marks for the twelve gate portals. They had nowhere to go.

"I think this is the time you are expected to drop your weapons," Elfgon stated flatly.

The brigands complied.

"You will pay for this effrontery, you Ancient Relic!" Jason shook a fist at Elfgon. "You should have disappeared with your kind years ago."

"Jason, that is hardly complimentary. And to think I thought we were friends," Elfgon baited, not in the least intimidated by his posturing. "It is too bad, really. It seems our time grows short to get to know each other better. I hear the gallows being nailed as we speak. Perhaps you would rather cross swords?"

Elfgon took a step forward with his hands open and free of his scabbard. He blatantly stepped past the first mule header towards Jason. The brigand instantly dropped his mule leads and reached for Elfgon in a sudden lurch. His arms crossed around Elfgon's neck and shoulders in an attempt at a Half Nelson. As he sought to close his grip, Elfgon exploded into motion. He allowed his body to just drop as dead weight; then he smoothly arose, spinning in place. In the instant, he was suddenly face-to-face with the brigand. Never slowing, Elfgon smiled as his hands slipped, open palm, inside the arms trying to close about his neck. His arms followed upward shooting through the hold. The brigand never saw the slamming knee into his inner thigh, hitting the nerve bundle there. The jolt set him up for Elfgon's arms rounding back down to pound into his sides. Elfgon's forearm plowed into the union of the brigand's throat and lower jaw, dropping him to the ground.

"Your turn, Jason," Elfgon said. His eyes burned with the inner anger Elfgon held in control.

Jason saw death there. "I surrender! Hamilton, stop him!"

"Aye, ye heard him, men."

It only took a minute for the group to be bound and headed towards the stockade. Hamilton had Jason brought to Elfgon's combatant. "It seems only right that Jason should help carry the thief what tried to defend him, aye men?" Hamilton asked. He stood over the bandit's body. "He be not getting up on his own with a broken neck."

CHAPTER TWENTY SIX

Everard watched as Jason and his small troop entered the village gates. Everything seemed to be going well. He waited for an hour watching for the sign that they were inside the village and ready for the assault. An hour passed turning dusk to dark. The sign was not given—it should have been. After two hours, Everard was certain something had gone wrong. He left one of his lieutenants to continue watching while he reported to Luanta.

Showing no reaction towards Jason, Luanta pondered a few moments, "I have an idea how to create a diversion at the gates. Set your men in two groups. Have the first circle to the north and attack the farmhouses there. Set them on fire. Encourage the men to create a lot of noise and disturbance. They have been patient. And the more screaming the villagers hear of their own, the more defenders will flock to the northern walls." Luanta made sure Everard understood before she continued, "The second group will remain in the forest before the front gates. When the disturbance to the north is loud and visible, have the second group mount their attack on the front gates. Have them stay just beyond arrow range."

Everard nodded his understanding. "The farmers not already behind the village walls will seek shelter at the north gate. Would you have the men follow?"

"No. They are also not to get within range of defender arrows. These two forays will draw any floating defenders in the village to the walls. They will provide enough diversion for me to get to the orchard between Skon's Hall and the village. You will not want to be within the walls until the demons' darkness passes over you. I would not want your men mistaken as defenders."

A shared chortle followed, and then the two separated to be about their parts.

It took only half an hour before the northern sky began to show the wavering glow of flames. The screams of the few farm families still without the walls were mingled with the bellows of panicking livestock.

When the second group charged the gate, Luanta flew to the south and over the wall into the orchard. She knew her spot, having observed it from the forest hills earlier in the day.

She took a moment to survey the orchard and the ramparts of Skon's Hall beyond the treetops. There was an excited beat to her heart like none ever felt before. "Your time is up, Skon. Now meet your end and never will I be thwarted again. You will pay dearly for my enslavement to the Wherants. Too bad he does not want you. I would cherish each scream of fear, each tremor of pain you shed in his pits of darkness." Luanta laughed out loud as she knelt down and removed the black box from her bag. She caressed the ebony surface gently as she rehearsed the vision in her mind of exactly how to place and open the box. Languishing in hateful patience, she set the box in its place and lifted the lid slightly. All was quiet; all was still. She removed the lid entirely and set it to the side of the box: Nothing happened.

A sudden profound fear smashed into Luanta's heart. "What is wro…?" Her question went unfinished as there was an impact of strange sensations on and within her being. It was like the concussion of innumerable thunders simultaneously rolling through a storm, yet all was silent. Total, complete silence reigned. The air was still as if time had stopped. Luanta looked up into the night sky. Then she heard it: the sound of far off winds fraught in fantastic fury. The sound came from every direction. It encompassed the entire hills circling the valley of Skon's Hall bouncing from the mountain walls beyond. "They are coming!" she said in a whisper so quietly only her lips moved mouthing the words. Fear, as she had never sensed it, shrouded her being. She flew to the upper parts of a large apple tree and watched as a distant darkness slowly imploded upon the entire valley.

Razon leapt up from bed screaming, holding his hands to his chest as if trying to keep his lungs and heart within his rib cage. "It has happened, the darkness! I saw it! The demons come!"

Cynderet rushed to his side. She noted his agitation but was unsure what his ramblings were saying. "What is it?" she pleaded.

At the sudden outburst, Ashley exploded from her sleep on the cot. She threw back the covers and lurched to her feet savagely twisting her ankle as she landed doing an unnatural split as the throw rug slipped from beneath her. It took a few minutes for the pain to register as she remained down with her mouth open and eyes wide looking to Cynderet striving to quiet Lord Razon wild eyed and struggling to arise.

Razon turned to Cynderet and held her firmly by the shoulders. "You must help me get to Skon. I will not see my friend die without me at his side. It is because of me this has all come about. You must help me!"

Realizing he was at least coherent, Cynderet strove to quiet him. "Lord

Razon, you are too weak! You cannot make but a step from this bed. You have not the strength!"

"Damn! If only I had the ring!" He looked down at Ashley trying now to get to her feet. Tears of pain coursed down her cheeks, but not a sound did she utter through her clenched teeth. "I am so sorry, Ashley. Again, I have brought pain to your eyes." He turned back to Cynderet, supporting his teetering body. "Cynderet, you must help me to the walls. Grab my sword. There now, hand it to me and help me secure my scabbard belt."

As soon as Razon had his belt on, he reached a stabilizing arm to Ashley who clung tentatively to the end of the bed.

There was a sudden pounding of heavy steps coming quickly down the Hall. Razon strove to draw his sword. His arm could not extend fully enough for want of strength. The door resounded one warning pound of heavy fist before it was thrust open by Serenten. He had two pole weapons firmly in one hand. The other reached out for Cynderet.

"Child, they are coming. Take your place beside me. I will defend you until breath is gone from these lungs and my heart ceases to beat!"

"Help him, instead, my friend. He must take his place beside Lord Skon. I will aid Ashley. She has hurt her ankle."

Serenten surveyed what was about in the room and complied. He handed Cynderet one of the weapons and gathered Razon to his massive body and lifted him over his shoulder. "Undignified it may be, but it is fast and secure. Keep your sword still." Turning back to Cynderet, he noted her questioning study of the weapon now in her arms. "It is the weapon of the Council Guard. You may need it. Come quickly! We may never make the walls as it is."

Cynderet went to aid Ashley. The pole arm seemed to be always in the way. "This weapon is too cumbersome!" she pleaded.

"Let me use it as a crutch, Cynderet. You go after Lord Razon. You need to keep up with them. You do not know your way around as I do."

"I can find Serenten and Razon in the deepest darkness—even beyond this earth. You are the one I must walk beside. Come, take the pole in one hand and I will aid you as well."

Cynderet and Ashley made it to the outer ramparts to find everyone just watching. Most had not even drawn their weapons yet. Her eyes followed the stares of the others to the distance. The hills surrounding the valley were gone from sight. There was nothing to be seen but darkness. A growing wave robbing all light from any source as it approached the outer perimeters of the village fields drew even the night into absolute darkness.

Yet it was the sound that struck fear in the hearts of all, a wind of fury bearing the wailing of an immense multitude. The evil of the demons' armies of hell could be felt hurtling upon the slightest breeze beginning to wave the rampart flags of Skon's Hall: a breeze foretelling of the deluge growing stronger by the moment.

*****

Strike felt the opening of the box. He cursed Luanta for the fool she was. He heard the immediate screams of Razon as he leapt from his bed. "Ah, now I find you." Strike listened intently to his sounds in order to locate him fully. "I must get the Ring of Radiant before it is too late!" Strike melted into the granite walls of Skon's Hall. Slowly, he drew his body through the porousness of the granite. He reached the inside surface finding himself in the stable area. He had to go up. He had heard Razon say he wanted to be with Skon on the ramparts. Slowly, Strike began to ascend the upward ramp to the main floor.

*****

Laura felt the give in the order of things around the valley's perimeter. She rose almost in slow motion from her reading chair in her subterranean chambers.

"They come," Missive said. "Almost a thousand years, and now the demons have returned to earth. The Lions of Radiant will not awaken without the Ring of Radiant. The Master Ring does not even know."

Laura did not answer while she buckled her sword belt. She put the spell book she had been studying into a side purse.

"Well, we will have to send as many back to their hell as possible, aye, my Ancient Friend?"

It was a familiar man's voice. Missive turned to the mirror behind him. A small man in monk's robes finished extruding himself from the far corner mirror.

Laura turned at the voice as well. "Wolfie, you are here!" she almost giggled as she rushed to the welcoming arms of her brother.

"Aye. The affairs of state grew tiring compared to the needs of my sister and her fine husband." Taking instant command, he said, "Come, shall we lend a hand? I think light will be the most important spell in this effort. And bring your spell book of infra-vision as well, aye?”

“My very thoughts, I have them.”

“Let us go then.”

The darkness sealed up the lower forest edge and was coming quickly now. Elfgon could see into the darkness with his infra-vision affording no trouble identifying forward ranks of demon minions. “Arrow fodder before the main forces of evil,” he remarked to himself.

“What be ye saying, Elfgon?” Hamilton asked in his command voice, striving with military demeanor to thwart the growing fear within him. Watching the quickly encroaching void of light, he knew he would be helpless being blinded in the dark. And so many upon these walls depended upon his being in command of the moment, his being their leader.

“Come beside me, Hamilton. I have a gift for you.”

Hamilton did as bidden;. He watched Elfgon kneel at his pack pushed up against the village wall.

Elfgon drew from his pack a strange earthen vial. From its body extended two fragile looking necks long and intertwined like the necks of geese. The markings were completely foreign to Hamilton.

“I have but this one left of my people,” Elfgon said, placing the strange vial in Hamilton’s hand. “Break the two necks with your teeth, allowing not a drop to spill upon your lips or the ground. Drink deeply and swallow. In the times of shared darkness and light when the elves persevered to maintain a balance, this was a vial of courage and sight within both realms. It will aid you to see in the coming dark, and it will allow you to keep command of your forces until the end. Now drink, my friend, for we have little time left.”

Hamilton looked at Elfgon a moment. Elfgon winked;. It was just as Hamilton had seen him wink so many times in earlier conflicts. It was his way of saying, “Trust me or not, it is up to you.” Hamilton put both necks well within his mouth and crushed the fragile necks with his teeth. He noted there were no shards of pottery, only a smoothness, as of powder. He sealed his lips tight about the vial on his lips and tilted his head back to consume fully the contents. He swallowed all in a single gulp. It burned. It burned like fire down into the pit of his stomach. The heat beaded sweat upon his forehead and upper lip. He felt heat course down his back and into his loins. It stopped. Just stopped. Hamilton looked to Elfgon.

“About now, I should think,” Elfgon said to him. A smile cracked his face.

Never had Hamilton felt such a rush of senses and emotions. His muscles seemed to swell of their own. A calming radiated through his being. His chest pectorals tightened in definition as they would after a determined workout, yet instead of fatigue, he was invigorated. He looked with a growing passion and fire into the coming darkness. He saw! Turning to Elfgon one last time, he said, "So that is what we will fight."

"Nay, my friend. The real enemy follows behind. These are just to warm our arm and bloody our swords until they get here."

Hamilton gave a wry look. He understood so much now and there was no time left to share it. He gave Elfgon a salute, stating, "Aye. I go to my men now."

"Fight well. I will see you in the battlements of our fathers where warriors gather around the fires of new life."

"Aye. We will compare notes, aye?"

Elfgon did not watch him leave. He simply listened to each fading step away. "My fathers," he whispered, "soon, I will eat again the venison of the giant stag and wear the ceremonial robes of dire wolves. I come. Allow my last battle to be long and well-fought. I come with the end of many spirits of the dark soon to fall to my blade."

Landsfall and Patrick heard the deafening rush of winds heightened by the venturi of the canyon's walls. The winds screamed like a multitude of bitter cries of the insane. Landsfall patted a shaken Patrick on the shoulder. With no words, he signaled it was time to do a rearward guerrilla action by slaying as many of the brigands as possible before the actual attack on Skon's Hall was mounted.

Patrick felt his fear diminish with the opportunity for action. He was worried for Ashley and the others at the Hall. Now he would do something for their defense. He followed Landsfall's example by putting his dagger in his teeth. Not having a sword as Landsfall, he placed a lead bullet in his sling and set it in his hand for quick use.

Together, they slithered down the hillock and into the trees just at the limits of Everard's brigands. The wind stole all sound here. The first two brigands fell without any others noticing, one with a slit throat; the other, a lead bullet perfectly to that area just in front of the ear where the hair ends and whiskers begin.

Two more fell before complete darkness enveloped the entire area.

*****

Cynderet watched as the darkness crashed like a silent wave upon the outer walls of the village. She was not sure but thought she saw the swirling of bright colors as it hit the front gates. Then there was the blasting of a battle horn.

"That be Hamilton giving a rally to his men at the walls," someone said behind her. "We best be giving him our response to know he fights not alone."

There was an answering blast from the battlements. Throughout the village came several last answering calls.

Skon moved further down the wall to keep his men rallied. Blue Song, his bastard sword, was held firmly in his iron fist. Cynderet had never noticed before, but the sword glowed now, a determined light matching the stern visage of its wielder. She did not know where Quick and Ryan were, yet she was confident that Quick was about somewhere close, guarding the back of his lord.

She looked to her right. Beyond Ashley were Razon and Serenten. Two newly found friends, yet such was their bond that she knew Serenten would die alongside Razon with no hesitation or qualm. "You are free now. I release you of any bond you may feel towards me." She sent Serenten.

"My Child, I think I have been so since of my own choice. When I sought to save you from the Table. Yet, it is good to know you know it as well."

She felt his smile for her and returned the sentiment.

Ashley was beside her. She held herself up bravely, leaning her back to the wall for support. At her left hand rested the pole arm and gripped within her right was the dagger used to slay Razon's crystalline assailant. Despite her pain in standing, Ashley showed no weakness of resolve. Cynderet felt a tremendous surge of pride. "Even in the end, these, my friends, my family, stand forthright, willing to die for all they believe in." Suddenly, she knew what she must do. "Yes, Reht. Now is the time of my choice. I choose my friends. If I die, I die with them."

"Then let us be about our work."

CHAPTER TWENTY SEVEN

Cynderet stood before the great portals of Council Peak. They were opened and unguarded. Everything was quiet. She looked around her and found no one in sight. She could read no Hert or Energy Feeder sensations in the city. Suddenly, there was movement. A shadow crept out from under a low-lying shrub.

It was a cat. It began stalking across the large open area before the portals to a tree on the far side. Cynderet looked up the tree to see what the cat was after. The pale sun shining directly into her eyes robbed her of visual acuity. She opened her mind to sense what was there. The birds felt her warning and flew off. The cat stopped in anticipation of later arrivals; waiting until other prey arrived.

Cynderet was confused. If she could read the cat and send to the birds, why were there no Hert or Energy Feeder sensations? She dared not turn to Reht with the question, not here at Council Peak, the center of the Table's power.

"Why not?" he asked.

It set her back. "There is great danger here. You could be hurt again," she responded protectively.

"Think, Little One. They want you. It matters not at all that I am included in the lot."

"They know I must come," she said, knowing it was a trap. She remembered her mission. It was a desperate time for all she had come to love. "We have no choice," she said to Reht. "I am glad, if it is to be this way that we walk openly together again."

She entered the portals. She opened her mind to the sensations within the great foyer leading to the stairs. There was nothing, not even the Table was to be found. "This is not possible," she reasoned. "The Table is hiding all from me. It plays me for a childish fool. It may be right." She ascended the first flight then, the next. At the landing of each, she took time to send ahead. Each time, it was the same: nothing.

At the lower landing of the last flight, Cynderet knew she was being allowed easy access. The last time she had reached this point to the top, she had needed Reht's help to ascend because of the voices screaming at her. They were not here now. The voices and emotions had been too strong and too real to just disappear. There were no visions of centuries of feet climbing these stairs. Even if the spirits had departed, the stone of the steps would still speak to her. All remained still, nothing. Then she knew. "The Table is masking it all from me. It wants me to enter completely unprepared."

Instead of climbing up the last flight, she sat down. She turned and looked out at the vista of the city. She had an idea. She allowed herself to see nothing but the physical structures. They had not changed since the last time she was here at Council Peak; had it only been a few weeks ago? She looked out over the city. It was almost the same as then. Except the shadows!

Last time she had seen them like this, she had watched the shadows of the day's progression slide away as if into the walls of homes. Now there was a difference. It took her a while to figure it out. She saw it: the difference. The shadows were not moving at all!

She looked to the sky. The weak sun was still in its same position—the same position as when she had looked into the tree. She looked at the cat she had seen going up towards the tree. It had not moved any further then when she watched it when newly arrived. "The Table has stopped time?" she asked Reht. "The Table is so strong it has stopped time!"

"This does not feel right," Reht responded. "I felt the Table's power throughout the city my entire life here. Now I feel nothing. If it is masking everyone from you, it is masking itself as well. It feels as absent as when in the mountains with Serenten. The Table had no power there, remember?"

"Yes. So how did it become so powerful now?" Cynderet asked. This was beginning to overwhelm her determination. The Table was good at that, she recalled. "Every time I begin to feel renewed hope or determination, the Table manages to crush it, or me."

She thought about the time she had gained a sense of strength, thinking of how she would model herself after that girl fighting the brigands in the forest. That girl was now her friend Ashley. Cynderet reminded herself she was here to save Ashley and the others.

"I had to leave the city to find peace," she mumbled to herself. "That was when I found you, Reht. I had escaped the Table's power by going beyond its limits to send."

Cynderet remembered how humiliated she felt when the Table had violated her private thoughts in her nest room. "I ran to Serenten and sought to get away. He led me back to the mountain forests beyond the city." Cynderet remembered the clear stream and the coolness of the forest glade. It was so pleasant beyond the Table's power. "Wait! That is what is wrong," she said, taking a moment to see the idea through. "The Table could not find me once out of the city. It sent the Eldresses to find me. It has no power beyond the limits of the hills. How could it now have the power to stop time?"

"You are right, Little One. The Table cannot stop time. It has only built a lie around you," Reht agreed. "See beyond the lie. Look for truth."

Cynderet was beginning to open her mind to find the truth to the situation when she was overwhelmed by a sick feeling of time lost. Panic grew swiftly because she was not able to save her friends at Skon's Hall. She jumped up and, with no other thought than to save them, ran up the next four steps before Reht spoke.

"Stop, Cynderet. It is the Table again," he urged. "It has sent this fear to you. Now is your chance. Look!"

She stopped. She closed an iron band around her fear. She looked again to the unchanging picture surrounding her at Council Peak. She imagined it as a painting. One she did not like. She took a knife and sliced through it.

She had a moment's clear vision before the Table thrust another lie upon her. In that instant, she saw the Eldress Council around the Table chanting and feeding. She also saw the Ring of Radiant held by its chain in the hand of the Captain of the Council Guard—the one who tried to kill Serenten. He was standing just outside the Table's inner circle, just outside a large hole in the flooring. The spirit voices were screaming in fear and anguish, in intensities she had never experienced before. The black drapes were parted, revealing large clear containers with bodies of Energy Feeder youths suspended in liquid.

Linnet. Linnet was one of them. Her body was pale, her eyes closed in death, but her spirit was not dead. Cynderet heard her voice amongst the others now that she knew what to listen for. It was impossible to understand words—the anguish was too strong.

"Cynderet. They are sending the spirits of these children through the hole in the floor within the Table." Reht spoke.

The Table closed the scene with its next lie. It enclosed her within a room of blank walls in an effort to blind her.

"You cannot deceive me any longer!" she yelled with a strength she had never suspected herself to have. She drew her hands together in her mind, and as if parting curtains, she forced a parting in the walls, throwing them open. She did not stop there. Two steps at a time, she raced up the stairs. There was no hesitation; her time was now.

The Table lashed out at her. The stairs collapsed upon each other, forming a steep stepless slide. Cynderet felt her feet slip beneath her. She was losing her footing and sliding back down to the landing. She could think of nothing to do to overcome the steep surface. She slipped and lost her balance falling to the ground in her downward grind. Each effort to slow down only led to more distance lost. I have to stop myself, she thought. She was quickly reaching the landing she had just left. She drew upon the stone of the landing creating a retaining wall to cease her backwards momentum. Her feet touched it, ending her descent. With no thought, only action, she turned again to face the stone slide. Her feet metamorphosed into bird claws, her claw like nails grasping firm hold upon the roughness of the stone itself.

The Table threw a giant cat at her. It was hungry. It studied her only for a moment and leapt into its pounce.

Cynderet turned into a hummingbird and shot beneath its extended body. "Why did I never think to fly before?" she asked herself as the cat was left behind her. She flew into the upper portal just as a fine mesh net was dropped upon her, forcing her to the floor.

The Table hurried to move the youth spirits into the hole.

Cynderet felt the utter darkness of the Lightless Plane emanating within the hole opened to receive the spirits. It sickened her as the fright of the spirits keened and twirled about to enter the void. "I have to do something. I have to stop the Table." Her pent-up frustration turned to hot anger. She became flame and burned through the netting, freeing herself instantly.

The Table abandoned trying to deposit the spirit youths and sought to deposit Razon's ring instead.

The Table prompted the Hert to drop the Ring of Radiant into the hole. He took too long.

Cynderet had forgotten about the ring. She was indecisive while she watched.

The Hert was thrown into the hole by the power of the Table. The Hert had no chance to respond as the Table crammed him forcefully downward to his doom. The ring, held by its chain, plummeted after him.

Cynderet lunged from her mind's tongues of flame and became an arrow, piercing the neck space of the ring's chain. She was almost through the neck loop when she dropped a hook behind her and carried the chain clear of the hole.

In un-satiated anger, the Table struck out at her. "You shall never thwart my power!" it screamed as it encapsulated Cynderet in a tar-like goo.

For a moment, she was disoriented and blind. Whatever she did, she knew the Ring of Radiant must not be released. She felt the Table's thought as it burst into laughter. Cynderet knew she was being thrust into the hole in the capsule of tar. She drew in all the air she could and swelled the goo into a huge bubble. It lodged its width inside the hole, ceasing to fall.

A flaming javelin pierced the bubble setting the tar on fire. Cynderet moved quickly, just avoiding the javelin's wicked head. She was falling again with flame all about her. She saw the darkness below reaching to envelop her. She could distinguish arms and bodies of the creatures below as variations of heat in the darkness, creatures she could never have imagined. They were anxiously grasping for her.

Cynderet refused to see it end this way. There were too many lives at stake. "It will not end here like this!" she screamed inside. Rage erupted as from a magma vent within her being. "This battle is not over!" she bellowed to those beings just moments from grasping her. It was her turn to strike out as the magma's heat burst from her soul—action took command. She grasped the flaming javelin with a powerful hand and arm, biceps swelled, wrist tendons tightened about the shaft. She blew a kiss of white heat into the javelin's flame and with all her strength shot it down at an unbelievable speed.

The creatures below had no chance to move. The javelin exploded upon impact into a million white-hot shards, which light died instantly—not the heat. Screams of pain and the hissing of burning flesh were just discernible to her ears as the awful stench reached her. Her continuing fall was plummeting her almost to the invisible flames.

Cynderet felt the heat sear her face. "What can rise without burning in this heat?" she asked in desperation.

"Ash!" Her descent stopped instantly as thought became reality in her mind. She began a rapid upward drift upon the heat waves of the flames from below.

Cynderet took advantage of the Table's momentary confusion and transformed into a stone shot from Patrick's sling. Her ascent hastened as she drew the Ring of Radiant within the center of the stone. She was not finished yet. There was a battle with the Table to end, once and for all.

The Table read her thoughts and smugly sealed up the hole with a stone plug.

Cynderet felt a strange sensation emanating from the Table. It was not the usual boastful confidence. She felt its sense of apprehension. Things were not going at all as it had expected.

Cynderet reacted without hesitation. She hardened herself into a fine steel quarrel fired from a powerful crossbow. She shot upward and out. The stone plug the Table had used to seal the hole exploded outward. The Eldresses were thrown away from the Table by its concussion. Cynderet felt another foreign feeling from the Table in its moment of alarm as its nursing mothers were unexpectedly blasted from its feeding.

The Table recognized a change in Cynderet. Her fear was gone. She had not been afraid since she parted the walls like a curtain. She had simply been dealing with each trial as it came, never even considering the Table itself.

Clear of the hole, Cynderet noted the Eldresses scattered about the region behind the Table. She struck out, attacking the Table directly. She mushroomed the particles of the plug into a giant capstone as she propelled out of the dust cloud into the fresh air above. She dropped the capstone on the Table.

The Table countered by converting the capstone into fine dust. It mustered its power together to fling Cynderet from Council Peak into the city itself.

She never hesitated a moment.

The Table saw Cynderet working her hands together into a ball while hurtling through the air on her back. The Table felt the ionic change in the ambient air about itself. It was helpless as bolts of static electricity sparkled in the lingering dust cloud. The Table shuddered, defenseless. It knew not the heavens. It screamed as Cynderet threw the electrical charge she had gathered and saw it hit the dust cloud about the Table. The explosion shot the Eldresses and pieces of the Table against the cylinders holding the youth spirits of several generations; anything combustible burst into flame.

The cylinders were shattered open. The fluids drenched the Eldresses dousing the flames eating their clothing. Cynderet felt the exuberant elation of the spirits as they were released. Emotional energy overwhelmed Cynderet's senses. Every space flowed with power; all was spirit, steam, or flame.

Cynderet halted her flight before hitting anything. She continued to feel of the spirits.

Suddenly, the spirits were gone. Telepathically, all was quiet. Wherever they went, it was not to the Lightless Plane, to Lord Wherant, as had been planned. They had been freed to finish the process of death.

Cynderet felt herself begin to fall back to earth. She became a thistle seed blowing on the wind with the Ring of Radiant protected within her seed coat. She settled gently to the ground and reverted to herself again. She closed her mind's eye and looked around her with the natural eye. She was standing just within the upper entry portal where she had been netted as a hummingbird. Everything was on fire on Council Peak. Council Guards were just appearing, rushing out from their barracks to save the Eldresses from the encroaching flames. The fluids of the cylinders had saved them. Cynderet looked to the cylinders. They were shattered, their contents now freed and gone.

"The Table is dead." Reht spoke softly as Cynderet took in the rest of the scene.

"Aye. Your constant aid of ideas allowed me to destroy it," Cynderet answered, thankful for his help. A sense of relief swelled within her as the realization that the Table was gone grew.

"Little One, I had little or nothing to do with it. You were so busy thinking and fighting on your own. I never had a chance to interject a thought. And when you could not think of an idea for a moment, I had no idea either. This was all you."

CHAPTER TWENTY EIGHT

Landsfall and Patrick remained side-by- side as the darkness overwhelmed them. Thinking it was the end for them, they openly charged the last two brigands before them. It was a desperate act, yet successfully carried out—six enemies down.

The darkness enveloped them. Landsfall grabbed Patrick's jersey and hauled him along towards a tree he had seen close by. Once Landsfall's grasping through the short distance of darkness yielded the location of the tree, they positioned themselves on the downward side. Suddenly, there was the pounding of feet, thousands of feet—the sound absolutely engulfing them. With it came the jostling of bodies; the dust from the rushing feet filled the air. It was difficult to breathe. All was in total darkness to Landsfall and Patrick. They felt the bodies of creatures passing by them in haste, their cries keening as they charged in the darkness towards the village.

Landsfall and Patrick knew they would die any moment—they were prepared for it. Their weapons were out: Landsfall, his bastard sword, and Patrick, a short sword he had picked up from a fallen foe. They readied themselves for unseen conflict and death. The rushing horde continued to pass. There came no attack on either of them. It was as if the horde could not see them.

After several moments, Landsfall yelled in Patrick's ear, "They be thinkin' we be brigands. Put yer back ta mine, we be strikin' out at these creatures of hell as they pass us by."

"I be not able ta see!"

"It matters not as long as ye remain at my back. We be the only two of Skon's Hall here. This tree be providin' us some protection. I have wrapped a cord about my waist. Secure the opposite end ta yer belt for if ye slip or we be separated we be never findin' each other again."

"Aye," Patrick felt for Landsfall's shoulder and keeping his sleeve in hand he followed it until he found the cord. As soon as he secured it as directed, he backed into Landsfall's back. Together, they began striking out in earnest at any body which touched them going by. They fought totally by feel. The creatures streamed by endlessly. Their arms grew weary from the constant wielding of their weapons. Patrick's short sword was small compared to Landsfall's bastard sword, yet so close were the enemy, it did not matter;. Patrick felt his efforts strike many an impassioned creature passing in haste to breach the village defenses.

Suddenly, the creatures ceased passing in close proximity. The two could still hear the keening cries in the dark around them, yet none made the so familiar contact with them.

There was a heavy feeling settling its ponderous weight upon both of them. Then a deep gravelly voice spoke clearly to their ears. "What is this? Two humans lost on the wrong side of the walls?" the voice asked, rumbling like far off thunder. "It must be the darkness which confuses you as to where you are."

Both strained to see in the dark in futile effort to identify this mocking voice.

"There is no need for you to see me. Just know your fate is now mine. And I decree it to be in the pits of my minions."

Patrick was ready to die, to give up his life for the folks at Skon's Hall. Capture was not an option he had considered. He felt a devastation of spirit he had never known before. It was answered by an invisible net dropping over him and Landsfall. He felt Landsfall drop behind him under the weight of the net.

"Drop, boy, lest the net drop ye ta yer damage."

Patrick did as he was told. He felt the net settle tightly about them both.

The demon who had captured them stopped several of his minions and forced them to secure the netting and hoist the two humans upon their shoulders. With a wicked slap of his whip on their backs, the minions carried the two back in the direction the minions had come from.

"Where be 'em tak'n us?" Patrick cried, panic beginning to edge his voice.

"I know not, boy, but panic be not the answer," Landsfall's voice was firm and reassuring. "Hold yer fear. Force yerself ta be still till I figure an effort for us."

Landsfall seemed to be searching for something. There was a grunt of pain as he was jabbed savagely in the back by an unseen porter.

"Found it," he whispered hoarsely. "Be holdin' tight ta me, Patrick. This be happening fast. Whatever happens be not let'n go of me!"

There was a sudden movement of Landsfall's arm. He threw something to the ground. His rebounding shoulder drove into Patrick's midsection driving the air from his lungs, yet he held on with an iron grip.

A bright light shown for an instant revealing the forest still around them. Then darkness closed in again. There was a slipping sound as something slithered through the leaves on the ground from the trees and brush around them. Patrick struggled futilely to see. The rustling noise was all around them. The demonic minions bellowed in pain and fear. Their voices were choked into silence. The net with its human cargo remained lifted. The sound stopped and so did movement. Whatever it was, it did not touch Landsfall or Patrick. Wherever they were, they were going no further.

Elfgon fought alone just behind the front gate. The undaunted demonic hordes rushed past on either side of him. A prayer continued to play in his heart to stay alive long enough to meet the demons themselves once the minions were by him. He had adapted lines of this prayer to a chant as he fought. The rhythm aided his breathing and perseverance. His elfin vision allowed him to see clearly in the darkness. He quickly dispatched the two minions confronting him while doing a backward movement to get his back up against the wall and halt possible attack at his unprotected rear. He found himself in a portal frame where the door had been blown out. As he backed in, he lost his balance stumbling over a body. A third minion pressed him as he fell. Elfgon hit the stone flooring in a spin on his buttocks. He struck out at the minion's legs as he spun around again. The minion screamed, falling back through the portal. His right leg was severed through to the bone just below the knee. His life's blood shot in squirts from a leg artery. Elfgon used the momentary respite to move. He stood, hidden in the stonework of the doorframe. He waited for the demons. It was not a long wait.

Elfgon recognized the burly human coming up the ramp. It was the brigand leader Everard with a corpulent mass of demonic evil waddling beside him. Both detected Elfgon simultaneously. The obesity of the demon prevented it from entering the portal. Everard slipped in and engaged Elfgon's sword with nonhuman speed.

Elfgon threw himself from the wall for space and time to reappraise his foe's blade. "There is magic here. No human is this fast!" his voice hoarse from combat.

"To be sure," Everard answered. "Your death will end in magic, befitting for an elf, I think." He attacked as a streak of movement: two flicks and a lunge with his blade.

Elfgon parried the first, knew he had been hit by the second, and recognized the sword combination in time to block the lunge with a hard, downward stroke. Elfgon tried to slip his blade up and in as Everard recovered. So fast was Everard's blade, he parried and flicked Elfgon's shoulder.

Elfgon knew he was in serious trouble. Few humans were a match for a well-trained sword elf, yet Everard was even faster than any elf he could remember. Elfgon did a reverse somersault over the dead minion beneath him. Instead of engaging Everard, he continued his attempt at distance by ducking into the gate tower portal.

Everard was soon in the portal behind him, his sword ready. Watching the distance quickly being lost, Elfgon noted the sword hit still in Everard's scabbard!

Elfgon took a second set of stairs at a flat run. He had to buy a moment to think. Everard had a sword in his hand and the exact hilt still in its scabbard. There were a lot of swords, true, but not of this hilt's craftsmanship. It had to be a twin.

Elfgon could hear Everard running up the stairs behind him. It was a man's pace. Elfgon ducked into the upper rampart portal and slammed the door shut. He braced it with a body as Everard slammed into it with his shoulder. Elfgon stepped clear and readied his sword. He remembered Razon's assassin. "Could there be two? Two what?" he asked himself. Then it came, just as Everard shattered the door with a pulverizing blow of his fist: a shape-changer, Everard's sword was actually his, its, own arm.

Not waiting for the sword to reform, Elfgon attacked. His effort was simple: to sever the arm from Everard's body. Instead of chopping down as a normal attack form, Elfgon struck low to high. It hit, raising Everard's arm as the blade began to immerge from the fist. The blade elongated quick as thought. Elfgon was beyond thought, having already decided his attack. He spun and struck down hard.

Everard's elongated blade drove itself into the stone flooring of the rampart.

Elfgon used the momentum to reverse his arm, bringing his blade into a flick across Everard's throat.

Everard's jugular spurt black liquid in a vile pulse.

Elfgon spun to avoid its contact.

Everard withdrew his sword arm from the stone;. In vicious strokes, he pounded Elfgon. Black blood spewed from his neck.

Elfgon held his sword as a shield against the blows: one, two, and three. He was driven to his knees. The fourth came down hard. Elfgon angled his blade forcing Everard's blade to slide down its edge. Elfgon reversed his wrist in a tight flick driving his sword tip deep into Everard's throat in hopes of an instant kill. He could think of no other way to best this creature.

Everard rebounded from the misdirection of his sword. He reversed himself and struck a lightening tip at Elfgon.

Elfgon was pinned close as his blade was still inserted deeply in Everard's throat. Elfgon tried to dodge the riposte taking it in the shoulder instead of the heart as intended. He felt the blade bite deep, then nothing.

The sword of Everard was gone. Everard was gone. He simply vanished into nothingness. There was no white powder. Whatever magic gave Everard life must have garnered him back as he died. Elfgon's sword dropped to the stone flooring, having been freed in Everard's disappearance.

Elfgon took up his sword though struggling to keep his balance as he gasped for air. He stumbled to the inner wall and looked down to the demon still without the tower portal below.

The huge mass looked up and snarled at Elfgon. In a mighty lunge, the demon vaulted the rampart wall. His weight's impact on the floor at Elfgon's feet shattered the surface stonework, sending a reverberation through the rampart.

Elfgon attacked in a double strike at the huge creature's left leg. His sword bit deep. The demon's leg collapsed, throwing the creature in a sprawl.

The demon responded with amazing singleness of thought. As he fell, he struck out his monstrous arm and threw Elfgon to the floor beside him.

Elfgon had lost a lot of blood from Everard's hits. He was swept to the floor like a rag doll. Unconsciousness followed the bounce of his head on the stone's flooring.

The demon rolled his massive weight upon Elfgon, pinning him helpless beneath his bulk. The demon raised a giant fist and drove it towards Elfgon's chest. There was a sudden climatic clap in the air as if the heavens imploded and exploded in instantaneous succession just as the demon's blow hit its mark.

Hamilton cursed his newfound vision into the darkness, for as he fought, he saw each of his men slain, trying to defend themselves in blindness against an unseen enemy. Two died fighting each other, never even knowing whom it was they fought. Though he cursed his vision, he never forgot who to take his anger out on. A growing circle of minions lay around him;. He no longer had use of his left arm as the shoulder muscles had been deeply sliced. He let it hang, his shield still protecting his left side. The securing straps held to his forearm and hand.

Two minions replaced the one he just killed. They struck in alternating blows, forcing Hamilton to fend the first and then the second by swinging his sword and rotating his body to bring the shield to bear parrying the other. He knew he could not keep this up, yet his fatigue would not allow fresh thought.

He parried the next blow and swung his body to bring the shield up for the next. His legs wavered beneath him as he did so, forcing him to do a half circle. He let the momentum carry him through full circle, expecting the killing blow to his exposed back as he came back around. It did not come. He gripped his sword tight and low. As he came full circle, he struck low to high. Hamilton's sword drove its edge into the minion's rib cage deeply into its lung.

The other minion struck, hitting Hamilton on the side.

Hamilton fell with his momentum, drawing the dead minion on top of him, his sword still jammed in its ribs.

*****

Strike managed to shuttle from the stable up to the portal of the forward tower without detection. He remained sure of Razon's location listening through the walls as he went. Although it took several precious minutes, his melding into the wall allowed him to verify that Razon remained where he was. Thrice, Skon's men rushed by, forcing him to stay within the wall's surface. Each time he reminded himself, it was Razon he had to get. He did not have time to deal with petty matters. "If I do not get the ring, this will all be for naught." He was not sure why the Ring of Radiant had not acted yet, it should have. He had no choice but to continue. For the hundredth time in the past couple days, he cursed Luanta. "The ring is my power to return to the Halls of Darkness. Without it, I am stuck on this glaring sphere of light. It blinds me!" He melded into the outer wall of the tower.

Strike congealed on the outside of the tower wall. The rampart opened up to him on the other side. He saw Razon fighting side-by-side with a giant Hert. Razon was in serious trouble with two streams of blood issuing from below his jersey. "He is fighting as he dies," Strike mused. "Berenice may have done her job well, after all. From where I stand though, I see no one getting by that Hert fighting at Razon's side."

Strike studied the maneuvers of the two combatants and their minion adversaries enough to see his approach. He melded into the wall Razon used as his back protection and slithered towards him as he battled with a minion.

Razon's sword drove deeply into his foe. His arm was hyperextended and he did not have the strength to pull it out without leaving the wall's protection. He stepped forwards to allow his arm some freedom before his next foe arrived—coming at his front. There was just enough time to draw and return. He never saw the stone fist that pounded a single blow into his exposed rib cage. He felt the ribs cave in and his lung collapse driving him to his knees. Razon could not speak as bubbles frothed from his mouth.

Strike savagely pulled Razon to him. He crushed the wrist in an effort to get the ring from his finger. It was not there. Strike looked up to Razon. What he saw instead was the driving butt end of the Hert's pole arm taking him in his chest as he was presently exposed from the wall. The strength of the blow threw him into the tower wall he had just left.

Strike charged Serenten in an explosion of pent-up rage. He knew Luanta had set him up. This Hert would pay until he could catch her.

Serenten's entire mass of muscle swelled. The adrenaline coursed through his body as never before. His closest friend was dying—this demon killed him—the same kind of hellish creature that stole him as a child from his Hert home. There would be death here!

Strike plowed into Serenten; only Serenten was not there. Serenten spun to the side of Strike's path and, using Strike's own momentum, drove the shaft of his weapon into Strike's back. The power smashed him into the rampart wall again. The wall shook forming a shallow bowl-like impression as Strike impacted its surface.

Strike thought to turn around and charge again when he was awash by a dousing of water soaking him in the wall's impression. Peripheral vision allowed him to see a small man in monk robes putting a bucket down. Strike never saw the bolt of cold shot from the lady at the monk's side. He was frozen in place, still affixed to the wall.

The very pores of the stone were closed to him as he tried to meld further into the wall. The ice sealed him in place. A second blast of cold froze him solid. All he could do was watch.

Laura rushed to Razon; a vial was placed to his lips. The small man in woolen robes knelt beside Razon and, placing an open palm on his head, saying a prayer. No minion got past the giant Hert to interfere with the ministrations for Razon;. With fist and weapon, the pile of dead grew below the ramparts as Serenten's rage slew them as fast as they came. Soon, there was a wide berth around the small group. The minions would let the demons behind take care of this giant.

*****

Ryan saw the first demon arrive at the ramparts. Blue Skon met it. The bastard sword Blue's Song never ceased to glow its brightness. No blood could seal its radiance. Skon and the demon met, exchanging powerful blows. Skon had been fighting for over an hour. The demon was fresh, yet neither seemed to slacken before the other. It was impossible for Ryan to see into the darkness. He saw only the silhouettes of the two combatants cast by Blue's Song.

"Where is Quick?" Ryan asked himself. He heard a scream behind him. He turned quickly to see shadows of Ashley falling to a second demon's blows. Ryan charged the demon drawing his sword in an arc from his shoulder down onto the demon's arm. The demon took the blow as if struck by a stick;. The sword's edge did not penetrate the demon's flesh.

The demon's arm dropped as Ryan's sword finished its downward arc. Then the demon's arm slammed back up again into Ryan's body. Ryan was lifted from his feet and flung into the rampart wall. Stunned, he felt panic surge through his heart. He was helpless. He had struck his best effort and had not even hurt his foe.

The demon turned on Ryan, having forgotten Ashley on the stone flooring.

Ryan was frozen in fear, unable to move.

The demon drew closer and reached down, picking Ryan up bodily. "Now die, pathetic coward," it hissed.

Ashley felt her dagger fly from her hand—her wrist a motion of magical perfection. A bright meteor she watched as the dagger drove deeply into the base of the demon's powerful neck.

The demon bellowed in pain. Dropping Ryan like a sack, it reached its hands behind its neck to grasp the killing blade from its body. Struggling to get a hold of the blade, the demon found no effort would withdraw it. He turned and faced Ashley. It would not die without killing her too!

There was a flash of light—only a heart's beat in duration then a second, a third, each just before the demon's next step. It screamed in exquisite fury. It sought desperately to kill. It took one last step to Ashley and stooped and picked her up to crush her in its arms. The glint of light flashed a last time as the demon dropped her. It fell about her in death and silence.

Ryan could voice no sound. Tears of anguish burst from his eyes as he saw the demon smother upon Ashley. He buried himself into the protective darkness of the rampart wall and shuddered spasmodically. Blackness shrouded him as he slipped from consciousness.

*****

Cynderet saw the vastness of the demons' destruction in their assault of Skon's Hall. The village was a shambles. Blue Skon quickly weakened, embattled with two demons himself. Laura knelt over Razon in what appeared to be a protective glass dome. A strange little man in woolen robes was firing a blast of cold into a flying demon diving towards them. The last desperate defenses would be over in just a few moments. There were too many of the creatures from hell. More still were arriving at the outer gates of the village and many flying in on grand wings. The hall's own were dead, wounded, or exhausted—all fought valiantly as death was but a moment away for each of them. All of them except those captured alive.

Going out the gates was a long line of villagers in nets being ported off on the backs of the minions. The demons were carrying off those still alive into their realm of darkness.

Cynderet rushed beside Laura. She pulled the chain from around her neck and took off the Ring of Radiant. "I hope it is not too late." She spoke to Laura's mind.

Laura did not react in defense. She understood what Cynderet was doing and complied with her send. She lifted Razon's crushed wrist and hand. The fingers were bent and twisted.

Cynderet strove to ignore the gruesome damage and placed the ring on Razon's finger. Nothing happened.

Laura and Cynderet exchanged desperate glances. Laura looked past Cynderet to the battle going on around them. Wolfie fired the bolt of cold from his wand just as the winged demon's claws smote the glass dome.

The creature bounced off and hit the tower wall, shattering like ice to fall on the stone floor. Skon took a chopping blow on his shield. It drove him to his knees. The second one repeated the blow, forcing Skon to buckle beneath. Laura screamed as the third blow hit. She seemed to melt through the dome to protect her husband. With an open palm, she drove her hand into the air in front of her. Simultaneously, Missive did the same motion from her shoulder. Twin lightning bolts shot from their palms into to the striking demon.

He erupted in sparks. The second demon attacked her; two more were coming from behind this new one.

Cynderet did not watch further. She looked down to her father, his face twisted in the thralls of death. Cynderet entered his mind. He was succumbing to the gloating of demons. Their telepathic strength was choking him. Their darkness had reduced his spirit to a mere speck of life's light.

Cynderet encapsulated that last spark in a crystal. Like a glow-stone, it shone ever so faintly. The demons saw her and attacked. She had no time or way to fight;. She had to save her father.

Reht suddenly stood before her and the glow-stone. In his hands was the pole arm of the Council Hert, yet never had she seen one shine with the radiance of this one. As it arched through the air before the first demon, an arc of light pierced the darkness. Its beaming edge grew until it looked like a sickle. It pierced the rugged flesh of the demon, taking it across the chest. Its scream of pain was cut short as it burst into a shower of sparks and vanished. Reht turned to the second.

Cynderet did not watch. Instead, she washed the glow-stone with tears as she nuzzled it into her cheek. "Father, you cannot die," she breathed passionately. She cradled the glow-stone of Razon's life in her two hands. She blew upon it like a candle trying to intensify its flame.

Its intensity grew. With a growing hope, she continued to blow. With each breath, the light shone brighter. The glow-stone burst apart and Razon's light drove the darkness from his being. Cynderet was thrown from his mind as warriors arose in the most glorious armor from the heightening brightness.

Cynderet looked upon Razon's withered body lying at her knees. She still held his hand as she had after putting the ring on his finger. The finger curled. He clenched his ring fist. The mangled hand was healed. A gauntlet suddenly appeared around the fist, radiant gold in its color. From there, his flesh seemed to metamorphosis into full armor. The Ring of Radiant remained exposed on the finger of his gauntlet.

Razon arose. He held his fist up, the ring high. Upon his chest was emblazoned a leaping lion before a radiant sun. His face stern, determined, and alive.

A pillar of light shot from the ring high into the air. The darkness of the demons wavered. There was a shudder in the air. Then followed a series of several pulsing light waves deep into the darkness over the village. Colors, in a multitude of hues, coursed through the darkness. They pulsed back to the ring and the darkness returned. Everything was dark. There was no light anywhere. Even the magic light of Laura's spells was gone. Cynderet was falling into despair. "We cannot just end like this!" she cried.

"Nor shall we!" Razon said still standing above her crouching form. His hand of reassurance rested on her shoulder, and with his right fist fully raised into the darkness, he said in his command voice, "Now!" The ring shot its radiant pillar high and full into the air. Light exploded into the darkness—a full circle of light, immediately turning the night into the brightness of day over the village. In its light rode the Golden Knights Cynderet saw in Razon's mind just as she was thrown out. Their swords were brands of color—intense in hue and variety. They attacked the creatures of hell with abandon.

Demons and minions disappeared as they were struck down. The demons and minions on the ramparts were the first to disappear then followed the ranks behind them.

Cynderet saw their darkness collect in a distant bank of black clouds. The clouds grew and grew, swelling, twirling, twisting in ever increasing speed. A heart of color arose in the very center of the storm's being. The creatures of evil where lifted high into the air and flung into the growing storm's heart of color by the growing intensity of the storm. The light grew ever stronger as the demons' ranks diminished.

Luanta continued to watch in awe as the light display pulsed, beat upon beat.

The ramparts of Skon's Hall were clear to her vision in the new light. She was sure the man standing with his fist in the air was Lord Razon. She felt her defeat in a sense of shock. "How?" she kept asking herself, unable to fathom this turn of battle.

A deep blackness gathered about her. A calm voice above her answered her plea, "The Ring of Radiant."

Fear buried itself in the deepest reaches of her being. She knew—she knew with the surety of prophesy. It was the Lord Wherant himself. She looked up into the blackness.

His calm voice in contradiction to what was happening captivated her as a spell. "This day is lost. My turn will come again—later. But you—you will never see it."

Luanta felt the calmness shatter as a fine porcelain vase might shatter in innumerable shards. His gentle voice belied the visions suddenly coming to her mind—visions of her new destination.

"Think not that you will escape me in this defeat. This is the doing of your prideful ineptitude." He roared a laugh of the hell-bound dead. "You are mine and you will pay for this!" His darkness swelled around her, thrusting her into the black's invisible heart.

She feltherself lifted and carried away. The speed of the flight increased every moment until she felt herself begin to circle—huge, sickening cycles about the heart of color centered above Lord Razon, Prince of The Light Forest and Commander of the Lions of Light.

The circles began to constrict, to tighten upon themselves. Luanta could hardly breathe. There was not enough air to suck into her craving lungs;. Dizziness swirled about her failing consciousness.

Cynderet watched as the last bulk of blackness lifted from the apple orchard just from outside the village. It slammed into the swelling clouds swirling with all the evil caught within the storm's immense clouds. All began to swirl ever faster and faster. As it did so, the darkness condensed into deepest blackness. No light penetrated as the heart of color and light constricted; the light pulsated about the darkness, forcing it ever faster and tighter in blackness of the storm.

A blackest of swirling fingers descended from the clouds. It touched down in the orchard before Skon's Hall. Unseen by any the little black box burst open to receive the funnel's finger. Down the blackness went into the box. Faster and faster, the blackness rushed downward, passing through the box to its own place. The light from the Ring of Radiant pulsed around until all the blackness disappeared. The box was gone.

There was only the light. It congealed upon itself as the Golden Knights rode their mounts back into the pillar of light. The last entered, and the light diminished back into the Ring of Radiant.

Now only Razon remained of the Golden Knights. Razon, standing tall, no evidence of mortal wounds. His stern visage looked down upon Cynderet kneeling at his feet never having moved during the entire ordeal.

Tears coursed her cheeks, her eyes studying Razon's face.

Razon's fist descended slowly, opening as it dropped towards Cynderet. It joined its brother to rest on her other shoulder as he looked into her eyes and smiled. It was a warm and tender smile that spoke so much only the heart could comprehend it all.

Razon removed his ring and gauntlet from his right hand and held his hand towards her, palm up. "Stand, Cynderet. Arise, Daughter of Radiant."

At first Cynderet was uncertain what to do. She looked from Razon's face to his extended hand and back to his face again. The words began to register. "Daughter of Radiant?" she asked. "Then you know who I really am?"

"Aye, Child. My Child. I think I have known since I saw the green of your eyes that afternoon in the forest. It took Serenten to convince me." Razon smiled. "Cynderet, you are Heir to the Light Forest. You are the daughter of its Crown Prince. Arise and take your rightful place.

"It is your place to take, Father. Not mine."

"You do not fully understand yet. My time here as a mortal is done. You blew breath into the glowstone of my life. It was you who allowed me to pass from death into the realm of the Golden Knights: The Lions of Light we are. I must take my place with them. It is you who made it possible. You returned the Ring of Radiant to me as I died." Razon opened Cynderet's right palm.

He placed the ring in it along with its chain. "The Ring of Radiant is passed down to you. I am its own Lion of Light. You made this possible as well. The others arose from their place from the Master Ring of Radiant of my father. The king's ring was called upon to usher forth its knights by this ring, your ring."

Razon raised his sword in salute. He turned his eyes to Laura and Blue Skon struggling to get back to his own feet. They were both alive. Skon's injuries would heal. He faced Cynderet again. "Go to them, my daughter. They need you."

Razon took a step backwards as he dropped his sword in formal fashion to Lord Blue Skon and Lady Laura. Wolfie stood alongside, noting the Finest detail to this ceremonial.

"Lord Blue Skon and Lady Laura, I present my daughter, Cynderet, Crown Princess of the Light Forest and Holder of the Lesser Ring of Radiant. Care for her as you have me. Teach her the meaning of loyalty and faith as you have me.

And when the time comes, see her to my father." Razon raised and sheathed his sword. His smile, the only thanks he could offer. Razon turned. He now faced the giant Serenten. Cynderet felt the closing of Serenten's mind to her, sealing her from witnessing what was shared between these two, her defenders.

Then Razon was gone.

Cynderet had difficulty in seeing through her cleansing tears, yet she found warmth of heart and a sense of outreaching she had never experienced before. She did not wipe at her tears. For the first time, she cried tears of joy, tears of purpose. Her father, a man she hardly knew, was gone. Yet within the Ring of Radiant, he remained with her as her Lion of Light. And around her, he had bequeathed his legacy of friends. They needed her. She needed them.

Cynderet turned. She found herself immersed in Laura's arms, Blue Skon standing beside them. Behind her, she read Serenten's helping Ashley up to her feet.

Ashley leaned against him for support as she worked hard to hide her own emotions.

All this did Wolfgang the Meek note—all this to record in the Annals of Wisshard.

CHAPTER TWENTY NINE

Wolfie found Elfgon prostate on the upper ramparts of the gate tower. Dawn was just clearing the eastern hilltops. Close beside him was the sword of Everard, still in its scabbard. All other evidence of the shape-changer and the demon were gone.

Wolfie could tell by the dried blood on his shoulder and the horrible dent, a permanent impression of a huge fist, in Elfgon's breastplate that Elfgon was seriously injured. He breathed though. He was still alive.

Wolfie placed his palm on Elfgon's head and said a prayer. He allowed his energy of being to penetrate deeply into Elfgon. He sealed the wounds and bound Elfgon's punctured lung. He set the broken ribs with his mind. He cleansed Elfgon's wounds, visiting each site with meticulous care of thought. When he was sure each injury had been tended to, he brought his energy of being back out and lifted his hand from Elfgon's head.

Elfgon felt the warmth of the new day on his face. The light of day's newness brought memories of earlier days when such mornings, such feelings of life, were commonplace—morns when playful elfin children ran amongst the trees and danced in the early morning rays. Elfgon felt the effervescing joy of life as only an Elf can. He opened his eyes to see a bundle of woolen rags sitting next to him. No. It was a hermit's habit. Then his eyes focused better and he knew he was looking at Wolfie in his woolens. "When did you get here?" Elfgon asked. "I could have used your help up here. At least until I died."

"Accept my sincerest apologies. I would have been at your side had I not been so preoccupied trying to stay at everyone else's. However, you did not die. Here you are, and now well on the road to full healing.

"The last I remember was a losing fight with a demon."

"Aye. I found his good parting kiss on your breastplate. I think the Ring of Radiant's timing is what saved you from death."

Elfgon could not help a face-shattering smile. "So Razon did find it and save us in the end."

"Aye. More than you realize, he saved us. Yet it was his daughter, Cynderet, who actually regained the ring."

"Razon's daughter?" Elfgon asked not sure he heard right.

"Aye. Razon's daughter. Crown Heir to the Light Forest."

"Then it is as I feared. Razon is gone?"

"Aye. To us." Wolfie spoke quietly. "Yet to Cynderet, and to the Halls of Radiant, he remains always. He is a Lion of Light."

"Aye. I am glad of it. Of the Lions of Light, I know a little history. It is as he would want it then. He has met his charge and accepted it."

"Aye. Come, I will help you up. There are others we need yet to find."

Wolfie helped Elfgon up, and the two wove a winding course to the rampart stairs and down.

There were village and minion dead all around. Of the demons, they found nothing. Just inside the inner gates, they found a great slaughter of minions. Within the midst was the body of a single human: Captain Hamilton Harm, his shield remained strapped to his arm and his sword firm in death's grasp.

"A hero for sure is Skon's Captain," Elfgon said.

"I think an Elfin song of praise be due this one. His memory should be joined with the others of this countryside. He died a Soldier's Valiant."

They searched the rest of the day, healing whom they could, trying to identify those they could not. There seemed to be many missing. The village population, they were sure, had been much greater than the number they found among the living and dead.

Laura and Blue Skon joined them around midmorning, having cared for those of the hall they could. A feeling of desperation seemed to follow them. Serenten, Cynderet, and Ashley also aided in the dismal work. All shared in the happier moments of finding villagers alive in their places of refuge.

Ashley was quiet and distant. Elfgon felt sure the reason. He too felt a heavy loss. Neither Patrick nor Landsfall had turned up. Where were they? Where were the others of the village?

It was dusk when they found out. With very heavy hearts, they were finishing the last tasks of daylight when they heard a commotion near the front gates. The guards seemed to be yelling a cheer.

Serenten and Cynderet were the first to arrive. The others were as close behind as their wounds would allow. From the ramparts, they saw a line of villagers coming in from the forest. Haggard, still wide-eyed, and shaken yet alive. The line continued to grow. Towards the rear, several walked two and three abreast, the stronger aiding the wounded. Rear most came a man walking his familiar stallion, his modeling sidekick behind. Both their horses carried the weakest.

Ashley burst out in tears of joy. She began a confused hobbling dance, trying to figure the fastest way down. Serenten grabbed her in his powerful arms and swept her down the rampart stairs towards her brother. So caught up in knowing Patrick was still alive, she never ceased her hollers of heart's voice. For the next several days, her throat would be sore. She would never believe the others speaking of her continuous noise of glee.

Patrick handed his reins to Landsfall and ran to meet Serenten and embrace his sister. "We be able ta save these folks from demon slavery!" Patrick bellowed in wonderment. "'Em demons just vanished and left these folks wander'n all tied in lines. Me and Landsfall brung 'em back."

"Yes, and we are both still alive!" Ashley added, giving Patrick a hug, he would never forget. It marked the passing of childhood for both of them. It also sealed the family bond they would share for life.

Laura watched with tears streaming down her cheeks. She held tightly to both Cynderet and Skon. Wolfie watched beside them. He marveled at the strength of his sister. She remained a lady and a power of love even after all that had happened. Even after knowing her son Ryan was gone. And Quick. They were not found among the living or the dead.

*****

Deep in the rocks of the granite peaks overlooking Skon's Hall, a cold mass of living stone melded into the mother rock. Blind and stranded, the creature forsook self-pity. It would take years to recover his sight and mend his fractures of body, but he would mend. And when healed, he would resume his pursuit of the Ring of Radiant, that ring he had seen given to the girl, Cynderet. He would have no trouble recognizing her; her visage was the last thing he saw as the blinding brightness of the ring's power etched the scene on his mind with the finality of a closing curtain. He would find her. She was his only way home.

About the Author

Lowell Duane Pabst has been sharing stories for as long as he can remember. His first written story, done in the third grade, was noted as "Anti-Climatic" by his teacher. He considered that a compliment and continued sharing stories one way or another. He considers himself a jack-of-all-trades having finally become a master of one in teaching high school until retirement. Even there, though, he taught many subjects during each year. Starting out in Vocational Agriculture, he evolved through business, chorus, and dramatic arts to teaching English and Social Science with Creative Writing on the side.

Mr. Pabst has been a theatre director of several major plays and musicals in local theatre. He has been a professional auto racetrack announcer, announced high school football, and continues to be deeply involved in serving in his faith in Jesus Christ.

Mr. Pabst feels the wide range of experience and associations have done much to fuel his passion for writing. Fantasy is a major medium in his writing though he also writes in other genres and non-fiction short stories.

www.ingramcontent.com/pod-product-compliance
Lightning Source LLC
Chambersburg PA
CBHW041047310726
48978CB00011BA/459